THE DEVIL IN
GREEN

Also by Mark Chadbourn

The Kingdom of the Serpent:
Jack of Ravens

The Dark Age:
The Devil in Green
The Queen of Sinister
The Hounds of Avalon

The Age of Misrule:
World's End
Darkest Hour
Always Forever

Underground
Nocturne
The Eternal
Testimony
Scissorman

For more information about the author and his work, visit:
www.markchadbourn.com

THE DARK AGE

1

THE DEVIL IN GREEN

MARK CHADBOURN

an imprint of Prometheus Books
Amherst, NY

Published 2010 by Pyr®, an imprint of Prometheus Books

Inquiries should be addressed to
Pyr
59 John Glenn Drive
Amherst, New York 14228–2119
VOICE: 716–691–0133
FAX: 716–691–0137
WWW.PYRSF.COM

14 13 12 11 10   5 4 3 2 1

Library of Congress Cataloging-in-Publication Data

Chadbourn, Mark.
    The devil in green / by Mark Chadbourn.
        p. cm. — (The Dark Age ; bk. 1)
    First published: London : Gollancz, an imprint of Orion Publishing Group, 2002.
    ISBN 978–1–61614–198–1 (pbk.)
    1. Mythology, Celtic—Fiction. I. Title.

PR6053.H23D48 2010
823'.914—dc22

                                                        2010003562

Printed in the United States

For Elizabeth, Betsy, and Joe

CONTENTS

ACKNOWLEDGMENTS

Allan Beacham, Labhras de Faoite, Alanna Morrigan, Faith Peters, and the other regular visitors to the Mark Chadbourn message board, and all the many people who've e-mailed me or written to me during the course of the Age of Misrule; Greta for discussions about balance and the Craft; Howard's House Hotel, Salisbury; and finally to the staff of Salisbury Cathedral, who answered all my impertinent questions with good grace.

For more information on the author and his work, please visit:

www.markchadbourn.net

CHRONICLES OF THE FALLEN WORLD

One night, the world we knew slipped quietly away. Humanity awoke to find itself in a place mysteriously changed. Fabulous Beasts soared over the cities, their fiery breath reddening the clouds. Supernatural creatures stalked the countryside—imps and shape-shifters, blood-sucking revenants, men who became wolves, or wolves who became men, strange beasts whose roars filled the night with ice; and more, too many to comprehend. Magic was alive and in everything.

No one had any idea why it happened—by order of some Higher Power, or a random, meaningless result of the shifting seasons of Existence—but the shock was too great for society. All faith was lost in the things people had counted on to keep them safe—the politicians, the law, the old religions. None of it mattered in a world where things beyond reason could sweep out of the night to destroy lives in the blink of an eye.

Above all were the gods—miraculous beings emerging from hazy race memories and the depths of ancient mythologies, so far beyond us that we were reduced to the level of beasts, frightened and powerless. They had been here before, long, long ago, responsible for our wildest dreams and darkest nightmares, but now that they were back they were determined to stay forever. In the days after their arrival, as the world became a land of myth, these gods battled for supremacy in a terrible conflict that shattered civilisation. Death and destruction lay everywhere.

Blinking and cowed, the survivors emerged from the chaos of this Age of Misrule into a world substantially changed, the familiar patterns of life gone: communications devastated, anarchy ranging across the land, society thrown into a new Dark Age where superstition held sway. Existence itself had been transformed: magic and technology now worked side by side. There were new rules to observe, new boundaries to obey, and mankind was no longer at the top of the evolutionary tree.

A time of wonder and terror, miracles and torment, in which man's survival was no longer guaranteed.

chapter one

IN THESE TIMES

"It is not bad luck, but right and just that you have found yourselves travelling this road, far from the beaten track followed by others. It is right that you should learn all things and develop the unshakeable heart of well-rounded truth, unlike the opinions of men that contain no truth at all. You shall learn how mere appearances seem as though they actually exist."

Parmenides

The weight of a man's soul is greatest in the dark hours before dawn. On a night when even the moon and stars were obscured, Mallory carried the burden of his own intangible more heavily than ever. He was in the thrall of an image, a burst of fire in the night like the purifying flame of some Fabulous Beast. It was clear when he closed his eyes, floating ghostly across his consciousness when he opened them, both mysterious and haunting. Yet a deeply buried part of him knew exactly what it meant, and that same part would never allow it to be examined.

He had briefly been distracted by the passage of a man in his midtwenties who looked unusually frail, as if gripped by some wasting illness. He was hunched over the neck of his horse, buffeted by a harsh wind hurling the first cold stones of rain. Autumn was drawing in. Mallory was protected from the elements in his Porsche, which he had reversed behind a hedgerow so that it couldn't be seen from the road; he'd felt the need to clear his head before continuing on to his destination.

Briefly, he caught his reflection in the rearview mirror: shoulder-length brown hair framing a good-looking face that took its note from an ironic disposition. It sent a shiver through him, and he looked quickly away.

Obliquely, Mallory wondered if Salisbury was no longer there, like the rumours he had heard of Newcastle and some of the villages in the Scottish borders. The night had been so impenetrable as he drove south that the whole world could have been wiped away.

If he'd had a choice in the matter, he would have travelled in daylight. The countryside was filled with gangs armed with shotguns and knives, raiding villages and the outskirts of towns for food; life had become infinitely more brutal since everything had turned sour. But it was the other things that cast more disturbing shadows across life. The silhouettes of little men moving slowly across the open fields under the stars. The thing he'd glimpsed up close once, emerging from an abandoned pig farm: eyes like saucers, scales that glinted in the moonlight and fingers that were too, too long. It only confirmed the stories that kept everyone confined to their homes once the sun set: the night didn't belong to man anymore.

Mallory watched the traveller's slow progress and wondered obliquely what was on his mind.

The rider bowed his head into the rising storm, pulling his waterproof cloak tighter around him as the gusts of wind threatened to unseat him. Seeking shelter was undoubtedly the wise thing to do, but the hard weight of his fear wouldn't let him. To rest in a place where he could be cornered was more than he could bear to consider; at least on the road he had the *chance* to flee. Single-minded determination was the only thing that kept him going. He didn't even glance behind him, because he knew his imagination would conjure faces in the trees and hedgerows, the rustling noises of pursuit, the presence of something coming up hard to drag him from his horse.

Nothing there, he told himself.

He'd planned his journey to skirt Salisbury Plain—it was a no-man's-land and anyone who was stupid enough to venture in never came out again—yet even the surrounding countryside felt unbearably dangerous. But if he made it to Salisbury, it would all be worth it. Finally: salvation, redemption, hope.

The thunder made him start so sharply that he almost jumped from the saddle. It was the roar of a giant beast bearing down on him. The lightning came a few seconds later, turning the inky fields and clustering trees to stark white.

Nothing there, he confirmed with relief.

To his right, the stern mount of Old Sarum rose up in silhouette. Soon he might see a few flickering lights—candles, probably, to light loved ones home. Perhaps someone had even got a store of oil to keep a generator running. He was surprised at how much that simple thought gave him a thrill.

More thunder, another flash of light. His thighs were numb beneath sodden denim; he couldn't feel his fingers. He wished it were still high summer.

The wind deadened his ears and started to play tricks on him. A gust eddying around the cochlea became a song performed by a string quartet; a breeze penetrating deeper was the whisper of an old friend. The blood banging around inside his head only added to the dislocation that made him ignore his most vital night sense. When the high-pitched whistle came, it was nothing more than the protest of the trees' uppermost branches.

The second time the whistle rose, he clung on to the desensitised state pro-

tecting him from the night fears; but the third blast gave
it was closer, and had an insistence that suggested purpo
bring himself to look around. He gave a futile spur to
ness made it immune. Even his illusion of having the f
taken from him.

A *whistle is nothing to be scared of*, he told himself, while
picturing the bands of skinhead men with blue tattoos and dead eyes, sig
to each other that it was time for the attack. He was armed for defence, but he
wasn't ready; he never had been a violent man, but he could learn to change. The
kitchen knife was in a makeshift scabbard of insulating tape against his thick
hiking socks and the cricket bat with the nails hammered through it was slung
over his back in a loop of washing line. Which would be the best for use on
horseback?

The whistle became insistent and continual, the high-pitched screech
somehow unnatural, not the product of men or musical instrument. Suddenly it
was *all* he could hear, and it was like nothing he had ever heard before. It was
growing louder, the unfortunate pitch making him feel sick and disoriented; he
wanted to plug his ears or sing loudly to drown it out.

Instead, he forged on. So near to Salisbury, with its medieval cathedral rising
up to proclaim the majesty of God, with its ordered streets, its gentility, its cafés
and pubs, intelligence and history. Salisbury, the New Jerusalem in the West.

Whistling is nothing compared to what I've been through, he thought, but the
notion only made him feel worse.

As the road drove down steeply, the trees drew in to create a funnel chan-
nelling the blasting wind. He felt like ice, and not just because of the weather.
To add to his discomfort, the rain started, quickly becoming a downpour.

Shortly before he passed the first stretch of abandoned houses, he allowed his
gaze—stupidly—to wander away to the field on his right. A flash of lightning
brought it up like snow: across it dark shapes bounded; not men.

He raced through the possibilities of what he might have seen, but nothing
matched the reality and the impossibilities were infinitely more terrifying. Salisbury grew distant.

The whistling pierced deep into his brain, no longer a single sound but a
chorus of alien voices. Now he wanted to claw at his ears until they bled. It was
a hunting call.

He urged himself not to look around, but the magnetism was irresistible.
Tears blurred his eyes as he turned, and he had to blink them away before he
could see what was closing in on him. Another flash of lightning. Across the
countryside, the shapes fluttered eerily like paper blown in the wind, drawing in
on the road; some were already amongst the nearby trees, dancing around the

winging from the branches. Their whistling grew louder as they neared, of them, perhaps even more than a hundred. They had his scent.

He dug his heels hard into the weary horse's flanks, but all he could get out it was a burst of steaming breath and a shake of sweat. A cry caught in his throat. He wanted to wish himself somewhere else, he wanted his parents, but the shakes that swept through him drove everything away.

Though the blasting wind made his eyes sting, he kept his gaze fixed on the wet road ahead, but soon his peripheral vision was picking up motion. He was caught in a pincer movement. Some of them could have had him then, but they were waiting for the others to catch up. Briefly, the hellish whistling faded, but that was only because it was drowned beneath the constant low shriek that rolled out of his own mouth. Dignity no longer mattered, only his poor, pathetic life.

And then the things were at the side of the road, tracking the horse with wild bounds. With rolling eyes and flaring nostrils, his mount found some reservoir of energy.

In a brief instant of lucidity, he remembered the cricket bat. His panic made him yank at it so wildly that the clothesline caught around his neck. Frantically, he tried to rip it free, but it was plastic and wouldn't break. His actions became even more lunatic until, miraculously, the makeshift weapon came loose. He whirled, ready to beat off the first of the wave.

One of the things was already at his side. It moved with the easy grace and awkwardness of a monkey, long arms flipping it forward as fast as the horse could gallop. It had orange-red fur like an orangutan and it reeked of rotting fish. Then it turned its head toward him and it had the face of a child.

It said, in its infant voice, "Your mother has cancer. You will never see her again."

He almost fell from the horse in shock. A thought . . . a secret fear . . . plucked from the depths of his mind. The creature bared its teeth—a horrifying image in the innocent face—and then launched itself at him. He brought the bat down sharply, but as the creature caught on to the saddle its long arm snaked up, snatched the bat from his grip, and snapped it in two with the force of one hand.

His shrieks rose above the wind as he attempted to slap the thing away with the hand that wasn't clutching the reins. It was an emasculated gesture, filled with hopelessness; the creature didn't even attempt to defend itself. It brought its young-boy face up closer and the big eyes blinked. As he stared into their depths, he was sickened by the incongruous sight of something hideously old and filled with ancient fury. The beast bared its teeth again, ready to attack.

He threw back his head and cried out to God. In a burst of blind luck, his flailing arms caught the creature under the chin just as it jumped and it flipped head over tail behind him. It did him little good; the other beasts were already preparing to rush in.

Above the wind and the whistling came the throaty rumble of a car engine. At first he barely recognised it, so lost to his terror was he; and it had been an age since he had heard that sound. But as it roared closer and bright light splayed all around him, he looked back in disbelief. Twin beams cut a swathe through the creatures as they scrambled to avoid the light. Whoever was driving floored the pedal, swerving across the road to hit the beasts slowest at getting out of the way. He winced: their screams actually sounded like those of small children.

A body slammed across the hood, leaving a deep dent. Another turned part of the windshield to frost. Others were flattened, midscream, beneath the wheels.

The headlights burned toward him as the car accelerated. He wasn't going to be torn apart by a pack of supernatural creatures, he was going to be run down in a world where you rarely saw a car anymore. The irony didn't really have much time to register.

At the last moment, the car swerved until it was running alongside him. The black Porsche was still bright with showroom gleam. His mount jumped and shied in terror, almost throwing him under the wheels.

The passenger window slid down electronically and Mallory leaned across the seat while steering blindly; the rider squinted to make out his face. "Are you doing this for sport?" Mallory called out.

The rider gave a comical goldfish gulp, his comprehension flowing treacle-thick.

Mallory shook his head dismissively, then readjusted the wheel as the car drifted dangerously close to the horse. "You'd better get off that and get in here," he called again.

His words broke through the rider's fug. Along the weed-clogged pavement the creatures were jumping up and down, their whistling unbearably shrill and threatening. The horse didn't want to be reined in, but the rider slowed it enough to dismount, wincing as he landed awkwardly on his left ankle. Mallory brought the Porsche to a screeching halt and flung the passenger door open. The rider gazed worriedly after his departing mount until Mallory yelled, "It'll be fine. It's not horse meat they're after. You've got about two seconds to get in—"

The rider dived in and slammed the door. The creatures bounded closer in fury; it seemed as if they might even risk the light. As the car jolted off with a spin of wheels, the rider threw his head forward into his hands, sobbing, "Thank God."

"Don't thank Him yet. I've been running on empty for the last mile or so. We'll never make it to Salisbury." The rider noted Mallory's expensive black over-coat that looked as new as the car and couldn't mask his discomfort that both had plainly been looted.

Mallory checked over his shoulder before reversing the Porsche at high speed, eventually swinging it around sharply through a hundred and eighty degrees. The rider clutched his stomach and groaned. "Now, let's see if we can get some of those bastards." Indecent pleasure crackled through Mallory's voice.

He hit the accelerator, popped the clutch, and at the same time launched the car toward the edge of the road. Golden sparks showered all around as the undercarriage raked up the curb. The rider squealed as the expensive car tore through long grass and bushes, then squealed more as the creatures failed to get out of the way. They slammed against the already fractured windshield, their bodies bursting to coat the glass with blood so black it resembled ink.

The beasts were too intelligent to be victims for long. One of them dropped from an overhanging branch, clutching on to the windshield with its phenomenally long arms. It fumbled for the spot where the glass was most frosted and hammered sharply. Tiny cubes showered over the rider, who threw up his hands to protect himself. The creature drove its arm through the hole it had created and clawed toward his face. The rider squealed again like a teenage girl and attempted to scramble into the back of the car. His eyes fixed on a shotgun lying across the rear seat just as Mallory shouted, "Use the gun!"

The creature tore chunks out of the windshield and thrust its head partway into the car. The black eyes ranged wildly in the freckled, pink-cheeked face, the teeth snapping furiously.

"I can't use a gun!" the rider shrieked.

"Give it here!" Mallory said with irritation. "It's already loaded."

The rider snatched up the shotgun and threw it at the driver as if it were red hot. Mallory cursed before grabbing it, and then in one simple movement he shouldered it, aimed, and pulled the trigger. The thunderous blast in the confines of the car made their ears ring. The creature's faceless body flapped at the windshield like a piece of cloth before the air currents dragged it away behind.

The cold night air rushing through the hole cleared the rider's senses. "Where can we go?" he whimpered.

Mallory accelerated from the trees along the road out of Salisbury. He pointed to the silhouette of Old Sarum towering over the landscape.

The car died on them on the steep slope to the parking lot between the high banks of prehistoric ramparts constructed for defence more than 2,500 years earlier. Jumping into the driving rain, Mallory and the rider headed along the road, which ran straight for around four hundred and fifty feet to a wooden bridge across a deep inner ditch. Beyond were the ruins of the Norman castle built in the heart of the Iron Age hill-fort. Although the car hadn't taken them far, they'd earned themselves enough breathing space to cover the remaining distance on foot.

"Shouldn't be long till dawn," Mallory said as they ran, head down against the deluge. "They'll leave us alone at first light."

The rider was finding it hard to keep up with his twisted ankle. "How do you know?"

"I don't."

"Are you sure we'll find somewhere to hide out up there?"

"No, but we haven't got much choice, have we? Unless you want to stand and fight?"

The rider didn't answer.

They came to the wooden bridge barred by a gate with signs warning of the dangers of crumbling ancient monuments. Mallory laughed, then hauled himself over, yanking the rider behind him.

The whistling assailed them as they ran through the broken remains of the gatehouse; the wild shapes were already loping along the road past the parking lot. Lightning revealed the bleak interior of the inner bailey: a flimsy wooden ticket office and shop to their right, and then a wide expanse of sodden grass and ruins that were barely more than four feet high in most places.

"Shit, fuck and bastard," Mallory said.

The rider whimpered. "What do we do now?"

"Firstly, you stop getting on my nerves by whining. Secondly . . ." Mallory scanned the site as best he could in the storm, then with a resigned sigh broke into a run. The rider jumped and followed, looking over his shoulder so much that he slipped and fell several times.

Mallory picked out the shattered block of the keep on the far side of the inner bailey. It was useless for any kind of serious defence, but it was the best place to make a stand until the shotgun shells ran out. They found an area protected on three sides by the only remaining high walls on the site, which also served to shelter them from the worst of the storm.

"We're going to die," the rider moaned.

"Yep." Mallory began to count out the remaining cartridges; there weren't as many as he had thought.

"You don't seem bothered!"

Through an iron grille, Mallory could just make out frantic activity near the gateway. He positioned the shotgun to pick off one or two as they advanced across the open space, then waited. After five minutes it was clear the things weren't coming in.

"They've stayed at the gate." Even as Mallory spoke, the wind picked up the insistent whistling, now moving around the ramparts as if searching for access. It became increasingly sharp, frustrated. Mallory sank back down into the lee of the wall.

"Why aren't they coming in?" The rider looked at Mallory accusingly, as if he were lying.

"I don't know," Mallory snapped. "Maybe they don't like the décor."

It was so dark in their defensive position that they could only see the pale glow of their faces and hands. Above and around them, the wind howled mercilessly, drowning out their ragged breathing but not the whistling, which, though muted, still set their teeth on edge.

After a while, they'd calmed down enough to entertain conversation.

"I'm Jez Miller." The rider appeared keen for some kind of connection, comfort, someone to tell him things weren't as bad as he feared, though he realised instinctively he was talking to the wrong person.

"Mallory."

"It's lucky you came along when you did."

"That's one way of looking at it." Mallory examined Miller surreptitiously. Though in his midtwenties, he had the face of a man twenty years older, lined through screwing up his features in despair, hollow-cheeked from lack of sustenance, made worse by scruffy shoulder-length hair already turning grey.

"Where did you get the car?" Miller asked, plucking at his sodden trousers.

"Stole it. In Marlborough."

Miller thought for a second until the realisation hit him. "You drove across Salisbury Plain!" An uninterested silence hung in the dark. "You don't see many cars these days. Everyone's trying to save petrol, for emergencies."

"It was an emergency. I had to get out of Marlborough. Dull as ditchwater, that place."

Miller couldn't read Mallory at all and that plainly made him uncomfortable. "So you were going to Salisbury?"

"I heard they were hiring down at the cathedral. At least, that's the word going around. Thought I'd take a look."

Miller started in surprise. "Me too!" Excitedly, he scrabbled around to face Mallory. "You're going to be a knight?"

"If the pay's right. These days food, drink, and shelter would probably swing it."

"I couldn't believe it when I heard! I thought the Church had gone the same way as everything else. You know, with all that's been happening . . ." He struggled for a second. "With the gods . . . what they call gods . . . all that happening every day . . . all the time . . . people said there wasn't any need for a Church. Why should you believe in a God who never shows up when all that's going on around you? That's what they said."

"You a Christian, then?"

"I wasn't particularly. I mean, I was christened, but I never went to church. I'm a Christian now. God's the only one who can save us." Miller slipped his fingers around the crucifix he'd picked up from the broken window of the jeweller's.

"Well, it's not as if we can save ourselves."

Miller wrinkled his brow at the odd tone in Mallory's voice. "You don't believe."

"I don't believe in anything."

"How can you say that?"

Mallory gave a low laugh. "Everyone else is doing a good job believing. You said it yourself—miracles all over the place. I'm the only unbeliever in a born-again world." He laughed louder, amused at the concept.

"But how can you work for the Church . . . how can you be a knight?"

"They're paying men to do a job—to protect their clerics. The new Knights Templar. That sounds like a good deal. A bit of strong-arm stuff here and there, nothing too taxing. These days, it's all scratching in the fields to feed the masses, or making things, or sewing—all the rubbish people think's necessary to get us back on our feet. If I had a list of ways to spend my remaining days, planting potatoes would not be on it."

"They won't have you."

"I'm betting they will. They'll have anybody they can get, these days."

"That's cynical."

Mallory grunted. "We'll see."

Miller scratched on the floor, listening to the rise and fall of the whistling as it moved around the ramparts. "What are they?" he asked eventually.

"No idea."

"Where did all these things come from?"

"No idea."

"One of my mates saw a dragon." When Mallory didn't respond, Miller pressed on, "Why are we being made to suffer like this?"

"You say *made* as if there's some intelligence behind it. The sooner you accept there isn't, the easier your life will be. Things happen, you deal with them and move on to the next. That's the way it goes. You're not being victimised. You don't have to lead some deviantly perfect lifestyle just to get a reward in some next life. You make the most of what you've got here. It's about survival."

"If that's all there is, what's the point?"

Mallory's laugh suggested that the answer was ridiculously obvious.

Miller became depressed by Mallory's attitude. Everything about Miller said he wanted to be uplifted, to be told there was some meaning to all the suffering everyone was going through. "Is Marlborough your home?"

"No." Mallory considered leaving it there, but then took pity on Miller. "London. I wasn't born there, but that's where I spent most of my life."

"Is it true the whole place has been destroyed? That's what people say."

"I got out before the shit hit the fan. Went north. Birmingham for a while." His voice trailed away.

"No family?" Mallory's silence told Miller this was a question too far. "I'm from Swindon," Miller continued, to fill the gap. "My mum and dad are still there, and my sister. I suppose I could have stuck it out, too. Life isn't *so* bad. People are pulling together, setting up systems. They've just about got the food distribution sorted out. I reckon they should get through this winter OK." He paused as the harsh memories returned. "Not like last winter."

The thoughts stilled him for a while, but he found it hard to deal with the pauses that magnified the dim whistling outside. "I had to get out in the end. My girlfriend, Sue . . . we were going to get married, been in love for ages . . . couldn't imagine being with anyone else." His voice took on a bleak tone. "Then one day she dumped me, just like that. Said she was moving in with this complete moron . . . a thug . . . God knows what sort of things he was involved in. And she'd always hated him, that was the mad thing! But she said he made her feel safe."

"These are dangerous times. People do what they have to, to survive."

"But I didn't make her feel safe, you know?" Miller made no attempt to hide his devastation; he reminded Mallory of a child, emotional, almost innocent.

"That's what made you decide to come down here, to sign up?"

Mallory obviously wasn't really interested; it was a friendly gesture, but after the rigours of the night it felt to Miller as if Mallory had clapped his arms around him. "Partly. I mean, I'd been thinking about it for a long time. I knew I wanted to do something. To give something back. So many people were making sacrifices for the greater good and I didn't feel as if I was doing anything at all. I know you don't believe, but it felt as if God had put us through all this suffering and spared some of us for a reason."

Mallory made a faint derisive noise.

"No, really. Sometimes when you sit back and think about it, you can see patterns."

"There aren't any patterns, just illusions of patterns. It's the human condition to join the dots into something cohesive when all there is . . . is a big mass of dots."

"I can't believe that, Mallory. When you see some of the goodness that has come out of all this . . . the goodness people have exhibited to others. They could have wallowed in self-preservation." His voice became harder as he went on, "Just done things to survive, like you said."

"Well, I'm not going to try to change your mind."

Miller's shoulders sagged so that the rainwater ran from his crown to drip into his lap. He suddenly looked burdened by some awful weight. "It's hard to be scared all the time, do you know what I mean? Life was difficult enough before everything changed, but now there's just . . . threat . . . everywhere, all the time. It wears you down." He trembled with a deep, juddering sigh. "Why isn't the government doing something? Where's the army, the police?"

"I don't think they exist anymore."

"But if it's left to people like us, what's going to become of us all?"

Mallory couldn't answer that.

They sat in silence for a while until Mallory said, "Well, it's not all bad."

"What do you mean?" Miller mumbled.

"No more *Stars in Their Eyes*."

Miller brightened. "Or Euro-disco."

"Or public-school boys getting drunk at Henley, or . . ." He made an expansive gesture, just caught in a flash of lightning. The depressive mood evaporated with their laughter.

It was echoed by another laugh away in the dark, only this one was an old man's, low and throaty. Miller yelped in shock, pushing himself back until he felt the stones hard against him. The shotgun clattered as Mallory scraped it up and swung it in an arc, waiting for another sound to pinpoint the target.

"I've got a gun," he said.

The laugh sounded again, slow and eerie, though with a faint muffled echo as if it were coming through the wall.

"Who's there?" Miller whined. He shivered at the haunting, otherworldly quality of the laughter.

"My names are legion," the old man said.

Miller started to whimper the Lord's Prayer.

"He's playing with you," Mallory said. "Aren't you?"

The old man laughed again. "No fooling you, Son of Adam."

"No!" Miller said. "He's lying! It *is* the Devil! And he always lies!"

"There are devils and there are devils," the old man snorted. "You must know the Devil by the deed."

Miller hugged his knees to his chest. "What are you?"

"Not of the Sons of Adam." The statement was simple, but edged with an unaccountable menace.

Not wishing to antagonise whatever was nearby, Mallory's tone became slightly less offensive. "What do you want?"

"The question, more likely, is what do *you* want? My home has looked out over this place since before your kind rose up."

"We didn't realise," Miller protested. "We don't want to trespass—"

"We're sheltering," Mallory said. "We'll be gone at first light, if that's all right with you."

"Perhaps it isn't and perhaps it is. I would have to say, in this day and age I'm not wholly sure where the boundaries lie. You may be trespassing, and then again you may not."

"We'll pay you," Miller said. "Anything!"

"No." Mallory's voice was sharp, cutting Miller dead.

"You're very cautious," the old man said slyly, "but are you as wise as you seem, I wonder?"

Mallory replaced the shotgun on the floor, instinctively knowing it was useless. "You like questions——"

"I like questions and games and riddles because that's what everything is about, is it not? One big riddle, and you trying to find out what the answer is." He chuckled. "Trying to find out what the question is."

"And you have all the answers, I suppose," Mallory said.

"Many, many, many. Not all, no. But more than you, Son of Adam."

The wind dropped a little, the crashing rain becoming a mere patter. Mallory remained tense. "Do you want something of us?"

A long silence was eventually ended by words that were heavily measured. "Curiosity was my motivation. Few venture up this hill in these times. I had a desire to witness the extent of the bravery in our latest visitors." A smack of mockery.

Tension filled the air, driving Mallory into silence. It felt as if they were in the jungle with some wild animal padding slowly around them, content in the knowledge that it could attack at any time. Mallory decided it was better to engage the old man in conversation rather than allow any lulls where other ideas might surface.

"Perhaps you'd like to provide us with some answers, as we're so sadly lacking," he said.

The old man mused on this for a time, then said, "Answers I can give, and questions too. But if you seek my advice, it's this: keep your head down doing honest work and give offence to none. Avoid drawing unwanted attention at all costs."

"What kind of attention?"

"Ah, you should know by now," the old man said with a cunning tone, "that when the mouse gets noticed by the cat, it won't leave him alone . . . until he's long gone."

"What's going to happen?" Miller was whimpering again.

"Many things," the old man said, pretending it was a question for him, purely for the sake of malice. With another chuckle, he added, "The wormfood will come up for air, and the quick will go down for a way out, but find none. There'll be a man with three hands, and one with one eye. Some will be bereft in more profound areas. Friends will be found in unlikely places, but where friends should really be, there will at times be none. And consider this: a religion isn't as good as its god, only as good as its followers."

"Is that supposed to help?" Mallory said.

"The joy of a riddle is twofold: in the solving, or in the enlightenment that comes from hindsight. Riddles are lights to be shone in the darkest corners, where all secrets hide."

"Secrets?"

"Everybody has secrets," the old man said pointedly.

"Thank you for your guidance," Mallory said with irony. "We'll take it with us when we leave."

"Oh, you will be back, Son of Adam. Back here, and back there. Sylvie doesn't love you anymore. It's a hopeless case." Then, "Your sins will always find you out."

The tension in the air dropped slowly until they realised they were alone, which was an odd way of considering it because they had no idea where the presence had been. Slowly, Miller's body folded until his face was in his hands. "What did he mean?" he said bleakly. When Mallory didn't answer, he asked, "What was that?"

"Probably best not to talk about it right now." Mallory illuminated his watch. The green glow painted his face a ghastly shade, the shadows defining the skull beneath.

"He can still hear us?"

"I think he . . . and what he represents . . . can always hear us." He stood up, shaking the kinks from his limbs. "It should be dawn any minute." The whistling no longer floated around the building; instead they could just make out birdsong dimly coming over the ramparts. "Want to risk it?"

"I guess."

"*I tell you this. No eternal reward will forgive us for wasting the dawn.*" Mallory cracked his knuckles.

"What's that?"

"Words from an old singer."

"You like music?"

"That's a funny question. Doesn't everyone?"

"No, not really," Miller said.

They walked out into the inner bailey, the ruins and windswept trees now grey ghosts. The rain had blown away and there was an optimistic bloom to the edge of the sky. The monkey-creatures were nowhere to be seen.

The morning had the fresh smell of wet vegetation. Mallory took a deep breath, still surprised at how sweet the air tasted now that it was pollution-free. They made their way back along the track and prepared to walk the short distance into Salisbury. As they breached the crest of the hill and headed down into the city, the mother sky turned golden, framing the majestic spire of the cathedral protruding through the treetops ahead. Miller was overcome with a rush of Glory and turned to Mallory, beaming; Mallory shook his head and looked away.

The corpses of the monkey-creatures ploughed up by the car had vanished. A little further on they came across Miller's horse, grazing at the side of the road. Miller patted its flank affectionately.

"We can take it in turns to ride," Miller said brightly.

"It's all yours. I like a good walk of a morning, gets the blood flowing."

They took the empty road slowly and within the hour the outskirts of Salisbury drew around them. It was still odd for both of them to see the empty houses and factories, the abandoned petrol stations and corner shops without any of the trappings of the modern world. No vehicles moved, no electric lights burned, no fast-food wrappers blew up and down the streets. Instead there was the smell of woodsmoke hanging in the air and some homes were illuminated by candlelight. The air of the makeshift lay across the city: handmade signs pointing to the farmers' market or the council offices, piles of wood obviously prepared for nighttime beacons, repairs carried out to broken windows with plastic sheets. Wild dogs roamed the streets and furtive rats skulked out of front gardens.

They came upon a sentry box roughly constructed out of crates and perspex. A grey-faced man in an adapted police uniform was boiling some water on a small fire. As they approached, he rose suspiciously, holding a handmade truncheon close to his thigh.

"What's your business?" His eyes were hard on their faces.

"We're going to the cathedral," Miller said with bright innocence, "to become knights."

The guard didn't attempt to hide his disdain. "Good luck," he sneered, rolling his eyes.

"The police are still going?" Mallory asked.

The guard glanced down at the uniform, which had SPM sewn on to the left breast. "I used to be with the force," he said. "Still got my warrant card. These days it's the Salisbury People's Militia." He waved them through, nodding toward the spire. "I don't think you'll get lost."

"Have many people come to join up?" Miller asked as he rode by.

The guard laughed indecently loudly. "I shouldn't worry about having to queue."

"It's early days yet," Miller said when they were out of the guard's earshot.

"Look on the bright side," Mallory replied wryly. "At least the standards will be low."

At that same time of day, the outskirts of the city were deserted. In the bright dawn light, it could have been any time before everything changed; the fabric was, in the main, intact, although a few shops had been burned out in looting, and others had been adapted to fill more immediate needs. An electrical goods

26

store had been converted into a cobblers and leatherworkers. A video shop now housed carpenters and builders.

They made their way down Castle Street and before they had got to the end of it they could hear loud voices, jocularity, cursing, life going on. The farmers' market was in the process of being set up, with red-faced workers loading piles of cabbages and bags of potatoes on creaking stalls. Many places appeared to have quickly established a local economy and regular food supply, but everyone was still fearing the winter, Miller noted. Mallory pointed out that nothing would have worked if the population hadn't been decimated.

Their attention was caught by an area of brightly coloured tents and tepees on a park on the other side of a river bridge. They clustered tightly together like a nomadic enclave within the wider city. A flag bearing red and white intertwined dragons flew over the largest tent.

They followed the High Street past the shells of Woolworth's and Waterstone's. The horse's hooves echoed dully on the flagstones; the atmosphere in that area was strangely melancholic.

But as they came up to High Street Gate, the historic entrance to the Cathedral Close, they were confronted by ten-foot-high gates of welded metal sheets, the ancient stone surround topped with lethal spikes and rolls of barbed wire. Beyond it, the cathedral looked like a fortress under siege.

chapter two

OPUS DEI

"A man's character is his fate."
Heraclitus

The reinforced gates were rust eaten, stained, and covered with foul graffiti. Mallory tried to decide whether they had been erected out of fear, or strength; to keep the outside world at bay, or to keep those inside pure. Whichever was the right answer, first impressions were not of an open religion welcoming all souls into a place of refuge from the storm of life. He'd only been there a moment and he already doubted the judgment of those in charge. Situation normal.

He could feel Miller's uncertain gaze on his back, urging him to do something to dispel the disappointment his companion was starting to feel. With a shrug, Mallory strode up and hammered on the gates. When the metallic echoes had died, a young man with a shaven head and an incongruously cherubic face peered over the stone battlements.

"Who goes?" he called, with a faint lisp.

Mallory turned back to Miller. "Well, that's scared me off."

"We want to join you," Miller shouted.

The guard eyed them suspiciously, focusing particular attention on Mallory.

"We want to be knights," Miller pressed. His voice held a faint note of panic at the possibility that after all he'd been through he might still be turned away.

"Wait there." The guard bobbed down. Several minutes later, they heard the scrape of metal bars being drawn on the other side. The gates creaked open just wide enough for Mallory and Miller to pass through in single file. On the other side were five men armed with medieval weaponry: pikes, swords, and an axe, which Mallory guessed had been taken from some local museum.

The guard stepped forward. "Enter with humility before God." An implied threat lay in his words.

Mallory looked at him askance. "Does everyone talk like that around here?"

Miller gazed back at the fortified gate uncomfortably. "Why all that?" he asked.

"Times are hard." It wasn't enough of an answer, but the guard turned away before Miller could ask him any more.

Mallory was intrigued by what he saw within the compound. He'd seen photos of the cathedral in the old days, had even caught the last of a TV Christmas carol service broadcast from there, seen through an alcoholic haze after a late night at the pub. The serenity of the expansive lawns that had once surrounded the cathedral was long gone. Now wooden shacks clustered tightly, some of which appeared to have been knocked up overnight, offering little protection from the elements. Mallory also spied vegetable and herb gardens, stables, a small mill, and more. The grass was now little more than churned mud with large cart ruts running amongst the huts. The entire scene had an odd medieval flavour that discomfited him.

The houses appeared to consist of only a single room, two at the most, with small windows that could not have allowed much light inside. They were arranged, more or less, on a grid pattern, the cathedral's own village, although there were still a few remaining lawns around the grand building to form a barrier between the sacred and the profane.

Once they were well within the site, they could see that fortifications had been continued on all sides to create a well-defended compound. Most of the wall was original, constructed in the fourteenth century with the stone from the deserted cathedral at Old Sarum, but where gaps had appeared over the years, makeshift barriers had now been thrown up. Abandoned cars, crushed and tattered, building rubble, corrugated sheets, had all been riveted together to become remarkably sturdy. Of the original gates, three remained, all as secure as the one through which Mallory and Miller had passed.

Enclosed within the new fortifications were several imposing piles that lined the Cathedral Close, including the museums on the western edge, which appeared to have been pressed into Church use. The weight of history was palpable, from Malmesbury House, partly built by Sir Christopher Wren and where Charles II and Handel had both stayed, to the grand Mompesson House with its Queen Anne façade, through the many stately buildings that had offered services to the Church. Beyond the houses, the enclosure ran down to the banks of the Avon past a larger cultivated area providing food for the residents.

And at the centre of it was the cathedral itself. Dedicated to the Virgin Mary, the grey stone of the gothic medieval building gleamed in the morning light, its perpendicular lines leading the eye toward the four-hundred-foot spire that spoke proudly of the Glory of Almighty God. Even in that broken world, it still had the power to inspire.

They were led through a door near the west front to an area next to the cloisters that had once held a café. The surly guard guided them to a windowless room containing three dining chairs and a table. He sent in some water and bread before leaving them alone for the next hour.

"What do you think?" Miller asked in an excited whisper.

Mallory tore a chunk off the bread and inspected it cautiously before chewing. "They're worse off than I imagined."

"What do you mean?"

"All that graffiti on the walls—looks as if they've had a falling out with the locals. And the walls themselves, what message are they sending out?"

Miller wasn't going to be deterred. "Still, it's great to be here, finally," he said with a blissful smile.

"You really are a glass-half-full kind of person, aren't you." Mallory spun one of the chairs and straddled it. "They'd better not bury us in rules and regulations. You know how it is with God people. Thou shalt not do this, thou shalt not do that. Bottom line for me: no vows of celibacy, no abstinence from the demon drink."

"We might not get accepted."

"Right," Mallory said sarcastically. "We're going to get accepted."

"How can you be sure? They might think we're not . . . devout enough. We're supposed to be champions of God's Word."

"So what does God want? That His Word gets out there. Do you think He really cares if it's being transmitted by some cynical money-grabbing toe rag who doesn't believe one syllable of it?"

"Of course it matters!" Miller stared at Mallory in disbelief.

"Why? The job's still getting done. People are still being led away from the dark side to the Path of Righteousness. Or is it more ideologically pure if the unbeliever doesn't do it and they all stay damned?"

"It . . . matters!" Miller looked as if he was about to burst into tears again. Mallory's weary attempt to backtrack was interrupted when the door swung open, revealing a man in his late forties, balding on top, but with long, bushy grey hair. He carried with him an air of tranquillity underpinned by a good-natured, open attitude visible in his untroubled smile. He wore the long black robes of a monk.

"My name is James," he said. "I realise things may seem strange to you here. It's strange for all of us."

"We want to be knights," Miller said firmly.

"It's my job to greet the new arrivals," James continued. "Help them adjust to the very different life we have here, facilitate an easy transition from the world without to the one we are attempting to build here in the cathedral precinct."

"So you're the official counsellor," Mallory said.

James didn't appear troubled by the less than deferential tone. "I suppose that's one way of describing my work." The cast of his smile suggested he knew exactly what game Mallory was playing. "Come, walk with me and I'll show you the sights, introduce you to a few people. And I'll explain why things are the way they are."

"Getting your apologies in first?" Mallory said.

"I think it's true to say things are probably not how you expected them, how we all expected them to be. But everyone is still coming to terms with the Fall." The euphemism for the chaos that had descended on the world made Mallory smile. James continued, "It has necessitated a particular approach which may be . . . surprising at first impression."

Mallory gestured for him to lead the way. "I love surprises."

James took them into the cathedral nave, crossing himself briefly as he faced the altar. Inside, the building was even bigger than Mallory had imagined. The magnificent vaulted roof soared so high over their heads it made them dizzy when they looked up, dwarfing them beneath the majesty of God as the original architects had intended. Further down the quire, a few men knelt in silent prayer.

"It will be packed at vespers," James noted with a sweep of his hand from wall to wall.

"I haven't seen any women since I came in," Mallory said.

"No." James appeared uncomfortable at this observation, but he didn't give Mallory time to follow up. "This is the last outpost of Christianity, at least in Great Britain. Within this compound you will find Anglicans, Catholics, Methodists, High Church, Low Church, representatives of the fringe evangelical movements, all worshipping side by side in a manner that could never have been anticipated at a time when the Church was thriving. Then, there were too many rivalries. Now we are all forced to work together for the common good." He smiled benignly at Mallory. "I'm sure there is a lesson in there somewhere."

"The last outpost?" Miller appeared to be hearing James's words in a time-delay.

"What happened over the past year and a half shattered the Church." James led them slowly along the nave. "Even in our darkest moment we could never have foreseen . . ." He shook his head dismally.

"It obviously wasn't as strong as you thought," Mallory said.

"The Church remains as indefatigable as always," James parried.

"Then perhaps the people didn't live up to your expectations."

James thought about this for a moment, but did not deny it. "With miracles happening on every street corner all day every day, with gods . . . things that call themselves gods . . . answering the calls of anyone who petitioned them, it was understandable that there would be a period of confusion."

Miller turned in a slow circle, dumbfounded. "This is all that's left?"

"The congregations fragmented. Yes, some became more devout because of the upheaval they witnessed, but many lost their way." He took a second or two to choose his words, but could find no easy way to say it. "Including many of our ministers."

The sun gleamed through the stained-glass windows, but without any electric lights to illuminate the loftier regions there was still an atmosphere of gloom.

"With the lines of communication shattered, the situation rapidly became untenable," James continued. "Belief was withering on the vine. The leaders . . . the remaining leaders . . . of the various churches held an emergency conference, a crisis meeting, at Winchester." He had led them to the Trinity Chapel where the window glowed in blues and reds in the morning sun. Slender pillars of marble rose up on either side to support a daringly designed roof of sharply pointed arches. "It was decided that a period of retrenchment was necessary. The Church would fortress itself if necessary, reestablish its strength before taking the Word back out to the country."

Mallory examined the images on the windows. The design was called *Prisoners of Conscience*. "You really think you can do it?"

"If faith is undiminished, anything can be achieved." James watched him carefully. "And why are you here?"

Mallory didn't look at him. "Food, shelter. Security."

"Is that what you believe?"

"You *are* looking for knights?" Miller ventured hopefully.

James turned to him with a pleasant aspect. "At the same Council of Winchester, the decision was taken to reestablish the Knights Templar. Do you know of them?"

"A bit," Miller said uncertainly.

"According to historical sources, most notably the Frankish historian Guillaume de Tyre, the Knights Templar were formed by nine knights under the leadership of Hugues de Payen in 1118," James began. "After Jerusalem fell to the Crusaders in 1099, it became a Christian city and the nine, under the name of the Poor Knights of Christ and the Temple of Solomon, vowed to devote themselves to the protection of all pilgrims travelling along the dangerous roads to the Christian shrines. They took quarters next to the temple and from then on became known as the Knights Templar."

James led them from the Trinity Chapel into the presbytery and then into the quire, the "church within a church" where the canons' stalls faced each other beneath the shining pipes of the organ.

"Ten years after their establishment, their fame had spread," James continued. "No lesser an authority than Saint Bernard, the abbot of Clairvaux, wrote a tract declaring the Templars to be the epitome and apotheosis of Christian values. They were soon officially recognised and incorporated as a religious-military order, Christ's militia, if you will, soldier-mystics, warrior-monks, combining the spirituality of the Church with a fighting ability that struck terror into Christianity's enemies."

"Until the God-fearing royals of Europe had the Church brand them heretics," Mallory noted wryly, "because they had the misfortune to become too successful, right? Too rich and powerful . . . a challenge to the established order. Had their leader slowly roasted alive in the square of some French city . . . nice . . . had the knights hunted down and slaughtered, launched a propaganda assault to completely destroy their reputation."

"You're obviously an educated man. But don't confuse the Church with the people who claim to administer God's Word," James cautioned. "Humans are fallible."

"Pardon me for pointing it out, but you seem to have had your fair share of the fallible in your history," Mallory countered, unmoved.

"We are all fallible." James turned his attention to the high altar at the focal point of the cathedral. "The decision to reestablish the Knights Templar was taken for practical reasons, and for symbolic ones. The new Knights Templar will protect our missionaries as they move out across the country. It's a dangerous land out there . . . worldly threats, supernatural threats, spiritual threats . . ."

"That's a tough job," Mallory said. "You'll need tough men."

"Tough, yes. Not just physically or psychologically, but spiritually. It will be demanding, with little reward in this world." There was pity in his smile. "Many who wish to join will not be suitable. You need to understand that. But there will always be a role here for people willing to carry out God's Word."

"Not many perks, though," Mallory said.

James laughed. "Sorry, no company cars! On the plus side, the Council decided not to continue with the strict rules under which the original Templars existed—shaven heads, beards, poverty, chastity, and obedience—though we have adopted a distinctive dress for our knights so that everyone will know them when they see them coming."

Mallory pointed to James's habit. "You've got your own strict dress code as well."

"Indeed. It was felt, with the various . . . strands . . . of the Church coming together, that a uniformity was necessary to bind everyone here into a single community." He was choosing his words carefully, Mallory noted.

"You had some friction, then? A little local rivalry?"

"There was a danger of that, yes. So it was decided that we adopt elements of the Rule of Saint Benedict, which was written in the sixth century as a guide to the spiritual and administrative life of a monastery. Although we are not a monastic order—we are a chapter of canons—it was agreed that a certain level of . . . discipline was necessary." He didn't appear wholly to agree with this, although he attempted to mask it with a smile. "But you'll find out all about that later."

As they turned to leave the quire, they were confronted by two men who had been making their way toward the altar. One of them was very old, possibly in his eighties, Mallory estimated. Hunched over his walking stick, he resembled a crane, both awkward and frail; he didn't appear to have the strength to walk any distance at all. Helping him along was a man in his late twenties with shoulder-length black hair and a long, pointed nose that reminded Mallory of some forest animal.

James knelt and formally kissed the hand of the old man. "Our bishop," he said when he rose.

The old man smiled; his eyes were uncannily bright and sharp. "Cornelius," he amended in a rural Scottish accent. "New arrivals?"

"More recruits for the knights," James said. "They're growing fast. It shouldn't be long before we have a full complement."

"Then our community here owes you our gratitude," Cornelius said to Mallory and Miller. "You are our future. Your bravery will not go unrewarded."

He began his slow progress along the aisle, but his companion held back. With a surreptitious glance at the bishop, he caught James's arm and said, "The dogs have started to gather."

James's expression darkened. "Surely they won't make their move yet." He, too, glanced after the bishop. "Surely not yet."

"They're driven by ideology. Common sense doesn't come into it." He moved off quickly to catch the bishop's arm.

"Who was that?" Mallory asked.

"Julian. A good man. He's the precentor, responsible for the choir, the music, and a few other recently added duties, mainly to do with the services and spiritual life of the cathedral. He's one of the four Principal Persons who oversee the Chapter of Canons, our guiding body."

James appeared briefly distracted, then, sensing Mallory's interest, shepherded them quickly away before they could ask any more questions.

James took them throughout the main body of the cathedral and its ancillary buildings; it was important, he said, for every new arrival to understand both the facts and the symbolism of their new home. "This will be our Jerusalem," he said. "In England's green and pleasant land." He detailed the history of the cathedral from its construction between 1220 and 1258 following the decision to move it from its original location at Old Sarum, through to modern times, so that by the end Mallory thought he was going to go insane if he heard another date.

"The new cathedral was entrusted to Nicholas of Ely, a master mason, who encoded many mysteries in the sacred geometry of the building, utilising the vast secret knowledge of numbers, angles, and harmonics passed down through the masonic guilds of medieval times," James commented as they stood in the south quire aisle. "They say the great secrets of our religion were locked in the stone, but much of the knowledge has since been lost. Who knows what the length of this column, or the angle of that beam, was meant to imply? What we do know is that the building itself was seen as an act of worship. Here, God is in the detail and in the greater design."

"Is that why you made your base here?" Mallory asked. "What was wrong with Winchester? Or Glastonbury?"

James thought deeply before replying. "Those places were certainly considered, as were several others. In the end, the decision was made to come to Salisbury for one very important reason."

Mallory read his face. "But you're not going to tell us what it is."

James grew serious. "We like to keep a few secrets." He winced as if he'd said too much, and Mallory was intrigued to see him change direction, leading them now up a winding stone stairway rising from the south transept.

"We have an excellent library here," James said rather awkwardly, as if continuing the previous conversation. "Its most famous item is a copy of the Magna Carta, but it has long been praised by academics for its ancient manuscripts, including a page of the Old Testament in Latin from the eighth century and two Gallican psalters from the tenth century."

"I'll have to book those out on a quiet night," Mallory said.

"The more important books are less well known," James continued. "Within, there are sacred texts the outside world has never been allowed to see since the cathedral was established. Indeed, part of its reason for existing was as guardian and protector of old truths—or lies, depending on your point of view."

"Surely the great Church wasn't afraid of a few words on paper?" Mallory said. "Or was it that these things were too dangerous for the common man to find out?"

James laughed quietly. "I'm just a lowly member here. But I've heard it said that the potency arises not from any individual volume, each of which presents one particular view, but in the totality. Each is a fragment that together reveal a large secret."

Miller appeared troubled at this. "Religious secrets?" he asked anxiously.

"Not wholly," James replied. "The library also contains a collection of the earliest scientific, mathematical, and medical books, including William Harvey's *De Motu Cordis*, which identified the circulation of the blood for the first time. They were bequeathed by Seth Ward, who became bishop in 1667. But before that he'd been Professor of Astronomy at Oxford and a founding member of the Royal Society."

"I thought scientists and the religious were always at each other's throats," Mallory said.

"Apparently not in the old days." James's smile was enigmatic.

At the top of the stairs they were confronted by two men installing large locks in the door that led to the library; through the opening they could see the stacks of ancient books and smell the warm atmosphere of dusty paper. The workers were being overseen by a man in his late fifties, overweight beneath his black robes, with a balding pate and a goatee beard. His eyes were dark and piercing and instantly fell on the new faces.

"Good morning, Stefan," James said brightly. "What have we here?"

"The library is now off-limits, on the orders of the bishop." Stefan tried to return James's smile, but it was an awkward attempt that looked out of place on his face. The shadows under his eyes suggested a saturnine nature, and he quickly returned to a gloomy countenance.

"Oh?" James said, puzzled. "I can't understand that. The library is a vital resource for everyone here."

"Nevertheless, the decision has been made. Requests for specific books can be presented to the librarian, who will put them to the new library committee for consideration."

"That sounds like an unwieldy process. How often does the committee meet?"

"We haven't yet reached agreement on all the details, but as chairman of the committee I will certainly do my best to expedite matters."

James nodded and smiled, but as he moved Mallory and Miller on, he was plainly uncomfortable with what he had heard.

"Looks as if your back-to-basics approach is gathering speed." Mallory couldn't resist prodding. "What next—services in Latin?"

"I think I'll raise this with the bishop myself," James said. "Those books are so important in these days when knowledge is at a premium. The people here need—" He waved a hand to dismiss his thoughts, though they obviously lay heavily on him.

"Stefan's another big shot?" Mallory said.

"He's the chancellor. He looks after the education of everyone here. Like all the Principal Persons, he was instrumental in bringing the Church to Salisbury."

As they exited the cathedral, it was as if some tremendous gravity was reluctantly releasing them. Outside, there was an ethereal quality to the bright morning sunlight. James took them into the sprawling mass of houses, now fully alive with men of all ages cutting wood, feeding cattle and chickens, and cleaning out pigsties. "This is where we house all those who have come to us since we established our new base," James noted. "As you can see, we've just about reached the limits of occupation. Quite what we're going to do from here is open to debate, though we are loathe to allow our own to live beyond the walls for fear of victimisation."

"Is there much of that?" Miller asked apprehensively.

"Not a great deal, though there have been several severe incidents. There are some who see us as a threat, others who feel our time is done. In the light of all that has happened, it appears everyone has their own peculiar belief system to try to make sense of the upheaval. I think they feel let down by the Church because we did not explain the events, or care for them in their hour of need, or simply because they feel what we offer has no relevance to the difficult times we all live in. What need do we have for a hidden, mysterious God when solid, physical gods have walked amongst us? Obviously the answers to that question are easy for us to voice, but who has the time or inclination for theological argument? The only way we can win them back is by playing a long game, by letting the Word filter out organically. And that is where the knights come into the equation."

Finally, James took them to an area at the rear of the former Salisbury and South Wiltshire Museum where the knights were sequestered. Several men were learning the art of sword fighting, while others attacked scarecrows with halberds. All faces were intense and deeply introspective, the movements fluid and powerful. Distinctive uniforms marked them out: black shirts bearing the Templar cross in red against a white square on the breast and right shoulder, hard-wearing black trousers, heavy-duty boots, and black belts.

There was another cadre of knights removed from the core group who duelled with each other with a frightening ferocity, at times lithe, then vicious, their speed and dazzling turns and dives revealing skills that set them apart. Their uniforms were also slightly different, with a blue stripe gleaming on the left shoulder.

The commander stood off to one side, watching the activity, his authority apparent in his rigid bearing. Up close, Blaine had a face that registered such little emotion that at times he resembled a wax dummy. He was in his mid-forties, his black hair badly dyed. Hard muscles filled out a uniform carrying the red Templar cross more prominently on the front. His heavy brows cast a shadow around his eyes so that he appeared on the verge of sickness, yet there was a street-hardness about him that gave a commanding presence.

He remained impassive when James introduced him as Blaine. "It won't be a free ride here," he said, with a Belfast accent. "We had a couple in who thought they'd get fed and watered without having to give anything back. They didn't last the week."

"We'll do what's expected of us," Mallory said.

"You see that you do . . . if you want to stay here. You're getting a shot at something people would give their right arm for. There's not much of value out there anymore. But in the next few years you'll see that being a knight will be a mark of respect. The country will come to love you. But you have to earn it."

"What do we need to do?" Miller asked. The knights had adopted a routine akin to tai chi, with measured, graceful movements, the weapons whipping rapidly around their bodies a hairsbreadth from causing them harm. Their movements looked easy yet unbelievably difficult at the same time. "How long did it take them to learn that?" Miller continued, agog.

Blaine's gaze flickered lazily toward James. "You're sure you want to give them a shot?"

"I always go on first impressions. Besides, if we are here for anything, it is to offer hope, to take in those who come to us . . . for whatever reason . . . and give them a chance."

Blaine grunted in a way that implied his complete disagreement with everything James had said, yet without seeming the slightest bit disrespectful. He turned back to Miller. "You'll get full training. It'll be hard, and fast. We need men out there quickly. I warn you, a lot aren't up to it. We need to get you to the peak of physical fitness. You have to learn how to use weapons you've probably only seen in museums. You've got to learn skills—medicine, astronomy, herbalism, cookery—"

"And don't forget the spiritual guidance," James said, with a smile.

"And you'll need to know the Good Book back to front," Blaine continued without missing a beat. "The poor . . ." He fumbled for an acceptable word. ". . . people out there will be looking to you for guidance. They don't want you telling them that Thou Shalt Not Pick Your Nose is one of the Ten Commandments."

"Don't worry," Mallory said. "We'll make sure they don't covet any oxen."

Blaine laid his gaze heavily on Mallory; it said, *I've already got you marked as a troublemaker, and you'll have it knocked out of you in a day.*

Mallory didn't flinch.

James was winningly courteous as he took his leave. "These are desperate times, but also momentous," he said. "I feel that the Chinese were correct when they said there are no crises, only opportunities. This is an opportunity to re-energise Christianity and to bring it into the lives of the people once again." After Blaine, his gentleness was even more pronounced.

Blaine summoned his second-in-command to lead them to their quarters. Hipgrave had barely broken into his thirties, and he appeared much younger. His features carried a permanent sneer, but it looked theatrical, as if he thought it gave him gravitas. "You'll be out of here before the week's through," he said in a light voice attempting to disguise its upper-middle-class origins.

"Thanks for the vote of confidence." Mallory hadn't seen anything he couldn't handle.

Hipgrave gripped Mallory's upper arm and spun him round. "The knights may be temporal but they operate along strict military lines. There is a chain of command. Insubordination is punished. There's no room in the ranks for weak links."

Miller flinched, knowing that if Mallory remained true to his nature they could both be ejected. But despite a brief moment of tension, Mallory stayed calm and Hipgrave strutted off in front.

"Please, Mallory," Miller whispered, "don't ruin this for me. You don't know how much I need it."

"Give me credit," Mallory replied. "I've got some self-control—I'm not a complete thug."

Their footsteps echoed along empty corridors as Hipgrave led them to the second floor of the old museum and into a large room at the front overlooking the Cathedral Close. Ten camp beds were laid out at regular intervals beneath medieval wall tapestries. Two other men were already billeted there. One of them, a muscular, good-looking black man, was cleaning his boots with furious brush strokes while the other, a rangy white man in his early fifties, knelt in prayer at a tiny altar beside his bed. They rose and faced the new arrivals for Hipgrave's cursory introductions. Daniels was in his late thirties, intelligent, with an air of amused sophistication. Gardener, in contrast, was a Geordie with a rough working-class attitude, long greying hair tied in a ponytail, and a face that had the leathery appearance of meat left out for days in the sun.

When Hipgrave had departed, Mallory chose a bed from the remaining eight and lay on it, staring at the ceiling.

"I wouldn't get used to that position if I were you," Daniels said wryly. He'd resumed polishing his boots with a verve that bordered on obsession.

"They work you hard?"

"We're twinned with a Soviet Gulag. Their idea of downtime is a face-wash with river water and a turnip to gnaw on."

"Don't listen to him. He's a soft Southern bastard. Drinks wine with his little finger stuck out," Gardener called over.

"At least I know what wine is, you beer-swelling Philistine."

"Aye, you whine all the time."

Daniels walked over to Gardener, brandishing his brush. "You know, you'd think some of my innate style and breeding would have rubbed off on you after the weeks we've been stuck here, but I'm starting to think you'll remain a troglodyte forever."

"You know you're not supposed to use big words around me. Now bugger off, I'm trying to pray."

Despite their fractiousness, it was obvious to Mallory that a deep affection underpinned their relationship, a clear case of opposites attracting. In his voice and body language, Daniels seemed gay, though Gardener, as far as Mallory could tell, was straight—at least, he sported a worn wedding ring—and they obviously came from different backgrounds. But the camaraderie made him think it might not be so bad there after all.

Mallory and Miller were allowed only half an hour to settle in before another knight was sent to fetch them. He had red hair and freckles and a fastidious manner that irritated Mallory the moment the knight opened his mouth. He had been ordered to give them a wealth of instructions, none of which he was prepared to repeat, so they had no choice but to listen.

"Everything here is based around discipline," he said, "to focus the mind. Your day will be mapped out for you, and it's a long day, believe me. This isn't a place for the lazy."

He marched ahead of them with the stiff gait of a well-drilled military man, which made Mallory's loose-limbed amble seem even more lazy. Miller hopped and skipped to keep up like a pony on a rope.

"The knights, however, have a slightly different timetable from the rest," the red-headed man continued. "There's a lot of studying, a lot of training. For most people out there—" He motioned toward the sprawl of wooden huts visible through the window. "—the day begins at six a.m. with prime. That's a full service in the cathedral, plainsong, the works. The prayer and chant continues through the day, seven days a week. Terce at nine a.m., sext at midday, none in midafternoon, vespers at the end of the afternoon, and compline at dusk. After that, everyone retires to their rooms for *the great silence* and the cathedral is locked. At midnight everyone rises for the night office, followed immediately by the lauds of the dead. It lasts about two hours in total, and then you're off on the cycle again. You will be expected to attend services when you are not involved with your other duties."

Mallory glanced at Miller; the younger man was clearly enthralled at the strict routine that left Mallory feeling an uncomfortable mixture of depression and defiance.

"Your routine will be individually tailored, depending on where your strengths and weaknesses lie," the knight continued. "For the first week or so, it will mainly centre on physical fitness and weapons training." He eyed them askance. "To see if you have what it takes to meet the exacting standards required of a Knight Templar."

Mallory knew enough about the military mind-set to understand what that meant: they could look forward to days of gruelling and unnecessary exercises to see if they had the strength of character to continue. And then Blaine—a military man at some level, Mallory guessed—would begin the long task of breaking their spirit so they would obey orders without question.

"After that period, the physical and weapons training will be confined to the early morning, after prime. Then you'll be studying herbalism for treatment of wounds out in the field. The supply of drugs won't last long and there's no infrastructure to manufacture any more. Astronomy is . . . difficult." His jaw set. "But you'll need to navigate by the stars. And then there's the Bible study and philosophy classes. Those are the main ones."

He brought them into a large oak-panelled room on the first floor. On one wall was fixed a plain wooden sign carved with the legend: *"Let nothing have precedence over divine office"—The Rule of St Benedict.*

At the other end of the room was a heavily fortified door beside a window that opened onto a small office stacked with boxes. The knight hammered on the windowsill to attract the attention of a man with a scar that turned his left eye into a permanent squint. He was introduced as Wainwright, the knights' quartermaster.

"Two uniforms?" he said, mentally measuring Mallory and Miller before disappearing into the bowels of the store. He returned a second later.

"Perfect for a torchlight rally," Mallory said, holding the black shirt up for size.

"Uniforms are to be worn at all times," the red-haired knight said. "And that means *all times*. Being caught without it means the disciplinary procedure."

Mallory considered asking what this entailed, but he knew it would only depress him further.

The rest of the day was spent in a process that fell somewhere between induction and confession: names, education, abilities, criminal record, past transgressions, hopes, fears. Miller gave them a detailed account of his relationship with his parents and the breakdown of his romance, the catalyst that had propelled him toward Salisbury. Mallory changed his story several times, often during the same strand, before delivering a complex list of dates, times, names, and anecdotes that would have taken days of investigation before it was discovered that it made no sense at all.

"They were very nice," Miller said afterward, as they picked their way amongst the huts toward the refectory, a large, newly constructed building a stone's throw from the cathedral.

"When you say *nice*, do you mean prying, interfering, compulsive control freaks?"

Miller looked at him, puzzled. "No. Nice. They were nice. Didn't you think they were nice?"

"I worry about you, Miller. You're going to be the first person ever to die of unadulterated optimism."

Miller sighed. "I don't know why you came here, Mallory. We're going to be part of something big and good. Something important. All you've done is criticise. You're a cynic."

"You say that as if it's a bad thing."

"Look, there's Daniels." Miller nodded toward the knight sauntering ahead of them; he carried himself with confidence, seemingly above the bustle he passed. Mallory noted how many looked at Daniels with respect, if not awe; was it the uniform or the person? "Come on, let's catch him up," Miller continued.

"So how long have you been here, Daniels?" Miller asked as he skipped up beside him.

"Two months." He eyed Miller's skittishness wryly. "It was this or the circus."

"That must be when the call first went out. Where were you?"

Daniels looked bemused at Miller's effervescent questioning. "Bristol."

"I heard some of the cities were tough in the early days," Mallory said.

A shadow crossed Daniels's face. "It was, in some parts, for a while. The riots had died out by the time the call filtered through—no one had the energy left. But there were still some parts of the city you didn't go into, if you know what I mean." He looked across the huts at the darkening sky.

Daniels had an impressive charisma that underscored his bearing. Mallory could imagine him in his civilian days, well groomed, wearing expensive, fashionable clothes, maybe in some professional job; maybe a lawyer.

"How are you finding it?" Miller had such a bright-eyed-puppy manner that Daniels couldn't help but lighten.

"Hard, but rewarding." He smiled. "You'll enjoy it here."

"Any missions yet?"

"No, but it's only a matter of time. They want to be sure before they send anyone out there."

"What made you come?" Mallory asked.

"You don't think I came out of obligation? An overarching desire to give something back to Christianity? To the world?" Daniels eyed Mallory as if he knew exactly what was going through the new arrival's head.

"Don't mind him," Miller said. "He's just an old cynic."

"No," Mallory replied. "I don't."

Daniels shrugged in an unconcerned way. "My partner was killed in the fighting. We'd been together for a while. It left . . . a big hole." He chose his words carefully. "There was nothing for me in Bristol. I thought there might be something for me here."

"I'm sorry," Miller said. "Were you planning on getting married?"

"Gareth was the religious one," Daniels said directly to Mallory. "He was the one who went to church every week. I could take it or leave it. But he died with such dignity. Faith right up to the last. That was my moment of epiphany."

"That's a good enough reason," Mallory said.

With some kind of unspoken agreement made amongst them, they set off together for the refectory.

"You don't seem much of a Christian, Mallory," Daniels noted wryly.

"I'm not much of anything."

"Yes, he is," Miller said brightly. "He just doesn't know it yet." He proceeded to tell Daniels how Mallory had saved him.

"Self-preservation," Mallory said. "Two were a better defence against those things."

"Pants on fire," Miller gibed.

They joined the queue filing into the refectory. The aroma of spiced hot food floated out into the cooling twilight, setting their stomachs rumbling. The air was filled with the hubbub of optimistic voices, the sound of people who still couldn't believe they were getting a square meal.

"Tell me," Mallory said to Daniels, "when we met Blaine earlier, there was another group of knights in training, away from the main lot. They had a blue flash on their left shoulders."

"The Blues? They're the élite. I think they used to be squaddies stationed at one of the army camps out on Salisbury Plain—it would take me years to get to their level of training. Blaine keeps them apart from the rest of us, but that's OK by me—you can see it in their eyes." He waved a pointing finger in front of Mallory's face. "Army eyes. You know what I mean?" Mallory did. "Anyway, they're involved in some ongoing mission. They go off for days at a time. Come back exhausted and filthy."

"Oh?"

"Don't bother asking questions, Mallory. You'll soon find that no one tells you anything here."

The refectory was a long, narrow barn with a high roof and open beams permeated by the smell of new wood. They picked up trays and cutlery before passing by tables at one end where the kitchen staff loaded up plastic plates with a stew of carrots, potatoes, parsnips, and oatmeal; bread; and a small lump of cheese.

"No meat?" Mallory protested.

"Once a week," Daniels said, "They're keeping a tight rein on supplies. Just in case."

"In case of what?"

Daniels shrugged.

They sat together at the end of a long trestle table reserved for the knights, away to one side. On the other tables, about a hundred and fifty people packed into the first sitting, their freedom from the day's chores making their conversation animated. Gardener joined them soon after, taking a seat opposite Mallory with a gruff silence.

"What did you do in the old days, Gardener?" Miller asked chirpily.

"Binman." Gardener stuffed an enormous mound of vegetables into his mouth. "And I tell you," he mumbled, "this is better than having your hands covered in maggots and shit every morning."

"I don't want to hear about your sex life, Gardener," Daniels said.

"I hear the Blues headed off hell for leather at noon," Gardener continued. "Don't know what got them all fired up, but Blaine had a face that could curdle cream. And Hipgrave was pissed off because Blaine didn't send him out as leader. Again."

"He is *so* desperate," Daniels said.

"You know what he did this morning—" Gardener cut off his sour comment when he spotted Hipgrave heading across the room with his tray. The captain had lost his sneer and appeared uncomfortable in the crowd. He hesitated briefly when he noticed Gardener and the others watching him and then veered off his path to another table so he wouldn't have to sit near them.

"Thanks for small bloody mercies," Gardener muttered.

Mallory spotted a table on the far side of the room where all the diners sat in complete silence, intermittently praying and eating. He pointed it out to Daniels.

"Headbangers," Daniels said, chewing slowly on a piece of potato. "The price we pay for bringing all of the Lord's flock under one roof."

"Leave them alone." Gardener continued to tuck into his dinner with gusto.

"You would say that—you're one of them." Daniels turned to Mallory. "They're Born-Agains, or evangelicals, or whatever it is they call themselves. They have a hard-line view of the Lord's Word—"

"They stick to the text of the Gospel," Gardener said, "unlike some of the weak-willed people in here."

"There are so many branches of the Church in here . . . sects—cults, even . . ." Daniels shook his head. "Some of them, they're like a different religion. I don't know where they're coming from at all."

"You don't have a monopoly on God's Word," Gardener noted. "It's open to different interpretations."

Mallory stabbed a chunk of parsnip with his knife, then thought twice about eating it. He noticed Miller looking dreamily around the refectory. "You're going to say this is like Disneyland for you, aren't you?" he said.

Miller grinned at how easily Mallory had read his thoughts. "Well, it is a wonderful place. All these people . . . all this hope . . . and faith . . . under one roof. It's what I wanted to find. I just never really expected I would." A shadow crossed his face.

"But?"

"It's a bit weird, too." He looked guilty at this observation.

"You don't know the half of it." Gardener had so much in his mouth that he spat a lump of mushed vegetables back onto the plate with his words.

Daniels shook his head wearily. "I'm asking Blaine to include etiquette in his tiresome list of lessons to be taught."

"There's been talk," Gardener said. "Some strange stuff happening around here."

"Oh, here we go again." Daniels rolled his eyes. "Lights in the sky. Mysterious this and strange that. Usually reported by people who've had the Toronto Blessing one time too many."

"You're a cynical bastard, Daniels, and no mistaking." Gardener swallowed his mouthful and stifled a belch. "See? Etiquette."

"Heavenly," Daniels replied. "Which finishing school did you go to again?"

"What strange stuff?" Miller said.

Gardener leaned across the table conspiratorially. "Ghosts, for one. And not just one. Some old bishop . . . Seth Ward, someone said . . . he was seen crossing the nave. One of the brothers saw a man's face pressed up against the windows in what used to be the old cafeteria . . . all hideous, like. A cowled figure in the cloisters . . ."

"I can't believe you fall for that nonsense!" Daniels said.

"How different is it from the manifestation of the Holy Spirit?" Gardener waved his fork in Daniels's face.

Daniels batted it away. "Very different. It's not real for a start."

"And there were lights, floating over the altar," Gardener continued. "Beeson heard voices when he was praying in the cathedral . . . calling to him, saying . . . worrying things."

"What kind of things?" Daniels said.

"I don't know."

"No, because it's a story, and a feeble one at that. They never have any detail. Just someone heard this, or someone saw that."

"Don't believe it, then," Gardener said with a shrug. "See if I care." He turned to Miller and Mallory. "But the smart folk here think it's wise to keep your wits about you, and to stay away from the lonely places at night—"

"Has anyone been hurt yet?" Daniels asked.

"No."

"Then why are you making out like it's the Amityville Horror? You're such an old woman, Gardener."

Gardener smiled tightly at Miller and Mallory. "You know what it's like out there in the world. And it's the same in here. Nothing's what it seems."

Their conversation was disrupted by a commotion near the door. Diners peeled away to allow a small entourage to move slowly into the room. At its centre was the bishop, walking with the aid of a cane and the support of two attendants. Julian and Stefan followed behind. All eyes followed Cornelius's excruciating progress.

Daniels's brow furrowed. "He normally eats in the palace."

"He looks as if he hasn't got the strength to get across the room," Mallory said.

"His legs are a bit shaky, but don't go underestimating him. He's sharp as a pin," Gardener said.

"What are the others like?" Mallory's attention was fixed on Stefan.

Daniels pointed with a carrot impaled on his knife. "Stefan's a bit of a cold fish. He used to be some businessman up in Manchester before he saw the light, I think. Julian's OK. A bit too quiet for me, thoughtful, you know, but he's got a very liberal view of life. He wasn't involved in the Church before the Fall, but they promoted him out of nowhere because he's brilliant, or so they say. Very learned about philosophy, comparative religion. I don't know if he was an academic, but he's a sharp guy, definitely."

Cornelius made his way to a table not too far from the door, which was hastily vacated for him. His attendants lowered him into a chair while Stefan brought over a plate of food that he proffered with a formal bow.

"This is a show," Mallory said quietly. "A little spin-doctoring. To let the common man know the bishop is just an ordinary joe. He's not larging it in the palace. He can eat vegetable mush with the rest of the suckers."

"Be respectful," Miller hissed.

Mallory began to mop up his gravy with his bread while gently fantasising about pizza.

"And that is Gibson," Daniels said, pointing to the last imposing figure in the group. He must have been twenty-five stone, with a comically jolly face that appeared to be permanently on the point of a guffaw. His cheeks were bright red, his hair tight grey curls; large silver-framed spectacles surrounded eyes fixed in a humorous squint.

"Don't tell me," Mallory said, "he's the Canon of the Pies."

"The treasurer, actually. Looks after all the ornaments, vestments, and gold plate tucked away in the vaults." Daniels smiled as he ate. "But he does oversee the kitchens as well."

"So we're in their hands." Mallory didn't attempt to hide his dismissiveness.

"Them and their advisors," Gardener said gruffly. "There's a whole bunch of arse-kissers following them around, whispering in their ears. Keeping them informed, supposedly, because the top dogs don't have time to spend finding out what the rest of us are thinking. But the arse-kissers are guiding them, really. They're the power behind the throne."

Daniels snorted. "Oh, not that routine again! You're only upset because they're not whispering about you."

"It's true. You've got to watch out who you're talking to round here. Everybody's got some sort of thing going on."

"*Thing?*" Daniels shook his head and sighed.

"Come on, you know it's true," Gardener said. "This whole place is split down the middle. The modernisers think we should build on the state the Church had reached just before the change, make it acceptable to modern thinking. The traditionalists want a hard-line approach. Everybody's plotting."

"Well, as much as I'm enjoying your comedy double-act," Mallory said, "I don't think I can stare at these vegetables anymore without gnawing on my own arm."

"You should eat it up," Gardener said, cleaning up the last of the gravy on his plate. "You'll be desperate for it tomorrow when Blaine's got you scrambling over that assault course."

"It's not as if you've got anywhere to go," Daniels said. "It's compline next, or had you forgotten? You'll soon get used to realising you have no time of your own."

Mallory rocked back in his chair. "You know, this place is just too much fun."

Despite Mallory's disgruntlement, the atmosphere in the cathedral was deeply affecting. Outside, dusk had fallen, the darkness licking over a chilly landscape freed from electric lights. Inside, the stone walls basked in an ethereal golden glow from hundreds of candles. Incense and tallow smoke cocooned the worshippers who stood shoulder to shoulder along the nave and the quire. The plainsong rose up, filling the vast vault with a mesmerising, heady sound that reached deep into Mallory, tugging at emotions he barely thought he still had. It was a single voice made by hundreds of people, simple and pure yet powerful on so many levels. Mallory glanced over at Miller to see tears streaming down his cheeks.

Briefly, Mallory felt a sense of belonging that put all the unpleasantness of his past life into the shade. Perhaps there still was a chance for him: a fresh start, although he'd long ago given up that childlike whimsy of believing that some Higher Power took enough of an interest in the ants that swarmed the earth to give them a second chance. The fleeting hope, that weak thing he thought he'd scoured from his system, was a simple by-product of the perfect confluence of music and moment, he told himself. But still, it tugged at him.

He was examining the odd thoughts pulled from him by the intensity of faith when his concentration was broken by a figure he could just glimpse on the edge of the congregation, slightly ahead of him and away to the left. His face was obscured by his black cowl pulled far forward, unusual in itself as everyone else there went bareheaded. But there was no other reason why Mallory's attention should be drawn to him so powerfully that he couldn't look away. The figure was still, his shoulders slightly hunched. He didn't appear to be singing, merely watching or perhaps listening, deep in thought.

Mallory couldn't understand why the figure made him feel uneasy, or why the tingling that had started in the small of his back was slowly spreading up his spine. Some deeply buried part of him was trying to break out of his subconscious to issue a warning.

As he watched for some sign that would give him an explanation for his reaction, the figure began to turn toward him, as if he sensed Mallory's eyes upon him. Inexplicably, this filled Mallory with dread. He didn't want to see the face inside that cowl.

He looked down at his hands, then up toward the altar, and when he did finally glance back, the figure was gone.

Outside in the night, Mallory tugged Miller away from the uplifted worshippers streaming back to their huts for a few hours' grace before the whole round started again. He found a shadowed spot next to the cathedral walls and said, "Let's hit the town. We can dump our uniforms and explore. There's got to be some life out there. Maybe we'll find someone who'll take pity on us and buy us a beer." He knew his bravado was a response to the sobering but stupid fear he had felt in the service.

"Are you crazy? You heard what they said—being caught without the uniform—"

"We're not going to get caught."

"—is a punishable offence. And we're not supposed to go out of the compound after curfew. I don't even know if we're supposed to go out there at all."

"I told you, we're not going to get caught. Who's to know? Don't you want to find out what your new neighbours are like?"

Miller protested fulsomely, clearly afraid of jeopardising everything he felt he'd gained, but Mallory chipped away at him on the way back to their quarters so that by the time they arrived, Miller reluctantly agreed to the secret foray.

Daniels and Gardener still hadn't returned, so they quickly changed into their street clothes and slipped out. "How are we going to get away?" Miller hissed as they flitted from hut to hut.

"I had a look around earlier. There's a spot not far from the gate where we can slip over the wall. When we come back we can give the guard some bullshit about being on a secret mission or something. He's bound to let us in." Miller didn't look convinced, but he allowed himself to be swayed by Mallory's confidence.

The camp was still as they made their way past the gate. But before they could climb the ladder to the runway around the top of the wall, the sound of running feet and frantic raised voices rapidly approached from the other side. Mallory pushed Miller back into the shadows.

An insistent cry hailed the guard. Mallory couldn't make out what was said, but the guard responded by hand-winding an old-fashioned klaxon before opening the gates.

Nine knights rushed in through the widening gap, the blue flash on their shoulders clear in the flickering flame of the torch mounted above the gate. Their swords were drawn as they constantly scanned all around with their *army eyes*. They were in a terrible state, their uniforms torn and charred, their bare skin covered with cuts and bruises; some had bound deeper wounds with makeshift bandages torn from their shirts, the material now stained black. Their faces were grim with determination.

In the middle of the group, two knights hauled what Mallory at first thought was burned log. It was only when he saw its rolling white eyes that he realised it was a man, his skin seared black; Miller turned away from the smell of cooked flesh. The knight was still alive, but he wouldn't be for long.

The ones at the rear gathered around one of their number who had a wooden box clutched tightly to his chest. They drove hard into the compound then yelled at the guard to close the gates.

A group of five men hurried from the direction of the cathedral to meet them. The only one Mallory recognised was Stefan, his balding head gleaming like a skull. Ignoring the suffering of the wounded knight, he went directly to the captain and said something in hushed, insistent tones that Mallory couldn't make out. The captain nodded and motioned to the one with the box; Stefan barked an order to his four assistants and then the whole group moved speedily in the direction of the cathedral.

When they'd gone, Miller whispered dismally, "That poor man!"

"Looks as if he stood a little too close to the barbecue." Mallory stared at the silhouette of the cathedral blocking out the stars, trying to make sense of what he'd seen. "What was in the box?" he mused to himself. "What was so important?" After a moment, he set off for the ladder. "Ah, who cares? Come on, let's hit the town."

They climbed quickly, keeping one eye out for the guard. When they reached the top, Mallory led Miller to a part of the wall that was lower than the rest where they could easily drop down to the street. They paused for a moment at the foot of the wall, and when they were sure no one had seen them, they ran toward the town, keeping well to the shadows.

Once the walls had been swallowed by the dark at their backs, Miller heard Mallory's voice floating back to him as they ran. "You know how you get that little tingling sensation when something's going to end in tears? Or is that just me?"

chapter three

THE EVIDENCE OF THINGS
NOT SEEN

*"Just as children seem foolish to adults,
so humans seem foolish to the gods."*
Heraclitus

Salisbury's streets were oddly otherworldly in a flood of light from flaming torches that had been attached to the now-useless lampposts; their sizzling pitch added a spicy quality to the cooling air. More people milled around than Mallory would have expected with the encroaching night. Many shops remained open, their trade carried out by candlelight. Friends chatted beneath the crackling torches, freed from the rigour of days that had become unduly hard. Children played in the gutter without fear of cars or buses, although the occasional horse-drawn cart moved by them at an alarming clip. Outside the Maltings shopping centre, a teenager strummed on a guitar while his friends danced or drank homemade cider. Others flirted or kissed each other in the shadows.

The population had adapted remarkably well to the inversion of their lives. Indeed, from the good humour evident all around, they appeared to be relishing it. Mallory and Miller moved through them, watching silently, enjoying the normality.

Near Poultry Cross, where tradesmen had hawked their goods for centuries, a man with lank grey hair to his shoulders stood on an old kitchen chair and preached passionately to a small detached crowd. He seemed to be proclaiming the glory of a god that lived at the bottom of his garden. Further on, three women prayed silently around a picture of George Clooney framed with wild flowers. At the marketplace, there were more individuals preaching to no one at all, or large groups singing of the wonder of some deity or other.

"They're crazy," Miller muttered.

"Your God's more real, is that it?" Mallory noted.

"Yes." Miller knew Mallory was baiting him but couldn't resist responding. "He's been worshipped for millennia, not ten months."

"So in a couple of thousand years, old Clooney—"

"Oh, shut up." Miller tried to stop there, but he couldn't. "There's a whole coherent philosophy behind Christianity—" His ears burned at Mallory's laughter. "There is!"

"You don't have to sell it to me, Miller. Just don't try pretending you're better than these poor sods."

They continued to wander, exploring the sights. As a new city, Salisbury had the benefit of being planned on a rectangular checkerboard pattern like some Roman metropolis. Most people gathered in a small square that ran from the market to the Maltings and up to Crane Street and New Street, a continuous thoroughfare that was the closest to the cathedral.

As Mallory and Miller wandered along the path at the side of the culverted river, watching the trout, grayling, and dace swim in the light of an occasional torch, they were disturbed by the sounds of a scuffle coming from further along the lonely path where no light burned. Mallory was ready to ignore it, but when Miller jumped to investigate he felt a weary obligation to follow.

Barely visible in the gloom, three men were hunched over a still shape on the floor. Before Mallory could utter a caution, Miller was already yelling, "Leave him alone!"

Against his better judgment, Mallory ran in behind Miller, who was rapidly closing on the three. The gang half-heartedly squared up to him, then saw Mallory behind and decided it was too much trouble. They turned and ran off into the dark, but not before Mallory saw that they were all wearing black T-shirts marked with a bright red V from shoulders to navel.

"Have you lost your mind?" Mallory said.

Miller was kneeling next to the shape on the floor: a young man crumpled in a growing pool of blood. "We're knights. We're supposed to help people in trouble."

"I'm going to have to have a word with you about the difference between fantasy and reality." Mallory checked the victim's pulse. "Dead."

"Poor man. Who shall we tell?"

"No one."

"We can't leave him here," Miller said. "He'll have a family—"

"Someone will find him soon enough. Listen, we're strangers here. They're likely to think we did it. Not everyone has a naïve belief that all people speak the truth." He knelt down and started to go through the victim's pockets.

"What are you doing?" Miller said, aghast.

Mallory fished out a wallet and went through the contents. "Look at this. They've got their own currency going on here. A local economy." He took the amateurishly printed notes and stuffed them in his pockets.

"You can't do that!"

"He can't take it with him."

"You're as bad as the people who killed him!"

"No, I'm not, because I *didn't kill him*. Come on, we'll have a drink on him."

"I will not," Miller said peevishly.

"Then you can sit beside me while *I* have a drink. You've got to get your head around how the world works these days, Miller."

"What, without ethics or morals?"

"Something like that." Mallory sighed. "No, I don't mean that. But you've got to be hard, Miller. There's no safety net in this world anymore. No Welfare State to help you out. Everybody's watching their own backs—that's the only way to survive."

"I don't believe you, and you'll never convince me otherwise. Basic human nature is decent."

"And then you woke up. Are you coming or not?" Mallory walked back toward the lights. Miller hovered for a moment, sad and angry at the same time, then followed.

They found a pub overlooking the market square. The bright green doors of the Cornmarket Inn were thrown open to the night, tempting passersby into the smoky interior lit by just enough candles and torches to provide shadows for those who preferred to drink out of plain view. The customers were a mixed bunch: some rural workers, grime on their clothes and grass seeds in their lace-holes, some weary-eyed traders and shopkeepers who had finished up for the night, and a large group who all appeared to know each other. They ranged from teenagers to pensioner age, but the smattering of dreadlocks and shaved heads, hippie jewellery and colourful clothes made Mallory think of New Age travellers.

True to his word, Miller eschewed a drink, but he appeared happy enough surrounded by the high-spirited pub-goers. Mallory ordered a pint of ale brewed in the pub's back room and they retreated to the only free table.

"What do you think those Blues were up to?" Mallory mused as he sipped on his beer. "The *élite* group," he added with mockery.

Miller didn't appear to have given it a second thought. "Nothing for us to worry about."

Mallory looked at him in disbelief. "Of course it's something for us to worry about. *Everything* is something for us to worry about."

"Blaine—"

"The bishop, the canons, all of them . . . You don't put your trust in people who set themselves up as leaders, Miller. In religion, in politics, in the military, in business . . . the simple act of seeking high office is a signifier of a peculiar, unreliable, controlling, unpleasant pathology that means they shouldn't be *allowed* any kind of power. And I'll keep saying that over and over again until everyone on this planet listens."

"That's ridiculous. If we followed that line of thought we wouldn't have any leaders at all."

"And your point is?"

"You can't have a religion without leaders—"

"Who says?"

Miller squirmed with irritation. "I hate it when you do this. Why are you picking on me?"

"Because your life's just too perfect, Miller. You need to be brought down to everyone else's level. Just see me as your own personal tormentor, a living horse-hair shirt for the soul."

Miller took a deep breath. "You can't have a religion without leaders because you need discipline—"

"No, you don't."

"—to help the followers find the true path to God through all the confusion."

"You can do it yourself." Mallory jabbed a finger sharply into Miller's sternum.

"No, I can't."

"You just don't think you can. You can do anything you want, Miller."

"Thanks for the vote of confidence, but you don't know me. Besides, that sounds faintly blasphemous."

Miller started to brood over what Mallory had said, chewing on the nail of one of his little fingers. Mallory returned to his beer, hiding his smile, but after a moment he was drawn back to the neo-hippies whose humour was both infectious and comforting. Mallory realised how rarely he had heard anyone laugh in recent times.

His attention fell on a woman who was doing nothing out of the ordinary but who had a presence like a beacon. He realised he'd been aware of her from the moment he walked in the pub, even though he couldn't recall looking at her; all around people were glancing at her as if they couldn't tear their eyes away. She was in her mid- to late twenties, wearing a faded hippie dress beneath a bright pink mohair sweater; a clutter of beads and necklaces hung around her neck. The others in her group, even the older ones, deferred to her, nodding intently when she was serious, laughing at her jokes. Mallory liked the sharp, questioning intelligence he saw in her face, but it was coupled with a knowing quality around the eyes that was deeply sexy. To him that was a winning combination.

"Do you like her?" He had been so lost in his appraisal that he hadn't noticed Miller studying him.

"She's put together OK."

Miller chuckled. "Is it the hair?"

"I wouldn't be so shallow as to be attracted by the merely physical."

"You make me laugh, Mallory!" Miller put his hands behind his head. "What I see is long brown hair that you just want to touch, full lips that curl up at the corners, and big, big eyes—"

"Steady on, Miller. They'll have to hose you down when we get back."

The woman stared at Miller, her brow furrowing; she'd obviously caught him watching and talking about her. Miller blushed furiously and looked away. Mallory jabbed a thumb at him, then raised one eyebrow at the woman. She shook her head wearily.

"Mallory!" Miller protested. "She thinks I'm after her now!"

"That'll teach you to stare." Mallory chortled to himself before downing the remainder of his pint in one go.

"You're such a *lad*." Miller sighed, becoming gloomy as memories surfaced. "Did I tell you I was going to get married?"

"Yes."

"Sue and me had been going out since we were at school. I thought we'd always be together. No great beauty . . . not too smart, either . . . but that didn't matter. She really made me laugh. She didn't mind that I was a brickie's mate, didn't nag me to get a better job." He was staring at the floor, lost to his thoughts. "You know how it is when you're with someone so close it's like you're with yourself?"

"No."

"You don't have to put on any act," Miller continued dismally, "you can be the same sad loser you know you are without pretending to be anybody else and they still love you."

"I said, no." Mallory pretended to concentrate on his glass while surreptitiously watching the woman, wishing he were in a position where he could talk to her.

"At least, I thought it was like that," Miller continued to himself. "But I was just fooling myself, wasn't I? Maybe if I'd acted like somebody else she'd still be with me . . . and everything would be all right again."

He mumbled something else that sounded as if he thought it was important, but Mallory's attention was deflected by sudden activity outside the window: a flash of a figure running by in the dark, then another, then several people sprinting. It was a perfectly mundane image, but a tingle of apprehension ran up his spine nonetheless.

Others had noticed it. An old man in a window seat pressed his face against the glass. Someone else ran out into the street and grabbed hold of a passing teenager who at first struggled to get free before pointing behind him, gabbling animatedly.

Miller's chattering in his ear was a distant drone; Mallory was drawn by the scenario unravelling outside.

As the teenager ran off, the man who had emerged from the pub looked back down the street. A subtle change crept across his face, amused detachment giving way to incomprehension, then a dull, implacable fear.

"I think we need to see this," Mallory said quietly.

As he replaced his glass on the table, other drinkers were already making their way out onto the street. Mallory pushed his way into the centre of the road with Miller trailing behind him. They were instantly transfixed.

Though it was a dark, moonless night with heavy cloud cover, the sky was filled with light. Flashes of angry fire illuminated the clouds, every now and then bursting through to form pillars of flame that rammed down to the earth. Occasionally, it limned a shape moving with serpentine grace on large batlike wings that beat the air lazily. Mallory thought he glimpsed the shimmer of jewels on its skin, rich sapphires, emeralds, and rubies; echoes of another image surfaced from the depths of his subconscious, of fire in the dark. Whatever it was, it was filled with power, but there was something in the way it moved that suggested a terrifying fury: it was hunting.

But that wasn't the worst thing. Behind it, along the horizon but sweeping forward, Mallory could make out something he could only describe as a presence: a thick white mist was unfurling like cloth, billowing at its central point and folding around at the edges so that it had an unnatural substance and life. It moved quickly across the landscape toward the city. Occasionally, the mist would take on aspects of a face—hollow eyes, a roaring mouth—before some other disturbing shape appeared; Mallory saw something that resembled an animal, another that looked like a bird. Gradually, it coalesced into a smoky horned figure towering over the city, insubstantial but filled with primal fears.

"The Devil," Miller whispered, terrified, "and the Serpent."

The air was infused with a palpable sense of dread. Everyone standing on that chill, dark street could only look up at it and remember years of religious imagery, laid on them since childhood, of damnation and torment. Whatever it was, it had come from the outer dark to the city, and its intent appeared apparent. Those of a Christian bent crossed themselves, and some who had not called themselves Christian for a long time did so, too.

Miller was whimpering quietly, whispering, "The Devil . . . the Devil . . ." until it became a mantra of Evil rippling through the crowd.

Even Mallory, who thought he was numb to most things, felt a crackle of fear as he looked up at the ancient image. He didn't know what it was, or tried to tell himself he didn't, but he knew he could feel the presence of a cold, alien intellect, and the threat it brought with it.

"The Devil's come to town." Someone laughed, though without humour.

It drifted for a moment in the thermals above the cooling city before breaking up as something dark at its core drove forward with a monstrous purpose. Screams rang throughout Salisbury, one voice lifting up in terror.

Mallory glanced back in the direction of the cathedral. Miller's sagging expression showed they both shared the same thought: even if they got back to the gates, there was little chance they'd be able to get inside in time.

"Come with us." The voice at Mallory's shoulder was low, warm, and accentless, though insistent. He looked into the face of the woman he'd been admiring, and for the briefest instant he was so dazzled by her large, dark eyes that the threat faded into the background.

"You've got a concrete bunker with ten-foot-thick walls?" he said.

"Something like that." Her gaze felt as if it was cutting through all his carefully prepared defences and he quickly looked away.

A teenager with dreadlocks bleached a brilliant white appeared beside her. "Come on, let's move." His eyes flickered furtively toward the Devil in the sky.

The group Mallory had decided were New Age travellers headed quickly down the street, the woman at the heart of them, pausing only briefly to see if Mallory was following.

"What are we going to do?" Miller asked anxiously.

"Stand here or run." Mallory didn't wait to see Miller's choice.

They veered away from the cathedral along Crane Street, over the river bridge to Queen Elizabeth Gardens where the tent city sprawled. The cries had become a nerve-jangling chorus, rising up all around as though everyone in the city was aware of what was bearing down on them. The horned shape had dissipated, to be replaced by a rushing wind that had substance and its own inner darkness screaming in at roof height. Chimney pots crashed down, sending slates showering into the street. The glass of streetlights exploded as if crushed by a malicious hand.

As they ran toward the tents, they were all knocked from their feet by the shock wave of a powerful blast. Rubble rained down all around, most of it reduced to less than the size of a fist. With ringing ears, Mallory looked back to see part of the shopping quarter on fire, a column of thick black smoke rising up to the serpentine winged creature, now clearly visible.

"A Fabulous Beast." The woman sat nearby, rubbing at her temple, which was now streaked with brick dust. "And it's angry?" She threw off her daze and hauled Miller to his feet, urging him to move. Mallory was surprised to feel a twinge of jealousy for the touch of her hand. "We need to get within the camp," she said, which Mallory found faintly ridiculous when the only shelter there was a thin covering of canvas or plastic.

The travellers surged into the camp before scuttling beneath trees to avoid the still-raining debris that took out more than one tent. The bursts of fire screaming from the sky were like some hellish vision of a wartime air raid, but the dark presence that fell across everything was far worse; it was as if shadowy fingers were plucking at their souls.

"We can't stay here!" Miller squealed impotently. "We need to find a hiding place!"

"Chill." The dreadlocked teen slapped a hand on Miller's shoulder, pressing him down. "We're safe, if we don't get brained by a flying brick. See—protected." He pointed to a post hung with strings of crystals, feathers, and small animal bones. Similar posts were staked out around the perimeter as far as Mallory could see.

"Kill me now," he said. "We're doomed." He tried to discern the location of what the woman had called the Fabulous Beast, but the glare from numerous torches lighting the camp made it difficult to see. The devil-wind rushed around the boundaries of the camp before delving back into the city.

"Can't you feel it?" Miller rubbed at his skin as if he had scabies. Mallory could: the touch of some intelligence so far beyond him he couldn't begin to categorise it, creeping through the labyrinth of his mind, swinging open locked doors, bringing wild panic into the civilised centres, dark and hateful and very, very old. Despite himself, he shuffled back until he felt the security of a tree trunk.

Gradually, the panic passed. The Fabulous Beast and the dark wind accompanying it had focused on another part of the city.

"It won't come this way. We can't be seen," the woman said, to reassure him.

"Right. We pretend we're trees. Or do we just cover our eyes really, really tight?" Mallory watched the sky, having decided he'd run for cover under the river bridge when the things came back. "What's your name?" he asked.

"Sophie Tallent."

"Mallory. And that person trying to burrow under the soil is Miller. You're the boss?"

"Here? No, of course not."

"You really believe this . . ." He nodded to the posts. ". . . is going to keep you safe?"

"Do you see the Fabulous Beast and that other thing attacking us?"

"And if you wish hard enough the sun might come up tomorrow." He grabbed Miller roughly by the collar of his jacket and lifted him off the ground. "Come on—we might still be able to make the compound."

As they moved toward the perimeter, they were surprised by the insistence in Sophie's voice as she called, "Don't cross the boundary!" She was right behind them, one imploring arm stretched out. "You'll be seen. Really. You need to believe—"

Her voice was drowned out by the rushing wind sweeping through the streets at hurricane force. Hidden in the noise was the sound of screaming voices that brought a chill to Mallory's spine. A building collapsed nearby. The force rushed toward the cathedral, dragging what seemed like all hell in its wake. When it reached its destination, there was a sound of thunder and a metallic crashing before it soared high into the air. Screeching, it continued to circle the cathedral compound.

Pale and shaking, Miller made the sign of the cross.

"Let's sit. You can't go out there till things have quietened down," Sophie said.

Every rational argument told Mallory to ignore her, but he was already under her spell; the attraction had been instantaneous—he had never met anyone he wanted to know so keenly, though he couldn't put his finger on exactly what it was that entranced him. With a shove, he encouraged Miller to follow her toward the fire, though they both continually glanced over their shoulders at the oppressive presence over the city.

By the time they found a quiet spot away from the other pockets of travellers and sat down, Mallory had almost started to believe that the thing wouldn't attack. They were joined by the dreadlocked teenager who appeared to be less of a friend and more of an assistant to Sophie. He introduced himself as Rick.

Miller crossed himself again, craning his neck upward fearfully. "That's the Devil," he said, hoping someone would dissuade him of the notion.

"It was certainly scary," Sophie said, "though I'm not much of a believer in the Devil myself." She leaned over and gave Miller's hand a reassuring squeeze. "You're safe here." He visibly calmed at her touch.

Miller looked to Mallory for support. "It's like in Revelations. The Last Days. The Church has collapsed . . . I mean, it's not gone," he added guiltily, "but it's barely hanging on. We've had war, and starvation, and . . . and . . ." Panic crossed his face once more. "It *was* the Devil . . . you saw it . . . you *felt* it . . . the fear. Everything's ending." He hugged his arms around himself tightly, staring blankly into the middle distance.

In a glance, something passed briefly between Sophie and Rick, then she leaned over and rested a small crystal from a pouch at her waist against Miller's forehead. There was an instant reaction: Miller's posture shifted, his shoulders loosening, his features becoming brighter, almost as if a shadow had been drawn from his face. Mallory looked at her curiously, but she studiously avoided his eyes.

"This is like a little town," Miller said with incongruous brightness. "How long are you staying here?"

"For good." A breeze caught Sophie's hair. Despite the now-faint screeching high above them, a surprising tranquillity lay over the camp. Sophie noticed Mallory's recognition of the calm. "There's a deep spirituality in the land here," she said. "That's why we've come. That's why we'll continue to come, from all parts of the country."

"A ley line—" Rick began.

Mallory snorted derisively.

"I might have expected that response before the Fall," Sophie said, "but things are different now, surely you know that? We've got our technology back, but these days spirituality is just as potent a force—"

Miller nodded. "The power of prayer."

"There's an energy in the land, an energy that runs through us, too. You can call it spirit, or soul, but everything is tied together by it—" Sophie's face hardened slightly at Mallory's dismissive laughter. "I believe in it because I *feel* it," she said, "and because it works."

"It's Sophie's power source." Rick smiled at them. "Her battery. You should see what she can do." The awe in the teenager's voice was affecting.

The discussion touched something in Miller. "It's true, Mallory. Back in Swindon, I saw an old woman lay her hands on a baby that was about to die . . . and it lived. It's like, if you believe in something strongly enough, you can tap into something, make it real. All the atheists used to say there was no evidence of God, but now He's here, answering prayers." A notion dawned on him. "Perhaps it's because these really are the Last Days. Good and Evil preparing for the last battle . . ."

"They've been saying the Last Days are here ever since the Book of Revelation was written, Miller. I'm not going to start running my life around something composed at a time before underwear had been invented." He waved away Miller's hurt expression. "These days, everybody's desperate to find something to believe in," he continued. "They can't face what a nightmare the world's turned into . . . how many people have died . . . how *hard* it's become. It's made children of everyone. They're wishing for a way out because the alternative is decades . . . at the very least . . . of hardship and suffering as we try to crawl back to some measure of the society we had before. Look around . . . we're back in the Dark Ages."

Sophie listened carefully, but gave no sign of what she was thinking. "And what do you believe in, Mallory?" she asked.

"Nothing. That's what I believe in."

"Everyone believes in something. But sometimes they don't recognise what they put their faith in. Money, drugs, sex—"

"That works for me."

Her eyes narrowed as she examined his face. "No, it's none of those things. There's something there, but I can't tell exactly . . ."

He had the sudden, uncomfortable feeling that she was trying to read his mind. He broke eye contact. "You're just being dazzled by my charisma and earthy sex appeal."

She smiled ironically. "That must be what it is."

Miller hugged his knees. The firelight actually gave some colour to his normally pallid face. "Who are you people?"

"Pagans, philosophers," Rick began. "Environmentalists, travellers, free-thinkers—"

"There's a movement going on all over the country, Mallory. We're just one sign of it," Sophie said passionately. "We're rebuilding a new Celtic Nation from the ground up. You don't have to have Celtic blood to be a part of it, but we're using that ancient culture as a template—"

"If you're trying to get some kind of historical credence, you're off to a bad start," Mallory interrupted. "There was no Celtic Nation, just a bunch of tribes—"

"With a similar culture, music, belief system—"

"Fragmentary. The Romantics built them up into something bigger . . . a fantasy . . ."

"Exactly." She leaned forward, emphasising the word with a blow of her palm to the ground. "You've obviously read the right books, Mallory, but you're missing the point. We *want* an ideal. The system we had before was woefully bereft. It worked for a few, the élite, the Establishment, and disenfranchised the many. We've got a chance here to start with a clean slate and we want something better."

"So you're going to cover yourself with blue paint and go into war naked?"

Her smile was a challenge. "If we have to. I love to see cynics proved wrong, Mallory. As an aside, don't go basing your views of the Celts on the writings of some tired old Romans. The victors write history and they disempower the vanquished. What we want is a society of equality, a strong community that looks after the weakest members, that's close to nature, that emphasises the arts and spirituality over making money and personal greed—"

"Well, when you put it like that . . ."

She watched him cautiously with those big, unnaturally dark eyes, slowly getting the measure of him. He relished her attention, enjoyed the fact that, liked or disliked, he had somehow been raised above the herd in her eyes. "If we don't do it, there'll be plenty ready to take us back to the old, failed ways," she said.

"OK, that seems a reasonable motivation," Mallory conceded, "but all this other stuff . . ." He waved a dismissive hand toward the perimeter posts.

"It's part of the human condition to be arrogant." Her smile was as confrontational as Mallory's words. "Everyone thinks they know *exactly* how the world works. Everyone." Irony laced her comments. "What do you think that suggests? We're all fumbling in the dark toward an answer."

The calming atmosphere in the camp had almost made them forget the devastation going on in the city beyond. Occasionally, they would be distracted by a sudden pillar of fire, or when the wind with its chilling voices rushed close by, but generally they felt cosseted in an atmosphere of security that made Mallory face up to the possibility there might be something in the travellers' magical thinking.

They continued their conversation well into the night. Mallory enjoyed the challenge of sparring with Sophie's sharp intellect, and it soon became apparent that Sophie found something intriguing in Mallory, too, though whether she liked him was a different matter. She maintained eye contact, spoke to him much more than she did to Miller, and underneath it all there was definite sexual tension.

Sophie spoke warmly of her background, growing up in Cambridge, father a doctor, mother a lawyer, studying English at university before feeling there was more to life. She committed herself to campaigning: for the environment, for Amnesty International, was briefly arrested during a protest against the World Trade Organisation that got out of hand. Mallory was taken by the rich depth of her beliefs and the passion she exhibited. She was so full of life he felt revitalised being next to her.

He, in return, told her nothing, but he did it in a humorous enough way to win her over.

Other members of the community came and went during the night hours, occasionally bringing them food—roasted vegetables, branded snacks that had a desirable rarity post-Fall—and cider. They were uncommonly cheerful; most of the people Mallory encountered in life were surly, suspicious, broken, or downright violent. Probably all on drugs, he thought, yet he felt oddly disturbed that they were genuinely pleased to see him, and never once questioned who he was or from where he came.

At one point, an impromptu music session broke out, with guitars, harmonicas, saxophones, and makeshift percussion, intermingling old pop songs and traditional folk tunes. It was the first time he had heard them since the Fall and he was surprised at how powerfully they tugged at his emotions.

But there was also something about the idyll that irritated Mallory: they had no right to be so content when the rest of the world had a cast of misery. "So who's in charge here?" he said. "Or is it one of those idealistic communes where everything starts to fall apart the moment the washing-up rota comes into play?"

Sophie thought briefly, then said to Rick, "How is she?"

"She'll probably be asleep."

"Let's check. She likes the night." She stood up and motioned for Mallory and Miller to follow. They picked their way amongst the tents, past many smaller fires, to a larger tent outside which two torches blazed.

Sophie disappeared inside, emerging a moment later to say, "She'll see you."

The interior of the tent was shadowy, warm, and perfumed with lavender. The front section contained a few chairs, rugs, pot plants—one of them cannabis,

Mallory noted—and ornaments with a faintly occult bent, including the skull of a cow.

The second section lay behind a purple velvet drape. Here, it was even gloomier and it took a second or two for their eyes to adjust. There was a large wooden bed that appeared medieval in origin and must have been brought from somewhere in the city, and on it lay a woman in her late forties, her long black hair streaked with silver. Despite the heat emanating from a brazier in one corner, she sprawled beneath several thick blankets. Her face was nearly white and drawn, as though she had some debilitating illness. Her gaze, though, was incisive, and she fixed instantly on Mallory.

"This is Melanie," Sophie said quietly.

Mallory introduced himself and Miller. The woman gave off a peaceful air, as if whatever lay in the ground at that site had been absorbed by her.

"I hope my friends have been looking after you." Her voice was hoarse, almost a whisper.

"You've got a good crowd here," Mallory said.

That appeared to please her. "Sophie seems to think the two of you are very likeable, too."

Mallory glanced at Sophie, who blushed and looked away.

"We're trying to fit in with the locals," Melanie continued. "We want people to see that what we're doing here is right." She ended her sentence with a deep, tremulous breath.

"Mallory here is very sceptical." Sophie eyed him slyly. "He doesn't believe in ley lines or the power in the land. And he especially doesn't believe we can create a boundary that will make us invisible to Fabulous Beasts."

"Sophie, dear, not everyone is a forward thinker, even in this newly enlightened age." She smiled weakly. "I'm sorry, Mr. Mallory, I'm teasing you. If you're hard and fast in your views, I wouldn't dream of trying to change them. But this is the way it was told to me. Millennia ago, the power in the land flowed freely through everything and everyone. We call it the Blue Fire, but it has many other names: chi to the Chinese . . ." She waved a hand to suggest this wasn't important. "It healed, but it could also be destructive when used against the enemies of life. It could be shaped and directed by will alone and it could cause effects at a distance."

"Magic, in a word," Mallory said.

"Very perceptive," Sophie said, with mild sarcasm.

"The Blue Fire formed a global network that kept the world . . . nature . . . healthy. It was fuelled by spirituality, by the faith of ancient people in tune with the land. They erected the standing stones and established the old sacred places at points where the Blue Fire was the strongest. But as civilisation advanced we lost touch with the energy. It became increasingly dormant, and the land suffered accordingly. There were still people who could use it to achieve things, but it was hard work and the effects were both hit or miss and not particularly great. The Craft, we call it. The great Wiccan tradition."

Miller gasped audibly and took a step back. Mallory saw a glimmer of panic in his face. *Please don't shout "Burn the witch!"* Mallory thought.

Melanie smiled at his reaction. "Forget the old clichés. We're not all *double, double, toil and trouble.* This is a religion, if you will. We have our rituals, the same as the Christian Church. We have our ministers and silly little trappings that make us feel happy. And we do good works. But I digress—"

"The Blue Fire is back in force." Sophie's eyes gleamed, her voice quiet but intense. "And we can do great things again."

"Just like that," Mallory said.

"Yes. Just like that." She looked to Melanie. "When everything changed with the Fall, it regained its old vitality. The Fall was a signifier that we'd moved into a new age—"

"The dawning of the Age of Aquarius," Mallory joked.

"Not everyone has the ability to work subtle magics, in the same way that not everyone can be an artist. But those who are able are very, very able. Super-charged," Melanie said.

"I remain to be convinced," Mallory said.

"Of course you do," Melanie replied. "This is a hard topic for many people to swallow. They get taught things when they're young . . . things about the way the world works . . . and they don't like to give them up easily. It makes them feel uneasy. Destabilised." Melanie nodded to Sophie. "Darling, be a dear and tell Mr. Mallory about Ruth Gallagher." Her eyelids drooped shut.

"I've heard that name," Miller said.

"You should have. Everyone should have, but the word is still getting round." Sophie tried to read Mallory's face to see if he had become any more receptive. "After the Fall, there was a group of people who fought for humanity. They were heroes. And one of them was Ruth Gallagher. The gods gifted her with a tremendous power. She became an ultimate adept at the Craft—"

"An Über-witch." Mallory couldn't restrain himself, but Sophie was unfazed.

"She could do amazing things. She could shake the world if she wanted. After the final battle, she set out across the land, spreading the word, teaching those who came to her. And Melanie was one of the first. They met in the Midlands, near Warwick, and Melanie took to it phenomenally. Her potential was off the scale. And she taught me."

"And Sophie's potential is great, too." Melanie's eyes were open once more, but she looked even more weary.

"I still think you're fooling yourself," Mallory said. "But I'll bite. Go on, show me."

"No," Sophie said indignantly.

"We don't perform, Mr. Mallory." Melanie threw a scrawny arm over her eyes. "We use the Craft sparingly and for the right reasons. We use it as Christians would prayer. It's not something to be taken lightly."

"Oh, well, then, that's all right. You *can* show me, you just don't feel like it," Mallory said. "You've convinced me. I'm a believer."

"Are you always like this?" Sophie's eyes blazed.

"Actually, he is," Miller said.

Mallory flashed him a look that suggested he was a traitor. "As you said earlier, everyone out there thinks they know the way the world works. And they're all wrong. So why should you be right?"

Miller moved to the foot of Melanie's bed. His curiosity had been caught by the way the blankets were lying; it didn't look right. "If you don't mind me asking," he said gently, "what's wrong with you?"

Sophie's face grew hard. "What's wrong with her?" Rick suddenly appeared near to tears. "She was trying to do some good and she was attacked and beaten for it!"

"I'm sorry," Miller said. "We have access to medical care . . . well, herbs and the like. If we can help—"

"There's not much that can be done, I'm afraid." Melanie gently pulled back the blankets. Both her legs were missing from the knee.

Miller recoiled. "My God, what happened?"

"She was attacked by a group of bastards from the cathedral!" Rick said, his eyes brimming over.

Miller blanched and glanced at Mallory in disbelief.

"We were at Stonehenge," Sophie continued, her face like stone. "It used to be a dead site . . . all the energy leeched from it because of exploitation . . . but after the Fall it came back with force. We were investigating some reports that a Fabulous Beast had settled in the area when—"

"They came out of nowhere!" Rick raged. "Black-shirted bastards with a red cross on the front—we've seen them around the cathedral! Think they're some kind of knights—"

"No!" Miller exclaimed, waving his hands as if he were trying to waft away the notion.

"They did that?" Mallory said.

"They tried to drive us off," Sophie replied. "Came at us on horseback with swords and pikes and all sorts of medieval weaponry."

"I couldn't get out of the way in time," Melanie said. "I fell beneath the hooves. They weren't able to save my legs."

"No," Miller repeated, backing toward the purple drapes. "I don't believe it." Sophie, Rick, and Melanie looked at him in puzzlement.

"It's true," Sophie said. "We wouldn't make something like that up. They knew who we were—unbelievers—and they rode her down. They didn't try to help or anything, just drove us away. They didn't care if we lived or died."

"No," Miller said again. "We're knights—we're from the cathedral. And no one there would do anything like that."

Mallory's heart sank. Miller's denial was too strong, bolstered by his own need to believe that there was no truth in the story. Mallory had been focusing on Rick's face; the puzzlement hung there for an instant while he processed what Miller had said and then his features hardened.

"Is this true?" Sophie said directly to Mallory. A hint of betrayal chilled her eyes.

"We only signed up today," Mallory replied.

Rick looked as if he would leap across the room and attack them. "They're all the same!" he raged. "They hate anyone who's not a Christian—"

"That's not true!" Miller protested, close to tears himself.

"Please," Melanie said weakly, "no arguments."

Mallory could see that the warm atmosphere had already evaporated. The extent of Melanie's tragedy meant any attempt to argue their innocence would be offensive. "Come on, Miller, this isn't the time," he said, grabbing the young knight's arm. Miller threw it off, preparing to defend his Faith further, and Mallory grabbed him tighter this time, dragging him back. "Get a grip," Mallory hissed in his ear. "Look at what's happened to her—have some heart."

"Yeah, get out of here," Rick said, "and tell your lot we'll never forget what they did."

Melanie closed her eyes; the strain was telling on her. Mallory tried to imagine the pain and horror of having two legs amputated without recourse to anaesthetic or an operating theatre. "Come on, Miller," he said, softening. Slowly, his companion unclenched and turned to go.

Miller paused at the drapes and said, "I'm sorry. I truly am." But the look on the faces of Sophie and Rick showed they both realised Melanie was probably dying and there were no words that could make amends for the crime that had been committed.

Sophie exited with them while Rick tended to Melanie. The frostiness of her mood made Mallory feel as if he'd lost something truly valuable; she didn't meet his eyes any more.

"I know it's not your fault," she said, "but I have a very real problem with anyone who subscribes to a belief system that condones something like that."

Mallory wanted to tell her he'd only signed up for a job of work, but at that point it would have sounded so pathetic it wouldn't have achieved anything. Instead he said, "I'm sorry things ended like this."

She didn't wait to hear any more.

As they trudged across the camp, the first light of dawn coloured the eastern sky. The screeching wind ended as if someone had flicked a switch, nor was there any sign of the Fabulous Beast.

Miller had been lost to his thoughts until he said, "It can't be true, Mallory. No one at the cathedral would stand by that kind of behaviour."

"I don't know, Miller—it only takes one bad apple . . . or one psycho . . . and everybody gets tarnished. Any club that has me as a member can't have a very strict vetting procedure."

"We should tell James . . . or Blaine—"

"Right, and say we dumped our uniforms and slipped out under cover of darkness to spend time with a bunch of witches. That should merit a crucifixion at least."

"Don't joke about that, Mallory!" Miller's emotions were all raging near the surface, but he managed to calm himself. "I'm sorry. But I'm not like you, Mallory. I believe in things, and it hurts me when you take the piss out of them."

"OK. I won't do it again."

Miller eyed him askance to see if he was joking, but couldn't begin to tell. Mallory's thoughts, however, had already turned to seeing Sophie again and ways that he might bridge the gulf that lay between them. It wasn't insurmountable, he was sure, but he would need time away from the strict regime of the cathedral.

When they walked along High Street up to the main entrance, what they saw brought them to an immediate halt. The enormous iron gates were bowed, almost torn asunder, hanging from their hinges by a sliver. The Devil had come calling.

chapter four

ENTERTAINING ANGELS UNAWARES

"No human being will ever know the Truth,
for even if they happened to say it by chance,
they would not know they had done so."

Xenophanes

September turned to October and with it came the first real chill of the approaching winter. The rooftops visible beyond the walls sparkled with frost as they emerged from the dawn mist, and the breath of the brethren formed pearly clouds when they trooped to the cathedral for prime. How the city's residents were coping with the first cold snap was a mystery, for since the night of the near destruction of the gates the bishop had ruled that no one should leave the compound.

The attack had shaken the cathedral to its core. A black, fearful mood lay over all, turning every conversation at the refectory tables, or in the leaky, cold shacks, or in the kitchens, or the herbarium, or the infirmary, to only one subject: the End Times had arrived.

At first, no one could quite grasp that what had been predicted and dissected for millennia had finally arrived and they were truly living in the age of the ultimate battle between good and evil, but gradually the desperate reality of their situation crept over them. Everyone in the cathedral who had seen the horned figure looming over the city or felt the scuttling touch of the presence's hideous intelligence in their mind had no doubt of the Adversary's black power. As the bishop pointed out in one of his sermons, there were no coincidences in God's world; the Adversary had come when the Church was at its weakest, but also at the point when it was preparing to break out as a potent force once more. "Evil is determined to prevent our resurgence," the bishop had said, "and so it is down to us to ensure that Evil does not triumph. *We* are God's champions at a time we thought was always in the distant future. But it is now, and we cannot fail, and with our Lord beside us, we shall not fail."

Yet while the bishop and the Church administration pored over ancient documents in the library, or discussed the signs and portents for any insight— sightings of the risen dead reported around the cathedral compound being one of the most prominent—many of the brethren were driven to frantic prayer. They felt cripplingly weak beside the strength they had seen exhibited, unprepared, fragmented, the rump of a once-mighty religion, and after the tribulations they had already suffered, they did not know if they had any resistance left. They reassured each other that their faith was strong, but the cold wind was in danger of winnowing the small flame of their fear into a blaze.

In the claustrophobic confines of the compound, grim and conflicting rumours circulated endlessly: the Dark Forces of the Prince of Lies were moving to wipe the Church from the land; it was the sign of the Second Coming; the apocalypse was at hand.

Expectations were high of another assault on the cathedral, and with each day that passed peacefully the tension increased. The Chapter of Canons authorised the reinforcement of the already sturdy walls from a supply of sheet metal, then trebled the number of guards and increased the frequency of patrols along the walkways around the battlements.

At the same time, the already rigorous routine of the knights was stepped up into a relentless round of weapons training, physical exertion, and tedious study that stretched from first light to compline. The only positive aspect for Mallory was that it kept him away from the hours of prayer and chanting that dominated every aspect of life for the brethren.

His trip into the city with Miller had given him a taste of what he was missing in the cathedral, but there was little chance of repeating the excursion. Though they had got back into the complex with ease, losing themselves among the team of workers repairing the badly damaged gates, the clampdown meant it would be too risky in the future. Suddenly Mallory felt like a prisoner.

"Do you think it was the Blues who attacked Melanie?" Miller whispered to Mallory as they watched the élite squad moving through their practice with machinelike efficiency. "They scare me."

Mallory leaned on his sword, a well-worn Reformation model. "Don't waste your time thinking about it, Miller. We're never going to find out, and even if we did we wouldn't be able to do anything."

"That's not right, Mallory. We can't just ignore something so wrong."

"Miller, sooner or later you're going to realise that the world is filled with injustice. It's situation normal. You might as well get wound up about stopping the rain."

"You two! What do you think you're doing?" They turned wearily at Hipgrave's clipped tones. The captain had been bawling out one of the novice knights for clumsy swordplay, even though he was barely out of his teens and had been suffering from malnutrition when he wandered into the cathedral an hour after Mallory and Miller. He was still painfully thin and weak thanks to the meagre diet offered in the refectory.

"Just taking a break," Mallory said.

Hipgrave stormed over and yelled into Mallory's face. "There's no break on the battlefield! Get fighting!"

Mallory didn't flinch. "You've seen *Full Metal Jacket*, haven't you?"

Hipgrave had clearly not encountered insubordination in his brief time as a captain. For a couple of seconds, he stared so blankly that Mallory could almost see the thoughts moving across his face. Finally, everything came together with the realisation of what Mallory had said, that the other Knights were watching, that he hadn't responded quickly enough or cleverly enough or with enough discipline. Unable to cope, he backed away and took his embarrassed irritation out on the knight he had just been berating. Yet his flushed cheeks revealed his awareness that his position had been undermined. Mallory expected a response sooner or later, probably when he didn't expect it; more, he didn't care.

"That bastard's the worst kind of bully." Gardener adjusted the bandages he had wrapped around his hands to help him grip the sword better. For someone in his fifties, he was leaner and fitter than many half his age. Mallory noted when it came to training that the Geordie had an attention to detail—like the bandages—that made him an effective force. "He won't do it to your face 'cause he's too weak. He needs taking down a peg," he added.

"If we were in 'Nam we could frag him," Mallory said wryly. "Full Metal Racket."

Hipgrave gave the order to fight and Mallory and Gardener stepped into the sequences of feints and strikes they had been learning. Beside them, Daniels lined up against Miller. There were twenty-seven of them in the novice group, a mixture of skills, ages, and social backgrounds. Most of the ones Mallory had encountered were decent enough, though they were all weak and pathetic according to Hipgrave.

"You know he's got a small penis?" Daniels said. His hardly strong blow brought Miller to his knees.

"How do you know?" Gardener grunted. "He always goes in a cubicle if there's anyone at the urinal. Never trust a man who does that—he's got something to hide."

"Aren't you Mr. Boa Constrictor-in-the-pants," Daniels gibed. "No, he's trying too hard. Overcompensating."

"If that's the case he probably needs a pair of tweezers to find it." Mallory grunted as Gardener came in with three blows in quick succession.

"I love this locker-room talk," Daniels said. He evaded Miller's strike lithely and made a mock blow that would have taken off his partner's head.

"It's like being in *Loaded* magazine around here," Miller said. "I bet the original Knights Templar weren't like this."

"'Course they were," Mallory said. "They had their candid charcoal sketches of Big Mary of Damascus, a goat's-skin full of mead after work, and then bared their arses to the passing camels before stumbling back home."

"You do realise we're God's Troopers," Daniels said sniffily. "We have forsaken all pleasures of the flesh. We get by on fresh air, a prayer, and a turnip."

"Bollocks to that," Gardener said. "If God wanted us to be eunuchs he wouldn't have given us . . . bollocks."

"You've obviously not been listening to some in your constituency, Gardener," Daniels said dryly. "Don't forget they're the no-sex-before-marriage and lose-a-hand-for-masturbation crowd."

"You'll be laughing out of the other side of your face when the Rapture leaves you here to get buggered by the army of the Antichrist." Gardener twisted, sidestepped, and knocked Mallory's sword from his hand. "'Course, you'd probably like that, you perverse bastard."

Mallory noticed Hipgrave hounding the young knight again, this time quietly but with obvious venom. The knight's eyes were wet. "Come on," Mallory said to Gardener, "let's have some fun."

He quickly whispered his idea. Gardener broke his usual dour expression with a grin, then rapidly and silently positioned himself behind Hipgrave, pretending to tie his boot.

"Hey! Hipgrave!" Mallory called.

Hipgrave turned suddenly at the insistence in Mallory's voice. Gardener was squatting so close to his legs that Hipgrave bumped against him, lost his balance, and tumbled to the ground in an ungainly tangle of arms and legs.

"There we go," Mallory said, "a dignity-free zone."

They expected some punishment, but after a brief outburst of cursing, Hipgrave stomped off to leave them alone with their training. Later, Mallory saw him in deep conversation with Blaine. As usual, the commander's face gave nothing away. His eyes moved in Mallory's direction only once, and then briefly, but they were cold and hard enough to inspire the briefest glimmer of regret.

Lunch was a small block of salty cheese and a lump of hard bread. Mallory and Miller found a table in the sun spilling through the windows that ran along one wall. The refectory had only just opened and they were the first diners, but it wouldn't be long before the tables were crammed; food was a high priority for everyone.

"So why haven't you been out to see Sophie?" Miller asked brightly. "I'd have thought you'd have sneaked over the walls a few times by now. Don't tell me you've lost interest. How fickle would that be?"

"Just biding my time."

"She was really nice . . . for a witch." His smile faded as he plucked the remaining crumbs from his plate.

"What's the matter? Afraid she'll turn you into a toad?"

"It's not that." He looked around uneasily. "You were right, the people around here wouldn't be very happy if they knew we'd been hanging out with witches. The Church has always had a strong line against them. *Suffer not a witch to live*, that's what it says. But she seemed all right. I should feel bad about liking her because of what she believes in . . . like, she's the enemy . . . but I don't."

"Christianity was made for you, Miller. You just love beating yourself up about all these little rules and regulations. Look, you know in your heart what's right. Don't let anyone try to tell you that you should or shouldn't like someone else."

Miller winced. "That sounds like blasphemy."

"Yeah, and according to some here, free will is blasphemy, even though it's the gift we were supposedly given. Look, it's simple . . . the Church hates witches because it nicked all their sacred places and all their worshippers, and it's afraid they're going to ask for them back."

"What do you mean?"

"Come on, Miller—if you're going to invest your life in this religion, you at least ought to know its history. When the Church first came here, it got its feet under the table by subterfuge. It built its places of worship on the sites that the people were already using, the old pagan places, the springs, the hilltops, whatever, in the belief that they'd just carry on coming. And all the Christian feast days were arranged on old pagan celebrations for the same reason. You don't think Christ was really born around the winter solstice, do you? At the point of rebirth and renewal in the old calendar—what an amazing coincidence. And isn't it strange that Easter—"

Miller smiled.

"What?"

"You're only telling me all this so I don't ask you any more questions about Sophie."

Mallory pushed his plate away and stretched. "If you don't want to learn from my great wisdom, that's up to you."

"If you really like her, Mallory, you should go for it. You only get one real chance for love. You can't let it slip away." Miller examined his empty plate dismally.

"Thanks for your advice, Miller. I always like to turn to experts for guidance." Mallory's attention was caught by James and the bishop's right-hand man, Julian. They came in separately, then both moved to the same secluded table without acknowledging each other. As they broke their bread they began a muttered conversation, heads bowed slightly so that no one could overhear them.

"I wish it hadn't happened with Sue," Miller mused to himself. "I wish she was here with me now." He chewed his lip, close to tears. "Mallory, I've got something to tell—"

"What do you think that's all about?" Mallory indicated James and Julian.

Miller shrugged. "They're having lunch."

"They're plotting. When we first came and James showed us around, Julian said something to him about somebody making their move . . . about dogs gathering."

Miller displayed a complete lack of interest, but Mallory was intrigued. Something was going on, and he wanted to know what it was.

"Why does Evil exist?" Peter began. "The Epicurean Paradox underlines the belief of many that the existence of Evil is incompatible with the existence of God. It goes like this: one, God is all-powerful; two, God is perfectly Good; three, Evil exists; four, if God exists, then there would be no Evil; five, there is Evil; six, therefore God does not exist."

Peter had been a deacon at the Catholic cathedral in Brentwood in Essex. From the sag of his skin, he had obviously been overweight at one time, but the hard life of the compound had taken some pounds off him. He had side-parted grey hair that, taken with his pallor, gave him a washed-out appearance, but it was the sadness in his features that characterised him; they reflected his belief that the world was a miserable place to be endured.

Peter's labour within the cathedral was to teach not only the scripture to the knights' new recruits, but also to explain the philosophy of the Christian Church. It was a task he relished, his demeanour even more gloriously lugubrious as he underlined the simple message that no one should expect any rewards in this world.

But whatever pleasures he got out of his office were wiped away whenever he saw Mallory slumped at one of the tables at the back. Most of the knights endured his lectures, nodding in the right places while they kept one eye on the angle of the sun. Mallory, though, asked questions. It wasn't as if he was eager for understanding of the Word of God. It was simply that he wanted to trip Peter up, to hamstring him with logic or garrotte him with a sharp line of philosophy. It was plain bloody-mindedness, Peter knew, and a childish desire to challenge authority that went against the entire teachings of the Church. Peter had endured it for many days—the constant questions about the historical truth of Jesus, the academic view that James was the true leader but politics had turned Jesus into the Messiah, the tortuous debates on the flawed and conflicting logic of the Bible, the pointed questioning about the atrocities the Church had been linked with, from the Inquisition to the collaboration with the Nazis—but his patience was not endless. Mallory was undoubtedly an educated man, but weren't they the worst kind? Oh, for the simple man who accepted the Message with the wide-eyed wonder of a child.

He noticed the expression Mallory always wore just before he launched into an argument, and quickly continued. "However, Saint Augustine presented the Free Will Defence: God created man with free will, thereby having the ability to do Good or Evil. Therefore, there is no assurance that man will not choose to do Evil. If God controlled the amount of Evil, or liberty, it would remove the gift of free will He had given to man. Quite simply, the existence of free will without Evil is an illogical impossibility. But even though man has the capacity to commit Evil, he can also perform acts of great goodness."

"I disagree." Mallory's challenging grin set Peter's teeth on edge.

"Why am I not surprised?"

"Mackie said the choice between perfect beings who always do Good, or free men who can do Good or Evil is a false dilemma, didn't he?"

"Yes," Peter sighed.

"And he also said there was an 'obvious better possibility' in which God could have created beings who always act freely, yet also have a predetermination to do Good. But he didn't, did he? So God doesn't exist."

"Not at all. Swinburne proposed a different approach: that there are advantages in the existence of Evil in the world. It gives men the opportunity to perform acts that show humanity at its best. Evil spurs mankind into action. Without Evil, we would live in a world where men could not show sympathy, compassion, forgiveness, or self-sacrifice."

"But—"

"Also, consider Hicks's 'soul-making' explanation," Peter continued hastily. "He said that man, who is made in the image of God but not in the likeness of God, is an incomplete being who must strive toward the perfect likeness of God. Qualities such as courage and love would not make sense in a world without Evil, because the world would be nothing more than a nursery paradise for children. Hicks's explanation is that Evil is necessary in order to build character and develop man into the likeness of God."

"That's a good argument. Why didn't Hitler use that in his defence? He was just doing God's work to get us all on track for—"

"You are not distracting me from my lesson today, Mallory." Peter maintained a pleasant façade but attempted to give steel to his words.

"So Hicks's argument is that this whole world is just one big classroom with a culture of disciplinarianism."

"Mallory . . ."

Mallory slid back cockily in his chair, settling in for a bout of tutor-baiting. "It's not a distraction to ask questions," he said.

"There is no need for questions. There is only a need for you to listen and heed."

"But surely a strong religion encourages debate. By answering the questions of doubters it will reveal its consistency and power and that can only lead more people into its open arms." Mallory nodded with faux-seriousness and it was that plain mockery that gave Peter the shocking urge to clip the grinning jackanapes around the ear. He wasn't prone to violence, ever, but Mallory brought out the worst in him.

"There is a time and a place. Perhaps you can encourage your brother knights to enter into these discussions in the free time you have on your hands." Peter smiled, knowing they had no free time at all. It wasn't very Christian to enjoy that barb, but he took the pleasure nonetheless.

Mallory also encouraged disruption in the others, and that was dangerous in a place that could exist only through discipline. Oddly, Miller, who followed him around like a dog, remained studious and intense, but Daniels and Gardener and some of the others who normally paid attention became distracted and lighter in mood.

Peter worked his way through the first part of the lesson, but instead of easing off, Mallory's baiting became progressively worse; something was eating away at him. As Peter weighed whether to continue, the decision was made for him. The door at the back swung open just enough for him to see Blaine, who must have been listening for a while. He signalled his intention to Peter before slipping away quietly.

Mallory moved through the corridors of the former museum with irritation. *Sent to the headmaster's office.* It was demeaning, and only added to his growing feeling that perhaps he should skip the cathedral and the knights; it hadn't turned out like he'd expected at all.

From rooms on either side came the drone of voices explaining herbalism, astronomy, basic field medicine, and other more esoteric subjects. The tutors were generally decent men and it was only Peter who received the brunt of Mallory's disruption, not because of who he was, but for what he said.

Blaine's room lay behind a thick oak door. Mallory hammered on it and loudly announced his name.

"Come." Blaine's Belfast tones echoed dully.

Blaine was as hard and emotionless as ever, sitting behind his desk with his hands splayed out on the blotter. Mallory only had a second to take this in before pain erupted across his shoulders. Briefly he glimpsed two of the Blues hitting out at him with cudgels from either side of the door before a blow caught him at the base of his skull and he blacked out.

When he came to a few moments later, the knights supported him by pinning his arms painfully behind his back. Blaine was standing only a foot away, peering into Mallory's face with a coldness that made him seem devoid of humanity. "You're a troublemaker, Mallory," he said. "Sooner or later I knew I'd get somebody like you."

Mallory almost couldn't resist making a smart comment, a pathological response that had got him into trouble many times before. He was only restrained this time by an ache in his jaw where one of the cudgels had given him a glancing blow.

"I could see it in your face the moment I set eyes on you," Blaine continued. "You don't like authority. You think you're bigger than you are. You think you're important. Well, you're not. Not at all." He returned to his desk and pulled from one of the drawers something that Mallory couldn't quite make out.

"You thought this was going to be an easy ride," Blaine said. "A bunch of soft Church people giving handouts to freeloaders. Well, they might be soft, but they're not stupid. They know how desperate things are. They're in the fight of their lives to save this religion, and they know they can't afford to be weak or they'll lose everything. They're good people, all of them, devout people, and they knew they wouldn't be up to some of the hard choices necessary to keep this Church going. That's why they hired me."

As Blaine approached, Mallory saw what he was weighing in his hand: a cosh, black leather on the outside, filled with something heavy, probably ball bearings. Mallory didn't have time to consider what lay ahead of him. Blaine brought the cosh down hard on Mallory's left shoulder blade. The pain made his knees crumple, but Blaine showed no emotion at all, neither sadistic pleasure nor contempt.

"They don't want to know what I do," Blaine said, without missing a beat. "They just want the job done. So I use my own initiative. I train up knights who can do the work out there and won't start crying the moment somebody steps on their toes."

The agony receded until Mallory's shoulder was enveloped by a dull ache. He made to respond, but Blaine brought the cosh down on his other shoulder so hard that Mallory thought he might black out again.

"You might think this is an overreaction," Blaine said. "It isn't. This place is based on discipline. That's the only thing that's going to hold it together through all the hard times ahead. You don't wait until little problems become big problems. You stamp on them early, get them sorted out. Lessons get learned, discipline is maintained."

"I can see why you chose a black shirt for your outfit."

He waited for the next blow, but Blaine held back. "You see, with your attitude, Mallory, I really should throw you out on your ear. Some would say you're not worth the trouble. But I don't see it that way. If I did that, you'd go out there, start bad-mouthing the knights all over the place, saying what a bunch of shirtlifters we are. And you see, the knights, they're only going to work if they've got a good reputation. The best reputation. Tough. Fair, of course, but tough. People will know not to mess with them, and because of them, not to mess with the Church. The way I see it, Mallory, I can't expel you. I can't send any failure into the world. I have to make everybody work out, one way or another. You're not going to leave, Mallory. We'll be watching you *very* closely from now on. You're going to turn out just the way I want."

"You really think you can make me?" Mallory sneered.

Blaine smiled. "Of course I can." The cosh came hard across Mallory's face. He felt his lip burst and then he blacked out again.

Mallory awoke on his bed, his body a web of aches; his face felt as if it had been hit by an iron. The first thing he saw was Daniels hunched over him.

"What happened to you?" Daniels said, with deep concern.

Mallory levered himself onto his elbows then noticed Hipgrave watching from the doorway. "I walked into a door," he said.

Hipgrave gave a curt nod and a smirk. Mallory felt a dull anger that his comment would be construed as acceptance of defeat, but it wasn't the time to make a stand. Blaine and the authorities had picked the wrong person to bully.

"You need treatment." Daniels helped him to his feet tenderly. "Come on— I'll take you down to the infirmary."

As they exited, Hipgrave said snidely, "The Lord watches over those who walk a cautious path."

"You going to tell me the truth?" Daniels asked, when they were outside.

"I was stupid. But now I'm smart."

Daniels eyed him cautiously then nodded faintly, understanding without needing to know the details. "These are indeed hard times."

Quietly seething, Mallory was barely aware of the disturbance as they walked across the compound. A large group had gathered in the shadow of the cathedral, their animated talk punctuated by cries hailing the Glory of God as they raised their hands toward the steeple.

Gardener was amongst them and broke away when he saw Daniels and Mallory. "You've got to see this." His face was transformed by wonder, stripping away the hardness of a tough life; Mallory thought he looked ten years younger.

He dragged them into the centre of the crowd where a grizzled, thickset man with a bald head staggered around in a daze. Occasionally he would stop, clasp his hands together, and raise his face to the sun. Tears streamed down his cheeks.

"Roy was blind," Gardener said in awe. "And look at him. He can see!"

"A miracle!" someone cried. "God is with us!" The note of relief in the voice revealed the subterranean fears of many in the compound.

"What happened?" Daniels asked, his eyes bright with the infectious fervour.

Roy dropped to his knees in front of Daniels, his palms pressed together in prayer. "Blind these thirty years!" A sob fractured his voice. He half turned and gestured toward the cathedral. "This morning I brought the relic into the new shrine. And now this!"

"What relic?"

Daniels's question triggered a ripple of murmuring through the crowd and as one they surged forward, with more joining by the second. Caught in the flow, Mallory and Daniels allowed themselves to be carried into the cathedral. In the Trinity Chapel a reliquary had been built out of bricks and wood. It was cordoned off by heavy-duty rope, but inside the framework Mallory could glimpse the chest he had seen the Blue Knights bringing into the compound on the night of the attack.

The crowd stood in awe, but its earlier noise had obviously alerted the authorities, for within moments the bishop and Julian were allowed through into the area next to the reliquary.

"We were hoping to make an announcement before vespers," Julian said when all eyes were on him, "but I suppose now is as good a time as any." He smiled devotedly at Cornelius. "The bishop will say a few words about what is obviously a momentous occasion, not only for our community here, but for Christianity itself."

Cornelius rested shakily on his cane. Though he looked frail, his eyes were bright with excitement. "Several weeks ago, the decision was taken to make this cathedral a haven for all surviving relics. Many from the Anglican branch may have long considered them of historical importance only, while our Catholic friends still believe they carry some part of the Lord's power." He took a long breath, his mouth dry. "We have all wrestled with the philosophy of our Faith in these changed times. But whichever way you approach this age in which we find ourselves, it is one of wonders. The Spirit affects the material world with a power that we could only have dreamed of before. In this world, then, where faith is an engine of change, what wonders could our relics bring?"

His smile brought gasps from the crowd as understanding of his words slowly surfaced. He gestured toward the reliquary. "In here lie the bones of Saint Cuthbert. Our brave knights faced undreamed-of dangers to bring them from Durham Cathedral. We prayed over them for seven days and nights. We had hopes . . . We had so many hopes."

With a trembling hand, he motioned for Roy to come forward. The tearful supplicant knelt before the bishop and kissed his hand with adoration.

"Word has just reached me of Brother Roy's cure. *I was eyes to the blind, and feet was I to the lame.*" He rested one hand on Roy's head. Tears streamed down faces on every side. "Let us hope this is only the first of many miracles. The light of the Lord shines brightly once more across this land of darkness.

"Even for the devout, faith is not always easy. We are tested at every turn, and over the last year and a half we have been tested more than ever. But now . . ." He paused for dramatic effect. ". . . faith has been renewed."

A loud cheer erupted.

"This is the first step in our mission to reaffirm the Word. Once more to bring the love of our Lord to the people. To build Jerusalem in England's green and pleasant land. *Let the heavens be glad, and let the earth rejoice: and let men say amongst the nations, the Lord reigneth.*"

The noise was deafening. Many fell to their knees, sobbing openly. Others hugged their fellows or bowed before the reliquary in quiet prayer.

As Mallory departed, a line began to build as those with ailments ranging from the minor to the debilitating waited to be cured.

Daniels brushed away a tear as they walked toward the infirmary. "Things are going to get better."

"You think?" Mallory breathed slowly; his ribs felt bruised, not cracked, but it wasn't worth taking any chances.

"We all need a little hope. That's what I came here for. That's why most people are here."

Mallory felt a surprising twinge. He'd locked himself in the present for so many months that whenever any echoes of the old days came back it felt like touching a live wire. "Do you miss your partner?"

Daniels looked startled by the question. "Every day. We'd been together eight years, since university. He was the first person I'd really felt anything for."

"Gary, wasn't it?"

"Gareth." He paused. "It feels strange saying his name again. You forget, with all the shit that happens in life. You don't have the time to think about what you shared. That's a mistake." He wiped his eye again. "Sorry. I'm a little emotional after all that with Roy."

"It's OK." Mallory felt oddly encouraged that Daniels felt no need to hide his sensitivity.

"What about you, Mallory? Anybody you left behind?"

"I don't think about the past. No point. It's gone. Same as there's no point thinking about the future. You just have to deal with what's going on around you."

"You see, that's what I'm talking about. I can't agree with that. We need to hold on to the good things from the past, to give us some perspective. Especially now, with all this." He gestured to the wide world.

"You just have to deal with things, Daniels. That's all it comes down to."

"No, that's wrong. Your memories are your guide. They let you create a framework so you can tell good from bad. Without that kind of compass, who knows how you're going to end up *dealing with things*? You see society out there: it's fallen apart. No rules or regulations. All we've got is what's inside us."

"That's all we ever had."

They reached Malmesbury House where the infirmary was situated. The grand Queen Anne façade sported a remarkable blue and gold sundial, the rococo interior too delicate for the use it had been assigned.

The infirmarian was a former surgeon named Warwick. He was in his fifties, with a brusque manner and the crystal pronunciation of a public-school education. Without any unnecessary chat, he made Mallory lie on a table in a white-tiled room filled with stainless-steel medical instruments oddly juxtaposed against jars of dried herbs and bottles of odd-looking concoctions. It was as if a modern doctor shared office space with an Elizabethan alchemist.

Mallory winced as Warwick examined the various bruises and abrasions. "So, with the back-to-basics thing that's going on here, can I expect some blood-letting and leeches?" he said.

"As much as I would like to oblige," Warwick replied tartly, "we still adhere to the basic tenets of modern medicine. Though there is an element of make-do, depending on what treatments are available." He checked Mallory's ribs closely then grunted, "No breaks. Who gave you a going over? Or is this part of basic training?"

"It was a test." Mallory saw Blaine's face and felt a dull burst of anger. "Which I passed with flying colours."

Warwick snorted and turned to the shelves that lined one wall. "Practising medicine in these times is difficult enough without dealing with self-inflicted injuries. If this happens again, you deal with it yourself." He delved into various jars before wrapping the contents in a small cloth package. "Infuse these in boiled water and drink it four times a day for the next three days."

Mallory sniffed at it; the contents were fragrant. "What's in it?"

"Would it really make any difference if I told you?"

Daniels surveyed the jars. "Heard any news from outside, Warwick?"

"Like what, exactly?"

"I know you hear everything in here. You get a snippet of information from everyone with an ailment. It's like a little spider's web, with you at the centre, collecting information."

"Thank you for the flattering analogy," Warwick said contemptuously.

"What about the government?" Daniels asked.

"Not heard anything."

"Somebody must be trying to put things back in place."

"Well, they obviously haven't got very far, have they?"

"No power on the horizon, then?"

Warwick removed a jar from Daniels's hands and replaced it on a shelf. "There's no oil coming in. They shut down most of the pits in the nineties. And I heard that all the nuclear power stations went off line during the Fall."

"Yeah, I wondered why we hadn't had a China syndrome experience," Daniels mused. "I hear you've got one of those clockwork radios tucked away."

Warwick shifted suspiciously. "Who told you that?"

"I just heard."

"You know how they feel about technology here." He rearranged the jars for a moment before adding, as if as an afterthought, "I've heard that all frequencies are dead. There's nothing coming in from the Continent at all."

"So either everybody's suffering the same all over the world," Daniels said, "or England's the only place with people left alive."

"Well, that's a thoroughly depressing thought," Warwick said, with a cold smile. "The survival of the human race might be down to us."

"And aren't we good representatives?" Mallory chipped in.

For the next three nights there were heavy frosts. The night office, the lauds of the dead and prime were all torturous in the freezing confines of the cathedral, where breath plumed white and the plainsong was disrupted by shivering until the mass of bodies raised the temperature a little. The bishop took the decision to limit the numbers of those who wished to pray before the bones of Saint Cuthbert due to the queues that built up throughout the day. Many, he said, were not seeking God's help with their ailments. They simply wanted a sign of God's power and it was wrong to test Him.

It was in the early evening that Miller overheard a commotion at the gates, which had not been opened since the attack. The torches blazing permanently around the entrance area cast a dull red light across the guards who leaned over the walls to talk animatedly with someone attempting to gain entrance.

The anxious note in the exchange drew Mallory from his path back to the barracks. He had a sense that here was something important, so he stood in the shadow of the nearest hut, stamping his feet against the cold.

After a few moments' debate, the guards sent word back for advice; they had obviously been told not to open the gates for anyone. The runner returned with James, who appeared agitated. He listened at the gate for a moment, then insisted it be opened. The guards were reluctant, but they eventually agreed to open the gates a crack so that whoever was outside could slip inside.

The visitor wore the black vest of a cleric and was shivering from the cold. He appeared so weak that he could barely stand, and his eyes had the glaze of the bone-weary or drugged.

Concerned, James grabbed the cleric's arm to lead him closer to a brazier that the guards used to warm themselves. The visitor's gait was slow and laboured, and even in the firelight his eyes didn't lose their dead expression. Intrigued, Mallory slipped as close as he could without being seen.

"—you sure?" James was asking.

"Near Stonehenge." The cleric sounded as if he was talking through depths of water.

James motioned to two of the guards to support the cleric, and then the four of them disappeared in the direction of the cathedral.

The summoning came at around eleven p.m. when Hipgrave appeared at the door, as bright and smart as if it were the middle of the day. "The operations room. Now," he barked. He disappeared swiftly, expecting mockery.

The operations room was a grand name for a room that contained only a wall map of the local area, a pile of useless phone directories, and a few chairs and a table. Blaine and Hipgrave were talking intensely near the window when the others entered. Hipgrave motioned for the new arrivals to take seats.

Blaine took up position near the map and surveyed them all carefully. "I hope you're ready for your first mission," he said in a manner that suggested he didn't think they were ready at all.

Mallory watched Blaine's face carefully, controlling the flame of his anger.

"Earlier this evening we received a visitor, a vicar from a parish in Norfolk," Blaine continued. "He'd been travelling to join us here with a companion, another vicar from an adjoining parish. With the way things are, it was remarkable they got more than ten miles from home. As it was, they reached Salisbury Plain. Nearly made it." He shook his head grimly.

"What happened?" Miller asked.

"Can't get much sense out of the one who turned up here. Shock, I suppose. Something attacked them on Salisbury Plain, not far from Stonehenge." He pointed to the map. "Here. He ran for his life, and I don't blame him. The other poor bastard scrambled as well—his name's Eric Gregory. Our man thinks he saw his friend get away, but he didn't hang around to find out what happened, understandably."

"You want us to bring the other one back." Daniels scanned the vast area of empty space on the map that signified Salisbury Plain. They were all thinking the same thing: it wasn't the fact that they'd be looking for a needle in a haystack, it was the prospect of what might be lying in wait out there in that liminal zone free of human life.

Back in the barracks, they lay on their bunks staring up into the dark. The atmosphere was thick with apprehension, but there was also a positive feeling that at last they were being given the chance to do something good. Only Mallory lacked any enthusiasm.

"Do you think we're up to it?" Miller asked.

"It doesn't take much to be up to a suicide mission," Mallory said.

"You're a bundle of laughs, Mallory," Gardener growled.

The joke had been too close to the truth. They all fell silent then, dwelling on thoughts too powerful to voice. Sleep did not come easily.

They were woken before dawn by Hipgrave, who would be leading the expedition. None of them were wholly pleased at that, particularly Mallory, who had already marked the captain as someone operating well beyond his capabilities, who knew it and whose desperation to be equal to the post only caused further problems.

The morning was bitterly cold with a sharp wind sweeping down into the compound from the Plain. Frost glistened on the rooftops of the huts and turned the cathedral building into silver and gold from the conflicting illumination of moonlight and torch. They stamped their feet and clapped their hands while Gardener furtively smoked a roll-up from some mysterious stash of tobacco that never seemed to diminish.

Eventually, they were led into the quartermaster's store where they were kitted out with thick hooded black cloaks woven by the brethren themselves, backpacks containing basic supplies (the rest of their needs were expected to be scavenged for on the way, as they had been taught in their survival classes), and, most importantly, a sword. These had all been retrieved from the museum's store and from a vast armoury at the Museum of the Duke of Edinburgh's Royal Berkshire and Wiltshire Regiment, which also lay within the compound.

The swords had all seen use in past conflicts, but the craftsmanship was expert, the balance perfect, the steel flawless. "Recognise this honour," Hipgrave said as he handed them out. "As knights, these will stay with you till you die. Your sword will be as vital to you as your right arm. Treat it that way. Look after it, sleep with it, lavish it with love and it'll look after you."

"I prefer my bed partners a little less skinny and a little less sharp," Mallory said. "Though there was this model once . . ."

Hipgrave fixed him with a cold eye. While the others fastened their scabbards across their backs for easy use while riding, he dragged Mallory over to one side. "I'll be watching you," he said, "especially now you're armed. One wrong move . . ."

"And what? You'll stab me in the back in front of all the others?"

Hipgrave couldn't control an unsure flickering of his eyes. Mallory laughed and joined the rest.

The horses were brought out from the stables at the back of the museum, all well fed and watered and ready for what could turn out to be a long journey. Three of them had two-man tents strapped to their backs.

After they had mounted, Hipgrave held up his hand for silence before saying a short prayer. He called for strength and courage in the face of the unknown, and for a safe return. Even Mallory found he couldn't argue with that.

They'd been locked behind the gates for so long that they would have felt uneasy even if they didn't have to venture into one of the most dangerous parts of the country. Blaine waited at the gates as they rode out, his hands behind his back, his face emotionless. He didn't wish them luck. Mallory had the feeling he didn't really care if they came back or not.

chapter five

INTO HELL

*"Even if you travel everywhere you will not find the limits
of the soul, so great is its nature."*
Heraclitus

Darkness lay across the city like the breathing of a sleeping child. Their horses' measured hoofbeats clattered with a lonely beat on the flagstones as they made their way down the High Street. Away to their left, the lanterns of the travellers' camp spoke of comfort and friendship, food, drink, and music: life. Mallory peered through gaps in the buildings to the tents in the hope that he might see someone awake. Miller caught him looking and flashed a knowing smile.

They watched the dark windows carefully and eyed every shadowy doorway and alley. The Devil was afoot, and now they were in his territory.

"It's better like this," Gardener said. He already had his hood pulled over his head so all that was visible was the red glow of his roll-up.

"It's freezing, it's nighttime, and we're heading for the next thing to hell," Daniels said gloomily. "I don't think *better* is the right word."

"I didn't mean that." Gardener's smoke mingled with the cloud of his breath. "I mean *this*." He gestured to the wider city. "No cars. No pollution. No bloody politicians or McDonalds or multi-bloody-national companies only interested in cash. Just peace, nature. Like God intended."

"There's always an enterprising Young Turk around the corner," Daniels said. "What's the matter, Gardener? Weren't you a capitalist in the old life?"

"I was a binman, you daft bugger. It was my job to clean up for the capitalists. I saw all the filth you left behind."

"Oh, you Communist," Daniels mocked.

"The Bible says enough about those who worship Mammon," Gardener countered. "You don't have to be a Communist to hate greedy bastards."

They passed St. Thomas's Church, the Guildhall, and the market, all still and dark, and made their way up Castle Street toward the ring road. The frost made the streets glitter, as unreal as a movie set. Without the streetlights, and the parked cars, and the stale exhaust fumes drifting in the air, everything seemed fake.

Beyond the city limits, they rode slowly in tight formation, all eyes watching the surrounding countryside, which was peppered here and there with the silent grassy mounds that marked the spiritual life of the ancients. The ordered fields had started to break down, becoming overgrown, with self-set trees sprouting here and there. The hedges were wild, the birds and animals abundant in the pesticide-free environment. Yet they all sensed there was more going on than they could see. Miller told them of his trials during his journey to the cathedral, of the monkey-creatures and the other things he had glimpsed at a distance. They listened attentively, without comment.

"What have you heard is out here?" Miller asked in the lull that followed his tale.

"The Wild Hunt rides at night, collecting souls." Gardener spoke with utmost confidence. "A black dog that's more than a dog."

"Ghosts." Daniels picked up his line. "Spirits . . . water spirits . . . tree spirits." He appeared a little embarrassed at saying these things, yet plainly believed in them.

"If this is the End Times, why has it been so quiet since the attack?" Miller said. "Maybe that was just a one-off. Maybe everyone's wrong . . . getting worked up for no reason." The note of hope in his voice was almost childlike.

"It was a calling card," Gardener said adamantly, "just to let us know what's coming up. This is the lull before the storm. Things will be going to hell in a handcart soon enough."

"Here we are!" Hipgrave's voice caught them unawares. He'd reined in his horse to point to grey shapes on a rise, almost lost against the background clouds and the rain.

"Stonehenge," Miller said redundantly.

Hipgrave trotted back to them. "We treat this area with extreme caution. No one goes into the circle—I have strict instructions from Blaine."

"I thought our instructions were to bring back the vicar," Mallory said. "You're saying you've got a whole load of other secret instructions?"

"They're not secret, they're operational." Hipgrave nudged his horse toward the stone circle. "You don't need to know."

They progressed cautiously, all of them feeling a tingle of excitement when the menhirs came fully into view.

"There's real power here," Daniels said. "Can you feel it?"

"What are you thinking, Mallory?" Miller asked, when he saw the faraway look on his friend's face.

Mallory shifted as if he'd been caught out. "I was thinking that it's returning to the days when Constable and Turner loved the place for its loneliness, and the special quality of the light and the atmosphere."

86

"I didn't know you were artistic," Miller said, surprised.

"That's because you don't know anything." Mallory spurred his horse away. He'd been struck by a strange notion: one of the outstanding mysteries of Stonehenge was why the builders had brought a special kind of bluestone all the way from mountains in southwest Wales. Three thousand years ago, it was a tremendous, seemingly unnecessary exercise, especially when there were more suitable stones close to hand. But after what Sophie had told him of the Blue Fire, he wondered if the bluestones had some special generating quality for the earth energy. He'd been quite dismissive during the conversation in the travellers' camp, but the concept of the invigorating lifeblood energy appealed to him.

They moved on to the English Heritage visitor centre, which was completely burned out. Scorch marks were evident all around the area, even in the tunnel that ran under the road. Hipgrave made them skirt the circle widely as if it were a sleeping beast, yet Mallory regularly caught him apprehensively scanning the clouds.

"Split up. Look around the site as fast as you can for any sign. We need to be out of here quick," he said.

They segmented the grassy field around the henge and each concentrated on one sector. After fifteen minutes of futile searching, Mallory's attention was caught by lightning on the horizon. A storm was approaching. Over in the next sector, Hipgrave stiffened and fixed his attention where the lightning had struck.

Maybe we can find a tree for him to shelter under, Mallory thought.

Three minutes later, the lightning struck again, though this time Mallory was aware it wasn't the brilliant white of any lightning he'd seen before; there was a ruddiness to it, perhaps even a hint of gold.

Mallory watched it curiously, waiting for the repeat, until Hipgrave thundered up beside him. The leader's face was taut. "We need to get out of here. Now."

"What's wrong?"

"What's wrong is we're trespassing!" Hipgrave spurred his horse to warn the others.

Mallory had no idea what he meant, but followed him nonetheless. Hipgrave had just spoken to Gardener when Miller called out on the northwestern side of the henge.

"Look here," he said when they galloped over. He pointed to a discarded bag and very obvious tracks leading away into the heart of the Plain. The bag was leather, embossed with the gold initials *E. G.*

"Eric Gregory," Miller said. "That's the name Blaine told us."

It was exactly what they'd hoped to find, yet Hipgrave barely gave Miller's discovery any attention. His neck craned in the direction of the lightning.

"Come on!" he said. "Move!"

Mallory followed his gaze to see a black shape just breaking the cloud cover; at that distance it resembled a fly.

Miller watched it dumbfounded until Hipgrave cuffed him on the side of his head. "Come on!" He set off in the direction of the tracks, quickly spurring his horse into a gallop, not waiting for anyone.

Miller stared at the bag in his hands, not really comprehending what was happening, until Gardener grabbed his collar and hauled him into his saddle.

"Look!" Daniels said in awe.

Another burst of energy. *Definitely not lightning*, Mallory thought again. He knew exactly what they were seeing, recalling the travellers' explanation as to why Melanie had been visiting Stonehenge when she was injured. The column of flame hit the ground and erupted, just as he had seen it do that first time in Salisbury. The Fabulous Beast approached on slow, heavy wing-strokes, its serpentine neck rising and falling with each beat.

For a brief moment, they were all transfixed. The creature carried mystery and wonder on its back; the very sight of it reached deep into the unconscious depths of their minds.

Another yell from Hipgrave finally stirred them and they spurred their horses into life, heading down the slope from Stonehenge into the heart of Salisbury Plain. Mallory estimated that the Beast was twenty miles away at least, but drawing closer rapidly. Occasionally, he could hear the sound of its wings, the jet engine roar of its flame bursts, each explosion followed by a shower of soil and rock and wood. Now they all knew why the Stonehenge visitor centre was burned out, and, as their wonder faded, what would happen to them if that searing breath came too close.

Lying low over their mounts' necks, they pushed on, the wind driving the rain into their faces until their skin stung and they could barely see.

The Plain passed by in a blur of green and grey. Eventually, they caught up with Hipgrave who herded them amongst old tank tracks into the once off-limits Ministry of Defence land. They finally came to rest under thick tree cover in a lower-lying area.

Mallory jumped down from his mount and ran to the tree line. In the distance, the Fabulous Beast was circling. "I think it's lost track of us," he said.

"Did it really see us? At that distance?" Miller said. "I mean, why was it after us?"

"They're stupid animals," Hipgrave said, dismounting. "They'll hunt anything."

Mallory wasn't convinced. From the very first sight of it, he'd instinctively felt there was an intelligence there. "It's definitely searching the area," he noted. He turned to Hipgrave. "You expected to see it."

"They like to follow certain routes—"

"Ley lines," Miller interjected, repeating the information he had learned at the pagan camp.

Hipgrave eyed him suspiciously, but didn't ask how he had come by this knowledge.

The trail was surprisingly easy to follow. Even the persistent rain had not washed away the regular footprints, and every now and then they were presented with items that pointed the way: a fountain pen engraved with the initials *E. G.*, a freshly broken shoelace, a page torn from an out-of-date Church diary, the writing illegible after the rain. Hipgrave was enthused by their progress, but Mallory felt oddly uneasy.

The route followed little logic, sometimes doubling back on itself. The suggestion was that the cleric was wandering, perhaps in a daze, and it would have left them completely lost in the uniformity of the Plain if they had not studied basic orienteering, as well as navigation by the sun and stars. The twisting track meant the miles passed slowly, but they also progressed with caution when they came to any area where they might be ambushed. Gardener grumbled that even in a daze the cleric was probably outpacing them.

"Where is this stupid bastard going?" Mallory muttered bitterly.

"You'd better hope something hasn't eaten him and is walking around in his boots," Gardener noted.

Daniels wrung out the sopping peak of his hood, sending a shower of water splashing onto the pommel of his saddle. "Well, isn't that a surprise—Gardener looking on the black side," he said.

"I'm not looking on the black side. I'm considering a possibility. These days, anything's a possibility." In the thin silvery light, Gardener's face appeared as grey as the heavy clouds that now lowered overhead.

Daniels snorted. "I know you well enough by now, Gardener. You think life's miserable—that's why you opt for that Old Testament morality. All the reward's in the next place. This one's just blood, piss, and mud, am I right?"

"You should get down to the pub more, Gardener," Mallory said distractedly. His attention was fixed on the trail ahead.

"Bloody amateur psychologists," Gardener said sourly.

"You know I'm right," Daniels continued. "All that fundamentalist Christianity you go for—it was right for a thousand years ago. Not now."

"Look around you," Gardener replied. "It *is* a thousand years ago."

"You really think the Fall was just the start of the apocalypse, Gardener?" Miller stared ahead gloomily.

"It's all there in Revelation. *The great dragon, that ancient serpent, who is called the Devil and Satan, the deceiver of the whole world—he was thrown down to the earth and his angels with him.* We've had war, we've had starvation, and there's talk of some plague doing the rounds. Death makes four—the pale horseman."

"What do you think, Daniels?" Miller asked.

Daniels appeared bored by the conversation. "I think fine wine, good food, and Italian furniture are the answer to all our earthly worries." He added, irritably, "Were you always like this, Gardener? Miserable, I mean."

Gardener grew introspective. "You don't choose who you are," he said after a while. "Life makes you the way you end up. You think you're going down one road, then something comes up . . . something you can't control . . . and you end up going down another. And then you get sent off on another journey, and then another, and then when you finally stop and look back, you're miles away from where you were."

His bleak tone put Daniels off pursuing the conversation, but Miller appeared oblivious to it. "What are you saying, Gardener?" he asked.

Gardener acted as if he were talking about something worthless. "We all need ways of making sense of this life. That's mine." As he considered this line, a shiver crossed his face. It appeared to prompt him, for he picked up the conversation again. "I married Jean when I was twenty. We'd already known each other for seven years. Met her on the Dodgems at Gateshead." A faint smile slipped out of the greyness. "She wasn't what you'd call pretty, but she'd got a mouth on her like a sailor. I liked that. She gave as good as she got. We had a few barneys in our life because of that mouth, I tell you, but there was never a dull moment."

He adjusted his hood so that his eerily glassy eyes retreated into shadow. "We always wanted kids . . . tried for years . . . until we found out I wasn't able. Jean took it well. We could have adopted, I suppose, but Jean said, 'We've still got each other.' We'd had the best times before. That's how we'd carry on into our retirement. Then Jean started feeling tired all the time . . . got ulcers in her mouth. I carried on doing the bins, came back after every shift, she'd mention it in passing. It wasn't important—she'd get over it." He shook his head. "All that time . . . wasted."

"What was it?" Miller asked quietly.

"Leukemia. Acute myeloid. Little chance of a cure, the doc said. We gave it a go. All that chemotherapy . . . her hair falling out . . . moods swinging like a bloody pendulum. I tell you, that foul mouth worked overtime." There was such affection in his voice that Miller winced. "She died. Here I am. I'm just passing time till I'm going to be with her again. No point looking for anyone else. Jean was the only one, for life. Without her, there's nothing here for me."

Nobody knew what to say. Daniels attempted a half-hearted apology, but it appeared pathetic against the weight of feeling that hung around Gardener. Yet Gardener himself seemed untouched by it. It was as if all his emotion had been considered and was now held in abeyance for some future time.

It was Gardener who eventually spoke first. He carefully surveyed the trail ahead, and then said, "What are you looking for, Mallory? You've been watching the way we're going as if you're expecting the King of Shit to come round the corner."

"When things are easy I start to worry."

"And you're calling me a pessimist." Gardener peered into the misty middle distance. "Though you'd have expected most of the footprints to have been washed away by now."

"It's all the things he dropped," Mallory said. "They're like signposts so we don't lose our way."

"Or perhaps you're just being paranoid," Daniels said. "What could possibly be the point? Who even knows we're looking for him?"

"Do you think we should mention this to Hipgrave?" Miller asked. As usual, the captain was trotting ahead, out of hearing range.

"Do you think he'd even listen?" Mallory replied.

As twilight approached rapidly, they considered making an early camp, but Hipgrave insisted that they press on. "We must be getting close to him now. How would we feel if he died of exposure tonight because we delayed? He might be just over the next rise."

Mallory made treasonous utterings, but the others accepted Hipgrave's view and continued against their better judgment as the light began to fade and the landscape slowly turned greyer. Soon after, they crested a ridge and saw a large hill looming up ahead of them.

"We've reached the edge of the Plain." Gardener pointed out a church steeple rising up due north.

Hipgrave rode back to them with the sodden map that had until then been of little use in the secretive heart of the army land. "That's Westbury Hill," he said. "On top, there's Bratton Camp, an Iron Age hill-fort. If we need to, we can make camp there."

"Look!" Miller said suddenly. They followed his pointing finger to a dark figure moving across the hilltop.

"That could be him," Hipgrave said. "Nobody else in their right mind would be roaming around a place like that now."

"I love these leaps of logic," Mallory said, to no one in particular.

Hipgrave spurred his horse toward the hill, with the others following close behind. It felt good finally to ride at speed, making them believe they were too fast for danger, once more untouchable.

Through the thin late-afternoon light, Westbury Hill loomed with seemingly unnatural steepness in the flat landscape, so heavily wooded around the lower reaches that they had to dismount and tether their horses. At Hipgrave's urging, they forged on, the breath burning in their lungs from the exertion of the climb. Finally, they reached the flat, treeless summit where the wind blew fiercely. In the twilight, they could just make out a figure picking its way over the banks and ditches of the hill-fort about half a mile away.

"I don't like it up here," Miller said. "There's a bad feeling."

As they moved uneasily across the open space, crows flapped all around, their eerie calls sounding like human cries for help.

"We were told to keep away from old hill-forts in one of Blaine's briefings," Daniels said.

Mallory recalled his experience on Old Sarum, and knew why.

"It was one of the classes before you joined us," Daniels continued. "They gave us a list of places we should approach with caution: hilltops, particularly where there were standing stones or ancient earthworks, some lakes and rivers, places that folklore linked with fairies or other supernatural creatures." He smiled thinly. "I presume they thought we might be corrupted by the sheer paganness of them."

The icy wind made the hilltop feel even more lonely. They came across a standing stone set in concrete with a plaque that said, *To commemorate the Battle of Ethandun, fought in this vicinity, May AD* 878 when King Alfred the Great defeated the Viking army, giving birth to the English nationhood.

The Iron Age defences made the going hard; pits and slippery banks lay hidden in the undergrowth, so they were constantly in danger of turning their ankles or breaking bones in a fall, but the uncomfortable atmosphere made them even more cautious. There was no longer any sign of the cleric.

Bratton Camp lay on the northwestern edge of the hilltop, overlooking a drop that was so steep and high it took their breath away. The B3098 was like a white snake far below. Next to the road, a giant factory that had scarred the ancient landscape now stood abandoned like some child's toy. In the last of the fading light, the shadows of clouds scudded across the surrounding fields.

"Look at that." Miller indicated an area of white on the steep slope below them. As they moved around, an enormous horse came into view, carved in the chalk that lay just beneath the scrubby grass.

"'The oldest white horse in Wiltshire,'" Gardener read from a sign, "'dating from 1778 but preceded by a much older version, date and origin unknown.'"

"Join the knights and see the sights," Mallory quipped, before adding, "What do you reckon, Daniels—Iron Age camp, ancient white horse, a standing stone, and undoubtedly lots of folklore? Are the alarm bells ringing?"

Hipgrave raised his voice above the howling wind. "Stop chatting—keep your minds on the mission. We need to fan out . . ." His order was cut off when he caught sight of movement from the corner of his eye.

The figure was disappearing behind an enormous earthwork that looked to

Mallory like a neolithic barrow mound: he glimpsed only white face, shock of white hair, black clothes, the fleeting glimpse of a dog collar.

"There he is!" Hipgrave said. "Halloooo!" he yelled, waving in the figure's direction.

But the figure had already disappeared. A few seconds later, they heard a muffled scream. They all stared into the growing gloom, listening intently.

"Quick!" Hipgrave barked. "He's in trouble! Let's get over there!"

Even in the heat of the moment, Mallory couldn't shake the feeling that what he had seen hadn't been quite right. It was a long way away and the light had been poor, but the vicar's white face had appeared oddly inhuman. Something in the shadows of the eyes and the black slash of the mouth had made it seem more an approximation of a man, perhaps not a man at all.

They ran across the fort, past the barrow mound. There was no longer any sign of the cleric.

"Take it easy," Mallory cautioned.

"No!" Hipgrave yelled back. "He might be in trouble!"

Yet even he was forced to come up sharp when he saw what emerged from the near dark on the other side of the fort. Ranged across the northern corner, branches had been roughly hammered into the ground and from them hung the skulls and dismembered carcasses of a variety of animals: badgers, foxes, rabbits, crows, smaller birds. Some were mere bones, picked clean by scavengers. Others were fresh kills, mouldering as they hung, glassy-eyed.

"What's going on?" Gardener said. The scene had an unnerving element of ritual about it.

"A warning," Mallory said. They eyed the grisly display warily, each of them trying to discern some meaning in the arrangement of carcasses. Though it was probably their imaginations, the wind appeared to pick up at that particular spot.

Drawing his sword, Hipgrave cautiously approached. The others followed, keeping watch on all sides.

Beyond the barrier, they could just make out a series of shadowy pits scattered seemingly randomly. They were surrounded by a complex arrangement of twisted bramble torn from another location, and more embedded branches that had been fashioned into lethal-looking spikes.

"It's a maze," Daniels said.

"What's behind all this?" Gardener said uncomfortably.

"Call out to him," Miller said, patently hoping they wouldn't have to venture further.

"I don't think it would be too good an idea to announce our presence." Mallory moved up beside Hipgrave to scrutinise the area more closely. "It's a trap. Got to be."

Hipgrave had already come around to the same way of thinking. "If he's in there, we've got to go in. It's our duty."

"I know," Mallory replied, "but the question is, is he really in there?"

"You think all this is some kind of elaborate plan to get at us?" Daniels said. "With all due respect to my esteemed colleagues, we're not worth the effort."

"Look, here." Mallory pointed to a route amongst the pits and barricades. "If you go carefully, you can enter. But you wouldn't be able to get out at speed. It'd be easy to slip into those pits—God knows what's at the bottom of them—or trip and get caught up in the brambles, or fall on those spikes. It's cunning, in a basic kind of way. Even worse if it's dark. We should leave it till morning."

Hipgrave fingered his chin nervously, but kept his implacable face turned toward the pits. Mallory could see that the captain didn't know what to do, and was desperate not to make the wrong decision.

"He looked all right when he went in, didn't he?" Mallory pressed. "We can afford to wait."

But just as he appeared to have swayed Hipgrave, Miller piped up, "Whatever built all this might have got him."

Mallory flashed him a black look, but it was already too late. "OK," Hipgrave ventured uncertainly. "We go in, but with extreme caution. Draw your swords."

"What kind of thing would do something like this?" Gardener said again. He sounded sickened.

"Maybe it's not here right now," Miller said, with forced brightness. "We could get the vicar, get out and be off."

"Maybe it's out hunting," Daniels said blackly, "for a few more little birds."

"Those are the things it *doesn't* eat," Mallory said. They all fell silent at that.

To his credit, Hipgrave led the way. The stink of decomposing animal flesh was unbearable as they passed the boundary line. Beyond it, the entire area felt different; it was almost too subtle to register, but it hummed away insistently deep in their subconscious: a sense of tension, a feeling of detachment as if they were just waking, or just falling asleep. The wind disappeared completely.

Mallory stuck close behind Hipgrave, followed by Daniels, then Miller, with Gardener bringing up the rear.

"I don't hear any sign of him," Hipgrave hissed. "He could have fallen into one of the pits . . . unconscious . . ."

Mallory wasn't listening for the cleric's cries—he no longer believed they would ever hear them.

At the first pit, they all peered inside in turn. The clustering shadows gave the illusion that it went down forever, though from the echoes of a displaced pebble Mallory guessed it was no more than fifteen feet deep. A damp, vegetative smell rose from within.

The construction of bramble and spike was complex and deadly, hinting at the arrays of barriers and barbed wire that littered First World War battlefields. It was impossible to tell what kind of intelligence could have established it, how long it had been in place. It was structured to form an impenetrable obstacle in some areas while simultaneously serving to direct them along a prescribed route that wasn't clearly visible from a distance. As they walked the precarious path amongst the pits—some of which were shallower than others, barely trenches— Mallory was struck by the design.

"It's like a ritual pattern you see in some ancient structures," he said. Hipgrave was clearly suspicious of this show of information. "It was symbolic, designed to put you in the right frame of mind before the revelation of some secret or mystery."

"Listen," Daniels interrupted. "Can you hear anything?"

They halted, bumping into each other nervously. The wind had picked up again faintly, soughing along the edges of the area so it was difficult to identify any other sounds. But as their ears adjusted, they could just make out another noise, low and rough, rising and falling.

"What is it?" Miller looked like a ghost in the twilight.

Mallory knew what it sounded like, and he could tell that Daniels and Gardener thought the same: breathing.

At their backs, darkness drew close to the horizon.

The path wound amongst the barriers until they were presented with a pit that hadn't been visible before. They knew instantly it was what they had been working toward. It stood alone, large and round where the others had been ragged holes torn from the turf and soil; its sides sloped down, but it was positioned so that the fading light allowed them to see the eighteen or so feet to the bottom where five dark holes indicated branching tunnels. More bleached skulls had been carefully placed around the perimeter, all looking out. Next to it, two tree branches had been strapped together with brambles in the shape of a tilting cross, a marker, and from it hung the tattered remnants of some kind of pelt.

"Oh Lord, I have a horrible feeling about this," Miller muttered.

"That makes two of us," Gardener said in a low, gruff voice that didn't draw attention to itself.

"If he's anywhere, he'll be down there," Hipgrave noted. He peered into the depths, then spied something. "Here!" He proudly showed them a shiny cuff link.

"There you go again," Mallory said.

Hipgrave drew himself up in a bid to imbue himself with some gravitas. "OK, Mallory, you'd better go down, check it out—"

"You can't send him down there!" Miller protested. "Not alone!"

"We're not going to risk all of us." Hipgrave's demeanour left no doubt that he had made his mind up; it was pointless Mallory arguing. "The sooner he gets down there, the sooner we can all get out of here."

Steeling himself, Mallory stepped over the edge and skidded down the slope in jerks. At the bottom it was cold and there was an unpleasant smell of decomposition drifting from one of the tunnels. He looked around: no footprints anywhere; there was no point mentioning it to Hipgrave—he'd long since given up listening to reason. The knights were all peering over the edge, their faces white. They all looked human, their emotions clear—apprehension, bravery, compassion, contempt—and he couldn't help thinking back to the glimpsed face of the cleric and the gulf between the two.

He moved around the tunnel entrances, trying to decide which one to explore, though he had no intention of venturing in too far. He could no longer hear what he had thought of as breathing. Perhaps he had been mistaken. Or perhaps it was simply holding its breath, waiting for him to draw near. He looked back up. Hipgrave gestured vehemently for him to press on.

"Bastard," he said under his breath.

He went around the tunnels again, listening, peering into the dark, smelling the air currents that came from them for any clue. Eventually, he chose one at random and edged his way in, his sword held out in front of him. With the fading light, the dark within became impenetrable after a matter of feet. The tunnel was small—his head brushed the ceiling and barely a quarter of an inch of space lay beyond his shoulders on either side—and the claustrophobia was palpable. Caught in there, he wouldn't stand much chance of getting out alive. He brushed the packed earth of the ceiling, afraid of a collapse. If Hipgrave wanted to investigate further, he'd have to do it properly, with a team and lights and supports.

Returning to the foot of the pit, he attempted to convey this information to Hipgrave in sign language, but if the captain understood he wasn't having any of it. He jabbed a finger in the direction of another tunnel. Cursing, louder this time, Mallory turned back.

The shape erupted out of one of the tunnels, hitting him like a wrecking ball. He went flying onto his back, seeing stars. He could hear the others yelling something, urging him to get up, get out, and then there was a tremendous weight on his chest and a sickening blast of hot, foul breath on his face. Slowly, his scrambled thoughts coalesced and he realised he was looking up into something that swirled with brilliant flecks, like a distant galaxy hanging in the cold void. They were eyes, he presumed, though he couldn't be sure, and if there was any human intelligence there he saw no sign of it.

Time locked, sealing him in that moment of connection with a presence he couldn't begin to comprehend; it was his only world, alien and terrifying.

But then the bubble burst and everything rushed in with an unbearable frenzy. The thing on him became a whirlwind; limbs lashed (he couldn't be sure if they were arms or legs or tentacles or something else), their sharpness tearing through his clothes, his skin. Desperately, he kicked and scrambled to free himself. Sickening sounds burst around him, at times high-pitched, then a low bass rumble, moving off the register; hot wetness suffused his clothing.

It lasted for only a few seconds and then the thing was away from him, bounding out of the pit with a single leap. Shattered by the attack, with blood seeping from him and the pain only just making its way to his brain, he was vaguely aware of the others yelling. Someone was shouting, "Attack! Attack!" over and over again. Someone else was urging them to scatter. A crashing and splintering as the barriers were torn up was followed by a scream of agony, suddenly cut off.

Mallory's consciousness returned with a lurch. However badly wounded he was—and he didn't want to begin to check—he knew he had to get out of there quickly before the thing returned. He threw himself to his feet only to feel his legs turn to jelly, pitching him back down onto the ground. His head spun; nausea turned his stomach upside down. With a tremendous effort, he managed to find enough equilibrium to get him to the side of the pit, where he hauled himself up on his hands and knees.

At the surface it was as unbearably dark as it had been at the bottom. Night had fallen, the thick cloud cover obscuring all moonlight. It made the sounds even worse: cries off in the blackness, panicked, pained, the terrible thrashing of something enormous and unimaginably wild moving too fast for its size.

One thought surfacing above all others: *We were led here, to find this.*

Briefly, he wondered what he was going to do, but there was no way out apart from the way he had come in. It was all he could do to pick out the path amongst the rubble of the smashed branches and torn bramble. He had taken some sharp blows to the head and it felt as if concussion was coming on fast. Every time he moved he lost more blood; he could feel it running into his trousers, puddling in his boots. It made him light-headed, broke his thought processes even more, so that he could only really concentrate on the here and now: getting out of there as quickly as possible.

He lurched along the path, desperately trying to keep his balance so he didn't plunge into one of the other pits, while at the same time continually wiping the stinging blood from his eyes. There was more frantic movement ahead, running, the sound of boots on grass, more crashing.

He blacked out briefly, waking to find himself face-down in the mud. Somewhere there were screams. It felt like a nightmare, as if he wasn't really there at all, merely watching himself going through inexplicable motions from a vantage point deep inside his head. Why was he trying to escape? Why was he there?

What was moving just beyond his perception? And then the image of the fire in the dark, urging him to go forward, not back.

Pulling himself to his feet once more, the brambles tore at his hands. One of the jagged branch-spikes ripped through his trousers into his calf. Away to his left he heard whimpering, instantly drowned out by the wind. "Miller?" he called out feebly.

Before he could turn in search, there was another explosion of movement as the hunting thing launched itself from the periphery of his field of vision. He ducked just in time, but he felt it pass only inches over him to crash into the barriers ten feet to his left. He scrambled on, almost slipped into another pit, and caught himself with his legs dangling over the abyss. More movement, more running, sounds bursting from periods of silence like explosions on a battlefield. His foot kicked something that bounced a few feet ahead of him: a severed hand, now caked in mud. It was impossible to tell which knight it belonged to, but the sight of it filled him with a deep dread, and he knew he would never be able to shake the image of it lying there, like discarded rubbish.

Somehow, he found himself near the display of skulls that marked the boundary, and then he was out, crossing the hill-fort, tripping over the holes in the turf, sliding down the ditches. He could barely walk, barely think. No one else was around, and he couldn't help believing they were all dead.

He was too weak to walk far. He went down the hillside head over heels, ricocheting off tree trunks, crashing through bushes that ripped at his skin and hair, using his body weight to keep the roll going as the only way to put distance between himself and the monstrous thing that still roamed the hilltop.

Finally, he came to a halt, lying on his back without the slightest strength to move, staring up into nothingness. The night was torn by sounds that could never have come from a human throat. Mallory felt as if he was in hell.

Consciousness came in the grey light of morning. His body was a web of agony and he was frozen to the bone, but he was still alive, though he didn't know how much longer that would be the case. From the state of his clothes he could tell he'd lost an inordinate amount of blood, and more leaked out each time he shifted. Shakes wracked his body repeatedly. His head felt stuffed with cotton wool as if he were on the verge of a debilitating migraine.

Nightmarish images flashed back from the previous night. He felt sick with shock and could barely believe he was still alive. A little joy filtered through, but it was dampened by the pain and his doubts for the safety of the others. He thought of the severed hand: one of them was certainly dead from blood loss. Could any of them have survived such an onslaught? He forced himself not to think about it, or the emotions that came with it.

Apprehensively, he peeled open his shirt. A gaping wound ran across his stomach, filled with blood. Other gashes lay open on his chest and arms, and for the first time he was thankful for the classes the Church authorities had inflicted on him during his training. Moving as carefully as he could, though still punctuated with devastating bursts of pain, he managed to free his haversack. At the bottom of it was the small medical kit they all carried with them for basic treatment on the road. First, he removed the small jar of antiseptic salve created in the medicines quarter that lay off the cathedral's herb garden. Unscrewing the lid, he recoiled from the potent odour, as strong as any smelling salts. Then he removed the tin that contained the large needle and sturdy thread. This was going to test his willpower.

Dipping three fingers into the jar of salve, he gingerly dabbed it on the stomach wound. The pain made him cry out, but he could instantly feel the area numbing. He left it a couple of minutes before threading the needle. He didn't have anything to sterilise it with, so he hoped the salve would do its job.

The first stitch was agony. His stomach turned as he watched it pulling the two flaps of flesh together. By the fourth stitch, the sight was not so disturbing and he learned to cope with the pain by chewing on the end of his leather belt. When he had finished, he tied a knot as he had been taught, then rested for five minutes before moving on to the next wound.

It took him an hour to finish the entire job. By then he felt like a shadow; he didn't want to guess how much blood he had lost. He really needed a transfusion, a few days' bed rest. Instead, he was lying on wet ground in the middle of the countryside. He just hoped he had the strength to mount his horse and reach one of the villages that bordered the Plain.

It took him fifteen minutes to get to his feet using a tree trunk as support, and even then he felt as if he was going to collapse with every step he took. At first, he lurched from tree to tree, pausing every now and then to dry-retch, but after a while he found it in himself to stagger unsupported. Even so, he lost his footing several times before he reached the bottom of the hill. There he found the remains of the horses; it looked as if they had been hacked to pieces by a chainsaw. He fought back the despair; it wouldn't help him. He'd just have to walk.

The day was a little brighter than the previous one, with no sign of rain, but it was still windy. He remembered where they had seen the church steeple poking above the trees and thought he would use that as a marker and head for it. Yet when he eventually skirted the foot of the hill there was no sign of the steeple anywhere. It made no sense to him at all, but he didn't have the energy to consider what it meant. Using the occasional glimpses of the sun as a guide, he set off in what was undoubtedly the right direction. In his weakened state he could barely keep his eyes on the horizon; his concentration was mainly occupied with staying on his feet, staying alive. Many times, his consciousness slipped sideways so that he was moving in a dream-state, observing his surroundings without being aware of them; this condition became more and more the norm, and the remaining rational part of him knew that he was dying.

He should have reached the neighbouring village within the half hour; it never materialised, nor did any of the roads he knew skirted that edge of the Plain. He wondered if he had somehow got turned around and was heading back into the wilderness, but the surrounding landscape told him otherwise. Rolling grassland lay all around, rich and fertile, punctuated by copses and small woods. The trees were oddly fully leafed, as if it were midsummer rather than crisp autumn, and there was an abundance of wild flowers scattered across the area in blues, reds, and yellows.

He slept regularly, usually where he stumbled, and on one occasion he attempted to eat some of the travel biscuits, but he immediately vomited them straight back up. In his daze, time skipped in haste. He would close his eyes in a moment's thought and clouds would have scudded across the sky, or the quality of the light would have changed.

He came to a small, winding track of well-trodden earth and without thinking began to follow it. It eventually led to a quaintly constructed small stone bridge over a tinkling brook where he was suddenly overcome with a tremendous thirst. He made his way tentatively down the side of the bridge, through the thick brookside vegetation, and scooped up handfuls of water, splashing it into his mouth and across his burning face. He was stunned at how wonderful it tasted, vibrant, with complex flavours, like no water he had ever sampled before. He immediately felt a little better, his thoughts sharper, his limbs a tad more energised. He continued along the track beyond the bridge with a little more vigour.

Twilight came sooner than he anticipated, the trees growing ghostly as the grassland turned grey. Most of the clouds had disappeared, so he could clearly see a crescent moon gleaming among myriad glittering stars. It was surprisingly balmy, with moths fluttering above the grass.

Where am I? he thought, without really giving the question much weight.

A little further on, he noticed a light glowing amongst the trees away to his left. Hope filled him that at last he might be able to find somewhere to rest. The path forked and he took the track that led directly toward the light, the other branch heading in a near-straight line across the landscape.

As he approached the trees, other lights became visible, like golden fireflies in the growing gloom. Lanterns had been strung amongst the branches and from their vicinity he could now hear voices, some raised though not threatening, others lower in conversation. It brought his consciousness another step back from the misty region where it had retreated, so that he was alert enough to experience surprise when he saw what lay ahead.

Amongst the trees, illuminated by the hanging lanterns, lay a large market stretching far into the depths of the wood. On the periphery there were only a few stalls and browsers, but further into the depths he could see that it was bustling. The air was filled with the aroma of smoke and barbecued meat, along with unusual perfumes and spices he couldn't quite identify. The raised voices were the traders encouraging people to examine their wares, and somewhere there was music, singing voices accompanying some stringed instrument that set his spirits soaring.

Obliquely, he knew how strange it was for a market to be held at that time of evening in such an isolated location, but he was so attracted by the sights and sounds it barely registered. Nor did he truly notice how unusual some of the market-goers were. They were dressed in ancient attire that echoed a range of periods—medieval robes and Elizabethan doublets, wide-brimmed hats, long cloaks, broad belts and thigh-high boots—while some were unusually tall and thin, and others uncommonly short. Their features were the most striking. Every face was filled with character, eyebrows too bushy, noses too pointed, eyes astonishingly bright or beady, so that they resembled pictures of people from another time rather than the familiar blandly modern features he was used to. Indeed, some of them were almost cartoonish in appearance, and if Mallory had looked closely, he would have seen that their skin had a strange waxy sheen, as if they were wearing masks over their true faces.

His attention wandered as he entered the market. The detail of his surroundings was almost hallucinogenic, the sights, sounds, and smells miasmic after the tranquillity of the countryside. But while he was lost in the swirl of life, he was unaware that many of those around watched him carefully and curiously, with only a hint of suspicion, and occasionally a hint of threat.

After the initial fascination had worn off, Mallory grabbed a passerby by the sleeve and mumbled, "Where is this place?"

The man he had stopped was thickset with a long bushy beard and piercing dark eyes. He wore a beige cloak, fastened at the throat with a gold clasp, over clothes that reminded Mallory of an Elizabethan pirate. "Why, this is the Market of Wishful Spirit," he said in an oddly inflected voice, as if Mallory were sub-educational. Mallory didn't notice how the man's words came a split second after his lips moved.

Mallory staggered on his way, his concentration coming and going. In that place, everything seemed like even more of a dream, the light from the lanterns too golden and hazy, the music growing louder then softer as though someone were tuning in a radio station.

Mallory's attention was briefly caught by the produce on sale at the stalls. On many there were items he might have expected—vegetables, clothes (though strange in appearance), gold and silver jewellery of unusual design, furs, perfumes in wondrously designed bottles of multicoloured glass—but others displayed goods that left him thinking it really *was* a dream. There was a rock in a gilded cage that spoke with the voice of a small boy, a purple jewel encasing a tiny man and a woman of dismal expression who hammered at the walls of their prison, a hat that supposedly made its wearer invisible, a mirror showing continually changing views of alien landscapes, and many more, some too astonishing to comprehend.

"Here! Over here!"

Mallory looked around at the call. A skeletal man in a black robe that appeared to be made of tatters was beckoning to him. Mallory drifted over.

"A Fragile Creature," the trader said in a rasping voice, "abroad in the Far Lands in these times. I thought I was mistaken."

"I need to get some medical help." Mallory supported himself on the edge of the trader's stall. The world was growing dark on the fringes.

"First examine my wares," the trader said. "They come from distant Kalash-stan on the edge of the Terminal Waste. Very rare, very wondrous."

"I don't have any money," Mallory said, distracted. He needed to move on and find someone to aid him quickly.

"There are many ways to pay," the trader said slyly. He held up a pair of scissors with long golden blades. "Here. The Extinction Shears that cut the weft of existence. Very rare, but within your grasp for a very small consideration. Very small, barely noticeable. Or here." This time he raised a face mask of a screaming man constructed from silver and studded with emeralds. "A Gon-Drunning. It will allow you to see into the dreams of your friends and enemies."

"No." Mallory looked around, bewildered. The darkness was even closer now, like the shadow of an enemy sweeping up on him from behind. "I have to go. I have to . . ."

The market began to swim. He was vaguely aware of the trader leaning forward to peer at him closely with predatory eyes, and then others nearby stopping to stare, smiling malignly as if a pretence were no longer necessary. They began to move forward just as the darkness rushed in and he collapsed to the ground.

chapter six
INTO HEAVEN

"Although we cannot choose what happens to us,
we can choose how we respond."
Epictetus

Mallory woke on a pile of furs on a long, low bed in the corner of a darkened room. The windows were flung open, revealing the silhouettes of trees beneath a starry sky. The perfumes of a summery wood floated in on the breeze.

Cautiously, he raised himself on his elbows. It took him a second or two to comprehend his state, but more important than his location was the realisation that he felt astonishingly well: refreshed, free from pain, his thoughts once again sharp and focused. He swung his legs off the bed and sat on the edge before examining the injuries on his chest. His clumsy stitches were all gone and the deep wounds themselves had almost healed. It didn't make sense to him at all. How long had he been unconscious?

In confusion, he went to the window. He was in a wing of a low building made of stone with a timber and thatched roof that stretched out for a hundred feet on either side; the architecture was unfamiliar. It was in a large clearing in a wood. Close-clipped grass ran down to the trees, and here and there torches blazed. There was no sign of life.

Instinctively, Mallory went for his sword—it was no longer there.

"No weapons are allowed in the Court of Peaceful Days."

Mallory whirled at the sound of the voice, though it was melodic and gentle. A woman stood in the open doorway, smiling enigmatically. When Mallory looked into her face, it took a while before he understood what he was seeing. At first he thought it was his mother, who had died ten years ago, then the Virgin Mary, then the dinner lady who was always kind to him during his lonely, troubled days at school. Finally, her features settled into those of a woman in her late forties, long black hair framing a face that was still beautiful, with lines of happiness around her mouth and eyes. She was wearing a dark blue dress that appeared to be made of velvet yet reflected the light of the torches filtering through the window. A mysterious quality to her made him feel instantly at ease.

"Where is this place?"

"The Court of Peaceful Days."

"I heard you the first time. But where is it? I walked for a while." His day's journey came back to him in flashes, impossible to place in any context. "On the way to Bath?"

"It is further away than you could have walked in a lifetime."

Her smile melted him instantly; he could no longer resist. "My injuries—?"

"We healed you. They were minor."

"They didn't feel minor."

"To us they were." She stretched out a supple arm; her hand was pale and delicate. "Come. Let us walk outside."

He took it, despite himself. Though he had almost recovered, he still felt as if he was existing in a dream. "Who are you?"

"My name is Rhiannon. The Court of Peaceful Days is my home."

"I'm Mallory."

"I know." She led him out into a long stone corridor. Guards were posted at regular intervals, dressed in a strange golden armour designed with an avian style. She nodded to each of them as she passed. Outside in the warm night she let go of his hand and they walked side by side across the grass until they reached a fountain of fire. The flames gushed out of a spout in the centre and rolled down into a surrounding pool, swirling like liquid against all the laws of physics. Even close to it, Mallory could feel no heat.

"Where *is* this place?" he whispered, suddenly overcome by awe.

"In the Far Lands. A heartbeat away from your own fields, yet as distant as the farthest star." She stood before him, still smiling benignly. "You were brought to me by some of the market people. They feared for your safety."

"When I was blacking out, I thought they were going to rob me. Or worse."

"Indeed, some of the traders come from far afield, and they have a predatory nature. But those who live within the remit of the Court of Peaceful Days would never harm anyone. That is our law, immutable, a law of all Existence, though recognised by few."

There was something about her that reminded him of Sophie, an odd combination of gentleness and power, perhaps. "As laws go, that's one of the best."

"It is a law of Existence." Rhiannon looked from the flames to the stars scattered overhead. "So simple when compared with the great philosophies, yet it is the only law that matters. We are all brothers and sisters of spirit, joined on levels Fragile Creatures can never comprehend."

Mallory looked back at the building. From his new perspective he could see that it was quite enormous. It stretched far back into the trees, and in parts, on the fringe of his vision, it appeared that the trees were growing in it and through it, were part of the very structure. Though the construction was simple, there was a breathtaking majesty to it that made him feel as if it had a slumbering life of its own, as peaceful and gentle as Rhiannon.

"Fairyland," he said. "That's what you're talking about."

"It has always existed, though for many generations of your kind the doors were locked." Her brow furrowed as she examined his face closely; Mallory had the strangest feeling she was looking deep into his mind. "Does it trouble you?" she asked.

"I'm not surprised by anything anymore."

Her smile returned. She motioned for him to follow her into the trees where the perfume of summer vegetation was more heady. Enough moonlight broke through the cover to allow them to see the nocturnal animals scurrying out of their path and the ghostly imprint of owls in the branches over their heads. Mallory was surprised to see glitter trails moving through the treetops, which he at first took to be fireflies, but which eventually revealed themselves to be tiny gossamer-winged people frolicking amongst the branches. They, too, made him feel powerfully happy, as if they radiated an energy field that altered his emotions. For the first time in ages he felt at ease. In his swirl of feelings, he suddenly felt like crying, and he hadn't cried in a long while. The thought of going back to the bleakness of his own home depressed him immensely.

"I think I'd like to stay here a while," he ventured.

She shook her head and looked away into the dark. "You have a job to do, Mallory. Every Fragile Creature has work of the greatest importance to do before they finally depart the Fixed Lands. A task that is unique to them, so important it is stitched into the fabric of Existence. And you cannot rest—none of you can rest—until your personal task has been completed." She paused. "There is always time to rest, when the work is done."

"What task?" he asked. "What use can I be?"

When she turned her face back to him, there was something profound locked in her eyes and her smile, but it was too enigmatic for him to decipher. She carried on amongst the trees in silence until they reached a large clearing where the moon appeared to have come down to earth, so milky and luminescent was the light reflected on the metallic items scattered all around. Swords were embedded in the ground. Shields lay like seashells; helms and breastplates, axes, spears, and other weapons Mallory didn't recognise had been discarded there. It was the detritus of some great battle.

"These remain here, so even at this, the most gentle of all the Courts . . . *especially* at this Court . . . we never forget," Rhiannon said gravely. "Suffering is always only a whisper away. Peace and happy days never last. Pain and war and despair will always rise up."

"That's a depressing view of life," Mallory said.

She disagreed forcefully. "Peace and happy days have their potency *because* of this dark side. Without it, the things we treasure would tarnish with boredom. They shine because we know the dark is always over the next rise."

"So you're justifying war . . . and suffering . . . ?" He was deeply surprised by her position after what he had seen of her so far.

"Justifying? No. Accepting. It is the way of Existence. There is a meaning for everything that happens. We deal with the unpleasant things in the same way that we celebrate the wondrous. And we must always deal with them. Never turn our backs, let them gain an upper hand, throw Existence out of balance so the darkness gains ascendancy, for that is what the darkness always wants."

He had a feeling she was no longer talking in abstract terms; indeed, was talking directly to him.

"We must be vigilant," she continued, "all of us, and even the gentlest must take a stand, on their own terms, when needs call."

She moved amongst the weapons of the dead before selecting a sword. She nodded knowingly as she weighed it in her hands, then handed it to him. Moonlight limned its edges so that it appeared as if a faint blue light was leaking out of the very fabric of the blade. Its handle was inlaid with silver and carved with two entwining dragons, like the flag he saw flying over the pagan camp.

"I have a sword," he said.

"Your sword is built to despatch the threats of the Fixed Lands. This is a sword of my people. It has a power that transcends the space it holds. Three great swords were forged from the very stuff of Existence, so our stories tell us. Three swords that can cleave the very foundations of life. One is the Sword of Nuada Airgetlamh—that stands alone and will not be seen again until the Dragon-Brother returns. The second is lost, believed corrupted, a danger to all who wield it. This is the third, and it is linked to your land in a fundamental way. Keep it close. It will bring you light and warmth in the dark days ahead."

"You're talking as if it's alive."

"It is, in the way that all things are alive, from the stones of the field to the clouds of the sky." She proffered the sword. Mallory hesitated before taking it, but when it slipped into his fingers it felt instantly comfortable. A tingling warmth spread through his palm into his arm. It felt as if the dragons on the handle were shifting to accommodate the unique musculature of his hand. "It is called Llyrwyn."

"It has a name?" Mallory said wryly.

"There is a reason it has a name, and that reason should be clear, if not now, then in good time."

"Why are you giving me a sword?"

"I told you, there is a meaning to everything that happens. You are not here by chance. In the terms of your world, you may have arrived a little earlier or a little later, but you would always have come here, to this spot. For the sword."

Mallory turned the blade over in his hand curiously. The faint blue glow wasn't a product of the moonlight at all—it truly was coming from the weapon. "I don't understand."

She moved her hand slowly to indicate the trees, the sky, the grass. "Everything is alive, everything is linked. There is a mind behind it all. We cannot know it, nor begin to know it, but it shapes us all . . . Fragile Creatures, Golden Ones . . . we are all part of it. And it demands champions. In its wisdom, it has decreed they come from the ranks of Fragile Creatures . . . of your kind, Mallory. They fight for the very essence of Existence, for Truth and Life. They are known in the Fixed Lands . . . in your world . . . as Brothers and Sisters of Dragons. At any time, five are chosen, though they may never be called to fight the enemies of Existence."

Mallory didn't like the way the conversation was going. "What are you saying?"

"The five who held that role throughout the troubles that devastated your land are broken, Mallory. Gone . . . to time long gone, to the Grey Lands, to different roles where the need for them is greater. A new five must arise."

He shook his head as if his own denial would prevent what she was saying from being true.

"You are the first, Mallory."

"That's ridiculous. It's so ridiculous it's laughable. Me, a champion?" The concept was absurd in so many different ways he couldn't begin to tell her.

"There is a need for you, Mallory. A great need. And you will be ready for it, though there may be more forging necessary. Existence does not choose its champions unwisely. You are a Brother of Dragons."

"A Brother of Dragons," he repeated with a disbelieving laugh. "OK, I'll bite. For now."

She gave him a scabbard, which he fastened to his belt, and then she motioned for him to follow her again. Mallory's mind was racing. He'd just about accepted that he was nowhere on earth, that he was in a place that had slipped into folklore as Fairyland and that the woman with him was of a race that simpler people had come to call fairies. But where he *really* was, and what she truly was, escaped him. What made him uneasy was the realisation that since the Fall the world was not simply at the mercy of isolated supernatural predators that looked as if they'd wandered in from *Grimm's Fairy Tales*. There were other powers, perhaps higher powers, that had some interest in humanity; mankind was no longer in control of its own future.

As they moved back through the trees toward the Court, he put his tumbling thoughts to one side and said, "Why are you helping me?"

"You were brought to me, and I never turn away a creature in need." She appeared to consider this for a while before adding, "My people have always had a relationship with your kind, sometimes friends, sometimes enemies, but always there."

An owl broke through the branches and circled her until she held out an arm for it to land. Her skin remained unscathed under its claws. She leaned toward it, apparently listening, as it made a series of strange sounds deep in its throat. "There is food and drink on the table if you wish to refresh yourself," she said as it took flight.

On the way back to the Court, Mallory thought he could sense a deep sadness underneath her calm, as if she had lost someone or something very dear to her. He found he had warmed to her with remarkable speed; she appeared uncomplicated and uncorrupted by cynicism.

In the Court, they walked for ten minutes along corridors where the only sound was the soft tread of their feet. Eventually, they entered a large hall with a beamed ceiling and luxuriant tapestries hanging on the stone walls. Food and drink were laid out on the table—silver dishes and platters containing seafood, spiced meats, breads and fruit, and decanters of a deep red wine—but there was no sign of any servants.

"Not many people here," he said.

"The Court of Peaceful Days is filled with life, but my subjects know I prefer silence to follow at my heels." She gestured for Mallory to sit. "Everything in my Court is given freely and without obligation."

"'Subjects?' You're the queen?" Mallory suddenly realised how hungry he was. He didn't know how long he had been out, but after the days of cathedral rations his stomach yearned for sophisticated food. He tore into the ham and bread, washing them down with a goblet full of red wine.

She took the seat at the head of the table but didn't touch the food, seemingly content to watch Mallory enjoy himself. "That is my responsibility."

"The queen of all Fairyland."

She laughed silently at his name for the land. "There are many Courts in the Far Lands, and each has its own queen or king, its own hierarchy, its rules and regulations, petty rivalries and intrigues, loves and vendettas."

Once he had taken the edge off his hunger, Mallory sat back and looked at her in the light of the latest information. "When everything went pear-shaped a while back, everyone was talking about gods carrying out miracles all over the place. That was your people?"

She nodded slowly. "We were worshipped when your race was in its infancy. The tribes called us the Tuatha Dé Danann. We are known to ourselves, in your tongue, as the Golden Ones."

"Why did everything change?"

She gestured dismissively as if it were a minor question. "The seasons turned. It was time once again for an age of wonder, of magic. We returned to the land we knew, and that many of us loved."

Mallory selected a sharp silver knife and began to quarter an apple. "Your kind were supposed to be everywhere during the troubles, but since then there's hardly been any sign of you."

"My people have detached themselves from Fragile Creatures once again. After the rigours of the Great Battle, when suffering and hardship were felt on all sides, the decision was taken to withdraw amongst ourselves, to concentrate on our own affairs. But we can no more leave Fragile Creatures alone than your kind, good Mallory, can leave the Golden Ones alone. Isolationism never works. We are all bound. We must find ways to exist together."

Mallory poured himself another glass of wine. The velvety warmth of it was spreading through his limbs. "I wouldn't hold your breath. My own people can't get on together."

She stared introspectively into the warm shadows in the corner of the room. "We are all bound, Mallory. Freedom to act independently is an illusion. Obligations and responsibilities tie our hands, as do love and friendship. And good men can no more turn their backs on need than cowards can face danger."

Mallory finished his apple and pushed himself back from the table, replete. "That's a very optimistic view of human nature."

She rose without replying and he trailed behind her out of the room into another chamber, heavily carpeted and filled with sumptuous cushions. She stretched out, catlike, upon them. "Threats lurk where you least expect them, Mallory," she said.

He slipped into the cushions, cocooned by every aspect of that place; he didn't want to go back to the hardship of the cathedral, or of his world. He wanted to stay there forever, listening to her voice, letting her take care of him.

"Your wounds were caused by something terrible," she continued, "even to my own people. It has no business being in the Fixed Lands, or the Far Lands, for that matter. It crawled up from the edge of Existence, where even worse things have been stirring. Your kind have been noticed." This last comment sounded like a tolling bell.

"But that thing's been left behind," he said. "I'm never going to go within a million miles of it again."

"Pick the pearls from my words, Mallory," she warned. "And beware."

He pressed her further, but she would say no more. Her statement, though, remained with him, niggling at the back of his head, spoiling the comfort he felt. In a bid to forget, he questioned her about her kind. She told him of four fabulous cities that haunted her nomadic people's memories, an ancient homeland they could never return to and the terrible sadness that knowledge engendered in all of them. And she told of the wonders the Golden Ones had seen: astonishing creatures that soared on the sun's rays, breathtaking worlds where the very fabric changed shape with thought, the play of light on oceans greater than the Milky Way, *the great sweep of Existence*. Tears sprang to her eyes as the stories flowed from her, memories of amazement that cast a pall over her current life.

"We have lost so much, and I fear we will never regain it," she said, and the terrible regret in her voice made Mallory's chest heavy.

At some point, her voice became like music, lulling him to sleep. He dreamed of worlds of colour and sound, bright and infinitely interesting, of nobility and passion and magic, and when he woke with tears in the corners of his eyes he resolved not to return to his world of bleakness and dismal low horizons.

The room was empty. He stretched, surprised at how wonderfully rested he felt. The corridor without had the stillness and fragrance of early morning. He wandered along it, searching for Rhiannon to ask her if he could stay at the Court, but the whole place appeared deserted; not even the guards were visible. He took branching corridors in the hope of finding some central area, but the building was like a labyrinth and he quickly became quite lost.

After a while, he came upon an atrium big enough to contain trees at least eighty feet tall. Sunlight streamed through the crystal glass high overhead, yet the space was cool and airy. A grassy banked stream babbled through the centre of the room, while birds sang in the branches and rabbits and squirrels ran wild amongst the trunks.

In the very heart of the atrium was a pillar of marble so white it glowed. Mallory felt oddly drawn to it, but as he approached, a disturbing whispering broke out on the edge of his consciousness. He couldn't quite make out what was being said, but still it unnerved him. He had an impression of strange intelligences, so alien he could barely comprehend what form they might take. *Turn away*, he told himself, fearing that his own mind would be burned by any further contact; but the pillar pulled him in.

Yet when he came within a foot of it, the subtle whispering faded away and there was only an abiding silence in his head. The marble was hypnotic in its blankness. As he stared at it he began to feel as if he was floating in a world of white with no up or down, no horizon. Peace descended on him.

He didn't know how long he was like that, but time had certainly passed when he realised he was seeing something in the nothingness. Shapes coalesced like twilight shadows on snow, taking on substance, clarity, depth, and eventually context, until he realised with a shock that he was looking at Miller lying on a muddy trail, his dead, glassy eyes staring up at the grey sky.

His cry broke the spell. When he looked around, Rhiannon was standing at his shoulder. "I just saw . . ."

She nodded slowly, her face grave.

The pillar was just white marble again. "A hallucination? Or did I see what was really happening back on earth?"

"The Wish-Post looks into you as you look into it," she said. "What you saw is the road not travelled. You are thinking about not returning?"

He didn't answer, but she could see the truth in his face.

"Your vision showed you the state of Existence if you stay here."

"Is it for real?"

She took his hand; her fingers were cool and calming.

"He was going to die sooner or later anyway," he continued, without meeting her eyes.

"I know what happened to you, Mallory. What you did." No accusation marked her face, only pity, and somehow that was worse. He turned away, sick at what had been laid bare.

Her fingers grew tighter, more supportive. "As above, so below. As without, so within. The rules of Existence are simple, Mallory, and unyielding. To everything there is an opposite, though it may often remain hidden, and these opposites are continually at war. We choose our sides, make our stand, and hope for the best."

"How do you know what happened to me?" Briefly, he thought he might cry.

"Some of us have the ability to peer into Fragile Creatures. But your essence, Mallory, is so raw that any of us could see. There is a battle raging in your heart, the same battle that sweeps through all Existence. Which side you take is within your control, but you will pay the consequences of your choice."

"I don't know what you're talking about."

"There is no need to lie to me, Mallory." Her voice was so gentle that his feelings surged again. He had the sudden, aching desire to put his head in her lap so she could stroke his hair, tell him of good and noble things. "Your bitterness and despair consume you. Do not let them."

"What do you know?" he said defensively. He made to break free from her hand, but couldn't bring himself to do it.

"Let me show you something else." She turned him so he was once again staring into the Wish-Post. He had obviously become attuned to the object for he quickly fell into the swirling whiteness. He dreaded seeing Miller's dead face again, but this time the snowstorm fell away to show a woman leading a pack of ragtag travellers along a muddy track. It was Sophie Tallent.

"Why are you showing me this?" he asked.

"You know, Mallory."

As Sophie and her band crested a rise, a dark smudge appeared on the horizon, and though it appeared insubstantial, Mallory knew instantly it was the thing they had faced at Bratton Camp.

"Now you're trying to tell me that if I don't go back, she'll die too?" he said acidly. "You really do want me out of here."

"No." Rhiannon pulled him gently away from the pillar; it felt as if white tendrils were withdrawing from his mind. "It is important that you are free to weigh what lies within you, and to make your choices accordingly. Good or bad, the choice is the important thing. But it is also important you have all the information to make your decision."

Following the flight of a bird, Mallory let his gaze rise up to the crystal roof. The way the sunlight shimmered through the glass brought a tremendously evocative memory of his childhood rushing up from deep within him with such force that it literally took his breath away. He was at his grandparents' farm just outside Worcester on a sun-drenched summer Sunday morning, with the light forming starbursts through the branches of the trees as they swayed in the breeze. The air was heavy with the fruity farmyard smell and he could still taste the saltiness of the home-cured bacon on his tongue. His parents were back in the house with his little sister, but he'd gone walking with his grandfather. It was one of his favourite pastimes. The old man with the lantern jaw and snowy hair had told vivid country tales with a rich Worcestershire accent, filling Mallory with an appreciation of the seemingly mystical power of nature, of the epic cycles of the seasons and the strangely intelligent actions of the animals and birds that surrounded the farm.

On that morning, they had walked the ancient cart track to the thick wood clustering the hillside where his grandfather had once terrified him by telling him that all the trees had spirits, and they watched him as he passed. In the middle of the track they had come across a chaffinch writhing in the dust and grass seed. It might have been clipped by a car on the road down in the valley or winged by a raptor, but it was undoubtedly dying. The seven-year-old Mallory had been deeply upset by its death throes, more so when his grandfather had told him there was nothing they could do to save it. Yet his grandfather had gently picked up the bird and held it securely, stroking its head with his thumb.

"Grandpa, you're getting blood on your shirt," Mallory had pointed out. But his grandfather had ignored the needless stain, only whistling soothingly to the bird, still stroking its head until it eventually passed away. When he finally laid it to rest in the shade of a hedgerow, Mallory had been shocked to see deep scratches in the old man's palms where the bird's talons had clawed out their fear.

"Why did you let it hurt you?" Mallory had asked. "It was going to die anyway."

His grandfather had leaned down until he could look deeply into Mallory's face, and what Mallory saw in his blue eyes had been strange and mysterious. "Every second is as valuable as the one that went before, lad, and we do our best to prove that. We've got no other job in this world," he had said, smiling, not really caring if Mallory understood or not.

And Mallory hadn't understood, but there in the Court of Peaceful Days he had the overwhelming yet incomprehensible belief that it was more important than anything else he had ever been told. Desperately, he grasped for the meaning, but it was as elusive as the shimmer of the sunbeams through the glass, and eventually the memory retreated to its hiding place.

"This place," he began, "it's affecting me . . . making me remember things . . ."

"Peace has that effect."

"How long before I have to make my decision?" he said.

"As long as you require. Time here is not the same as in your land. The breath between seconds can be an uncrossable gulf. Centuries can pass in the blink of an eye." She led him out of the atrium into the cool, shady corridor beyond.

"Then I could stay here forever and what you showed me might never happen," he said desperately.

Her sad smile told him that was not an option.

She left him alone to wander out into the lawned area that ran down to the thick wood surrounding the Court. The sun was pleasantly warm before the full heat of the day set in and the air was vibrant with birdsong. He found a grassy bank next to a stream and lay back with his hands behind his head, watching the clouds drifting across the blue sky. After a while, he realised it was spoilt: he couldn't appreciate the tranquillity, for his mind had been made up for him and it was already turning to what lay ahead.

An hour later, he trudged back to the Court with heavy legs. Rhiannon was waiting for him; she already appeared to know what his decision had been.

The kitchens prepared him a meal of bread, cheese, and fruit, which he stored in his haversack, and then Rhiannon led him into a large entrance hall he hadn't seen before. It had stone flags and wooden beams, and appeared home to as many birds and woodland animals as the atrium. In the centre, two blue and green globes hovered in midair, seemingly substantial, yet occasionally passing through each other as they spun.

Mallory was surprised how heavy his heart felt. He had been deeply moved after only a few hours in a strange place with a strange woman; it made no sense.

As they approached the large oaken door, it swung open of its own accord, revealing a winding path leading through a white gate before crossing green meadows that stretched to the horizon.

"Follow that path and it will lead you back to your world," Rhiannon said.

He considered asking how this could be, before accepting that the question was as pointless as everything else in his life. Instead, he asked the only question that mattered to him. "Would you mind if I came back here? One day?"

"The Court of Peaceful Days will always be here for you, Mallory. When you've walked your road and shed your burden, there will be peace waiting for you."

The words "Goodbye, Mum" popped into his head and he only just escaped the embarrassment of saying them aloud. Instead, he let his hand close around the dragon handle of his sword for comfort, and then he stepped over the threshold.

"Dark times lie ahead for you, Mallory," Rhiannon said. "You will find yourself in a labyrinth of opposing views, with peril on every side. Look to learning to understand the conflict."

He was about to ask what she meant by this when the door began to swing shut, and Rhiannon appeared to recede backward across the hall as if the image of her was being refracted through bottle glass. She allowed him a smile and a wave and then the door closed silently.

Mallory walked for an hour along the winding path through the idyllic countryside until he became aware that the weather had grown colder and the landscape was cast in muddy greys, greens, and browns instead of the vibrant colours of the start of his journey. The air smelled sourer; every sensation was muted after the heightened perceptions to which he had become accustomed. Yet there had been no sign of passing from there to here; the change had happened in the blink of an eye as if the two lands were merged.

As he skidded down a muddy slope, wondering how far he would have to walk and in which direction he needed to go, he heard voices carried faintly on the wind. He ran toward them until they lay on the other side of a ridge, and then he waited. A moment later, Sophie and the travellers came over the top, just as he had seen them in the Wish-Post.

She caught her breath in surprise, but then looked past him coldly. The others—a band of six, four men and two women—made no secret of their dislike for his uniform. Mallory could see that her first instinct was to ignore him, but she couldn't contain herself.

"You're not going to tell me you being here is a coincidence," she said sourly.

"Is that any way to talk to your rescuer?" Mallory retorted. He enjoyed manipulating the flash of annoyance on her face.

"I need your help like I need my eyes burned out," she replied, but he noticed she didn't lead the travellers past him.

"OK," he said, "but I was only doing my Good Samaritan bit. You're lost in the middle of Salisbury Plain with some very unsavoury things on the loose. And they're possibly very close on your trail."

"What makes you think we're lost?" a redheaded teenage girl said contemptuously.

"You're heading into the heart of the Plain and I don't think you'd really want to be doing that at this time of day. Not without tents, food, and heavy ordnance."

Sophie looked from Mallory to the sun that he had obviously read. Mallory could tell she was fighting the urge to be confrontational. "Perhaps we did make a slight mistake," she said. "And you would be able to lead us out of here, would you?"

"If you promise to say thank you."

"OK, I'm sorry," she snapped. "If you're offering to help us, we're very grateful. But we're not Christians and you stand no chance of converting us. So why would you want to help us?"

"I help everyone," Mallory said blithely. He thought for a moment, then added, "Except people with very bad body odour. And Chelsea fans. I've never forgiven them for David Mellor."

He marched off a few paces, then realised that no one was following him. Doubt was clear on their faces. A flash of their crippled leader slowly dying in bed mellowed him and he said, "I'm offering to get you back to Salisbury, after a short detour to pick up a friend, and I don't want anything in return. Understood?"

Sophie nodded. She silently reached an agreement with the others and they all set off together.

After they'd gone about half a mile, Mallory realised that Sophie had increased her pace so she was just behind his shoulder; the others trailed a few yards behind. He slowed, and she accepted the unspoken offer.

"What *were* you doing there?" she asked, without looking at him.

"Waiting for you."

"Don't lie."

"I'm not."

They walked a few more paces in silence before she snapped, "Have you lot been spying on us?"

"By *my lot*, I presume you mean the Knights Templar. Possibly. Quite frankly, I wouldn't put anything past some of the people involved." She was taken aback by his candidness, and for the first time looked him in the face. He stared back into her eyes, enjoying what he saw there. "If you're up for an unbelievable story, I'll tell you the truth."

He proceeded to describe his encounter with Rhiannon, although he left out the nightmare that preceded his journey to that other place. He ended the account with, "So, I was in Fairyland," and then waited for her laughter.

Instead, she appeared unduly serious. "The Celts called it Otherworld," she said, "or T'ir n'a n'Og, the Land of Always Summer. The place where the dead go."

"Well, I'm alive and kicking."

"The five who everyone says saved us in the war after the Fall," she said, impatient at his jokes, "they were supposed to have travelled to T'ir n'a n'Og."

"The five," he repeated. He'd heard all the stories about the heroes who had fought during the Fall and dismissed most of them as unbelievable, but now they took on a new significance. He wasn't in any mood to face up to what Rhiannon had told him about following in their footsteps, so he tried to make light of it instead. "We've come to a right state if I say, 'I was in Fairyland,' and you treat me like the sanest man on the planet."

"You were really there?" She looked at him in a different way that he found encouraging. "What was it like?"

"It was . . ." He pictured the Court of Peaceful Days and instantly felt a yearning that brought a swell of damp emotion. ". . . heavenly."

"I wish I'd seen it," she said dreamily.

"Maybe you will one day." He scanned the landscape carefully, trying to recall any landmarks from his vision that might reveal where Miller was. He hoped he would be in time. "So what are you doing out here?"

"We took a trip up to Stonehenge." She hugged her arms around her against the cold; she was poorly dressed for the time of year. Mallory took off his cloak and put it around her shoulders in a dismissive way so she didn't think he was doing anything so lame as being courteous. She attempted to fend it off at first, then relented, pulling it tight. She flashed a nervous glance back at the others, but none of them were paying any attention. "Thank you."

"Don't mention it. It's not really the time of year for trips, is it?"

"There's a problem with the ley. I can sense it . . . some of the others can, too, the ones who've worked on their abilities with the Craft. It's weakened, almost seems to be dying out, and it was so powerful before. Stonehenge is one of the main nodes of the Fiery Network. So is Avebury, and Saint Michael's Mount, but Stonehenge was close enough to investigate. We wanted to see if there was any sign of what was causing the problem."

"That's not very smart, indulging yourself like that. You know the risks on the Plain."

She bristled. "Indulgent? The earth is responsible for the well-being of the planet—and humanity, for that matter. We've taken it upon ourselves to be the guardians of the Fiery Network, as the Celts were, and the ancient people who were custodians of the land before them."

"The new Celtic Nation." His comment sounded more mocking than he had intended.

"Exactly," she said defiantly. "There's nothing wrong with continuing their traditions. They believed in the interconnectedness of everything, in being supportive of nature and the planet, which is perfectly sensible in my books."

"As well as slaughtering anyone who got in their way."

"That's right. So don't get on my tits." She swung the cloak around her with a flourish, and her delicate features disappeared into the depths of the cowl.

"A big, important mission in life. You couldn't just do stuff for food and beer like everyone else?"

"I'm not like you, Mallory."

"Yes, they broke the mold." He spotted a skeletal tree standing alone on a ridge that looked familiar. "Let's try over there," he said.

"What are you looking for?"

Mallory ignored her; it was the place, he was sure of it. He picked up his pace and called Miller's name, suddenly terrified he was too late. *Why does it matter?* he thought as he broke into a run. *The way things are, he's going to be dead soon enough anyway.* He didn't want to let it get to him—he didn't want anything to get to him. But it did. And he knew it in the speed that he was driving himself across the turf, the desperation that made the blood surge through his head, obscuring Sophie's yells.

He reached the tree and looked down the other side of the ridge. Miller lay in a crumpled heap where he had fallen, but his eyes were closed, not glassy. Mallory threw himself down the incline. Miller's eyelids flickered open at the vibrations in the ground.

"Mallory. I knew you'd come for me."

"Don't fool yourself, Miller. I was looking for a pub, and here you are littering the highways and byways."

Miller smiled, then coughed. Blood spattered across his chin. Mallory knelt down to examine Miller's wounds: his stomach was badly torn and he'd lost a great deal of blood, but hadn't had the benefit of the Court of Peaceful Days to put him right; and he still had both his hands. So it was Gardener, Daniels, or Hipgrave who lay dead somewhere in the vicinity of Bratton Camp.

Sophie let out a startled cry as she came over the ridge and saw Miller, but without a second thought she ran down and helped Mallory administer what treatment they could with the contents of his medicine pack.

"I didn't think I'd see you again," Miller muttered deliriously to Mallory. "I saw Daniels go down—it hit him in the face. I don't know what happened to Gardener, or Hipgrave." Tears came at the memory.

"Save your strength, Miller," Sophie said gently.

Miller tried to focus on her face. "Sophie? What are you doing here?" Then, "I knew you two would get together."

Mallory and Sophie didn't look at each other, but instead busied themselves stitching and daubing ointment. Miller couldn't feel their ministrations, and after a while drifted into a delirious semiconscious state.

Mallory pulled Sophie off to one side. "I don't think he's going to make it back."

"I might be able to help." She turned to the others. "We need vervain to quell the pain. And see if you can find any mallow, though we'll be lucky at this time of year." She reeled off another five or six plants unknown to Mallory, each containing some healing attribute. While the travellers headed off to find the items, Sophie said, "Give me some time on my own. I need to meditate."

Mallory watched her sitting alone on the top of the ridge, staring into the banks of grey clouds. She looked small in the wild landscape, and part of it, wrapped in the wind and the long grass, the oversized cloak giving her a fragility that only served to emphasise the simple beauty in her features. She remained there, unmoving, graceful, for fifteen minutes before slowly making her way back to him.

"This will work?" he said.

"If I focus correctly."

"You don't just say a spell?"

"Nothing would be that easy, would it?" The wind whipped a strand of hair across her face. "The words and the symbols of the ritual are a different kind of language that communicate with the subconscious where the ability lies."

He made to ask another question, but she put two fingers to his lips to silence him before moving on to Miller. Mallory took himself to the foot of the lonely tree where he could watch the proceedings. Her voice, chanting softly, escaped the whistle of the wind as she knelt over Miller's fragile form. After a while, she threw her head back and said something loudly; he didn't recognise or understand the word but it made his ears ring. He thought, though he couldn't be sure, that he heard an echo rolling across the bleak grasslands.

The ritual lasted fifteen minutes, and when she made her way back to him she looked exhausted. For a while, she sat next to him in silence, slowly drifting back from wherever she had been.

"Are you OK?" he asked.

"Sometimes it takes a lot out of you, depending on what you're trying to do."

No longer delirious, Miller appeared to be resting peacefully. "Did it do the trick?" Mallory said.

"It should be enough for you to get him back to the cathedral."

"Thanks." It was expressed with restraint, but the simple act of saying it warmed her to him.

"You're welcome."

The others drifted up and sat around quietly before Sophie arranged them into parties to search for wood to make a stretcher for Miller. It took them an hour to construct one, and by the time they set off they knew they wouldn't reach Salisbury before nightfall. Though none of them said anything, Mallory could see the fear buried in the travellers' faces.

They broke for dinner just as the sun was setting. They'd already agreed not to set up camp for the night. Mallory judged that they would be less of a target if they kept on the move, but either way he knew the odds of them making it home safely had shortened considerably.

The last of their provisions went quickly and when they picked up the march again, they were all still hungry. The sunset was a hallucinogenic mix of angry reds and florid purples, spectacular in its own way but oppressive. They watched the shadows race voraciously across the flat landscape with trepidation, wishing they had more weapons, torches, anything that could give them even the illusion of security.

Sophie stayed with Mallory at the head, undisputed leaders of the expedition. Though they couldn't be described as friendly, the travellers were less suspicious of Mallory because Sophie had accepted him. They trailed behind, taking it in turns to pull Miller's stretcher. Eventually night fell, but there was enough of a break in the clouds to allow moonlight to illuminate their way.

"I still can't believe how much the world's changed." Sophie snuggled deep in the cloak for warmth. "Yet there's been so much good with all the bad. Take the Craft—it was strong before, but nothing like now."

Mallory rarely took his eyes off the landscape as he continually tried to discern which shadows were benign and which posed a threat. He had already seen silhouettes circling them, low and bestial, but so far they had chosen to keep their distance.

"We've gone back to a time before science and reason and technology, when people relied on the power within them," Sophie continued. "What we have is so important, Mallory, yet we'd all lost sight of it. The Fall, for all the suffering, has let us forge a link with the people we used to be, and should be."

"Try telling that to someone whose family has just been wiped out by an illness that shouldn't exist in this day and age."

"I know, it's easy for me to say. But I'm just trying to see the big picture."

He laughed, then caught himself.

"What's so funny?"

"I wonder how my *friends* back at the cathedral would take my consorting with a witch."

She snorted derisively. "It's about time we got rid of all those stereotypes your lot foisted on us. We were the original religion—"

"You're not going to lay claim to that, are you? Murray and Gardener had an academic approach, but they made huge leaps of logic when they claimed there was a heritage for Wicca stretching back to prehistory."

"There might not be an unbroken line, although that's debatable. But there's still a basis of ancient traditions." She looked at him askance, a little surprised. "You're very well informed, Mallory. Did you have Burn the Witch classes at the cathedral?"

"I'm just well read, one of my very many strengths." Away to his right, something was keeping pace with them, staying low. He only caught sight of it when the ground rose slightly and it was briefly silhouetted against a moon-silvered cloud.

"One good thing about the Fall is that Wicca is in the ascendancy once again after centuries of repression."

"Don't get all whiny about it," he said. "You're in good company with all the beliefs Christianity has repressed over the last couple of millennia. Everything from tribal faiths in Africa to Taoism in the Far East."

"What's up with you, Mallory?" Incomprehension filled her voice. "You're not a Christian—you don't believe in anything, or so you said. So how can you do all this . . . fighting for something you don't believe in?"

"I told you—it's a job. It pays. It keeps me alive."

"You're a mercenary."

"Well, if you want to get into name-calling . . . witch."

She couldn't contain a smile at his ridiculous humour and had to look away. "Don't you take anything seriously?"

"Yes, sex and alcohol."

"I bet you're a bundle of laughs in bed."

"It's not supposed to be funny. With me it's a spiritual experience. You should try it sometime."

"I'd rather cut off an arm," she said, though he thought he saw the first glimmer that she might mean the opposite.

"Anyway, where's your broomstick?"

"I have one, but I don't use it how you think. And you'd better get any stereotypes out of your head quickly," she said. "No hooknosed crones carrying out nasty business over bubbling pots. We were the original wise women, offering advice and help to anyone in the tribes or villages. And we did good deeds, generally, because we all know that whatever we do is brought back to us threefold. It's all about balance, Mallory . . . a universal constant you can see just by opening your eyes and looking around. But not something your Christian colleagues would ever understand with their horsehair shirts and ascetic, sexually repressed lifestyles."

"Now who's dealing in stereotypes?"

Her rant was well rehearsed, and even though Mallory knew her arguments, he let her continue while he tried to keep track of whatever was stalking them.

"And we're not Satanists. Does *that* make me mad when I hear it. There is no Satan in the pagan religions—that's a Christian invention. No personification of pure evil. We look to nature for our guidance, where evil doesn't exist, just a dark side and a light side to everything. Our deity has two aspects: the horned male and the triple goddess of mother, maiden, and crone. Christianity demonised the male one, turned him into Satan with the horns and the tail and the cloven hooves, but he's really a god of nature, embodying aspects of the flora and fauna—"

"Sorry to interrupt your history lesson, Sophie, as interesting as it is, but we're about to be attacked." It seemed that his sword whispered as it slid out of the sheath; an aural trick, nothing else.

Before Sophie could say anything more, the shape loomed toward them. At first, it appeared to be on its knees, then loping like a wolf and finally upright. Mallory had the unnerving feeling it was floating an inch or so above the ground, its legs motionless.

One of the travellers had made the mistake of drifting off to one side. He was in his forties, but prematurely aged through drink and too many drugs, his hair thin on top but long and wiry down the back. He saw it first and let out a shriek that made Mallory's blood run cold. The traveller was rooted for a second, then half turned to run, but it was too late.

Coming up fast on him was a thing with the body of a man, but a head that was just a white skull with an angry red light seeping out of its hollow orbs. Its clothes were black, tattered in part as if it had been wrapped in a shroud, but gleaming black armour lay beneath.

The creature shimmered as it bore down on the traveller, appearing to change shape slightly so that its limbs elongated, the hands stretching into bony talons. It swung one and took the traveller's head off at the neck.

One of the girls fainted, hitting the turf as a dead weight. Mallory could feel the desperate eyes of the other travellers heavy on him.

The thing fell down on the corpse, tearing with its talons in a frenzy until the body fell apart. Then it ducked down into the soft tissue and began to feed so ravenously that the blood flew like rain.

Mallory's first reaction was to look after himself, but he couldn't do it. He gripped the sword with both hands and took a step forward.

At Mallory's movement, the creature raised its head, the bone now stained scarlet. Mallory wished it would let out some growl so he could characterise it as flesh and blood, but it was as silent as the grave. It launched itself toward him, eerily lighter than air as it tore across the distance between them.

The ghostliness wrong-footed him so that he wasn't ready for the force of impact. It felt as if someone had thrown a full oil drum at him. He went down underneath it as screams erupted all around.

It didn't use its talons immediately. Instead, those seething red eyes began to inspect him. Mallory had the feeling of being dissected, his hopes torn apart and thrown away, his fears peeled back. He could smell the traveller's fresh blood, but beneath it there was the odour of loam and rotting vegetation. It opened its mouth briefly, then closed it with a clack of bare teeth.

Mallory acted just as it launched its attack. When it shifted its weight to raise a bony hand he rolled to one side, brought up his knee, and levered it off him. The thing was already flinging itself back at him like a cornered wildcat. He tried to bring up the sword, but there wasn't room and he could only jam it crossways between them awkwardly. The creature's talons were just a flash. If Mallory hadn't snatched his head away instinctively it would now be bouncing alongside the traveller's.

He tried to fend it off with his left arm, but to his horror it brought its skull down sharply and closed those ferocious jaws on his forearm. He yelled with pain, but at the same time seized his opportunity to arc the sword around into the creature's ribs. It felt as if he'd swung it into the trunk of an oak tree.

But it did enough. The creature released its grip on his arm and recoiled, still silent even when Mallory yanked the sword out, bringing part of a bone with it. In that instant, Mallory knew no earthly sword would have had any effect; the dragon-sword sang in his hands, setting his nerve endings alight.

Now the thing hung back, floating eerily from side to side, its hideous red-stained skull cocked as it surveyed him in a new light. It only took a moment to size him up before it attacked again, unannounced and with rattlesnake speed. Mallory had the merest instant to respond; he shifted weight, parried, but it was like trying to fence with a cloud of claws and snapping jaws.

For fifteen minutes the battle raged back and forth. Occasionally, Mallory would sneak through the creature's defences to slice into his unbelievably dense body. More often it would catch him a glancing blow that would make his teeth ring, or raise droplets of blood with a rake of its talons. But with each wound, Mallory felt the dull rage within him grow colder and harder, focusing his mind, sharpening his reactions. He couldn't see Sophie or the travellers—even their cries were lost to him. Everything was centred on the grinning skull, the abomination that had no right to cause suffering when so much already existed.

He saw the opening, instantly dissected tactics and all possible responses, then acted with a swiftness that turned his sword arm to a blur. The dragon-sword drove into the creature's chest, and then Mallory gripped it with both hands and drove down with all his strength. It felt as if he was forcing the blade through stone.

As the thing began to split in two, Mallory snatched the sword free and slashed. The red skull flew free, rattled onto the ground, and bounced across the turf.

Mallory staggered back, catching his breath after the exertion, still shaking with the battle rage. Sophie stepped in to support him.

"Are you OK?" she said, with deep concern.

He steadied himself, then quickly herded her away from the carcass, still quivering with its death throes. "Let's get moving."

"You need to rest. We've got to treat your wounds." She gently dabbed at a deep cut on his forehead.

"Too risky. Anything else out here won't give us time to rest."

Reluctantly, she agreed. The travellers, who were now looking at Mallory with new eyes, grateful but awed, picked up Miller's stretcher and set off as fast as their weary legs would muster.

They hadn't gone far when the girl who had fainted cried out once more. Mallory followed the line of her pointing finger to the place of his battle. In a pool of moonlight, the creature was rising up from the ground, body rejoined, skull firmly reattached. It steadied itself for a second, then turned toward them.

"It's not going to let us go," the girl moaned.

Mallory cursed, feared he wouldn't have the strength and the luck to defeat it again, and wondered how many times he'd have to attempt it before the bony jaws were feeding on his own lights.

"Get moving," he said.

"What are you going to do?" Sophie said.

"Just get moving. I'll catch you up."

"You're stupid—"

Eyes blazing, he spun round, but his voice was low and moderated. "You've got a responsibility to these people who trust you. And you need to get Miller back. This is my job, for better or worse. You do yours."

She marshalled the others without further discussion. They headed off, but her voice floated back to him. "Catch us up, Mallory. We need you."

Then it was just him and the thing sweeping over the grass, black shroud flapping in the wind, jaw open in a silent scream.

He fought for a half hour this time, eventually stabbing the sword through its right eye socket before shattering its skull. He spent the next ten minutes chopping the body into chunks no bigger than a bag of sugar before lurching away, exhausted.

He caught up with the others, and this time they had fifteen minutes' grace before the thing came at them again.

Three more times he battled it. Each fight lasted longer, each time he grew weaker, picked up more wounds, undoing all the good works of the Court of Peaceful Days. After the last one he was convinced he wouldn't be able to do it again.

Sophie remained silent, but her eyes never left him. She understood his suffering and knew there was no point in discussing it, but in her silence there was a support that gave him an added reserve of strength.

The fluttering silhouette was against the now clear sky of the horizon when they came over a rise to find serendipity. Scattered across the downward slope were the picked-clean bones of soldiers, their shredded uniforms blowing in the breeze. A tank stood silently, a hole rupturing its side; Mallory had no idea what could have committed such a devastating attack. And beyond it was a covered truck, the driver's door sagging open where the occupant had been torn out.

Sophie saw it too, their hopes too fragile to voice. They ran down the slope toward it with the last of their energy. Mallory scrambled in and ducked under the steering column just as the creature whisked over the rise. He ripped out the ignition wires with ease—he'd done it enough times before—and sparked them. The lorry coughed, then fired.

The travellers had already piled into the back alongside Miller. Sophie took the seat next to Mallory.

"Everybody in?" He flicked the windshield wipers to clear several months' worth of dust.

"Put your foot down, OK?" Sophie hadn't shown a glimmer of fear throughout their ordeal, but Mallory could sense it just beneath the surface.

"Can't you do a spell or something?" he said, thumping the gear stick into first and lurching off.

"I told you, it doesn't work like that . . . not in the heat of things. I'll try to do something as we go." She closed her eyes, whispering a mantra as she meditated.

In the side mirror, Mallory saw the thing bearing down on them. Now the crimson skull appeared to be the only thing of substance, its body a ragged black sheet billowing in the wind as it rushed on with alarming speed. It wasn't far behind the truck now. Something about it made him feel sick: its relentlessness, the sheer inhumanity of its attacks, the way he couldn't be sure of its shape.

What is *it?* he said to himself, desperately urging the truck to go faster. He kept his foot to the floor as he rammed through the gears, but the vehicle felt as if it was running through mud. It slowly began to build speed, churning up the turf as it juddered and skidded.

In the mirror, the skull loomed up just to the left side of the rear lights. Mallory could hear the screams from the back and a crashing noise as someone lashed out with an object they'd obviously found in the back.

Just as the truck began to hit thirty miles per hour, there was a sickening scream followed by a tumult from the rear. Mallory could see the reflection of the thing hunched over a flailing shape pinned to the ground, ready to feed. It was the girl who had fainted.

"What's happening?" Sophie said anxiously.

Mallory set his jaw. "We've got away from it."

The rest of the journey passed in near silence as Sophie and the travellers mourned their two friends and Mallory turned over the events of the night, sickened that he hadn't been able to prevent the deaths. In one brief period of conversation, Sophie had thanked him "for being a good man," for his bravery and compassion, and he felt like such a fraud he couldn't look her in the face. She thought he was just exhibiting humility; another trait he didn't have.

They reached Salisbury at four a.m. The city was deserted, the houses and shops dark, not even a candle flame burning. Mallory expected someone to poke their head out at the long-lost sound of a combustion engine, but no one came to see.

Sophie pointed out the most unusual sight. There were barricades along some of the streets, and several doors and windows had been fitted with security covers. "It looks as if everyone's boarding themselves in," she said.

Apprehension tugged at Mallory's mind. What had been happening while they had been gone?

He pulled over on Castle Street so that the travellers could make their way to their camp without the guards on the cathedral walls seeing to whom he'd been giving a lift; no point making unnecessary trouble for himself. The remaining travellers came by one by one to thank him. He felt uncomfortable at the undiluted strength of their gratitude, yet touched, too, as he watched them troop sadly off in the direction of the tent city.

Sophie hung around until they were out of sight, then said, "You look a picture."

He leaned out to look in the side mirror. He was covered in blood and mud, his hair matted, a growth of beard shadowing his face. "At least all the relevant bits are there."

"I'm grateful for what you did for us, Mallory," she said. "You didn't have to help us . . . you could have abandoned us at any time. If all the knights are like you, I might have to reassess my judgement."

She looked even more attractive in the cold moonlight. He seriously thought about asking her to go with him, just drive off, but he knew she would never abandon her responsibilities.

"And I'll stand by you, if you ever need me," she continued. "I won't forget what you did."

She smiled properly for the first time on the journey. It was only a brief flash, but it was so honest it brought a shiver to his spine. "Don't I get a kiss?" he said, only half joking.

"Don't push it, Mallory. This isn't the Middle Ages where the shy, retiring damsel has to reward her knight." She slipped out, but before she closed the door she poked her head back in. "You know where I am." It wasn't much, but there was a substance to it that excited him.

He waited as she hurried down the street, hoping she'd turn back but sure she wouldn't; she knew he was watching her and she wouldn't give him that advantage. When she'd finally disappeared, he took a deep breath and moved the truck slowly in the direction of the cathedral.

But as he turned onto High Street and the final stretch to the compound gates, the shock of what he saw made him slam on the brakes.

Instead of the lone spire rising majestically from the cathedral's bulk, an enormous building of black stone now covered most of the area within the compound. The cathedral was still there at the core, but it had been expanded into a massive gothic construction that mirrored the original in the fundamentals, but had been elaborated into a feverish vision of gargoyles, towers, cupolas, stained-glass windows—some of them forty feet tall—statues, carvings, and insanely pitched roofs branching out all over the place. It would have taken decades to build with hundreds, if not thousands, of skilled craftsmen. The dislocation made him queasy; Mallory felt as if he had been transported back to the Otherworld, but everything else in the surroundings was as it always had been.

He let his eyes drift over what appeared to be a mad architect's dream. If the first cathedral had been an elegant vision of God's Glory, this was something much, much darker.

chapter seven
ALPHA AND OMEGA

"Appearances are a glimpse of what is hidden."

Anaxagoras

Mallory allowed the truck to trundle slowly up to the gates. Disbelief kept his gaze firmly fixed on the unbelievable, monumental construction; nothing, however bizarre, could begin to explain what he was seeing. When he did finally break his gaze, he saw guards ranged all along the walls, crossbows trained on him from several quarters. Everything had changed.

Cautiously, he turned off the engine and wound down the window. "It's me, Mallory. A knight," he yelled. "I've got another badly wounded knight in the back."

There was a long period of silence before a voice barked, "Get out!"

Slowly, he clambered onto the flagstones, hands raised.

"Move closer to the gates."

Two enormous torches blazing on either side of the entrance cast a shimmering pool of light in front of the gates. Mallory entered it tentatively, hoping the mud and blood didn't obscure too much of his uniform. For five minutes, he listened to dim chatter above as the guards debated whether to allow him entrance.

"Look, you can see I'm a knight," he protested. He spotted a guard he recognised. "You know me."

"Not good enough," the commander of the watch replied.

"What do you mean, 'Not good enough'?" His temper flared. "If you don't let me get my friend inside he might die, and then I'll make you bastards sorry."

His anger did little good. He was forced to remain there for another ten minutes until finally the gates opened a crack. "Approach carefully," a voice warned.

Mallory walked forward until he could see between the gates. The entire Blue squad waited on the other side, armed with swords and crossbows, a Second World War–era rifle and shotguns. "What is wrong with you?" he shouted.

The gates were flung open and the Blues surged out and around him. Some ran to the back of the truck. "He's telling the truth," one of them shouted back. "There's an injured knight here." They picked up Miller's stretcher and rushed it into the compound. Mallory was roughly manhandled inside, too, his protestations ignored. The gates slammed shut immediately behind him, heavy bars drawn across solemnly to seal it.

Mallory looked at these new defences, then at the faces of the Blues. What he saw there made him wary. "What's been going on here?" he asked.

No one would talk to him, and after a while he gave up asking questions and concentrated on the worries rattling through his mind.

From the gate he was led across a cobbled courtyard through a sturdy oak door with cast-iron fittings into a long stone corridor that hadn't been there days earlier. He had to tell himself again that he wasn't back in the Court of Peaceful Days, for there was something about the architecture that reminded him of that place, although the mood was significantly different.

Under heavily armed guard, they rushed him across tapestry-hung halls and up winding staircases to a debriefing room where he was thrust into a chair with two crossbows trained on him, as if he were not a knight at all, but a spy ready to betray the entire religion. After half an hour Blaine entered, looking tired and irritable. Behind him marched Stefan, proud and resolute. Mallory had had his doubts about the chancellor ever since he had heard the grim relish in Stefan's voice when he told James that the library was off-limits; his appearance there only confirmed Mallory's suspicions.

"What's happened to this place?" Mallory blurted.

Stefan eyed him suspiciously before retreating to a corner to watch like a raptor, his hands clasped behind his back.

"All the new buildings," Mallory continued. "Where did they come from? You couldn't have built them—"

"Where have you been?" The harsh tones of Blaine's Belfast accent were even more pronounced. His very demeanour threatened violence. "And where did you get that sword?"

"I found it," Mallory said, making light of the weapon. "We can never have too many swords, right?"

Mallory explained what had happened at Bratton Camp, but said nothing of the Court of Peaceful Days. "I was badly injured, on my last legs," he continued. "I was wandering for days before I summoned the strength to make it back here."

Blaine's eyes narrowed. "I'm surprised you did come back here."

"Despite what you might think, Blaine, this is the place for me," Mallory lied. The tension was palpable and he wasn't going to take any risks speaking his mind. "Did the others make it back?" he asked.

"You're the fourth, counting Miller."

"Who's missing?"

"Hipgrave." Blaine peered down into Mallory's face. "Any idea what happened to him?"

Mallory thought of the severed hand. "That thing must have got him—"

"Or you could have killed him in the confusion."

"I'm not going to kill one of our own!" Mallory protested.

Stefan's light cough was a signal for Blaine to step back. "Events have overtaken us while you were away," Stefan said, with a smile so insincere that Mallory couldn't believe he was even attempting it. "There are forces in this world . . . forces of the Adversary . . . ranged against a resurgent Church. He knows we are once again on the path to be the Guiding Light of the world, and he is prepared to do anything to destroy us." He made a strange hand gesture as he attempted to choose the right words. "Security is paramount. We cannot afford for our defences to be breached. We have to be sure you are still guided by the Glory of God."

"I'm telling the truth." Mallory looked from Stefan to Blaine and back, now even more unsettled.

"We've got people who can tell if you're who you say you are," Blaine said coldly.

"Who I say I am?" he echoed incredulously.

"To ensure you have not been corrupted by your encounter with the dark forces," Stefan corrected.

Mallory didn't understand their meaning, but the way they were saying it brought a trickle of cold sweat down his back.

"We held a grand synod," Stefan continued, "and took the advice of some of our Catholic brothers in establishing a new and very limited order of Inquisitors of Heretical Depravity. It has served Rome well for many centuries."

"The Inquisition?" Mallory said in disbelief.

"Oh, don't be put off by Godless propaganda or stories of medieval excess," Stefan replied. "The name 'Inquisition' merely comes from the Latin verb *inquiro*—to inquire into. There is nothing menacing about that at all. It is simply a way of gaining information through intensive questioning. By testing the defendant, if you will, through a trial of inquiry."

Stefan attempted to sound dismissive, but Mallory could tell what kind of Inquisition the chancellor had in mind, and it wasn't the essentially benign one that the Catholic Church had maintained throughout the twentieth century. Stefan's medieval turn of mind was plain for all to see. "Cornelius agreed to it?"

Stefan bowed his head. "The bishop is not well. The Lord watches over him, but his strength is fading fast. He is in no position to be concerned with the minutiae of the Church's day-to-day running. Our spiritual needs are all that matter to him."

"Have Daniels and Gardener been put through this?" The brief silence gave him his answer.

"This is the proper course of action. We need to be sure there aren't fifth columnists working against us within the brethren." Blaine sounded as if he was trying to convince himself. "This Church is the only good thing going in this world. There are a lot of people depending on us. We have to do what we can . . ." He realised his rambling was giving away his true thoughts and so he repeated, but with different meaning, "We have to do what we can." Mallory could see he was speaking from the heart: he believed completely in what he was doing—a soldier chosen to defend the Faith with any means necessary, however unpleasant.

"What is it?" Mallory still didn't accept the implication of what they were saying. "The rack?"

Stefan looked horrified, although there was no heart in the reaction. "Good Lord, what do you take us for? We have chosen men of integrity for this vital role, devout men who will ask the correct questions, that is all."

Mallory looked at Blaine; Blaine looked away.

Stefan turned to go, obviously eager not to be tainted by the unpleasantness that lay ahead. At the door he said, "Blaine was right, Mallory—this is a good thing. Everything we do is for the survival of the Church and the greater Glory of God. Answer with your heart and all will be well." He swept away.

Blaine paused at the door. "This isn't personal, Mallory. I think you're an untrustworthy bastard who needs to be kept in line, but I can do that myself. This is about something bigger . . . keeping the Church safe. I have a responsibility here and I'm going to see it through."

"That's all right, then," Mallory said acidly.

A flicker of the old hardness shone in Blaine's eyes. "You're too smart, Mallory. We don't need your type here. We need people who obey, who take orders. That's what the whole fucking religion's about." The flare of anger had already lost its edge when he was only halfway out. "Just tell the truth, Mallory. Don't make any rods for your own back."

Ten minutes later, three men walked in. They had the smart haircuts and mundanely handsome faces of catalogue models, so bland there was something resolutely sinister about them. Mallory could see instantly why they had been chosen: their floating irises and dead eyes gave away their penchant for dirty jobs.

The leader, the inquisitor-general as he introduced himself, was called Broderick. He was wiry with red hair and a pasty, papery complexion. His smile was so fake Mallory wanted to wipe it off with one blow.

He took Blaine's advice and answered truthfully, but they still punctuated their questions with hard knuckles just to let him know they could. At first they asked him about the mission and any encounters he might have had with "the forces of darkness." Eventually, though, they merely asked him to repeat the Lord's Prayer. Mallory got it right after a few promptings. He lost consciousness after fifty minutes.

He was woken with a bucket of icy water that washed some of the blood away. Blaine leaned against a wall, watching him cursorily.

"Did I pass?" The words came out strangely through Mallory's split lips.

"We had to be sure." Blaine motioned to the inquisitors to help Mallory to his feet. "They used to work for the security services in Belfast. Quite a coup, them turning up here."

"Yes, aren't we lucky?" Mallory shook off the helping hands and walked under his own strength. The pain in his ribs made it hard to breathe and his head rang with numerous aches; he had already been at a low ebb after his battles on Salisbury Plain. "This is the second time you've put me through the wringer. I'm starting to think you enjoy it."

Blaine didn't bite. "I would have thought by this time you'd have learned a little humility, Mallory. Now, you get yourself to the infirmary. I want you back on duty as soon as possible. We need every available hand for defence." Briefly, his shoulders sagged with the weight of responsibility. "You don't know how lucky you were getting inside here in one piece last night."

The dislocation Mallory had felt on his arrival returned with force. "What's been going on? Where did all the new buildings come from?"

Blaine was honestly puzzled. "What new buildings?"

"What new buildings! I'm talking about the four million tons of stone thrown up almost overnight. The new buildings!"

Blaine shook his head contemptuously. "You've had a long night, Mallory— you should have a lie down."

"Something's been going on here. The security's been stepped up—"

"You'll find out in due course. At least I don't have to worry about you trying to abscond anymore. You're stuck in here for the duration like the rest of us."

Mallory was disturbed by Blaine's reaction to his questions about the mysterious construction that now swathed the original cathedral building. Nothing made sense. The aches and pains reverberating through his body only contributed to the numbing effect of the transformed cathedral so that he felt as though he was floating through a dream. It took him nearly two hours to find the infirmary. A maze of corridors and rooms now linked the cathedral and Malmesbury House, some of them grand vaulted chambers with mighty columns, pristine as if newly built, others so decrepit they appeared on the verge of falling down. Early morning sunlight streamed through holes in the roof and ivy wound around pillars, while rats scurried amongst the shattered stone debris that littered the floor in some quarters. He found enormous deserted chapels, the stained-glass windows casting red, blue, yellow, and green swirls over the altars. He stumbled across the entrance to a subterranean ossuary so packed with bones that they spilled out into the corridor. There were crypts so vast their ends were lost in shadows and halls packed with graven images of men in monk's habits and bishop's mitres, knights and lords, none of whom he recognised. Even more confusing, when he back-tracked, the layout of the building appeared to be continually changing: corridors suddenly came to dead ends; rooms he had never seen before appeared around bends. And over it all lay a dense atmosphere—of reverence in the areas closer to the light, of unbearably claustrophobic repression in the dark.

Occasionally, he met a brother moving about his business and it soon became apparent that, like Blaine, none of them thought anything had changed. Only a supernatural force could have transformed the cathedral in such a manner, though how, and to what end, escaped him. Nor did he understand why he was the only one with clear vision. It made him feel even more apart than he had before, strung out and anxious with nothing to tether him to reality.

Finally, when he had just about consigned himself to being lost in the maze forever, he found himself inside Malmesbury House, an oasis of calm with its sophisticated décor. He couldn't shake the unnerving feeling that there was an intelligence to the newly appeared building that had presented the correct route to him only when it was ready.

When he entered the infirmary, Warwick was mixing a foul-smelling potion. After he had decanted the brew into a crystal bottle, he eyed Mallory suspiciously.

"Fell down the stairs again, I see," he said judgementally. "I told you I was not—"

"I had a meeting with the Inquisition."

Warwick's mood became contrite. He motioned for Mallory to lie on the table and began applying some stinging tincture to the cuts and abrasions.

"What's happened here?" Mallory said, wincing. He gave it one last try. "Who magicked up the new building?"

"Don't know what you're talking about," Warwick said brusquely. He tenderly checked Mallory's ribs. "No breaks again. Well done," he added acidly. "God looks after fools."

"The extension to the cathedral?" Mallory pressed futilely. "All the new rooms?"

"Did you get hit on the head?"

"For God's sake, it covers nearly the whole compound now."

Warwick helped lever him off the table. "You'd better go and have a lie down, old chap. I'll mix you up a sedative."

Warwick propelled Mallory toward a room at the back. It had a very high ceiling that gave it a restless air, a mood exacerbated by the lack of windows; torches burned in plates atop tall struts amongst the beds that lined both walls. It was too hot despite the time of year, and had the unpleasant aroma of the sick. Many of the men tossed and turned feverishly, though some lay still, as if dead.

"Mallory!"

He recognised Daniels's voice immediately. He was propped up in a bed at the far end, waving. As Mallory approached, he could see stained bandages covering the upper-left quarter of Daniels's head.

Mallory sat on the end of the bed, aching too much to stand any longer. "What happened to you?"

"Lost an eye." Daniels's hand half went to the bandages, then stopped. "It caught me a glancing blow, but it felt as if someone had rammed a carving knife into the socket." His good eye closed for a second.

"I'm sorry."

"We count our blessings, right? I was lucky to get out of there with my life. We all were. Gardener got me back. He's a good man." He leaned forward to slap Mallory on the arm with comradely good nature. Mallory winced. "But what about you!" Daniels said. "I was convinced you'd shuffled off this mortal coil in your usual iconoclastic, curmudgeonly manner. Should have known you've got too much piss and vinegar in you to give up the ghost, Mallory!"

"I had a good go, believe me. I got Miller back, too, you know?"

"Really? Thank the Lord. How is he?"

"He was in a bad way. I thought he'd be in here."

"This is the walking wounded. The slackers. They've got another ward for the serious. What about Hipgrave?"

"Dead, I think. At least, he's not back yet. I found a severed hand. Gardener's in one piece?" Daniels nodded. "Then it must have been Hipgrave's. I don't think he could have lost a hand out there and not bled to death."

"Shame. He was a detestable little shit who couldn't lead a drunk to the bar, but, you know . . ."

Mallory nodded, although he had to admit to himself that he didn't feel even that little bit of charity. They sat in silence for a moment, repressed memories of that night suddenly rushing back. Bizarrely, Mallory remembered the smell the most, like a wet dog, though sourer, with a rubbery under-odour.

"What was that thing?" he asked from his daze.

There was more silence, and when he looked up, Daniels had tears in his eye. "Sometimes I think we've got no right to be here, do you know what I mean?"

"I met someone on the way back," Mallory began tentatively, not sure how much he should give away. "They told me something had noticed us."

"What do you mean?"

"Some force . . . I don't know, exactly. I got the sense it was incredibly powerful . . . ancient. Evil." He stared at the hissing torch as he recalled Rhiannon's world. "That thing we met on Bratton Camp was linked to it in some way."

"The Adversary," Daniels said.

"I don't think so. The way she spoke, this was something else . . . something even worse, if that's possible. It sounded as if she was saying it was on the other side of the universe . . . *it crawled up from the edge of Existence* . . . but it's moving this way."

"It's nothing to do with the Adversary?" There was a dim note of despair in Daniels's voice.

"I don't know."

"Who told you all this?" Daniels asked.

Before Mallory could answer, they were both hailed in a gruff Geordie accent. Gardener strode toward them, beaming in a manner Mallory had never seen before. "Bloody hell, lad, I thought you were—"

"Yeah, yeah, we've just been through all that."

Gardener cuffed him genially on the shoulder and Mallory winced again.

"You landed a few bruises then," Daniels said, with what Mallory thought was unnecessary brightness.

"They're from our friends here. The Inquisition. I gather you haven't had the pleasure yet."

Daniels looked uncomfortable. "Sorry, Mallory. I heard about them, but they left us alone. I think they were too surprised we actually made it back . . . plus my injury . . ."

Mallory laughed. "You don't have to make excuses, Daniels. I know they don't like the cut of my jib. If there's some shit going around, I'm the one who's always going to get the first helping."

"Well, as long as you know it, laddie," Gardener joked.

Mallory's voice dropped to a conspiratorial whisper. "What I don't get is what the hell's happened and why nobody will talk to me about it." He eyed them hopefully, urging them to understand his meaning.

Daniels and Gardener both looked across the beds uneasily to make sure no one was listening. "We had the same thing when we got here," Daniels whispered. "They don't know, Mallory. They think everything's normal."

"They've been affected by whatever caused it," Gardener said. "They all think the place has always been like this. I tell you, I tried to explore the madhouse a few times, but it seems as though it's bigger than . . ." He picked his teeth rather than finish the sentence, so Mallory said it for him.

"Bigger than the land it's on."

Gardener nodded, but didn't meet Mallory's eye.

"And the layout keeps changing all the time," Mallory continued.

Once again Daniels looked unaccountably gloomy. "I like things to make sense—"

"Then why are you neck-deep in religion?" Mallory said bad-temperedly.

"—and there's no sense to this at all. There's no sense to anything in this world anymore. No rules. That's the one rule—there are no rules. And I hate it! How are you supposed to understand things if it can all change while you're sleeping?"

"It's either the Devil's work, or it's God's," Gardener said bluntly. "It's up to us to find out which. Personally, I'd plump for the latter. This is hallowed ground. The Devil can't have any influence here."

"Do you think you can come up with a more simple explanation?" Mallory said tartly.

Daniels lay wearily back on his pillow and closed his good eye. "Look, we've all got different beliefs here—there's no point arguing amongst ourselves. If we're the only ones who can see the truth, we've got to stick together until we find out what it means." He gave a low laugh. "And it's not as if you can run away, Mallory."

"Blaine said something along those lines. What's going on?"

"We're under siege," Gardener said.

"The kind of things we saw out on the Plain have moved into the city," Daniels added. "Every night they're roaming around the walls, sometimes during the day as well. Anybody who goes out doesn't come back."

"Blaine said I was lucky to get back here."

"He's right there, man," Gardener noted. "I just watched them send out three Blues. They didn't make it to the end of the street. There was something out there like dirty washing lying in the road. It came up, flapping around, like, and they all fell apart. Just like that. All fell apart. I tell you, it made me sick to see it."

"But they say the things don't touch any of the city people at all during the day. Most of the time, folk can just go about their business . . . though they're giving the cathedral compound a wide berth," Daniels said. "At night, it's a different matter, though. Anything's fair game then."

"Something's going on," Mallory said. "I don't believe that cleric we were following across the Plain was real at all. When I saw his face, it looked as if it was . . . made up or something. I reckon it was a setup from the start, to lead us to Bratton Camp."

"Why?" Daniels said. "So we'd get attacked by that thing?"

"I don't know. I've just got a gut feeling we've only seen the tip of the iceberg."

Before leaving the infirmary, Gardener and Mallory visited Miller. The younger knight was sleeping peacefully. Warwick had patched him up, but he'd lost a lot of blood and he'd need several days' recuperation.

"You did a good job bringing him in," Gardener said. "Couldn't have been easy, the state he was in."

"I need somebody to be my conscience," Mallory replied. "Was it hard getting Daniels back?"

"He was in a bit of a bad way . . . you know." He pointed to his temple. "Losing the eye hit him hard. It'd get any of us, wouldn't it? But he's a good bloke, Daniels, for a poof. He's got a good heart. He'd stand by you when times were hard, and that's all you really need in a mate, isn't it?"

Mallory couldn't disagree. But as he made his way back to his crib, his relief at the four of them surviving was already obscured by his growing worry that unseen events were taking place behind the scenes, with repercussions for all of them.

Blaine left Mallory alone for the remainder of the day. It gave him time to gain some respite from the dull ache throbbing through his body. He ate a bland lunch of vegetable stew in the refectory and noticed that the portions were all markedly smaller. If they were truly under siege, supplies would have to be conserved. He made no attempt to go to any of the services, relishing his disobedience like a boy skipping school; it was a small victory against the oppressive order, but it made him feel good nonetheless. Instead, he chose to dwell on his growing anger, not only with Blaine, but also with the higher Church authorities that had conspired in making what had been a simple exchange—work for food and board—into a thoroughly unpleasant experience. With enthusiasm, he began to plot ways in which he could get his own back.

He took supper with Gardener and was surprised to find two weeks had passed since they had set off on their mission, although he had only seemed to spend a few brief hours in the Court of Peaceful Days. It made him feel disoriented.

One other thing troubled him: the cleric who had wandered into the cathedral that night, setting them on their search for his missing colleague, was now missing himself. Since their last conversation, Gardener had found out that the cleric had spent the night in the infirmary, but in the morning his bed was empty. Common opinion suggested that he had wandered off in a daze, possibly to search for his friend, but the guards at the gate claimed that no one had exited the compound all night. Blaine had punished them anyway. It only confirmed Mallory's fears that they had been set up from the start, but why would such an elaborate plan have been put in motion just to entice a few knights into the danger zone?

After supper, Gardener invited Mallory to stand watch over the gates so he could see for himself what was happening. The mid-October night held a brittle cold and was suffused with the smell of woodsmoke from home fires. On the walkway running around the inside of the wall, Mallory felt a strange frisson looking out onto a city without a single electric light burning. Only a few flickering candles glowed like fireflies in the night. Yet the ghostly light cast by the full moon when it broke from the cloud cover was brighter and more affecting than any street lamp.

Duncan, the captain of the guards, was a middle-aged bearded man with a thick Birmingham accent. He met them deferentially as they walked to a position near the gates. His attitude reminded Mallory of the respect with which the knights were treated throughout the cathedral, but particularly amongst the guards who knew exactly what they had to endure under Blaine's leadership.

"I could swear it's colder in winter since the Fall. Do you remember the snow last Christmas?" Gardener said as they leaned on the top of the wall, looking out across the city. Their breath clouded, and they had their cloaks pulled around them for warmth.

"That's all we need—a new ice age," Mallory replied.

"What time does it start?" Gardener asked Duncan.

"They're already out there." Duncan indicated several points along the street, in doorways and deep shadows, but Mallory could see nothing. "They're like sentries—there all day and night."

Mallory couldn't understand how he had got past them; had they *let* him into the cathedral, and if so, why? Gardener sensed what he was thinking. "Daniels and me came in too," he said. "Don't ask me what's going on. Anybody else that tries to get in or out gets both barrels."

"The other things come at various points during the dark hours," Duncan continued. "They try to break down the walls . . . cause a bit of damage, but never manage anything too serious."

"That doesn't make any sense," Mallory said. "The things we saw out on Salisbury Plain would be in here in no time."

"They are kept out by the power of the Lord." Julian, the bishop's right-hand man, had come up behind them. He'd tied his long black hair into a ponytail, but that only served to emphasise the worry and exhaustion in his features. "Or the power of faith, or whatever you want to call it."

"Magic?" Mallory suggested mischievously.

Julian didn't appear offended. "Just words," he said dismissively. "Different ways of describing the same thing. Whatever you choose, in this new age the power of prayer and ritual has a dramatic and instant effect. Sacred land becomes empowered. Those things can't set foot within the cathedral compound."

Mallory thought for a second. "But why are they *trying* to get into the cathedral?"

"Why, they're opposed to everything we do," Julian replied, as if the answer were obvious.

"That seems to be the common view." Mallory made no attempt to hide his plain disregard for this approach.

Julian appeared momentarily troubled, as if Mallory had given voice to his own doubts, but the precentor brightened when he saw James clambering up the ladder to join them. Mallory had not seen the pleasant-natured brother since James's secretive meeting with Julian in the refectory.

"How goes it?" James said cheerily. He was red-cheeked and clapping his arms against his sides theatrically.

"Should bloody sell tickets up here," Gardener muttered.

"I come up here every night," James said, "in the hope that they will finally relent. Their patience must wear thin eventually."

Mallory disagreed. "Believe me, they're like a dog with a bone. They're not going to leave until we find some way to break them. I presume we haven't got a way?"

"Your commander has outlined several strategies," Julian began, before dispensing with the PR. "Nothing that yet looks like a workable solution. But we'll find it, in time."

"I love an optimist," Mallory said.

"I hear you've been consigned to the library?" Julian commented to James.

"Ah, yes. You can never have enough guards for dead trees." James attempted to mask his sarcasm with a smile, but failed miserably. He caught Julian's arm and said supportively and with honest compassion, "How is the bishop?"

"Forgive me for speaking disrespectfully, but Cornelius is a determined old bugger. He's not going to shuffle off easily." Julian's face suggested that the situation was graver than he suggested. "The vultures are still circling, however."

James's eyes flickered toward Mallory. Obviously this was not a subject to be discussed in front of others. "If we stand firm, we will abide," he said confidently.

"Over there." Gardener pointed down High Street to where shadows were congealing into small shapes, forming lines, ranks. Mallory squinted, not quite sure what he was seeing.

At first, it could easily have been a trick of the dark and the moonlight, but gradually order appeared out of the chaos of the night. The street was filled from wall to wall with tiny figures, though still too lost to the dark for any details to be visible. They remained there, stock still, for long moments until Mallory was convinced that was the end of the manifestation. But then, with no fanfare, they began to move forward in uniform step, an army in miniature.

Their procession was slow but deliberate. It took five minutes before they reached the crepuscular zone of the light cast by the torches blazing along the wall. As they emerged from the gloom, James gripped the wall with both hands and whispered, "Good Lord!"

The figures were no bigger than children of five or six, but were obviously fully formed adults. As the light first hit them they appeared burnished gold, but gradually their skin settled on a ghastly white. From their spectral faces huge eyes stared, wholly black and too large, so that they resembled alien insects; they looked like things that had lived below the earth for centuries, only just emerging from the dark. Their outfits were elaborate, part armour, part costumes: breastplates and metal helmets echoing conquistador design, the colour of dull brass; scarlet silk shirts beneath, and red cloaks, epaulettes, clasps, gauntlets, belts; the detail was hallucinogenic. One of them held a standard that reminded Mallory of a Roman legion's. On it was some form of alien writing and an image that appeared to form a circle, although it was difficult to discern detail at that distance.

Women stood amongst the ranks, too, their expressions as venomous as the males', and children, too. They all carried strange weapons—short swords, spears tipped with unpleasant-looking hooks, nasty daggers, and brutal axes. Some pulled carts, while a few rode on miniature horses. It could have been a picture from some child's fairy-tale book if not for the menacing atmosphere that hung over the whole scene, made infinitely more eerie by the silence of their progress. Mallory didn't hear so much as a footfall or a rustle of fabric.

Within twenty feet of the walls, they rushed forward, suddenly ferocious, snapping and snarling like wild dogs. Mallory gripped on to the side as the wall and walkway shook. For an instant he thought it was going to go down.

"The hoards of bloody hell!" Gardener said in a strained voice.

After the silence, the clattering of the weapons was deafening. Sparks flew where the swords and spears smashed against the wall's iron plates, now scarred from myriad attacks. The knights and clerics watched with thundering hearts for ten minutes and then the army mysteriously and quickly retreated as if some silent fanfare had been blown, melting back into the shadows as though they had never been there.

"Why do they keep doing that when they know they can't get in!" The anxiety broke Duncan's voice.

Mallory realised he was clutching the rim of the wall so hard his knuckles ached. It was plain there was no escape for any of them; he looked around and saw it in all their faces, though no one would have dared give voice to it.

"Is it always like this?" he asked.

"Nah. Different things on different nights." Duncan had managed to contain himself and now appeared embarrassed at his emotional outburst. "In the early days, we had a bunch of bloody loonies on horseback." His face blanched at the memory. "Though you'd never seen horses like these, with a pack of dogs running around their feet. They were mean bastards, I tell you." He caught himself. "Excuse my language, sirs, but they were. They'd come at the gates like all hell, and for a time there I thought they might actually break them down. They left after a while . . . probably realised they didn't stand a chance. Since then it's been one thing after another. I tell you, some of them I can't bear to look at. It's enough to give you nightmares." He clutched at a gold crucifix at his throat.

"What are we going to do?" Mallory mused to himself.

"We pray for God's guidance, as we always have," Julian said. "Life is filled with trials, but with the right approach, we overcome them."

Mallory studied Julian surreptitiously. Everything about the cleric gave the impression of a modern man—urbane, intelligent, insightful—so it was odd to hear him using a religious language that was almost medieval.

"Will we have enough food to see us through the winter?" he asked.

Julian chewed the inside of his lower lip in contemplation. "Procedures were put in place the moment we realised we might be in this for the long haul," he began. His words were so transparent there was no point in Mallory even stating the obvious.

As they stood there, Mallory felt a strange tingling along his spine that forced him to turn. It was instinct, a feeling of being watched, as inexplicable as anything else they had witnessed that night. The areas around the cathedral buildings were a place of whispers, which even the torches placed along the pathways failed to illuminate. It was impossible to determine any sign of life there, but he was convinced someone stood in the gloom, looking up at him. His heart began to beat faster as an uncontrollable rush of anxiety defeated any attempt to dismiss it as a primitive, irrational reaction to the fears of that night.

Just when the sensation became almost unbearable, it faded. A moment later, he saw a figure move across one of the illuminated pathways, but it appeared insubstantial, wavering as if seen through a heat haze. Even at that distance, and with the features hidden by a cowl, he recognised it immediately as the brother who had turned and looked at him during compline shortly after his arrival at the cathedral. As then, he was deeply unnerved for no reason he could explain.

Duncan interrupted his thoughts with a barked warning. A man, weak and staggering, was just passing through the shadows surrounding St. Thomas's Church on the other side of Bridge Street. "Bloody idiot," Duncan said. "Don't the locals know not to come around here anymore?"

"That's a knight," Gardener said at the same instant that they all saw the cross glowing through the gloom.

"It's Hipgrave." Mallory recognised the body language despite the rolling gait.

His confusion at Hipgrave's survival was washed away by the certain knowledge that the captain wouldn't last much longer. Already the shadows behind and around him were beginning to thicken.

"Poor bastard," Duncan said.

Gardener looked down, sickened. "I can't see this again."

Mallory tried to turn away himself, but he was rooted. For a few seconds, he wavered, before cursing, "Oh, bollocks to it." He prepared to lever himself over the edge.

Julian caught his arm. "You're mad!"

"It's the job I chose so I've only got myself to blame," Mallory replied, still wavering himself.

Gardener gave him a shove so hard he almost rolled over the top. "Stop gassing about it, then," he said, joining Mallory on the wall.

The silent acceptance of their responsibility flashed between them in a glance before they clambered over the top, hanging for a second before dropping to the ground. They hit the road running as fast as they could. Hipgrave was so dazed he hadn't seen them.

The miniature army was forming thick and fast, seemingly from the very shadows themselves, the gloom twisting and shaping as if it were Plasticine.

Mallory and Gardener reached Hipgrave together, each taking an arm. Their appearance shocked him from his daze, but he didn't have the strength to speak; his eyes rolled in fear.

"Don't worry, man," Gardener said to him. "We'll have you back in no time."

They both saw that was a lie the moment they started to haul Hipgrave toward the gates. The road was already blocked by the pale black-eyed people.

"I knew I shouldn't have let you talk me into this," Gardener said.

"Yeah, an old bloke like you should have more sense." Mallory looked around; the only way out was through the maze of ancient streets surrounding the cathedral compound. "This way. We might be able to find somewhere to hole up."

"You heard what they said, you stupid bastard. The only reason these fuckers can't get into the cathedral is because it's sacred ground. Anywhere else and they'll be in like shit off a shovel."

"Just shut up and run."

They each slipped an arm around Hipgrave's back to lift him and ran. As they headed into New Street, Mallory realised what they had to do. "We need to get through to the camp at Queen Elizabeth Gardens."

"Why?" Gardener grunted.

"Because it's protected, like the cathedral's protected."

"How can it be?"

"It just is." Mallory glanced back. The army had rounded the corner in pursuit, their eeriness magnified by their silence and speed, their small stature oddly making them even more threatening. They surged along New Street at a run, spreading out to cover the whole road, weapons lowered for use.

"How do you know?" Gardener pressed. His voice held a note of suspicion.

"I just do." Mallory didn't meet his eye.

They hauled Hipgrave as fast as they could into the nearby shopping precinct, taking refuge inside WHSmith's, which had been cleared out by looters. The first floor was pitch black, but they managed to find the door into the staff area and then made their way up to the roof. The army at their heels didn't relent, but Mallory's circuitous route got them to a point where they could make a break for the travellers' camp.

It was only then that Mallory noticed something that shocked him. "He's still got both his hands." Confused, he grabbed Hipgrave's wrists and held them out so Gardener could see.

"So?"

"I told you I found a severed hand at Bratton Camp. It had to be one of ours. It wasn't there on the way in, but it was when we came out."

Gardener waved him away; he didn't have time for such things. "Ah, you've got it all wrong-headed."

The mystery made Mallory's spine tingle. It hinted at something important just beyond his reach, the difference between life and death, if only he could access it.

When they crashed across the invisible boundary surrounding the camp, Mallory felt for the first time whatever protective force lay there. Outside, the air was charged with tension; inside, it felt so peaceful that he began to calm almost immediately.

"We're safe." Mallory reached out a calming hand, but Gardener knocked it away instinctively. It was only when the pale-skinned people surged around the invisible boundary before retreating back into the night that he began to relax.

Slowly coming to his senses, Gardener began to take in the unique mood of the camp, the flag with its entwining dragons, the colourfully dressed people cautiously venturing toward them. His face hardened. "What is this? Bloody travellers?"

"We're safe," Mallory repeated, recognising the signs of righteousness rising in Gardener's eyes.

"They're not Christians, you know." Gardener raised his sword menacingly toward the approaching travellers. "A lot of them are pagans . . . witches . . ."

Mallory recognised one of them from the group he brought back with Sophie from the Plain. Scab was unmistakable, with his shock of bright green hair and a T-shirt that bore the manifest colour sense of an LSD user.

"Back off!" Gardener yelled, brandishing his sword. "Back off!" The expression on his face was so terrifying that the youth blanched and froze in his tracks.

"Gardener, chill," Mallory said. "They're just normal—"

"Witches," Gardener said, with restrained fury. "Bloody Satan-worshippers. Come on, Mallory, you know the score. They're probably the reason the Adversary is after us. They're probably helping him!"

"You're talking bollocks now."

Gardener rounded on him, eyes blazing. Mallory could see in them the frightening depth of Gardener's bigotry, fuelled by fear and ignorance. "What's wrong with you?" Gardener snarled. "Are you on their side? Is this some kind of trap?"

"We're all on the same side," Mallory said as calmly as he could muster, "against that stuff out there." He waved his hands toward the dark city.

"No." Gardener was not ready to listen to reason. Mallory's heart leaped as Gardener began to back toward the boundary. One step beyond the invisible line and he would be easy prey. "The Bible says—"

"*Suffer not a witch to live*, I know. Fuck it, Gardener, I'm not going to get into some theological argument with you while we've got the Devil at our backs." Gardener halted; Mallory took a breath, relieved that his blatant manipulation had worked. "Remember why we're here." He gently lowered Hipgrave down to lie on the grass.

Gardener surveyed his wounded captain, clearly torn. Finally he said, "I'm not going to move from here. And if any of them come near me—"

"Fine, fine," Mallory interrupted hastily before any of the travellers heard Gardener announce that he was going to slice them into bloody chunks. "You stay here . . . guard Hipgrave. I'll . . . I'll . . ." He shook his head wearily. ". . . tell the enemy to keep their distance."

He marched up to Scab, who quavered at the insistence of his approach. Mallory shook his head curtly and said from the corner of his mouth, "Get out of here before he starts spouting scripture."

There was a split second before the youth registered Mallory's complicity, and then he lightened and hurried away amongst the tents.

Mallory and Gardener sat in uncomfortable silence for several hours. Their only hope of getting back to the cathedral was to wait until daybreak, but it was a long time in coming. For some reason no one could explain, Sophie was unavailable, but Mallory managed to get food and some basic medication for Hipgrave.

Eventually, he couldn't contain his desire to see Sophie any longer and went off in search of her. Rick, the dreadlocked youth Mallory had met on his first visit to the camp, was loitering outside the leader's tent under the fluttering two-dragon flag. He sucked anxiously on a joint as he wandered back and forth, jumping in shock when he saw Mallory.

"What do you want?" he said, with drug-fired paranoia.

"Peace on earth, goodwill to men. Where's Sophie?"

Rick jerked his head toward the tent door. "She hasn't got time for you. Not tonight."

"What's up? Big spell? Lots of nude dancing? I'm up for it."

Rick bristled. Before he could respond, the tent flaps were thrown open and Sophie stepped out. She looked pale and distracted, and Mallory thought she might have been crying. "I thought I heard your voice."

"What's wrong?" The sarcasm ebbed from his voice as he responded to her mood.

She took a gulping breath, her eyes widening. He was shocked to see the confidence and control falling from her until she resembled, briefly, a young girl lost in a frightening place. He stepped forward to comfort her, but she backed off, aware of Rick's eyes on her. He dropped his arms. It wasn't the time, or the place; and prejudice was everywhere. She composed herself quickly, weighed the moment, and turned her back on Rick, holding open the tent flap for Mallory to enter. Rick began to protest, but she flashed him a look so ferocious that the words died in his throat. He took a heavy hit on his joint and stomped away.

Inside, Sophie sagged, free from the need to present a front. Though concerned at the extent of her suffering, Mallory was secretly pleased that she made no attempt to hide her emotions from him. He hesitated, then reached out again. She let him place his hands on her shoulders, but didn't fold into him as he had hoped. "What's happened?" he asked.

She took another breath that blatantly suppressed a sob. "Melanie's dead." Her voice was like the wind under the door.

"I'm sorry." He cursed his awkwardness and inability to express honest emotion, but he couldn't think of anything else to say to connect with her.

She didn't seem to mind. "She was a good person, Mallory." She stared into the too-bright light of several candles blazing in one corner of the foyer. "Goddess, she was the only thing holding us all together." She pulled away from him, her knuckles involuntarily going to her mouth.

He replaced a supportive hand on her shoulder, and it lost its stiffness at his touch. "When did it happen?"

"An hour ago. I haven't told anyone yet . . . except Rick . . . haven't dared tell them." She looked up at him with moist eyes. "She was so strong, Mallory.

She had such a clear view of where we were going . . . what was expected of us . . . Everyone was relying on her."

"Don't think about that now," he said. "This is the time for grieving for her, for Melanie. Everything else comes later."

"We don't have that option. There's too much at stake. She wasn't just a friend, she was the leader of everybody here." She caught another breath. "They're all here *because* of her." There was a long pause, and then she said, "And now they're going to ask me to take over. But I'm not up to it, Mallory. I'm not up to it at all."

"Then don't do it. Leave."

She was plainly puzzled by this. "I can't walk away. I've got responsibilities now."

"You're telling me they can't get on without you?" He briefly entertained the fantasy that at daybreak he and Sophie could find a horse and ride away from the increasingly dangerous mess that was growing around them.

"I'm sure they could get on without me, but that's not the point. When you're part of a tribe there are structures in place to facilitate the survival of the community."

"And you're the wise-woman-in-waiting."

"My abilities with the Craft are important for everyone here. Melanie invested a lot of time and effort teaching me, and I accepted that role and the responsibilities that went along with it. It would be immoral to turn my back on people who are relying on me."

She noticed the anxiety in his features and caught herself. "Listen to me, going on about myself. Selfish bitch. Why are you here? Is there something wrong?"

Her concern triggered pent-up doubts and fears that surfaced unbidden; for the first time in a long while he felt there was someone with whom he could talk honestly. "We're in deep shit in the cathedral," he said, suddenly weary. "Those things have got us under siege . . . the food's getting low, and I can't see them finding a way out. There's something else going on, too, in the background. I can't figure out what it is, but I don't reckon it can be any good." His shoulders sagged at the release. "I think it's going to get really bad."

She forced a smile. "What a pair, eh? If this was before the Fall . . ." She caught herself; there was no point talking about could-have-beens. Yet in her comment Mallory sensed a connection: they were *a pair*, two people burdened by problems who would rather be a hundred miles away. Together.

The notion was underlined dramatically when she caught the neck of his cloak and pulled his head down to plant a firm kiss on his mouth. It was filled with passion, desperate yet restrained at the same time. It went on for a full minute, and Mallory responded in kind. After so long without female contact, he felt himself hardening instantly, but before it could develop into anything else, she broke the kiss and walked away a few steps.

"That was . . ." She had taken him so much by surprise he couldn't find the words.

"Life's too short for playing stupid games, Mallory," she said, lighting another candle to replace one that had guttered out in a pool of wax. "We both know there's something between us, despite our very obvious differences. There's no time for flirting."

"So does that mean we're *stepping out?*" His irony was a reaction to the feeling that he had lost control of the situation; and he always thought he was completely in charge.

"It was a recognition of what we feel, that's all. What happens from here is anybody's guess. Quite honestly, you might get on my tits—a likely prospect given your very unfortunate nature—and I'd be forced to curse you for all time."

Mallory really didn't know if she was joking.

"Now, thanks very much for the visit, but I've got a funeral to prepare." She peeked through the flap into the rear of the tent and when she looked back at him tears filled her eyes again. "Besides," she continued throatily, "I would think you'd be pretty much engrossed in sorting out your own crisis."

"Yeah. Any idea what's happening there?"

"Well, you've certainly pissed off someone in high places. At least it keeps you all in one place where you can't do any more damage." She couldn't mask her bitterness.

"Don't tar me with the same brush."

"You wear the uniform. You carry the weapons, eat the food, sleep under the same roof. Don't be naïve, Mallory. You might pretend to yourself that you're apart somehow—"

"They're not all bad," he protested. "Mostly, they're harmless. Well meaning."

"Then you ought to do something about the ones who aren't, oughtn't you? I thought you knights were supposed to be the police force of the New Christian Army. Or is it one rule for you, and one for the rest of us?"

Though hardly surprised by the strength of her response after Melanie's death, Mallory couldn't find any way to answer her. Instead, he peered out into the night. The red light of dawn tinted the horizon.

"We might stand a chance of getting back in daylight," he mused. "If we're lucky."

A startled cry followed by angry yells broke out not far away. Instinctively, Mallory knew what it was. He was already out of the tent and running before Sophie could enquire what was happening.

His worst fears were realised as he made it back to the camp boundary. One of the travellers lay facedown, unmoving though probably not dead, Mallory guessed. Worse, Gardener had Scab pinned against him, a dagger to his throat. Gardener was overcome with righteous anger.

Mallory motioned to the angry crowd of travellers to hold back, but that only convinced them to turn their rage on him.

"There's no talking to them, Mallory," Gardener shouted.

Mallory found himself herded closer to Gardener. With a sickening sense of fatalism, he saw Sophie approaching. "What are you doing, you Geordie idiot?" he snapped.

Scab rolled his eyes in abject fear. As he writhed, Gardener pricked him with the dagger as a warning and he almost fainted. "They offered me a drink," Gardener said darkly.

"Good call. After that it would have been lentil stew and then we'd all be on the way to hell."

"It was a potion. The bastards were trying to put a spell on me!"

"Or maybe it was just a drink." Mallory was shoulder to shoulder with Gardener now. About thirty travellers ranged in front of them. Some looked scared for Gardener's prisoner; others, who had patently had their fingers burned before, were murderous.

"Look at this one." Gardener motioned to a pentacle hanging on a chain around Scab's neck. "Devil-worshippers. The moment our backs were turned, they'd have had us."

Mallory cursed under his breath; the false propaganda Gardener had absorbed during his evangelical background was unshakeable. At that moment, Scab decided to break free, probably driven more by fear of what might happen than any real desire to escape. He kicked at Gardener's shins with his heels, writhed like a madman, and then attempted to yank his head down through Gardener's grip.

In the confusion, his neck was driven onto Gardener's dagger, or vice versa. A geyser of arterial blood arced toward the massed travellers.

The crowd was stunned into silence. Shock locked Gardener's face; Mallory wished he had seen some compassion there, or guilt, for his own peace of mind. Gardener took a step back, examining his crimson hands as if they belonged to someone else.

Mallory reacted instinctively. He stepped forward and hit Gardener so hard in the face he went down as if he'd been poleaxed. It was undoubtedly the best thing Mallory could have done, immediately deflating the furious rage that had enveloped the crowd and saving them from a lynching.

Instead, the travellers turned their attention to their comrade, who flopped like a dying fish in a pool of blood that seemed too big, too dark. Mallory knelt down to help, knowing there was nothing that could be done, but someone smacked him aside and he went over, seeing stars. When his vision cleared, Scab had stopped moving and everyone was staring at Mallory as if he had committed the murder himself.

Sophie threw herself through the crowd, all the grief of Melanie's death erupting in one instant. "See?" she screamed. "This is what happens if you do nothing! Nobody has the luxury of sitting on the fence! If you don't stand up for what you believe in, someone always pays the price."

There was no point in trying to calm her; he was lucky to get away with his life. Gardener was just coming around. Mallory gave him an unnecessarily rough shove that propelled him out of the camp and then collected Hipgrave, who had been slumped in a daze nearby, and dragged him away.

He could still hear the sound of crying, even when the camp had fallen from view.

As they hurried along the road in the ruddy light, Gardener began to say, "He deserved it," but Mallory turned on him so ferociously the words died on his lips.

His anger evaporated as he paused at the bridge, aware of the threat that lurked on the short route to the cathedral gates. A guard waved to him from a new section of the walls overlooking the river. His voice floated down. "Don't move!"

As they waited, a group of Blues ran out onto Crane Street at the turning to North Gate. They were armed with crossbows and longbows.

"What the bloody hell's going on?" Gardener said.

The group's captain barked an order and one of their number moved along the ranks with a torch. As he passed, the tips of the notched arrows burst into flames.

"Looks like it's a cremation for us," Mallory said. "And I'd got my eye on such a lovely headstone."

Gardener grunted, "I think—"

"I know what they're doing," Mallory snapped. "Get your arm around Hipgrave. And I just want to say that if these are the last moments of my life, I really am pig-sick I'm spending them linked to you two."

There was some communication between the captain and the guard who had moved out of sight near the North Gate. A second later, the guard reappeared and shouted, "Now!"

Mallory and Gardener moved as fast as they could; Hipgrave's heels didn't even touch the ground. The Blues raised their weapons. Mallory kept his vision trained directly ahead. The buildings on either side passed in a blur, still swathed in shadows, the dawn light only limning the edges.

Halfway along the street, the shadows became movement on either side. Still Mallory didn't look. Fear would take the strength from his legs, threat would deflect his single-minded purpose, and there would be little point in standing and fighting. Drained from the night's exertions, his breath burned in his throat.

The smell of something that had lain in damp soil rose up around him. He had the fleeting sense of fluttering wings, frightened birds in flight, of red brake-lights, of a striking cobra and a dog's snapping jaws.

Fire rained down all around them. Heat seared past Mallory's cheeks and brought starburst trails across his vision. The air was thick with the suffocating stink of burning tar.

Something lashed past the back of his neck, the backwash of air suggesting great weight, barely missing him. The sense of pursuit lay heavy on his back, relentless, drawing slightly closer with each second.

Twice he almost slipped on the slick flagstones as they turned into High Street, only righting himself at the last instant. Gardener kept pace, but Hipgrave swung wildly, threatening to overbalance them. The Blues retreated apace, still firing.

And then they were at the gates. The Blues backed in, leaving a small tunnel at their centre. Mallory and Gardener didn't stop until they heard the gates swing shut with a resounding clang, and then came the thunder of something heavy slamming into it.

They dropped Hipgrave unceremoniously. Gardener bowed his head in silent prayer, but Mallory looked up to the lightening sky, breathing deeply in relief.

But then he saw the grim faces of the Blues and the growing desperation of the brethren making their way to prime, and he realised the enormity of the trial that lay ahead for all of them.

chapter eight

A THORN IN THE FLESH

"Everything that happens is just and fair to the gods,
but humans regard some things as just and others as unjust."

Heraclitus

October passed like the tolling of a funeral bell. In the brethren's makeshift dormitories and the stone chambers of the knights' barracks, the nights crept by with bone-aching cold barely kept at bay by rough blankets. The days were bright and crisp, the wind whistling through the gothic architecture lowering over them with an unsettling character that hinted at sentience. Every night the attacks on the gate continued unabated. Every day brothers would creep up to the walkway to look desperately toward the city centre, knowing things were looking back at them, daring them to venture out into the seemingly empty street beyond. And over it all hung the oppressive presence of the Adversary, felt more than seen, but unmistakably there, watching, waiting, cold and hateful.

Within the cathedral compound, tensions rose at the realisation that the siege was not going to end, while the leaders hadn't yet identified a suitable plan to get them out of the predicament. Rations were tightened, and although there was an ample supply of water from the river, with winter just around the corner they all wondered how long they would be able to last.

Arguments broke out as tempers frayed, and it took all the ministering skills of the elder brethren to maintain the peace. Blaine had suggested posting the knights around the compound to keep order, but word had come down from Cornelius that he didn't want them used against their own; the knights had to remain pure in their ideals as an instrument of the Church.

To the majority of the brethren, Cornelius became an elusive figure, confined to his sick bed in the bishop's palace, tended by Julian and a small band of helpers, with reports of his condition occasionally sent down as if from On High. "Temperature raised, but doing fine." "Fever broken." "Took the air in the palace garden this morning," and the like. Rumours circulated as to what exactly was the root of his illness—everything from pneumonia and cholera to a brain tumour—but they all knew at heart it was his age. Whatever the hopeful spin placed on his condition by Julian, there was a dismal acceptance that he couldn't have long left.

In the upper echelons of the Church leadership, meanwhile, manoeuvrings for the succession continued in some quarters with unseemly openness. Stefan appeared to be the leading choice of one faction, though he professed no interest in the job, preferring "only to serve." His supporters were happy to class themselves as hard-liners, culled from the evangelical communities of Southern England and Unionist enclaves in Scotland. Stefan, however, kept his own views close to his chest.

Both Hipgrave and Miller recovered quickly under the able if curt treatment of Warwick in the infirmary. Exhaustion and hypothermia had been the only ailments afflicting Hipgrave, who had spent the days since the attack on Bratton Camp wandering randomly around Salisbury Plain. He had taken a blow to his head that had left him with a mild concussion, just enough to addle his thoughts before the weather took its toll on him. Blaine didn't put him through the mill of the Inquisition—it would not have been right for a captain of the knights to be seen to be doubted in current circumstances—but Hipgrave had been questioned extensively about what had happened. His ordeal had wiped away many of his memories of that night, but he still found it within himself to blame Mallory, Miller, Daniels, and Gardener for the failure of the mission.

"They were cowards," he told Blaine in front of the other four. "They ran at the first sign of danger, left me to deal with it on my own. Whatever happened to that poor man was their fault, and they should be punished accordingly."

Gardener protested, but Blaine silenced him angrily. Later, however, the four of them found it telling that for such a disciplinarian, Blaine didn't mete out any punishment. Hipgrave's outburst managed to sour any residual sense of camaraderie they all might have felt with him after the horrific experience they had shared that night. And it was a time when Hipgrave needed them. His dislocation at the mysterious transformation of the cathedral had been acute, and he'd made a fool of himself trying to convince everyone he spoke to of the change. Even Blaine eyed him with suspicion. Yet Hipgrave couldn't bring himself to talk to Mallory and the others for fear it would diminish his leadership.

But a strong bond was forged amongst Mallory, Miller, Gardener, and Daniels. They were outsiders in a community that was already outside of society, the only ones who could see the truth. Gardener made a grudging reconciliation with Mallory, though he "owed him a bloody big punch in the face." Whatever doubts they had about each other had to be overridden if they were going to survive in a place that continually tested their sanity.

Mallory spent much of his time attempting to piece together some overarching mystery he was sure lay behind the scenes. The others were not convinced. "Hello? Are you lot blind?" Mallory said after one particularly heated debate. "We were lured out of the cathedral by two ghost-clerics who disappeared the moment they'd got us where they wanted us. And then we were let back in—"

"What do you mean?" Gardener snapped. "We nearly got torn apart when we fetched Hipgrave."

"You've seen what's out there. Do you really think they couldn't have stopped us if they'd wanted? Jesus, they could have wiped us out in the blink of an eye. They let us back in," Mallory stressed. "They made a pretence of stopping us so we wouldn't be suspicious, but that was it."

There was a long silence while Mallory's theory washed over them. It was Daniels, fiddling with his eye patch nervously, who spoke first. "Why would the Adversary want to get us out and then let us back in—all of us, because we came back on three separate occasions?"

"And what's it got to do with all the new buildings appearing?" Miller asked. "There has to be a connection, right?"

The silence lasted longer this time, and none of them had any answers. But they knew that the only way of uncovering what was happening, and what it meant for all of them, was to work together.

It was October the twenty-eighth. Mallory and Miller had been despatched to the kitchens to see Gibson, whom Mallory had dubbed the Canon of the Pies. The place had been transformed along with the rest of the building and was now the size of half a football pitch, with a low, vaulted roof like a wine cellar supported by stone pillars. Woodburning ranges ran along one wall, drawing on the huge but limited supply of timber that had been amassed. Giant bubbling pans sent clouds of steam scented with spices and herbs drifting across the ceiling. The room echoed with the sound of clanging lids and chopping knives as twenty or more cooks and assistants prepared the day's meals.

Sweat beading his ruddy face, Gibson moved amongst the activity, chuckling at some joke no one else knew; his frame appeared as massive as ever despite the limited rations, nor had he lost any of his celebrated larger-than-life humour. With one podgy hand outstretched, he lumbered across the room to slap both of them on the shoulder in greeting. "Jolly good you could make it down here," he said, as if they had ambled along of their own accord. Laughter rumbled out like an avalanche as a vat of bubbling turnips steamed up his large-framed spectacles. Cleaning them on his robes, he motioned to a large door against the far wall. "The stores are through there, dear boys," he said theatrically. "Mr. Blaine suggested you might be able to help us with the conveyance of several large sacks of potatoes. I keep my little workers here so busy, they never do find the time to do those necessary chores." He wagged a chubby finger at Miller. "And no potatoes means no hearty meals to keep you boys big and strong."

"Straightaway, sir," Miller said brightly. Gibson appeared pleasantly amused by this.

As they headed down some steps into the basement stores, Mallory muttered sourly, "Do you have to be so deferential? You should have offered to stick a brush up your arse so you could sweep the floor while we're hauling and toting."

"It doesn't hurt to be polite. Besides, it makes people smile."

Mallory snorted. "Great. I get spud duty with Jesus' little ray of sunshine."

"You can be very hurtful sometimes, Mallory," Miller sniffed.

"No. This is hurtful." Mallory cuffed him around the back of the head.

"Ow!" Miller flashed him a black look and jumped a foot to his right to avoid another blow.

There was a fast movement at floor level when they swung open the storeroom door onto the dark interior. "Rats," Mallory noted. "The way things are, they'll be in the stew soon."

"How long do you think we can keep going?" Miller asked. As his eyes slowly adjusted to the gloom, he could see that the storeroom was vast, but in the great space the haphazard piles of sacks and crates appeared insignificant.

"I'm not looking forward to Christmas dinner."

"If we stand firm, whatever's out there might just give up and go away," Miller suggested hopefully.

Mallory began to investigate the sacks in search of the potatoes. "I love an optimist as much as the next man, Miller, but you've seen what we're up against. Those kinds of things don't give up, ever. They'll hang on until we're worn down."

"I don't understand why this is happening. We've not done anything wrong."

"That's always a matter of perspective."

A look of curiosity crossed Miller's face. "What did you do before the Fall, Mallory? Sometimes you sound like a historian, sometimes a philosopher, and sometimes . . ."

"Yes?"

". . . sometimes you act like a yob at closing time."

Mallory let out a belly laugh. He plucked a potato from a sack and tossed it in the air. "The only hope we've got is if our great leaders come up with a plan . . . a counterstrike . . . anything . . . that works. Do you have any faith in that?"

"I have lots of faith, Mallory." Miller attempted to shoulder the sack, but he wasn't strong enough. All he could do was drag it across the floor in jerks like some small child with a too-big toy. "You see, I have faith in people like you, Mallory. You're a man who gets things done. Why don't you turn your mind to a solution instead of being negative. As always."

Mallory tossed the potato another time, then hurled it into the shadows. It thudded against a wall and burst.

"You act as if you're apart from all this," Miller continued breathlessly, "as if you can just sit back and sneer and be snide. But we're all in it together, Mallory. If people help other people, things get done. Individuals have a responsibility to the community. No one can afford to stand alone, in here or out in the world."

"I'm sick of hearing about responsibility." Mallory grabbed another potato and threw it furiously into the dark. It splattered against the stone.

"Don't waste the supplies!"

"Ah, we'll all be dead before we get down to the last potato. They'll be roasting the youngest and tenderest of us in those big ovens long before that."

The silence prompted Mallory to turn. Miller was staring at him with a comical expression of horror. "This is a Christian community!" he protested.

"It's survival, Miller. That's what humans do."

"That's what beasts do."

Mallory plucked another potato from the sack, tossed it in the air, but caught himself before he threw it. He peered at the wall for a long moment, then marched over and began to rap it with his knuckles.

"What's wrong?" Miller asked.

Mallory turned to him and raised a finger. "A tunnel."

Miller's eyes widened. "Of course. Under the wall."

"Not just under the wall. To the travellers' camp. It stretches almost up to the cathedral compound now, on both sides of the river. We wouldn't need to dig far. And . . ." He paused in pride at his idea. ". . . the camp is protected. By magic, or faith, or whatever you want to call it, but the point is, it's safe ground. The travellers could help us get food in through the tunnel . . ." He paused. "After we've managed to build bridges with them. But they're good people . . ."

Miller looked uneasy. "You know how Gardener reacted. Do you think our people will be able to deal with the pagans?"

"You were the one preaching about the Brotherhood of Man, Miller, everybody working together. And oddly it dovetails with my philosophy, too. When it comes down to survival, people will do whatever it takes to keep living."

Miller thought about this for a moment, then smiled. "We need to tell someone. They should start on it straightaway."

Metallic crashing exploded from the kitchen as if someone had dropped a pile of pans. It was punctuated by a terrified yell. Mallory and Miller rushed upstairs and found the kitchen assistants clustered in one corner of the room. Gibson loomed over them, scrubbing his fingers through his tight grey curls. "What's going on here? What's going on?" he said in a flap.

One of the chief chefs clambered to his feet from where he had been sprawled on the stone flags. The way his features had been put together suggested he didn't have much time for nonsense, but he was now ashen-faced and his eyes darted around like a frightened animal's.

"It brushed right past him," said one of the assistants who had helped him to his feet.

"What in heaven's name brushed past him?" Gibson squealed.

The assistant glanced at two or three others in the circle. "You saw it too, right?" They nodded. The assistant was reticent to continue until Gibson prompted him with a rough shake of his shoulder. "It was a ghost," he said, obviously relieved that he'd got it out. "A ghost of a churchman of some kind . . . or a monk . . . hard to tell. I mean, it had the clothes on and everything."

"A ghost?" Gibson's expression suggested that everyone in the room was malingering.

"We saw it! All of us who were looking this way . . ."

"It was the face," the chef muttered. His eyes ranged around the kitchen but couldn't fix on anyone there. "It looked right at me. The eyes . . ." He turned and vomited down the side of the range, the heat cooking it instantly and filling the air with a repugnant stink.

"It was old Bishop Ward," one of the older assistants said. "I recognised him from the painting that used to hang in the library."

The chef wiped his mouth with the back of his hand. "When it looked at me, it felt as though my insides were being pulled right out through my eyes," he said.

"Did he say anything?" Miller asked.

"Not in so many words," the chef replied shakily. "But it felt as if it was telling me about death . . . about all our deaths. About the end of the world."

The study of the bishop's palace had the sumptuous feel of a Victorian gentleman's club: burnished leather high-backed chairs, books, dark wood panelling, Persian carpet, stone fireplace. It was a world away from the cold quarters the brethren endured. For many years it had been the cathedral school, but it had recently been reclaimed as a haven for the bishop from the privations experienced throughout the compound.

Mallory had spent a good half hour convincing the ancillary staff to allow him a few minutes with Julian, whom he then had to convince to allow him in to see Cornelius. Julian looked tired and distracted, but he was receptive to anything that might get them out of their current predicament. He had told Mallory to wait and he would be granted an audience once Cornelius was strong enough. That had been three hours ago.

The opening of the door suggested that the time had finally come, but it was only Blaine. Mallory instantly fell on the defensive. Blaine was sphinxlike, didn't even acknowledge Mallory, but the moment the ancillary left, his inscrutability vanished. "What do you think you're doing?" His voice was like stone. Mallory began to reply, but Blaine talked over him. "There's a chain of command here. You don't go bothering your betters with your half-baked *ideas*." The word was a sneer. "You come to me, and then I can tell you how much bollocks it is. Don't waste your time thinking—that's not what you're here for." Implicit threat filled every action. "Your trouble, Mallory, is you think you're better than anyone here. You're not. Nobody cares what you think." Blaine took a step forward, and Mallory had a sudden image of a Belfast backstreet, broken bottles and last orders.

The door opened and Julian breezed in, a little fresher, even managing a smile. "The bishop is ready for you now," he said.

Julian led them up imposing stone stairs to Cornelius's bedroom. The heavy drapes were drawn and it was oppressively warm despite the time of year: a fire blazed in the grate and candles flickered everywhere. The aroma of burning logs barely covered the atmosphere of sickness.

Cornelius was propped up in a large four-poster bed, his frame unbearably thin and fragile against the piles of cushions and brocade bedspread. He forced a weak smile in greeting and shakily beckoned for Mallory to come closer.

Only then did Mallory realise they were not alone. Stefan stood to one side, smiling insincerely, hands clasped in front of him in an attempt to appear penitent. "I took the liberty of inviting your commander-in-chief here," he said to Mallory. "I thought it only right you receive due recognition for your actions."

Every time Mallory saw Stefan, he liked him less, but at that moment he felt there was something unduly sinister about the chancellor. Mallory looked to Julian, who shifted uneasily. "I felt any suggestions should be heard by the Chapter of Canons," Julian said. "Stefan felt that would take too long to arrange, and that we here could easily assay its worth and decide if it should be taken forward."

"Tell us what you think, my son," Cornelius said so weakly that Mallory could barely hear him.

"A tunnel—"

"Is that it? We've already thrown that idea out," Blaine said contemptuously. "We haven't got the time or the facilities to dig a tunnel the length we would need to get to safety. If we go short, those things will be waiting to pick us off when we come up. And you try coming up under concrete and Tarmac when you haven't got power tools. If we go west we hit the river. We could never get under that."

Mallory allowed him to say his piece and then continued as if he hadn't spoken. "A tunnel under the wall into the camp to the northwest. It would be easy to dig. We wouldn't have to go under any water."

"Haven't you been listening—" Blaine began, but Stefan silenced him with a raised hand.

"Why that particular spot?" he said curiously.

"Because it's protected."

This intrigued Stefan greatly. "Protected? In what way?"

"In the same way that the cathedral and its grounds are protected."

"The cathedral is protected because of the Glory of God," Stefan said.

Mallory sensed the traps lining up before him. His position was already weak; he couldn't risk offending anyone. And the way Blaine had acted earlier, he felt there was more than his reputation at stake. "It seems, from what I've heard—"

"Where?" Stefan interrupted.

"Here and there." Mallory fixed his gaze on Stefan's and refused to break it. "That the strength of our belief . . . our faith . . . has . . . empowered the land so those things can't come on it. It's the same in the camp."

"They have accepted the Lord into their lives?" Stefan plainly knew otherwise.

"They have very strong beliefs."

"They are Christians?" Stefan's gaze didn't waver.

"No. They're a mixed bunch." He paused, but it was obvious Stefan wasn't going to let him get away with skirting over the issue. "Some nature-lovers. Probably . . . Odinists. Wiccans. Druids, maybe—"

"Pagans?" Stefan raised his eyes to look at the ceiling. "What you are saying sounds very much like blasphemy."

"Oh, for God's sake!" Julian snapped. "Does it matter who they are? If it provides us with a way out of this mess we're in, then we should go for it."

"I think the chancellor doesn't believe in equality of worship," Mallory noted, with a little more acid than he'd intended.

"We are at war, Mr. Mallory," Stefan replied, "for the very future of Christianity itself. We cannot afford insipid liberalism. Woolly ideas that appeared to work when times were good do not hold now."

"You believe the future of Christianity should starve rather than allow contact with the *corrupt*?" Mallory said.

"Of course not." Stefan moved his hands behind his back. "You are sure this camp is protected?"

"Yes."

"You have been there yourself?"

"I have."

Stefan nodded thoughtfully; Mallory felt there was a wealth of unspoken comment in that simple movement. Stefan turned to Cornelius, bowing his head deferentially. "I feel this is a matter we should discuss in private, your Grace," he said. His body language suggested Mallory had not only been forgotten, he had already been dismissed.

"We can't test what he says," Julian said. "We should just do it. What other options do we have? We need to start digging immediately."

Stefan smiled coldly. "In private," he repeated.

Blaine caught Mallory's eye and nodded sharply toward the exit. As Mallory left, the door closed firmly behind him.

The light was already starting to fade as Mallory made his way across the lawned area of peaceful walks and sheltering trees now enclosed by the transformed cathedral buildings. The air was cool and damp and fragrant with nature, and the garden would undoubtedly have felt tranquil if not for Mallory's growing awareness of troubling events developing just beyond his perception.

He found Daniels sitting on a bench with a young man who appeared to be hanging on Daniels's every word. The brother was in his late teens, with an open, good-looking face and long brown hair that framed it in such a way that he appeared almost angelic. Daniels was telling some tale in a voluble, entertaining way, and they were both engrossed, as much with each other as with the story. From their body language, half turned toward each other, Daniels's arm stretching out along the back of the bench, it was clear there was an attraction between them.

Daniels spotted Mallory and called him over with a wave. "Mallory, meet Lewis. He has this misguided belief that our leaders know what they're doing." Lewis smiled bashfully.

"Don't spoil him with your cynicism, Daniels." Mallory slumped onto the bench next to them.

"They established the knights," Lewis said shyly. "That was a stroke of genius. All the brothers know you're going to be our saviours."

Daniels and Mallory exchanged glances. "Better start praying," Mallory said drily.

"You're filled with the power of the Lord," Lewis pressed. "With belief and hidden knowledge and . . . and . . . bravery." He looked from Mallory to Daniels adoringly.

Mallory watched the stars start to appear in the dark blue sky. He had never expected things to go this way at all. He'd been running away to a simpler life, not trying to find even more responsibility, more trouble and suffering.

"Thank the Lord for the knights," he said sardonically.

Mallory was the first to the refectory, and took a table for them in a quiet corner. Miller joined him soon after, with Daniels and Gardener arriving together. Daniels was in unusually high spirits, enjoying some mocking banter with Gardener, who responded with dry wit and an impassive face. Mallory had overheard

Gardener defending Daniels to one of the fundamentalist brothers who had been objecting to something or other in a bigoted way. Daniels, too, had been steadfast and loyal in support of Gardener, especially when Mallory had complained about the events in the travellers' camp.

"Evening, Cyclops," Mallory said as Daniels sat down.

Daniels wasn't perturbed in the slightest. "You're just jealous because I've got this chick-magnet eye patch, you bony-arsed white boy."

"And it's no use to you at all," Mallory said.

"It's a benefit to all of us, Mallory," Gardener said, dunking his bread into his bowl of vegetable soup. "If I come up on his blindside I get to the food before he takes his greedy bastard portions."

"*Man*-sized portions," Daniels corrected. It was a lame joke now that the kitchen staff had cut the rations to subsistence level.

"I feel guilty about this," Miller said, looking around. "It's as if we're plotting."

"We're not plotting *against* the authorities," Gardener said with his mouth full. "If anything, we're plotting *for* them. We're the only ones who can see everything's changed here, so we're the only ones who can decide if anything needs to be done about it."

"I'm wondering if Stefan's got something to do with it," Mallory said.

"Stefan? He's the chancellor," Miller said naïvely.

"I don't trust him. He's manipulative. He's got some sort of scheme going on here—I think he reckons he can take over from Cornelius." Mallory could see the whole room from where he was sitting. It was slowly filling up, but he was mostly paying attention for Blaine or Hipgrave.

"He's certainly a slippery character," Daniels said, "but doing something like this? How could he? How could anybody?"

"Somebody made it happen," Mallory said. "I don't think it's a random manifestation."

"Look, we don't even know it's a bad thing," Gardener noted. "Maybe it is what I said . . . God's will, a miracle. That's no crazier than all the other stuff going on. Maybe that's the way of the world now—little miracles before the Fall, bloody big bastard miracles now."

"He has a point," Daniels said. "There's been no sign that it's anything bad."

"Not yet," Mallory said. He prodded at the unappetising chunks of indistinguishable vegetables. "But if you're right, why are the spirits growing restless?"

Miller told the others about the ghost in the kitchens that morning. "It's not a one-off," he added. "Down at the workshops they're all talking about it. Spooks all over the place. Old bishops, canons, scaring the stuffing out of people. It's getting worse, they say."

"Like I said, the dead are growing restless." Mallory looked around the table. "In this world we're stuck in, we need to start thinking with a medieval mind-set—not hard in this place. Signs and portents. We've got unquiet spirits. Something's bothering them. *The graves stood tenantless and the sheeted dead did squeak and gibber in the Roman streets.*"

"They know something we don't," Daniels said.

They all fell quiet for a long moment while they pushed their food around their bowls. It was Gardener who spoke first. "We wouldn't have spooks rising up if we were living in a miracle." He didn't raise his eyes from the table.

"Those things that have put us under siege . . . this . . ." Daniels motioned to the building around them. ". . . You really do think it's linked?"

"In some way," Mallory said, "but I'm betting it's not in as direct a way as you're saying. Those things can't get onto Church land . . . that's why they're pinning us down here. So I don't think they could have caused the cathedral to change."

Before they could debate the matter further, Julian walked in, looking brighter than Mallory had seen him in a long time. He marched to the centre of the now-busy room and climbed onto one of the long tables. "I have an announcement," he said in a voice that barely contained his joy. "The bishop . . . Cornelius . . . has turned the corner. He's on the road to recovery."

Mallory recalled how frail the bishop had appeared earlier; it was implausible that his health could have improved so quickly.

"We should all pray for his swift return to form . . . and for the guiding hand of Saint Cuthbert." A whisper ran around the room at the mention of the sacred relic that had invigorated the small community. "Yes, it's true. We transported Cornelius to our most holy relic earlier. The response was phenomenal. Strength flowed into his limbs, his eyes grew bright, his voice firm and confident. The sickness that had been tainting him for so long drifted away like mist in the rays of the sun." Emotion overcame Julian so that he had to wipe his cheeks with the back of his hand. "Cornelius is a remarkable man," he continued, speaking from the heart. "He held this community together in the earliest days. His vision guided us when we were at our weakest, when many were thinking of abandoning the Faith in those black days. Cornelius. All Cornelius. He has led us to this point where—current difficulties notwithstanding—we are on the verge of once again leading the Church, and God's Word, out into the world."

He stared into the rafters thoughtfully before continuing. "He probably wouldn't want me to tell you this, but he originally refused to be taken before the Saint Cuthbert relic. He felt it would be better for our morale if he fought and overcame the illness himself. He is an unselfish man." He shook his head slowly, almost talking to himself now. "Sadly, that was not to be. This afternoon he slipped into a coma . . . one from which it appeared he would not recover. The decision was taken then to transport him to the relic in the hope that he would be freed to continue his mission with us. And so it was. Praise the Lord." He wiped his eyes once more, stepped down, and swept out of the refectory.

There was a moment of silence before the room erupted in cheers and cries of "Hallelujah!" Only one man failed to join in the celebrations, Mallory noted: Stefan, who had walked in halfway through Julian's speech. Though he forced a smile when any of the jovial brothers appeared in his line of vision, his face was dark.

Blaine had instigated a shift-rota of cathedral patrols for the knights. It was clearly a propaganda exercise to provide the illusion of security.

That night it was the turn of Mallory and Daniels. They started their rounds just as the night office was beginning at midnight. The cathedral was ablaze with candles, the golden glow reaching up the walls until it was swallowed by the thick shadows engulfing the ceiling far overhead. They stood at the back, letting the seductive sway of the plainsong move their emotions like a tidal swell. The combination of light and sound, of emotion alive with the subtle nuances of voice, had more power than its component parts.

They eventually dragged themselves into the cloisters, the singing now ghostly through the walls. Yet silence and stillness hung over the square, so that at first they didn't dare speak; even their footsteps on the ancient stone sounded too loud. The open central area was a pool of moonlight that made the enclosing corridors appear even darker.

As they approached the chapter house, Daniels coughed self-consciously. "Sorry. I just wanted to hear my voice." He laughed in embarrassment. "Look at me—an educated, sophisticated, just all-round modern guy and I'm afraid of ghosts."

"We never really leave behind the children we were," Mallory replied. His own hand rested on the carved dragons of his sword. "Besides, these days it's probably smart to be scared."

"Stops you being blasé," Daniels agreed. His eyes darted around. "You know what I miss? Clubs. Music . . . new stuff, you know . . . and lights. I used to love clubs, went two or three times a week with Gareth."

"Yeah, I miss music," Mallory said, "and the football, movies, nipping out for a curry after the pub . . ." He thought for a second. "Getting a train, buying a newspaper on a rainy morning, maybe picking up a Mars Bar with it—"

"I hate Mars. Like eating sugar and glue."

"Buying a new book from your favourite author . . ."

"You could go on forever."

"It's the stupid little things that get to you the most." Mallory took a deep breath. "And what do we get in return—?"

"We get a life that's never boring."

The new structure began beyond the cloisters, the stone darker, more worn, as if thousands of feet and hands had trailed over it across thousands of years. Mallory still didn't like walking around the place. The constantly changing layout of corridors and stairs and rooms unnerved him—he couldn't get a handle on the floor plan at all—and there was an unsettling atmosphere that hung in the air like a bad smell.

They passed into a corridor that ran amongst a series of dormitories where the echoes were disturbingly distorted. Halfway along, Daniels caught Mallory's arm and hissed, "What was that?"

"Didn't hear anything," Mallory replied. His footsteps were still reverberating several seconds after he'd come to a halt.

Daniels's eyes had widened until the whites appeared to glow. "It sounded like someone calling my name."

"You're a big nancy-boy coward, Daniels," Mallory joked. "You're scaring yourself."

"No, it was definitely—"

He was cut short by a rustling sepulchral whispering that swept along the corridor like a breeze. Goosebumps sprang up on Mallory's arms. He could have sworn it was calling *his* name.

"It's just Gardener playing tricks on you," Mallory said. It sounded feeble and unconvincing the moment he voiced it.

"It was my name," Daniels stressed, looking up and down the deserted corridor. It unnerved Mallory even more that they had both heard something different. "We should investigate."

"Yeah, right," Mallory said. "Like I'm going to be a character in *Scream Ten*."

"It's our job," Daniels said. "We're supposed to be protecting everyone."

"OK. Off you go, then. I'll wait for the scream of agony. And when it comes I'll break with tradition and *not* come after you to find the bloody chunks. Go on. I'll be here, enjoying myself."

"You're a bastard, Mallory," Daniels said nervously. His sword rang as it slid out of the scabbard. He began to make his way back down the corridor.

"You're really going?" Mallory said, surprised.

"It's our *job*, Mallory." He disappeared into one of the rooms.

Mallory waited for ten minutes until he started to grow bored and then sighed and marched off to investigate. Except the doorway through which Daniels had passed now led into an alcove barely big enough for him to squeeze inside.

"Daniels?" he said tentatively. An unconscious shiver ran down his spine and he quickly backed into the centre of the corridor. The silence was almost unbearable; he could feel his chest tightening as anxiety insinuated its way inside him. Although he felt stupid doing it, he drew his own sword; the hum as it came free was almost comforting.

He had found through irritating experience that retracing one's steps rarely worked, so he pressed on along the corridor. As he neared the end of it, a cold blast of air brought him to a sudden halt; it was as if someone had opened a long-closed door. A second later, the whispering rustled along the walls again; it sounded like frozen lakes, like the tomb. And he was convinced it was calling his name.

He debated going back, but he couldn't be sure that whatever was there wasn't behind him. Oddly, his growing apprehension steeled his resolve.

At the end of the corridor, a short flight of worn steps led up to a deserted chapel. They were the night stairs, a regular fixture in monasteries allowing the monks to make their way speedily from the dormitories to the services so no time was lost for devotion.

He had his foot on the bottom step when a shape loomed up at the top. At first he thought it might be Daniels until he recalled the knight hadn't been wearing his cloak. The figure wore the black habit of a monk, the cowl pulled low over a shadowy space that hid the face. With a sudden wash of cold, he realised it was the same person he had seen twice before; except it wasn't a person. On the previous occasions, he had tried to convince himself it was one of the brothers; now he couldn't hide in that illusion. It took a step toward him; the whispering wrapped around it.

Mallory felt an overpowering dread coming off the figure that left him rooted, his limbs as cold as ice, his neck and back hot; it was his mind's natural revulsion to the supernatural. It was no ghost, he was sure of it, but he had no idea exactly what it was, only that it reeked of otherworldly threat. Yet how something like that could walk the hallowed ground escaped him.

He backed down to the corridor and levelled his sword at it. His action didn't deter its measured progress down the steps. His name echoed around him, the word insubstantial, the sentiment cold and hard and unyielding. It said, *Here is something that wants you, that will stop at nothing to get you.*

He considered striking out at it, but if the blow was futile it would leave him too close; it would be able to touch him and the thought of that was more than he could bear. As it closed on him, his dread increased until he could no longer look at the darkness where the face should be. It was more than simple fear of the unknown; a part of him somehow knew that here was a revelation too awful for him to accept; here were all the things he was frantically escaping.

And then he was running back down the corridor, through rooms unimaginable, waiting for the building to let him out into the night.

Mallory eventually found Daniels waiting outside the chapter house an hour later. The lauds of the dead was filtering through from the cathedral.

"Well, thank heavens for that," Daniels said tartly. "I thought I was going to have to send in a search party. Did you enjoy your rest period?"

"I tried to find you. I couldn't get out of the place." It had taken Mallory a long time to shake off the effects of what he had seen, and he certainly didn't feel like raising it again with Daniels.

"This place gives me the creeps." Daniels looked uncomfortably toward where the transformed building began. "It felt as though it was herding me out of there. I'd be a happy man if I didn't have to go in again."

Mallory followed his gaze. "I'll second that. But I bet you any money that if we want to find out what's happening here, that's exactly where we'll have to go."

The announcement was made the following day: digging would commence on November the first after plans had been drawn up and preliminary excavations opened. The haste to begin underlined the seriousness of their predicament. An uproarious outpouring of relief and optimism followed. The brothers flooded out of the cathedral into a light drizzle, eager to believe that the worst was over and they could get back to their primary mission of rebuilding God's kingdom.

By nine a.m the rain had become a downpour, the skies so slate grey over-head that in the oppressive shadow of the new buildings it almost seemed like night. Water cascaded from the mouths of gargoyles to gush noisily on the stone flags, or spouted off the ends of roofs to catch unawares any brother foolish enough to walk too close to the walls.

Classes continued for most of the knights, excepting the élite Blues, whom Blaine appeared to think no longer needed tuition. They were rarely seen by the other knights, always busy on some mysterious task Blaine had set them deep in the sprawling body of the cathedral buildings.

Mallory could barely keep his mind on the studies. Before, it had seemed irritating; now, it was merely irrelevant. The image of the monk moving slowly down the stairs played repeatedly in his mind, interspersed with thoughts of Sophie and a growing acceptance of his deep attraction to her. The two things pulled him back and forth, darkness and light, fear and love, combining with a general sense of paralysis at his inability to do anything productive that might get him out of that place. And that, he had decided, was what he wanted more than anything else: Sophie with him, miles between them and Salisbury, and damn the consequences. Even his desire for payback against Blaine and the Church authorities paled beside it.

He had doubts that he could ever convince her, especially after what had happened with Gardener, but he had a long-shot idea how he might make it work.

Mallory woke at first light, aching from the pointless, wearying tasks they were increasingly set. Miller was already sitting up in the thin grey light, his rough blankets pulled tightly around him against the cold.

"I think something bad's going to happen," Miller said bluntly.

"To be honest, that's not much of a revelation," Mallory said sleepily. "Under siege. The forces of hell at the gates. Food running out. And, I might add, having to wake up next to you every morning. This is the definition of bad."

"No, I think something bad's going to happen *today*."

Mallory rolled over; another few minutes' sleep would be good and luxuries were few and far between. "You're just spooked because it's Halloween."

"Exactly! It isn't just some stupid kids' holiday anymore, Mallory. Everything now is exactly how we were afraid it would be when we were children. Those things out there . . . this is their day!"

"Shut up, Miller. We're safe in here. Protected by the Blue Fire," he added sardonically. He pulled the blanket over his head. "Safe as houses till we starve to death."

Hipgrave pulled Mallory to one side after the herbalism class. He had appeared a different person since they had returned from their nightmarish excursion, more introspective, somehow.

"Can I have a word?" he said. His eyes darted around, uncomfortable at being seen with the black sheep.

"What's up?"

"What do *you* think's going on here, Mallory?"

"Why are you asking me?"

"Because you've got a different perspective on things. You know . . ." He floundered.

"An ungodly one," Mallory said.

Hipgrave nodded, oblivious to the humour. He'd developed a nervous habit of rubbing the knuckles on the back of his left hand; Mallory could see that one of them was sore and calluses had started to build up on the others. "This whole place . . ." He motioned a little too animatedly around the mysterious architecture. ". . . it's not right. No one seems to realise it's all changed . . . But they half remember . . . They talk about it being a result of the Glory of God." He paused. "But I don't see how it can be. It doesn't feel right." He stared off into the middle distance. "I can't talk to Blaine about it."

"I've got no answers, Hipgrave."

The captain's eyes held a devastating desperation that suggested life was slipping away from him. He clutched at Mallory's sleeve. "If we can sort this out, Mallory, everything will be all right." He held on for a second and then drifted slowly away.

"Hipgrave's losing it," Mallory said baldly. "Please excuse the complete lack of sympathy in my voice."

Miller, Daniels, and Gardener followed him across the grassy area that circumnavigated the sprawling cathedral buildings. It was only five p.m. and already dark; it seemed to be getting darker significantly earlier every day. Moonlight cast long, deep shadows all around.

"We gave him a chance to stand with us," Gardener said. "But he's too much of a shit to be decent."

"Well, aren't you the heart of compassion," Daniels jibed.

"You weren't so pleasant when he got Blaine to give you another ten laps on the circuit training." Gardener lit a roll-up, drawing the smoke in deeply.

"I think you're all being too hard on him," Miller ventured. "Yes, he has been unpleasant in the past, but he needs us now, and as Christians we need to give him support . . . extend the hand of friendship."

"Shut up, Miller," they all chanted in unison.

They reached the walls and climbed the ladder to the walkway. The guard greeted them with a curt nod and continued his rounds. "Halloween and all's hell," Mallory called out. He couldn't help a glance toward the pagan camp. A ruddy glow emanated from burning bonfires as they celebrated Samhain and the start of their New Year the following day.

"I'm hungry," Gardener grumbled.

"You're always hungry," Daniels said. He dropped the large bag he had been carrying and squatted down to delve into its contents.

"If they cut the servings any more, we'll just be getting bowls of hot water," Gardener continued. "Bloody turnips and swedes. Give me a bloody big steak, that's what I say."

"A curry," Mallory said. "Balti, preferably."

"Jerk pork." Daniels pulled out a crossbow and handed it to Miller. "Let's see if all that training paid off." He handed other crossbows to Mallory and Gardener.

"Won't they be annoyed at us for wasting ammunition?" Miller said.

"Don't worry, Miller. You can go out and reclaim them all when we're finished." Mallory drew the crossbow and fitted the bolt before looking through the sight as he moved it in an arc over the rooftops. "When you really need street lighting . . ." he sighed.

The guard wandered up. He had the worn features of someone who had worked too hard for too long. "It won't do any good, you know. You can't kill them. The best you can do is hurt them."

"Hurting is good," Mallory said.

"I don't know . . ." the guard mused. "Maybe I should talk this over with the captain."

Mallory clapped a comradely hand on his shoulder. "Look, we're all under pressure here. This is just a bit of aimless sport . . . a bit of R and R and some way to show we're not a waste of space . . . we're not beaten."

"Thumbing our noses," Gardener said in support.

The guard thought about this for a second, then nodded. "Go on. Give 'em hell." He wandered off whistling a Madonna song.

"Right," Gardener said quietly, "let's tear those bastards to pieces."

They knelt down to rest their crossbows on the top of the wall, aiming at the empty road ahead where the supernatural creatures would sooner or later make their nightly appearance. After a while, Miller began to mutter under his breath.

"For God's sake, Miller, what is it?" Mallory muttered.

"I'm not happy with this."

The other three all groaned together. "I'm having a post-traumatic stress disorder flashback," Daniels moaned. "Didn't we go through all this in the refectory? Didn't we talk *at length* before reaching a democratic agreement?"

"Yes, didn't we tell you you're a stupid bastard and to shut up?" Mallory added.

"They're living creatures," Miller protested.

"Debatable," Gardener said.

"They are. They move, they think—"

"But they don't have souls," Gardener said.

"Neither do dogs," Miller said. "But would you advocate sitting up here shooting at a few pets running around out there?"

"If they were the enemy," Mallory said.

"We're Christians," Miller said. "We shouldn't be going out inflicting pain on any living creature. We turn the other cheek . . . that's what we do."

"Eye for an eye," Gardener said. He cranked the bolt, ready to loose it. "They should be coming out any minute, right?"

"Regular as clockwork, so the guards say." Daniels armed his crossbow, too.

"I want to bag one of those little bastards," Gardener said. "Those black eyes they've got really give me the creeps. It's as though they're looking right into you."

There was a movement as if a curtain of mist had been peeled back across the street. In an instant the road was filled with the army of tiny people with their pale skin and large, black eyes. The manifestation was so eerie in its silence and speed that they all felt a frisson. Gardener shuddered as though the beings had come in response to his comments. Though they had shown bravado when they climbed onto the walls, none of them could hide the primal fear evinced by the army of alien men, women, and children in their odd clothes with their bizarre weapons of war.

It took a second or two for them to accept that the siege army was not making any attempt to advance as it had on previous days. Instead, they stood shoulder to shoulder, all hideous dark eyes turned toward the cathedral. An air of unsettling apprehension hung over the scene.

"What are they waiting for?" Daniels asked with irritation born of fear.

Gardener's finger gently caressed the crossbow trigger. "Praying to the Devil," he said. "A Halloween ritual. This is Evil's night."

Mallory felt growing unease. "I'm not sure . . ."

"They'll move soon enough," Gardener said. "Just wait till they get within range, then let rip. I'm going for that little shit on the horse. He looks as though he might be the leader."

"Something's wrong," Mallory said. He let his crossbow slip, then leaned forward so that he could get a better look. "They're waiting for something. It's as if they're listening . . ."

The white faces were turned up slightly, the moon making them glow with a spectral light. Their complete lack of movement was as frightening as their appearance. Gardener couldn't contain himself any longer. He loosed his bolt, but in his tense state his hand shook and it flew off course, embedding in a tiny wagon. The thud echoed across the silent street. Even then none of the creatures moved, nor even acknowledged they had been attacked.

"What *are* they doing?" Daniels said insistently.

"I don't like this," Miller whined.

"Wait," Mallory snapped. He had heard a sound, lost beneath the wind, something that had disturbed him, but it had come from his back, not from the city ahead. He turned and looked across the darkness engulfing the compound. Nothing moved. The only light came from the candles within the cathedral.

"What is it?" Daniels asked.

Mallory strained to catch what lay beneath the wind. "I thought I heard . . ."

"Look at that." Gardener's voice was so filled with repressed terror that they all felt queasy to hear it.

He was pointing over the rooftops. In the distance, rising up like grey smoke against the night sky, was the outline of a horned figure. It was massive, insubstantial, suggestive of great power. It had barely reached its full height when it began to break up and drift away. Instantly lights began to flare across the Stygian landscape beyond the city boundaries.

"Bonfires," Mallory said.

"What does it mean?" Miller whimpered.

"The Devil." Dread had turned Gardener into a shadow of his real self. "The Devil's here."

The noise behind them was now unmistakable and growing louder as voices rose up in support. Mallory heard terror, and disbelief, and grief. It was like wildfire, jumping from one person to the next. It was hard to tell which had the greater impetus—a desire to escape from the terrible threat looming over Salisbury or to respond to the alarm behind them—but they were all instantly in motion, skidding down the ladder and running across the compound to the source of the cries.

They found a small group milling around the cathedral doors. They were throwing their heads back and their hands up, wailing to the heavens. Mallory and the others drove through them to find Julian slumped against the base of the wall. Blood gleamed on his hands and face, so much blood that they were sickened to look at it.

At first, Mallory thought Julian had been stabbed, but as the precentor slowly pulled himself upright, it was clear it was his grief that had brought him to his knees. He didn't appear to be injured at all.

"What's happened?" Mallory yelled above the din. He grabbed Julian by the shoulders, shaking him a little too roughly to disperse the glaze of shock that covered his tearstained face.

Along the walls, the guards called the midnight hour. Slowly, Julian raised his left hand. In the half-light it appeared unnaturally dark; a drip slowly fell from his index finger and splashed in a band of light on the floor where they could see its colour and consistency.

Eventually, Julian found his voice, a cracked, pathetic thing that sounded like winter. "Cornelius has been murdered," he said.

chapter nine

THE WAY OF ALL THE EARTH

"There is a saying uttered in sacred rites that human beings
are in a sort of prison, from which we should not attempt to escape."

Plato

At first, it looked like a pile of abandoned laundry lying behind the altar. Only when Mallory closed on it did he see the white hand twisted upward from the clothes. In the stillness, the drip-drip-drip of blood falling from the altar table was unbearably loud.

"Oh, Lord!" Daniels hissed as he examined the body over Mallory's shoulders. It had been torn apart and was barely recognisable as a man.

Gardener and Miller helped Julian between them; he was almost delirious with shock. "He . . . he said he wanted to pray," the precentor stuttered. "He often came here on his own . . ." His voice ended in a small, strangled cry as his eyes fell on the body.

Miller dropped to his knees, eyes screwed tight so he couldn't see the polluting sight; he looked like a small boy praying at the side of his bed.

"Who'd do a thing like that?" Daniels said, aghast.

To Mallory, that was a question with ramifications to shatter the community: who *would* have committed such a terrible crime? Not any of the supernatural creatures that waited beyond the walls; they couldn't walk on the sacred ground. But could any of the brethren do such a thing? He couldn't imagine that either. The image of the army of tiny people waiting for something to happen lay heavily on his mind, along with the ghostly impression of the Devil appearing over Salisbury at the moment the murder was discovered. They knew. Somehow, in some way.

"Get back! Get back!" Blaine's harsh voice echoed into the far reaches of the cathedral roof. He arrived with Hipgrave dogging his steps, Blaine's face torn by a cornered-animal expression, part fury, part fear; he assimilated the entire scene in an instant, and it didn't seem to affect him at all. Mallory noted Blaine's response carefully. Hipgrave looked as if he'd just woken from the deepest sleep. "Who found him?" Blaine whirled, cold eyes flashing over each of them in turn.

Julian staggered forward. "Me. I did. I . . . I came looking for him . . . thought he might need a hand getting back to his residence. He still wasn't a hundred percent."

"He was like this?" Blaine snapped. "You didn't touch anything?"

"Well . . . I . . . I touched him. I tried to stop the blood. I tried to save him!" His voice rose to a sob, and then he covered his eyes, smearing Cornelius's blood across his face.

Blaine had no time for Julian's grief. "Did you see anybody else?"

Julian gulped air. "No . . . no . . ." he said, composing himself. "Look, we must do this later. We have to care for the body . . ." He covered his eyes again.

Blaine shook his head contemptuously, cursing under his breath but loud enough for Julian to hear. There was more activity further down the nave. The crowd that was hanging back from the awful scene parted like the Red Sea to allow Stefan to sweep through, followed closely by Gibson, the Canon of the Pies, sweating and blowing as he attempted to keep up.

Stefan was ashen-faced when he arrived, but his eyes had a dark avarice about them. Stefan silenced Blaine with a curt wave before he could open his mouth. He went directly to Cornelius's body and knelt beside it in prayer. There was a theatrical note to his action that irked Mallory, but no one else appeared to notice. After a long silence, Stefan dipped his hands in the blood and smeared it on his black robes. "We have lost something great and Godly this night," he said in a quiet, strained voice. Tears ran down his cheeks. "A devout man, the father of us all." He paused before booming angrily, "This crime shall be avenged!"

The act of pantomime was not lost on the crowd gathered further down the nave; cries of support echoed back. Stefan rose and addressed them directly. "This crime is not just against our beloved bishop, nor against us, but against Christianity itself. Someone . . . something . . . has aimed a blow at our very heart, hoping we will fall aside . . . that we shall turn our backs and flee to the shadows. That must not happen! The times ahead will be harder still, and we shall all be called on to stand firm. Trials and tribulations will be inflicted on all of us, but if we each fulfill our role, if we hold our heads high in the Glory of God, then we shall overcome. Go now, in the name of our Lord, Jesus Christ, and carry word of what has happened to all our brothers. Let the period of mourning begin. The time for action shall come."

His words were perfectly chosen. They resonated in the hearts of those watching and as one they turned and hurried from the cathedral.

"Good show," Gibson said when Stefan turned back to them. "*Gravitas*. Perfect. We need to steady the hand on the tiller in this dark time."

Mallory looked to Julian, who had as much right to leadership as Stefan, but Cornelius's advisor and friend sat hunched on a pew, broken by his grief. It was a time for the hard men, Mallory thought.

Blaine turned to Mallory and the knights. "You lot, find a sheet to wrap the . . . ah . . ." He struggled for a word with decorum, but could only come back to *body*. "Take it up to the infirmary and see what Warwick can find out. Then report to the great hall." He turned to Stefan. "I'm getting all the knights together . . . arming up. This might be the first strike in a war. Those things could be attacking even as we speak. We've got to be ready to knock 'em back."

"Well said, Mr. Blaine," Stefan agreed. "I have every faith in you to oversee our defence. Go to it."

Blaine marched away with Hipgrave scurrying and jumping behind him. Stefan and Gibson followed without a backward glance at Cornelius, as if he wasn't there at all.

"Hard men," Mallory said, echoing his earlier thought, "for hard times."

Miller was crying quietly, still in prayer with his eyes shut. He looked as though the final supports of his life had been kicked away. Gardener, too, looked tattered, uncommonly emotional; he wouldn't meet anyone's gaze.

"Better get to it, then." Daniels's shoulders had sagged. He tried to make a hopeful face at Mallory, but it wouldn't fix. "I suppose this isn't the end of it," he sighed.

"No," Mallory replied. "I'm betting it's just the start."

The infirmary was lit by several lanterns that gave an odd, too-bright distortion to all the white tiles. Warwick emerged from a back room wearing pristine white scrubs. He took one look at the leaking sheet slung between Mallory, Gardener, and Daniels, then down at his clothes and gritted his teeth.

"Get it on the table," he snapped.

The knights laid the body out carefully while Warwick stood in the background, muttering with irritation. But when the sopping shroud fell away revealing the face, the medic started, his eyes widening. He looked around at them as if someone was playing a particularly vicious prank on him.

"Murder," Gardener said grimly. "No suspects. Yet."

"What's it all coming to?" Warwick said under his breath. He gingerly lifted the sheet to see the extent of Cornelius's wounds, stared blankly for a moment, then dropped it.

"I think they were hoping for an autopsy," Daniels ventured.

"An autopsy?" Warwick raged. "He's dead. What more do they need to know?"

"What weapon was used. How the attack was carried out," Mallory said. "Who did it."

"I'm a surgeon, not a coroner. That kind of examination requires specialist knowledge."

Gardener snatched a towel from the side and threw it at him. "Do your best." There was so much repressed anger in his voice that Warwick's annoyed reaction was frozen. "From now on, we're all mucking in. Pulling together. We'll do what's expected of us. So get on with it."

172

Brooding, he stalked out of the room. Miller shifted uncomfortably. "Go on," Mallory said to him. "You don't have to hang around if you don't want to."

Miller forced a smile from his tear-streaked face and hurried after Gardener. Mallory and Daniels took up seats in the corner of the room while Warwick brought over a stainless-steel tray of instruments. After that, he called for his assistant, an old man with long white hair who, from his trembling hands, had overheard the news. He prepared to take notes with a precious Biro.

Warwick worked diligently, cutting and probing, occasionally cursing under his breath. His white gown quickly became stained.

"The first patient he's had who never complained," Daniels whispered behind his hand to Mallory.

As the time dragged on, Mallory's attention wandered. "Heard any news on your radio?" he said to Warwick.

Warwick's lips tightened and his eyes flickered toward his assistant. "I haven't got a radio."

"OK, heard any news from people passing through the infirmary," Mallory said pointedly.

"I have." Warwick gingerly held a pair of spring-loaded shears before attacking Cornelius's rib cage. "Still no news from abroad. But there has been . . . talk . . . of a government being established in Oxford."

Daniels grew alert. "The PM survived, then?"

"I don't know who's *in* the government, just that a government is being *set up*," Warwick said irritably. "There'll be some kind of order established within six months, so they say. The first aim is to get communications up and running, including food distribution, particularly to urban areas—"

"I can't believe anyone's crazy enough to stay in the cities," Mallory said. "What are they going to eat? They must have looted everything they can get their hands on by now."

"—and then they're hoping to get some kind of local power sources up and running, if they can," Warwick continued.

"How are they going to do that?" Daniels said. "I heard all the nuclear power stations had gone . . . wiped out somehow. There can't be any kind of oil or gas supplies—"

"I'm only reporting what I heard," Warwick snapped.

Daniels clapped his hands. "Things could be getting back to normal," he said enthusiastically.

"Whoop-de-doo." Mallory remained unmoved.

"What's wrong with you?"

"Don't you remember what it was like? Work, money, power-seeking, mundanity, no time for anyone to live or breathe . . ."

"You need to lighten up, Mallory. It was never as bad as all that."

"Yes, it was—you just get numb to it. You sink down into it, like a swamp, and forget there's fresh air above. The clock has been set back at zero, Daniels— it's a chance finally to get things right. It doesn't mean we have to take on board all the shit to get the good stuff back, but that's the way it's going to be if the same old people end up in charge again. They've got a vested interest in the society we had before. It made them fat and rich and powerful."

"You know what you are Mallory—an anarchist."

"You say that as though it's a bad thing."

"If you two have completed your irrelevant navel-gazing, I've finished here." Warwick covered the body with a little more reverence than he had shown before.

"What did you find?" Daniels asked.

"It's inconclusive."

"That's all you can say after all that?"

"He's been torn apart with such frenzy it's impossible to tell what weapon was used. It could just as easily have been a wild animal, if there were any indigenous species that could attack with this ferocity."

Daniels looked to Mallory. "So we've got someone in here who's such a mess in the head we can't tell if he's a man or an animal?"

"Now see what happens when you take red meat out of the diet." Mallory had a sudden overview of the whole situation that left him cold. "So we've got all those things outside the walls trapping us in here, and now we've got this psycho inside with us. I can think of a lot of clichés to describe our situation, but they all involve dumb animals being eaten up by smarter, wilder ones."

Daniels stared blankly into the middle distance. "What are we going to do now?"

The great hall had the uneasy atmosphere that permeated all the new buildings, but it was made even worse by the spiralling desperation and anxiety in the wake of Cornelius's murder. The vast expanse was filled with clustering shadows not even a row of blazing torches could dispel. The furthest the illumination reached was a row of hideous oversized gargoyles halfway up the wall. Whoever had designed them had made it seem as though they were looking down on those assembled below either disapprovingly or threateningly, depending on your perspective.

The knights stood in two ranks. Most shuffled and muttered apprehensively at what might now lie ahead for them. The Blues, though, were silent and disciplined, eyes fixed firmly ahead as if on parade. Mallory watched them with the wariness of a competing species. They were *too* professional, too far removed from the other knights; and probably too ruthless and violent as well, if Blaine had truly cast them in his own image. Why had he seen fit to create an élite force of knights? Why not simply train all knights to the same standard? And why were they so rarely seen around the cathedral? What special project did Blaine have them working on? The more he understood the hierarchies and powers within the cathedral, the more suspicious he became of them on every level.

Blaine marched in after they had been assembled for twenty minutes. He was accompanied by Hipgrave, who had managed to shake off some of the daze that had characterised him earlier, and the captain of the Blues, a muscular, square-jawed thirty-year-old by the name of Roeser.

Blaine didn't waste time getting to the crux of the matter. "You'll all have heard the news by now. The bishop is dead . . . murdered . . . perpetrator unknown. Others are dealing with the leadership fallout of such a great loss at such a difficult time. Our role in this is clearly defined and we must be single-minded about its execution, despite the many obvious distractions the days ahead must hold. Although security has been foremost in our minds ever since we established ourselves here in Salisbury, our defences have still been compromised. I will be launching an immediate inquiry to discover exactly what went wrong, and if there have been any lapses in the responsibilities of individuals, make no mistake, they will be severely punished.

"But the most pressing concern is to ensure that whoever carried out this atrocity is caught and brought to immediate justice before he can commit any further crimes. This will naturally entail some short-term loss of personal freedom. Some movement around the compound will be restricted. Premises and possessions may be searched and confiscated. There will undoubtedly be detailed questioning and cross-questioning. Patrols will have to be stepped up." He paused. "The use of lethal force will be approved. The safety of the brethren is our overarching concern. Unfortunately, that means we may have to take actions that go against our nature, but we make these sacrifices as Christians, for the benefit of others. It is our job sometimes to do unpleasant things so the brethren do not have to. That is the cross we bear.

"All of you are security-minded and will understand the necessity of these measures to prevent any more acts of unadulterated Evil. In this role, we will need to be seen to be acting with the utmost rigour and decorum. Anyone who lets the side down will not want to live, believe me. Captains Hipgrave and Roeser will oversee your allocation into effective units with particular responsibilities. A more structured shift pattern will be drawn up to accommodate these changes. One other thing: we shall be working alongside the Inquisition of Heretical Depravity and your full cooperation will be required." He nodded curtly and exited. It was a well-rehearsed speech that Mallory found quite chilling, the more so for its modulated language.

"He's left Hipgrave in charge? Blaine's crazy," Daniels whispered. "Look at him—he's falling apart. I wouldn't let Hipgrave oversee a Sunday school."

"I don't like the sound of any of this," Mallory said.

"Why not?" Gardener said sullenly. "It's necessary."

"Is it? Sounds to me like an overreaction. Or a chance for people who love control and discipline to seize more of it."

"We don't want any of that weak talk." There was an uncommonly harsh edge to Gardener's voice. "If we go soft now we won't stand a chance. You think those things out there are soft? You think the Devil's soft?"

"All right, Gardener, calm down." Daniels laid a steadying hand on his shoulder. "We're all in this together and we'll all play our part."

Mallory wanted to talk about how the *loss of personal freedom* and the involvement of the Inquisition in a criminal affair was more evidence of the medieval mentality that had infected the cathedral, but he bit his tongue. There were times when there was no arguing with Gardener.

Miller was pale and wide-eyed. "I've been thinking—"

"You don't learn, do you, Miller?" Mallory said.

"No one in this cathedral could have done that awful thing to the bishop," Miller continued. "You say those creatures outside can't come in here, but do we know that for sure? I think this is linked to the appearance of all the new buildings. Sometimes they seem as though they go on forever. The killer . . . the Devil . . . could be hiding in there."

They all thought about this for a moment until Mallory said, "Have you had a blow to the head, Miller? A good idea—unbelievable."

"We should tell Hipgrave . . ." Daniels began, until he saw the captain's blank expression as he wandered along the lines splitting the knights into groups.

"This is down to us," Gardener said, with fire. "We've got to search the place."

"We'll have to do it without Blaine knowing," Mallory said. "He'll think we're just skiving. Or worse, involved in some way. It'll be hard."

Gardener gripped his wrist forcefully. "We can do it."

Strands of luminescent mist drifted eerily across the rolling moor, collecting in the hollows where it turned with a life of its own. Boulders of dark grey granite were scattered here and there amongst clumps of spiky gorse and saplings swaying gently in the breeze. It was night. Across the sable sky a trail of stars swirled, diamond lights, cold and sharp. A full moon hung high overhead casting a bright light that painted the landscape silver and sent long black shadows stretching out across the stony path along which Mallory walked. It had the feel of late-summer-turning-autumn about it: still warm enough for shirtsleeves but with an encroaching chill.

Mallory paused to survey the moon and stars for a long period. They mesmerised him, spoke loudly of infinite wonder and distant magic. The air smelled so good, thick with the rich perfume of nighttime vegetation. His breathing was deep; he felt at peace.

He followed the path across the moor to a thick glade on a hill that rose up out of the flat countryside. The oak and ash, rowan and hawthorn were all ancient, their trunks twisted, their branches heavy and gnarled. Beneath their cover it was cooler, tranquil. Dry twigs crunched beneath his feet; the leaf mold felt like a carpet.

"Hello, Mallory."

Her voice sounded like the chime of a crystal glass, filling him with such a swell of emotion that he felt as if he was rising off the ground.

"Everything is so heightened here," he said.

"You'll get used to it."

Sophie leaned nonchalantly against an oak tree, her arms folded. He thought how beautiful she looked there, not just in the superficial qualities of her features, but in the complexity of intelligence he saw in her dark eyes; there were depths he could never plumb. Emotions rose in him mysteriously, the truth freed from the chains of conditioning and fear. In that potent place, the pure part of him that he kept tucked away, recognised connections not made on any physical plane, bonds that transcended consciousness.

"You look amazing," he said.

She laughed gently. "You are so going to regret saying that when you're out of this place."

The moon broke through the branches to highlight her, centre stage. "Why are we here?" he asked.

Once more dark and troubled, she looked away through the trees, out across the rolling moor. "I wanted to see you."

Her mood triggered his memory of the incident in the camp with Gardener, and all the blood. "I'm sorry for what happened," he said. "I felt bad about that. If I could have found any way to put it right . . ."

"I can see that now. Here, in this place, things are much clearer. That's why I came."

Puzzled, he looked around as if he were seeing the glade for the first time. "This place—"

"Here we strip away the barriers we put up against the world." She smiled again. "Well, you do. I'm used to it."

Perspective began creeping up on him. "Am I dreaming?"

"If you want to look at it with a limited perception, sure."

"You're as infuriating in my dreams as you are in real life."

"I try," she said.

"Are you practising your Craft? Is that what this is?"

"I don't practice anymore, Mallory. I'm a professional at this now." She stepped away from the tree and led the way deeper into the glade. Mallory followed her without a second thought. Her voice floated back to him, detached, ethereal. "So . . . now I've seen you . . . seen the truth in you . . . I forgive you."

"Thank you."

"But not those who you hang out with. Never that."

"No." He wanted to touch her hair, it looked so silky in the moonlight, but she was just a little too far ahead. "Where is this place?"

"Inside your head. Outside your head. Like I said, it depends on your perception." Her fingers brushed the trees as she passed as if she were caressing them.

"Can I kiss you?"

She chuckled quietly. "You want to bite down on those emotions, Mallory, or you're going to have no protection when you get back to the world."

"Well?" His unrestrained feelings burned through him like electricity. He recognised how deeply he felt about her, wanted to grab her and make love to her, do all the things he couldn't do in the real world of barriers and hardship and obligation. The purity of emotion was so overwhelming it was hallucinogenic, a drug he never wanted to give up. Did she feel the same way?

When she turned to face him, he saw for the first time the honesty in her that she had spoken about in him, and he realised that here, perhaps, was someone with whom he could spend the rest of his life. "Not this time," she said. "I want to be sure I have the measure of you. I choose my friends carefully, Mallory, but once my mind is made up I keep them close to me forever."

"You seem so much older than your age."

"Not older, wiser. I'm a wise woman. I've learned a lot in my few years, but there's a lot more to learn. Stick with me, Mallory—some of it might rub off."

"I'd like that."

This time she covered her mouth when she laughed. "You are going to be *so* sick the next time we meet face to face."

"You're in your camp . . . I'm trapped in the cathedral," he began. "Can we meet up like this again?"

"Very *Romeo and Juliet*, isn't it?" She looked a little sad at this. "Yes, we can meet again."

"How do I come here . . . contact you?"

"You don't. I'm in charge here, Mallory, don't forget that." Her laughter was infectious; he felt an honest smile for the first time in a long while. "I'll be back in touch."

She moved off through the trees, but although he tried to keep up, she drew ahead rapidly. "Don't go," he called.

Her voice came back like moonlight. "I'll be back." And then she was gone. And so was he.

Mallory woke in the best mood he had felt for a long time, not knowing why, but with the sense of something wonderful hovering just beyond his grasp. Even the biting cold of the room didn't dull his elation.

It was still two hours to daybreak, but the cathedral was already alive. Torches blazed around the cobbled meeting square at the heart of the new buildings. Breath formed white clouds as the knights stamped their boots and clapped their hands to keep warm. A group of about twenty brothers had assembled to one side where they were being given shovels, pickaxes, and wooden props.

Blaine marched along the ranks, wrapped in a thick cloak but with the hood pulled back so that everyone could see his eyes. He paused briefly at Mallory, allowing a silent warning to rise up in his face before he moved on. It was nothing new, but an uneasy thought crept up on Mallory: if things went bad a scapegoat would be needed, and he was the most likely candidate. It would be in his own interest to have a contingency plan for escape the moment the tunnel was completed.

"They're going to have their work cut out for them," Daniels whispered, nodding toward the digging party.

"I'd pick up a spade myself if I thought it would get me out of here any quicker," Mallory said.

"No talking." Hipgrave stood before them. His face was cold and hard and clear of the dazed attitude they had seen the previous day. He leaned between them and said quietly, "I've had a revelation. The Devil is here, in the cathedral. And it's up to us to exorcise him. It was the five of us, you see . . . the five points of the inverted pentacle. We were the ones who brought him in. We're the only ones who can get him out. We'll discuss this later." He walked away, casting only a cursory glance over the other knights.

"Lordy," Daniels said. "He's set up home in the bughouse."

An oppressive sense of claustrophobia fell across Mallory. The walls were closing in, shutting down options, filling him with a desperate feeling that he would never get out alive.

Blaine had them all on ceaseless patrols throughout the day to keep them occupied while plans were formulated. Meanwhile, other events were clearly taking place behind the scenes. From the roof, Mallory watched grim-faced elders hurrying back and forth between the bishop's palace and the new buildings, occasionally pausing to talk animatedly to each other. Every now and then a gaggle of six or seven would congregate, their voices rising in debate until they spotted someone drawing near. Stefan, however, was nowhere to be seen.

Up there, he had a clear view of the pagan camp where the Samhain bonfires still burned. Occasionally, he could smell cooking food and hear music drifting on the cold wind. Briefly, he entertained the fantasy that he could see Sophie and she could see him, but it only made him feel worse and he forced himself to stop.

As Mallory made his way down from the roof, he came across two of the brothers talking conspiratorially as they loitered in an alcove beneath one of the great staircases. There was something in their tone that made Mallory pause on the steps to listen.

"I'm getting out of here first chance I get—soon as that tunnel's open," one of them said in a Black Country accent.

"You can't turn your back on us," the other one, another Midlander, said. "You can't turn your back on the Lord!"

"When I first talked about coming down here, the missis said I was mad. We'd prayed all the way through that bloody nightmare after the Fall, and nothing. People died, people suffered. No Second Coming. There were miracles all over the shop, but for us . . . Christians . . . not a tweet. But I said to her, 'Don't expect miracles. Just know Jesus is with you. That's all we can ask of Him.'"

"That's right. That's exactly right."

"So she walked out on me and I came down here. But I kept my chin up . . . I kept my faith." His voice turned disconsolate at the end.

"Mickey—"

"Now look what's happened—it's gone from bad to bloody worse. This was supposed to be the big shining example—a new start, spreading the Word, bringing hope to the people." He laughed bitterly. "And now we're trapped, and we're going to be starving, and winter's coming in, and the Devil's at the gates, and now some bastard's picking us off inside! The bishop, I ask you! Not even he's safe! What's the bloody point if God doesn't even save him? You know what it says to me? Either He doesn't care or He isn't there."

"Mickey!"

"I've had enough, Glen. How long do you keep on praying before you realise no one's listening?"

There was something profoundly depressing in what Mallory had heard. He didn't hang around to hear the rest of the conversation.

By late afternoon, the wan, grey light had just about eked away. Blaine was locked in some meeting with the Church elders and Hipgrave was nowhere to be found, so the knights found themselves at an unusual loss. Most of them congregated in their dorms, trading rumours and making predictions, but Gardener pulled Mallory, Miller, and Daniels over to one side. "Fancy a party?"

"When you say 'party,'" Mallory replied wearily, "do you mean a hymn-singing, praying kind of party?"

"No," Gardener said. "I mean a drinking kind of party."

They all brightened, but he rebuffed their questions, insisting they had to follow him. There was a hint of snow in the air as they hurried outside and then into the sprawling complex. After a roundabout route, they eventually emerged through a door that led into the rear of the kitchens.

"How did you find this way?" Miller asked. "I didn't even know there was a door here."

"Did a bit of poking around earlier." Gardener clapped his hands and grinned at the prospect of what lay ahead.

The kitchens were comfortingly warm with the heat of the ranges still radiating after that evening's dinner, and the fragrant smell of vegetables and herbs hanging in the air. Exhausted after their most hectic period, the cooks and their assistants lounged around chatting next to the massive open hearth on which a cauldron of water bubbled over a log fire. They looked up briefly when the knights entered, but were too engrossed in their conversation to pay them any more attention.

Gardener caught the eye of one of the cooks who slyly slid out of the periphery of the group to come over. He had a shaven head and acne scars that gave him quite a frightening demeanour.

"You'll have me for the bleedin' high jump, Gardener," he whispered in a London accent.

Gardener pulled out a tobacco tin and waved it under his nose. "Do you want this or not?"

The cook went to grab it, but Gardener snatched it back at the last moment. "Oi!" the cook said. "Don't you go pissing me about, you Northern bastard."

"Just want to make sure you know the terms of the deal, laddie."

"'Course I bleedin' know. We went over them enough times." His eyes lit up as he succeeded in snatching the tin. "I haven't had a good smoke in a bleedin' year." He nodded toward a door not far from the one through which they had entered. "It's in there. Just keep it down. And if that fat bastard Gibson finds you, I had nothing to do with it, right?"

Gardener led them through the door and down some steps into a vast vaulted cellar filled with the heavy aroma of wine and wood. A single torch burned on the wall next to the door, but it cast enough light for them to see rows of barrels and racks of dusty bottles stretching into the shadows.

"Bloody hell!" Mallory said jubilantly. "We've got about three turnips to go around the whole cathedral and enough booze to swamp the city. Talk about getting your priorities right."

"I thought we needed a bit of cheering up, like," Gardener said. "It's the bishop's stash—for entertaining, I suppose. I think a load was brought in from all the local hotels when we set up here, but they've been brewing their own stuff for the last year, in case the water supply got polluted."

Mallory plucked a vintage bottle from the rack and used his Swiss Army knife to crack open the cork. "Here's to Cornelius, God rest his soul," he said, swigging a large mouthful from the neck. "A man after my own heart. *Let them drink wine!*"

"Should we be doing this?" Miller asked uncertainly.

"Yes, we should." Daniels moved slowly along the racks until he found a year and grape to his taste. "God's bountiful supply is for all men, not just the élite."

"Look at you," Mallory said, "a connoisseur!"

"You wouldn't know good taste if it kissed you on the behind, Mallory." Daniels sniffed the cork before letting the smallest amount settle on his tongue. "Wonderful. I had my own cellar in the old life," he added with his eyes closed, savouring the taste. "I was building up a nice little collection."

"Sorry for misunderstanding," Mallory said. "I just thought it was stuff you drank."

"Philistine."

"There's beer here too, y'know." Gardener caressed one of the casks. "Pretty good stuff according to that cockney bugger up there. They've done some nice porter, he says." Black liquid flowed from the tap into a tasting cup. "That hits the spot," he said, smacking his lips.

"See?" Mallory said to Daniels. "It isn't all bad. There are still plenty of little luxuries if you look carefully enough."

They pulled up some old packing crates into a circle and settled down. Once they began to talk, Miller came alive, the gloom that had descended on him since the bishop's death gradually evaporating. He hung on every word the others said, joining in when he could, nodding his support, smiling so widely Mallory was convinced his face would ache the following day.

Over the course of three hours, they got through several bottles of wine while Gardener had made Herculean inroads into one of the casks. In his merriment, he appeared a different person, his laughter rich and constant, his eyes disappearing in crinkles every time he showed his humour. He would sit on his crate and rock backward until the others were convinced he would fall off, but he always managed to catch himself with a jolt at the last moment.

They talked about music—Gardener loved the sixties sounds, Miller liked Slipknot and Marilyn Manson, Daniels preferred classical—about football (Daniels professed to know nothing about it), and TV, and radio (with Gardener wondering aloud what would be happening in *The Archers* right then), about food, and politics. And then, as they would have expected, they turned, in their cups, to their old lives, and the people who had meant much but were no longer with them. It wasn't maudlin in the slightest, just a fond remembrance of happier days, when problems existed without the stark simplicity of life or death.

Gardener spoke at length about his wife and a touring holiday they'd had in Scotland when they had finally reconciled themselves to never having children. "We were sad, like, but in a way, it was like this big bloody weight was lifted overnight," he mused. "We could get on with life again, start enjoying things."

Daniels discussed with unabashed joy the first trip he had made with his new partner, to the Greek Islands. "He told me on the second night that he was giving up his flat so he could move near me, if that was what I wanted," he said, with shining eyes. "Can you believe that? Even at that stage he was prepared to sacrifice what he had. He knew . . . we both knew . . . instantly."

Miller ventured a little information about his parents and his childhood in Swindon, but when he began to talk about the girlfriend who had abandoned him, he dried up and briefly turned gloomy again. But after a moment's silence, he piped up, unable to contain his emotion. "I'm so glad I found you all," he said. "I've never had friends like you. You saved my life . . ." He looked to Mallory. ". . . you've taught me things, you've cheered me up. You've been like family . . . better than family. This is what life is all about, you know." The honest swell of emotion brought tears to Miller's eyes and he blinked them away unselfconsciously. "If it all goes bad from here, it's been worthwhile."

"Don't talk so pissed-up," Gardener chided gently, though it was obvious he was touched by Miller's comments.

Mallory was about to join in the teasing of Miller when a movement caught his eye deep in the heart of the shadows at the back of the cellar. He held up a warning hand and the others grew instantly alert. "Who's there?" he called out.

His voice bounced off the arched ceiling and rustled around the casks. Nothing moved. Slowly, he stood up and drew his sword. The others followed suit, turning to face the back of the room.

As they stood alert, Miller suddenly shuddered. He looked around at the others with wide eyes. "Did you feel that? Cold . . . as if someone rubbed against me . . ."

The hairs on the back of Mallory's neck stood erect; iron filings filled his mouth and the back of his throat. He *could* feel something . . . an invisible presence . . . moving around them.

"It's over there," Daniels whispered, pointing to another part of the cellar.

"No, there." Gardener nodded to the opposite side of the room.

"It's all over," Mallory said.

Now they could see he was right: there was movement on every side just beyond the edge of the shadows. It seemed to Mallory that whatever was there wasn't quite in the world but rather a step removed, as if it were behind a veil trying to find a way through.

"Stand firm," Gardener said, all trace of drunkenness gone from him.

"It's the ghosts," Miller said in a hollow voice.

And once he said it, Mallory could see. The shadowy forms had the shape of men in long robes. They moved lethargically, roaming back and forth around the cellar's edge, seemingly oblivious to the knights. Pinpricks of green, the lamps of eyes, glowed with increasing force. They were coming closer.

"Bloody hell, let's get out of here," Gardener hissed. They dropped their bottles and cups and ran up the steps, slamming the door behind them.

They stumbled out into the biting cold of the night, where they rested against the stone walls, taking deep, calming breaths.

"Bloody hell, that was spooky," Gardener said.

"Did you feel it?" Daniels adjusted his eye patch. "They were coming for us. They wanted to—"

"Punish us," Mallory completed. They all understood it on some level they couldn't explain.

Miller looked from one to the other, his eyes wide and white in the dark. "I thought the demons couldn't get in here."

Despite himself, Mallory gave Miller a reassuring pat on the back. "Those things out there can't. These were different."

"How?" Miller said desperately.

A brief flurry of snow stung Mallory's face; the weather was taking a turn for the worse. "The things in there were wearing—"

"Habits and clerics' robes," Daniels interrupted. "They're our own."

Miller looked even more shocked at this. "But—"

"Who knows what the hell's going on around here?" Mallory said.

They shivered in silence until the wind died enough for them to hear the clamour of fighting just beyond the walls. The nightly attack was beginning to wind down.

"Let's take a look," Mallory said.

As they neared the walls, they were surprised to see frantic activity. The guards were desperately setting up sheet metal, hammering in nails to hold it in place.

"What's going on?" Daniels called out.

One of the guards turned, anxiety gnawing at his features. "Repairs. The wall started to buckle here." They all knew why he looked so worried: that had never happened before.

"Either they're getting stronger or we're getting weaker," Mallory said.

The guard turned back to his work, his voice echoing back to them. "They nearly broke it down," he said. "They nearly got in here."

chapter ten
AFTER THE FIRE,
A STILL, SMALL VOICE

"A fire takes on the aroma of whatever spice is thrown in it."
Heraclitus

The peal of bells at noon should have sounded joyful, yet it had an oddly leaden note to it as if it were heralding a warning instead of a celebration. The entire brotherhood, packed into the cathedral for the announcement, waited with a measure of hope. Mallory had already decided that what was to come was a foregone conclusion, though no one believed him. "Stefan hasn't got enough experience in the Church," Daniels said. "They'll go for a continuity candidate, somebody with the weight of Cornelius."

Mallory tried to explain that, as in all shifts of power, it would simply go to whoever wanted it badly enough. Daniels had countered that Stefan had professed he didn't want it at all—he was happy with his lot. Mallory praised him for a life untainted with cynicism—or reality. They agreed to differ.

The Church elders sat impassively in the quire, though Mallory thought he saw a hardness in some of their features that suggested which way the wind had blown.

It was Julian, the man who should have been Cornelius's anointed successor but who was probably too young and too pleasant, who made the announcement.

"The Chapter of Canons has deliberated long and hard over the last twenty-four hours. The choice of who should become our new bishop was never going to be easy." His voice was strong, filling the vast structure. "We took advice from some of the most learned and wisest members of our Church before reaching our decision. We considered the merits of many before coming to our conclusion. In the end, it was a harder decision than anyone dreamed, but it must be one that you all accept, for anything less than a united front could be the end of us."

Mallory thought it interesting that he made this point so early in his speech.

Julian took a deep breath before continuing, his gaze fixed on the sunlight breaking through the stained-glass windows. "There are some amongst you who probably feel we are rushing toward this with unseemly haste. Indeed, that was my own opinion. However, the case has been made that we are in a time of crisis . . . if not war . . . and that to leave the Church leaderless at this time would be

185

an abdication of responsibility with potentially lethal results. This is a time when we must all pull together, for our own survival and for the survival of the Church. The case, too, was made that the strongest leadership will be necessary. Thoughtful debate and a desire to consider all sides is a peacetime luxury. I accept now that we need a clear vision, a brave heart, and a strong stomach. An ability to call, perhaps, for sacrifices from us all. And who knows the importance of sacrifice better than we? Our Lord Jesus Christ died to redeem all mankind. Against that, the sacrifices demanded of us must seem petty. And so we shall stand firm, and do what is asked of us."

He appeared at that moment to be talking to himself. He caught himself after a long pause and fixed his attention back on the rapt audience. "The new bishop is well known to you, and I'm sure you're perfectly aware of the qualities we saw in him." He took a step to one side and made an awkward gesture that had more of the theatrical about it than any honest emotion. "Our new bishop is Stefan."

A ripple ran through the crowd, though whether it was appreciative or not was hard to tell. Mallory tried to catch Daniels's eye, but his friend pointedly avoided him.

Stefan emerged from the wings with an air of studied gravitas. "Thank you, Julian. I am truly humbled by the trust you have all placed in me, and I pray that I can find the strength to live up to expectations. This is not a position I wished for—I was content to serve in the role God had granted me—and certainly not in these terrible circumstances. But I will not shirk this calling. I will continue to serve God, and you, to the best of the abilities with which He has gifted me." He continued to move his gaze across the congregation as if he were speaking to each one personally. "There will be some changes . . . we need to be stronger if we are to avoid any more tragedies . . . but this is not the time to talk of them. The Chapter of Canons will convene shortly to discuss the new rules I have planned and an announcement will be made soon. Now, let us join together in prayer for my predecessor, Cornelius, a devout man who provided many lessons for us all."

As they bowed their heads, Daniels finally did look over. Mallory was surprised by what he saw in his face: it looked very much like fear.

The ceremony anointing Stefan had been stripped of pomp and ceremony under the circumstances and took less than an hour. Afterward, Mallory and Gardener went to inspect the digging. Piles of soil lay all around, but the diggers had now hit the expected obstacle of the gravel that provided the solid foundation for the cathedral.

"They need to make it deep and wide enough to bring provisions in," Gardener mused.

"And when they could have made it just wide enough for one man," Mallory said.

Gardener eyed him suspiciously. "You're not thinking of running out on us, are you?"

"With the way things have been going here, I can honestly say I'd rather be anywhere—even London."

"You're just a soft Southern shit, Mallory," Gardener deadpanned. "The first bit of bloody hardship and you fall apart."

"Well, I wasn't brought up wearing a horsehair shirt in a leaky hovel, you Northern bastard."

Gardener fixed himself a roll-up.

"Where do you get that supply of tobacco from, anyway?" Mallory asked.

"Don't ask me that, and I won't ask you what you did before you got here." Mallory winced; was it that obvious? "What do you think of the new boss, then?"

"Good choice, I reckon."

"Yeah? Can't see it myself."

"He's a tough bloke. That's what we need right now: somebody who can take control."

"That's what they said in the Weimar Republic."

Gardener inhaled the smoke deeply. "Sometimes, Mallory, I think you're from another bloody planet."

November advanced relentlessly. The nights were always bitter, the days harsher than anyone remembered from previous years. Winter threatened a furious assault.

Stefan quickly but cautiously exerted his control over the rule of the cathedral, though he did it with a smiling, always moderate face. The Inquisition was brought into the structure of authority alongside the knights, "to root out seditious elements amongst the brothers" so Stefan said, although Mallory saw no sign of treason; most were too broken for that. Yet Stefan made no overt move to change the day-to-day governance of life in the cathedral. Instead, he preferred to make daily pronouncements filled with platitudes about how spirits were high, how the brethren had grown even more devout, how the Lord was with them in the face of adversity.

The hangover from Cornelius's death was strong, affecting the mood deeply so that everyone expected something worse to come. The supplies were also diminishing rapidly, the dishes becoming more imaginative to utilise the sparse range of vegetables remaining in the stores. They'd even started slaughtering the milk-producing cows; the sheep, pigs, and chickens were already gone.

The detailed questioning of everyone in the cathedral regarding Cornelius's murder had continued unabated without any noticeable advances. There had been no further outbreaks of violence, but that did little to make anyone feel more secure.

Mallory, Miller, Daniels, and Gardener had been kept under such a strict timetable that they had not found any opportunities to search for the killer anywhere beyond the very edges of the shadowy shifting zone. "We've got to find some way to get in there—it's our responsibility," Miller urged at every opportunity, until he was shouted down by the other three every time the first few words came from his lips. Eventually, Mallory, as their unelected leader, was convinced that he should talk to Hipgrave, who, though plainly unstable, had the same object in mind and could manipulate the work rotas. Mallory silently resolved to put it off until the last moment.

The tunnel progressed slowly, through several collapses, much to the annoyance of everyone who saw the short distance that had to be traversed; there were simply no engineers in the cathedral, and in such a precarious environment best guesses didn't work. The dismal mood was made worse by the sounds of music and gaiety that floated over the wall from the travellers' camp beyond.

And every night the hordes of hell attacked with a vigour that had not been evident at the onset, as if they sensed that their moment was coming. Their tactics had changed too: instead of a frontal assault, they would sometimes storm Ste. Anne's Gate in the east, or Harnham Gate in the south. Occasionally, they would disrupt the metal sheeting or bring cracks to stone that had stood firm for centuries, prompting frenzied repairs. For so long the brethren had felt secure in their fortress. Now fear was rising that it was only a matter of time before the beasts broke through.

Blaine summoned the knights on the morning of November the thirteenth. It was a bright day, the first warm one for weeks, and that helped raise spirits a little.

Since Stefan's coronation, the knights' commander had rarely been seen, locking himself away with Hipgrave and Roeser to discuss strategy before debating it with Stefan and Broderick, whose role as leader of the Inquisition had earned him a place at the new bishop's right hand. That morning, Blaine had the bright-eyed look of someone finally ready for vengeance. He strode to the front of the great hall with purpose and a spring in his step. Hipgrave and Roeser took up positions behind him and to either side.

"I'm sure all this waiting around getting beaten on has annoyed you as much as it has me." He had a gleam in his eye and a faint, cruel smile on his lips. "Well, you'll be pleased to know that period is now officially over. We're not scared, we're not weak. We're men . . . men of God . . . and now we're going to show that we can't be forced to cower, or hide. That we're not going to be overrun. It's time for us to stand up proudly and *prove* who we are." He ground his teeth together so hard everyone on the front row heard it. "Now we strike back."

Hipgrave and Roeser disappeared to the back of the hall and returned with a long, low crate. They levered off the lid with a dagger, delved into the straw packing, and removed two rifles, both of which looked like Second World War issue. Hipgrave handed one to Blaine, who checked the loading mechanism and sighting.

"In the basement of the former regimental headquarters of the Royal Gloucestershire, Berkshire, and Wiltshire Regiment, now part of the cathedral compound, there is a store of weapons and a limited supply of ammunition," he said, still admiring the sighting. "They're not exactly top of the range, but they still pack a pretty big punch."

"Bastard didn't dish those out when we were riding into the danger zone," Mallory hissed to Daniels.

"He was saving them for people who mattered," Daniels replied wryly.

Blaine tossed the rifle back to Hipgrave, who deposited it back in the box. "For too long those devils have attacked us freely. They think we haven't got any teeth. Tonight we're going to show them that we have. Tonight we're going to make them scared of *us*, by hitting one of the most important, powerful demons out there. Prepare yourself for a tremendous victory. We gather on the rooftop at nineteen hundred hours precisely tomorrow night."

As he left the great hall, a ripple of impromptu applause ran through the knights. Even Mallory, who had no respect for the authority or badge, felt a wave of excitement at the thought of finally doing something after weeks of inactivity.

In the end, it was Hipgrave who made the first move. Mallory was finishing a small bowl of thin carrot soup after a hard morning of physical training and overseeing repairs to the walls when the captain crossed the refectory purposefully.

"Mallory," Hipgrave said with a curt nod, knowing they were being watched. But when he sat down he leaned across the table conspiratorially. "There's something I want you to see."

"I'm surprised you've found the time to come here. Blaine seems to be relying on you more and more."

Hipgrave gave a self-satisfied smile. "It often takes a crisis for someone's true worth to be recognised. But if anything, it's only made me more aware of my responsibilities. We have to flush that devil out before it strikes again, Mallory. And it will, make no mistake, because that's its nature." He rubbed his chin thoughtfully. Mallory could see the instability clearly upon him, in the long, odd pauses in his speech or the exaggerated gestures he often made to underline a point. It wouldn't take much for him to crack. "I have to be honest here, Mallory, you wouldn't have been my first choice to stand at my shoulder on this. You've not got the military mind. You're subversive and untrustworthy."

"Thanks," Mallory said, draining the last of his soup.

Hipgrave dropped a hand firmly on Mallory's wrist. "This is no joke, Mallory. We have been gifted with a tremendous responsibility. I spent a long time wrestling with why I was made to suffer by seeing the changes that happened in this place when everyone else was blind to it. Why I was made to be an outsider." Mallory realised this was the worst thing that could have happened to Hipgrave. "And then I realised it was because I had been chosen by the Lord, for a mission."

"Or it could have been a coincidence."

"In your world, Mallory. In my world, a world ruled by God, there are no coincidences. Everything that happens is through His Will. He chose me to be His instrument in ridding this holy place of Evil. And I choose you to help me. I have to choose you, because you have the God-given eyes to see clearly too. I don't profess to know the Lord's mind in this, and I cannot begin to understand what He sees in you, Mallory. But you fit into His plan somewhere, and I have to go along with that."

"Well, glad I'm not a fifth wheel."

"Now, come with me." Hipgrave walked a few paces ahead of Mallory as if he were leading him out for some menial task. Once they were away from the eyes of the brethren, he relaxed a little. "I've been doing some exploring myself. These new buildings are very strange indeed. They change their layout, you know. Not in any obvious way—I mean, if we want to get to the great hall we get there. It's just that sometimes the route is different. Three long corridors one day, two corridors and a set of stairs the next. I've been keeping detailed notes. But that's not the only thing."

He led Mallory into a small chapel on the periphery of the new section. There was a plain altar and cross at one end, and three rows of wooden chairs. At the back stood a small desk covered with masses of candles; most of them had burned right down, their wax set in a great white flood across the desk and onto the floor, like the lava flow of a volcano.

Hipgrave headed over to the wood-panelled wall behind the altar and began to work his way along it, tapping. When he found what he was looking for he turned to Mallory, smiling triumphantly, and said, "Watch this." He pressed the panel forcefully in the top two corners and it slid back silently. Mallory felt a rush of cold, dank air. "A secret passage," Hipgrave said redundantly.

He went to the back of the room, selected a candle with a little life, and lit it with his flint.

"Are you sure this is a good idea?" If the main corridors changed their route continually, Mallory didn't feel comfortable going into a secret network that might be even more unpredictable.

"No need to worry," Hipgrave replied breezily, "I've already investigated it. There are plenty of exit points along the way." He motioned for Mallory to follow him, then stepped into the dark, shielding the candle with his hand. Mallory considered leaving Hipgrave in there before accepting it would get him nowhere. Reluctantly, he followed.

The tunnel was just wide enough to walk along without brushing shoulders against the walls. After ten feet, a small flight of steps led down, and from then on it twisted and turned so much that Mallory had soon lost all sense of direction. It was damp with whistling, cold air currents suggesting large spaces somewhere ahead.

They'd been following it for ten minutes when another downward flight of stairs took them into a low-ceilinged room where expanses of *something* glowed white in the flickering candlelight. Hipgrave recoiled when he saw what was there.

Bones were heaped on all sides. The black eyeholes of skulls glared out from a confusion of skeletal remains so jumbled up that it was impossible to tell where one body ended and another began, or even if the skeletons were whole. The ghoulish display was oppressive.

"This wasn't here before," Hipgrave said.

"An ossuary." Mallory had been there before, briefly, on his first exploration of the new buildings. "They were popular in medieval times, particularly at monasteries . . . somewhere to store the remains of the people who had lived there. There's a famous one in the catacombs under Paris."

Hipgrave surveyed the immense size of the bone-heap stretching way beyond where the candlelight could reach. "There must have been a lot of people living here."

"Or it's been around for a very long time."

As they moved through it, Mallory was disturbed to see at the back of the piles some bones that didn't look human—too long, too twisted, a skull that appeared to have horns growing out of it. *Just a trick of the shifting shadows*, he told himself.

Hipgrave had been unnerved by the ossuary, too, for he remained silent for the next twenty minutes until Mallory was forced to ask him exactly where they were going.

"It's not the same route I followed before . . ."

Mallory's heart sank at the indecision in Hipgrave's voice; they were lost. "We should turn back—"

"No, no, we'll get there eventually."

Mallory was about to argue when Hipgrave let out a jubilant cry. He hurried forward and knelt down. As Mallory came up behind him, he saw what had caught Hipgrave's eye: a thin blue line of what looked like an electrical discharge crackling along the floor, up the walls, and across the ceiling. It was so faint as to be indiscernible unless you were actually upon it.

"What is that?" Mallory asked. He was surprised to feel a faint buzzing in his sword where it hung against his leg, as if it were responding to the energy.

"I don't know. But it's been in a few of the tunnels I've wandered down."

Mallory cautiously reached out across the blue line. A faint tingling buzzed in his fingers as they passed over it. The air on the other side felt different, almost silky. Instinctively, Mallory knew. "It's a boundary." *Between this world and the Otherworld*, he thought. His earlier suspicions had been true: for some reason, the cathedral compound had become a crossing-over point, where the world and Otherworld merged, and at the point of confluence there was chaos and unpredictability.

"That's what I thought," Hipgrave said, "and on the other side is where that Devil lives." He peered into the dark as if he could pierce it by effort alone. "The Devil has defined his territory of Evil. Who knows? Crossing over this line might warn him in some way."

"Then I've already triggered it," Mallory said. "We should get back."

"We'll return," Hipgrave continued dreamily, as if talking to himself, "the five of us, and we'll hunt it down. We'll kill it dead."

They were just turning to depart when the noise of metal clinking against stone echoed in the depths of the tunnel. As it approached them, the clinking became a consistent scraping. An image of a billhook being dragged along the wall sprang unbidden into Mallory's mind.

"Let's get out of here," Mallory hissed. His anxiety increased a notch when he saw that Hipgrave's eyes had become wide and distant.

"No, this is our chance," Hipgrave said quietly. He drew his sword and turned to face the crackling line of Blue Fire.

"You saw what it did to Cornelius," Mallory warned. "The two of us might not be up to it. Besides, this isn't the place to make a stand—there's not enough space to manoeuvre."

Hipgrave didn't appear to hear him. He stepped forward until the toe of his boot brushed the tiny sapphire sparks. A worrying thought leaped into Mallory's mind.

"Don't cross the line!" he said. "It's not sacred ground on the other side. We won't be protected."

"We have to stop the Devil," Hipgrave whispered.

Whoever was ahead of them was moving down the tunnel, the scrape of metal now accompanied by a heavy tread and hard breathing. Mallory thought he could occasionally glimpse golden sparks where the metallic object hit the wall.

"Come on, Hipgrave," he said as supportively as he could muster. "A good general knows when to retreat." He grabbed Hipgrave's arm and attempted to tug him back. Hipgrave resisted with the slow, measured strength of a sleepwalker. He held his sword out threateningly.

"WHO GOES THERE?" The voice boomed out with the sound and fury of a tolling bell. Mallory covered his ears and recoiled. Hipgrave blanched.

"I'm not scared," he said.

The growing noises suggested that the approaching figure should now be in sight, but Mallory could see nothing in the thick shadows.

"Hipgrave," Mallory pressed.

Hipgrave's sword arm wilted a little; he looked as if he was starting to comprehend Mallory's warnings. But then the haze crossed his eyes again and he took one step over the blue line. Mallory lunged for him and missed.

"I'm ready for you, Devil!" Hipgrave said, brandishing his sword.

A hand as big as a dinner plate shot from the shadows and clamped around Hipgrave's wrist. He yelled in fright; Mallory started. It had a studded leather band at its wrist and tattered brown cloth wrapped around fingers and palm in a makeshift glove. But what shocked Mallory the most was that where the forearm disappeared into the dark there was no sense of a body attached; it was as if the interloper only took on substance when it was in the light.

Hipgrave howled as the steely fingers dug into his flesh. Mallory threw his arms around Hipgrave's waist and attempted to drag him backward over the line. The hand held fast, and effortlessly; in fact, Mallory felt himself being pulled forward. It was too strong. Freeing one hand, he whipped out his sword and prodded into the dark. There was a fizz of blue and a tremendous howl that made his ears ring. Suddenly he was flying onto his back, with Hipgrave crashing on top of him.

Mallory half expected the attacker to pursue them even though they were on sacred ground, so he rolled over and dragged Hipgrave to his feet, propelling him back down the tunnel. Hipgrave was clutching his sword arm in pain where the skin was marred by five red marks.

"We'll be back," he grunted. "We've seen it now."

"It's seen us," Mallory corrected.

When they were a few yards away, he glanced back to see a large figure silhouetted against the lighter shadows, stooping to fits its frame in the constricting tunnel. Mallory didn't want to come back to face that thing at all.

They emerged from another tunnel on the edge of the cloisters, both still troubled by what they had seen. Hipgrave was rambling about exorcising the Devil, and seemed so distracted that he was barely aware Mallory was with him. Mallory took the earliest opportunity to slip away, first into the cathedral and then out into the twilight. As he crossed the lawns back to the dorm, he saw Daniels in deep conversation with his young friend Lewis—his lover, Mallory guessed. The teen appeared upset. Mallory tried not to look, but as he passed it was obvious all was not well between the two of them. The youth was tearful, his voice growing louder. Eventually he stormed away. Daniels noticed Mallory and came over morosely.

"Trouble?" Mallory said.

Daniels didn't meet his eye. "He's young—he doesn't understand." He fell silent, and when Mallory didn't press him for information, he added, "You haven't heard, then. Stefan is introducing some new *rules* to impose order. They were announced an hour ago in the cathedral. Where were you?"

"Carrying Hipgrave's drool cup. What kind of rules?"

"Reactionary rules." There was an edge to Daniels's voice that Mallory hadn't heard before.

"You know he comes from the fundamentalist wing. Don't tell me you're surprised."

"I was *hopeful*, Mallory. That's the kind of person I am—I always think everyone is as reasonable and erudite and downright charming as myself." He looked up at the icy stars. "It's going to be a hell of a winter."

"So what's he—"

"He doesn't want any *sodomites* polluting the religion. There are too many of us here, apparently—though most of them must be so far in the closet they've never seen the light of day. And God doesn't recognise us. We're sinful . . . we'll never be allowed into heaven."

"That's what you get for messing with religion, Daniels—it's just a prop for prejudice."

He swore under his breath with irritation. "I knew I shouldn't waste my time talking to you . . ."

Mallory caught him as he prepared to storm off. "You're right—I'm sorry, that was a cheap shot. Look, just lie low for a while. What can he do?"

"I don't know. But he had those thugs from the Inquisition with him when he made the announcement. I'm starting to get a bad feeling about this."

"For God's sake," Mallory said, "this is the pathetic rump of Christianity in Britain, here, within these four walls. He can't afford to start driving people out! There'll be nobody left."

"I suppose you're right. He's just making a point. I mean, he said we could stay if we renounced our sexuality, so he's not being completely hard-line about it."

194

"There you go."

Daniels rubbed his eyes wearily. "I was trying to explain it to Lewis. I said if we didn't flaunt it we could carry on. He said if God is love and we love each other, what's wrong with that?"

"He's got a point."

"The Bible says—"

"The Bible says a lot of nonsense amongst all the good stuff. You can justify any point of view with it. Same with the Koran. Look what happened out in Afghanistan."

"If we haven't got the Bible, Mallory, we haven't got anything."

"Yeah, I hear that all the time, and you know what? I don't believe it. When you come down to it, it's a book. Any religion has to be bigger than that."

"I'll try that one on Stefan the next time I see him," Daniels said sarcastically. "Look, I'm off to compline. Got to show willing in the current atmosphere. I'll see you later."

He headed off in the growing gloom, shoulders bowed. Mallory watched him go, sympathetic but not surprised. Daniels had been right: winter was going to be hard.

"What are you doing, Mallory?"

Miller's whisper floated out of the dark, startling Mallory, who was lying in his bunk, staring up at the ceiling. Further down the room, Gardener was snoring as loudly as a chain saw. Daniels had been tossing and turning for an hour, but now seemed to have drifted off.

"Thinking." He'd actually been tracing the pattern of the dragons on the hilt of his sword in the scabbard that hung from the bed-head. Its response to the Blue Fire barrier in the tunnels that afternoon had brought to a head his growing concerns about it. He recalled what Rhiannon had said about its importance when he had picked it up at the Court of Peaceful Days, but he still couldn't guess its true significance. Sometimes it felt alive in his grasp; when at rest in the scabbard it often appeared to be singing to him, the faint vibration he felt in his leg oddly comforting.

"You're always thinking, Mallory. I watch you, you know."

"You're starting to scare me now, Miller."

"All the people around here drift through what's happening, but you pay attention to everything and everybody." In the dark, Miller's voice sounded small, like a child's. "You try to pretend you don't care about anything, but I can tell you care a lot . . . even if you don't see it yourself."

"You sound like a bad self-help book." Mallory wondered if he could throw the sword away. At first it had seemed like a valuable, powerful form of protection, but increasingly it was just a reminder of the obligations Rhiannon had attempted to thrust on him: to be a hero, to fight for humanity as some kind of mythical knight, a *Brother of Dragons*. That had sounded pathetic at the time. Now it was simply irritating him, although he didn't quite know why he felt that way.

"We need you, Mallory."

The honesty in Miller's voice was affecting; Mallory couldn't come back with a joke. "You don't need me."

"You think that because you're strong, everyone else is strong, too, but that's not true. Some people need others to help them along. The strong help the weak—that's how it should be. Things are falling apart here, Mallory. We *need* you."

Miller's words were an uncomfortable piece of synchronicity with Mallory's own thoughts. He usually managed to keep his many doubts locked away behind a patina of arrogance, but at that moment he could barely contain them. "I was given this sword by someone who felt I should be a hero," he mused aloud. "I was in the wrong place at the wrong time, and they were acting as though I was meant to be there."

"Maybe it's true what they say—there aren't any coincidences. Everything that happens is meant to happen."

"Or maybe they just got the wrong bloke."

Silence consumed them for ten minutes until Miller said, "What do you see when you close your eyes at night, Mallory?"

A burst of fire in the dark, cleansing, like the flame of a Fabulous Beast. He didn't answer.

"Something bad happened to you before you came here, didn't it?"

Mallory tensed. "What makes you say that?"

"Like I said, I watch you. Little things you've said . . . the way you act . . . the way you won't talk about the life you had before."

"In this world we've got now, something bad has happened to everyone."

"It's not healthy to bottle these things up. It affects the way you act . . . stops you moving on . . . makes you give up on the life God has planned for you—"

"There you go with that evangelical crap again."

"You don't have to act with me, Mallory. You can tell me anything, get it off your chest. I'm your friend." A long pause. "Aren't I?"

Mallory sighed wearily. "I'm only saying this because the other two are asleep and it's dark. Yes, I like you, Miller, because you haven't let yourself get eaten up by cynicism like everyone else."

"Is that it?" Miller sounded disappointed. He covered himself hastily with, "Look, tell me what happened to you and I'll tell you something bad that happened to me. That's fair. That way we both benefit."

And Mallory almost did; the feeling that the awful burden that had crushed him for so long was about to be lifted was exhilarating. If he admitted it to himself, Miller was probably the only reason he had decided to stick around after his first beating at Blaine's hands. Whatever Blaine had said, he could have found some way to get out. But he saw in Miller something of himself, before all the misery. It gave him an odd sort of hope, but he didn't want to analyse it too closely. And that was the reason why he couldn't tell him: he couldn't spoil him.

"Go to sleep, Miller," he said.

He guessed from the silence that he'd hurt Miller's feelings, but he put it out of his mind; he was good at that these days. Gardener and Daniels were silent. The moon broke through the curtains in a band illuminating the far wall. It made him think, oddly, of Sophie. And then he fell asleep.

She was waiting for him in the silvery glade, filled with mysteries and cool, dark depths.

"How do you do this?" he asked. A summery breeze rustled the leaves above his head. "And, for that matter, where is this?"

"There are more worlds than the one you see around you, Mallory," she said, walking slowly around the ring of fungi that marked the perimeter of the clearing. "This one is at the same time in your head and encompassing everything . . . the universe . . . everything."

"Well, that's the kind of mystical bollocks I expect from you."

"You've learned a little sassiness since our last meeting, I see." She wasn't offended by his comment and that made him like her even more. "How do I come here? A few herbs, a little incense, some candle smoke, a small ritual . . . easy when you know how."

Recalling their previous meeting when his every emotion had been untrammelled, he struggled to keep control while maintaining a superficially blasé appearance. "And *why* do you come here to see me?" he said, leaning against a tree as nonchalantly as he could manage. But it was difficult; every fibre of him wanted to feel the sensation of her pressed against his body, forced inside him so he could consume all parts of her.

"It passes the time." She flashed him a sideways glance, quickly obscured by her hair.

"You said we should stop playing games." He tried to analyse why he felt so strongly about her, but it escaped all examination: too complex, too deep-seated, too many interrelated subtleties of intellect, emotion, and physical appearance. It was simply the way it was, and he had to accept it on those terms.

"I'm not. But," she added thoughtfully, "the travelling is half the fun of getting here."

"Then you haven't been doing it right."

The glade was filled with a crackling tension, both emotional and sexual. Mallory realised his breathing had become shallow, could see the same quick rise and fall in Sophie's chest. She kept her face turned away from him so he couldn't see her reactions. "And you've actually *had* a relationship before? Amazing."

He was hypnotised by the way she moved, in and out of the circle now, light and supple. "You've forgiven me, then?" he asked.

"Just about."

"We're trying to dig a tunnel into your camp."

She flashed him another look, more suspicious this time. "We heard the digging. What's going on?"

"We're starting to starve in there . . . you know those things won't let us in or out. Pretty soon people are going to start dying."

"And you expect . . . what? Sympathy? For the people who killed Melanie and Scab?"

Mallory walked into the centre of the circle, turning slowly to follow her. He could barely contain the electric charge in his limbs. "You're talking about prejudice now . . . the kind of thing you said your own people face. Yes, there are some unpleasant types in the cathedral . . . same as everywhere. But a lot of them are good, decent, possibly misguided, but—"

"And what are you asking?"

"For your help." She didn't show whether she had heard him. "You can trust me."

This time she looked up. "I think I *can* trust you, Mallory." She sounded surprised herself. "But how do I know I can trust the rest of the God Squad?"

"All they want is some food . . . a way to carry on believing in what they believe in. The same as you."

Mallory was intrigued to see what looked like moonlight glimmering where her bare feet had just trod. "So they dig under the wall . . . what then?"

"The food comes in through your camp to the tunnel. In return, they can offer something . . . I don't know. See it as trade between nation-states. They've got a good standard of health care . . . they know about herbs—"

"So do we."

"And they've got a massive wine cellar and a lake of beer."

"OK, you sold me." She laughed. "Whose idea was this?"

"Mine."

"Preaching peace and love between men, Mallory? There's hope for you yet."

"There might have been a slightly more selfish motivation." Hunger consumed him. In that place where there were no rules and no judgment, he finally accepted he didn't have to pretend.

Her eyes flashed in the moonlight. "Oh?" A faint smile.

"Well, you won't come to me . . ."

"Major engineering works, just to see me? How very romantic." She broke off from her dance and entered the circle to join him. There was nothing coy about her; she was as strong and confident as he was: an equal. All his repressed emotion rushed up and out: his consuming guilt, his fear, and, most of all, his love. At that moment, nothing else mattered—all Existence revolved around the two of them.

He grabbed her shoulders forcefully and pulled her forward. She propelled herself to him with the same hunger. This kiss was so much more than the tentative, desperate first one: it was voracious; all barriers crashed before it. Her skin was hot. Their lips were hard and bruising, their mouths moving with desire, hands raking each other's bodies.

Energy crackled between them: *Blue Fire*, Mallory thought, filling them, consuming them. From that point, there was no going back.

The next day dawned cold and grey, but Mallory took to it as if it was midsummer. He found time to go up onto the walls so he could look at the trees that lined the hillsides to the south of the city, bare black amid the evergreens. As he slowly made his way along the walkway, enjoying the peace away from the oppressive control of the knights, he became aware of two people talking below him. There was something in the tone of their conversation that caught his attention, a note of deep concern, perhaps of undue seriousness. He peered cautiously over the edge to see James and Julian so engrossed they were oblivious to his presence above them.

"It's outrageous," Julian said. "He should be using his position to bring the camps *together*. He doesn't have a mandate. The election was so close it could have gone either way. And after we all made such a big show of supporting him . . ."

"There'll be trouble. Some on our side won't toe the line indefinitely for the sake of unity," James said. He added hopefully, "Perhaps he won't go down that road. It's all rumour and innuendo—"

"It sounded pretty copper-bottomed when I heard it." Julian's voice snapped with repressed anger. "He could split the Church. How stupid is that? We're barely hanging on by our fingernails. To fragment us now could be . . ." He shook his head. Tears of anger flecked his eyes. "I can't believe this is happening so soon after Cornelius passed. He'd be outraged, after all he did to bring together all the conflicting factions. Good Lord, even the Baptists. I'm starting to think he should have been a little more exacting in his inclusion policy."

James clapped him on the shoulder supportively. "Things have been bad before. We'll pull through, God willing. If things are going the way you say, we have to make a stand. We *have* to. We can't let the Church be taken over in this way. It would be disastrous. The responsibility is on us to provide a counterbalance."

"And how do you think he'll respond to that?" Julian said. "For all his public pronouncements, he's never been one for compromise."

"Then we'll have a fight on our hands."

They walked away in the direction of the cathedral, leaving Mallory to ponder on the significance of what they had been discussing.

Most of the knights congregated on the roof at seven p.m., but the Blues were nowhere to be seen. There was an atmosphere of tense anticipation, though oddly hopeful as everyone prepared for the release of pent-up feelings of impotence and inadequacy. Although no one quite knew what it was hoped would be achieved by the planned strike-back, it felt good to be doing anything. And debate raged back and forth about exactly what they *were* doing; Blaine had given nothing away in his briefing. No one had any idea how they could hit the Adversary's forces from the restricted position of the roof of the cathedral buildings. And even if they could strike the creatures that attacked the walls, how could it possibly amount to the kind of earth-shaking blow Blaine had implied?

Mallory leaned on the stone wall that ran around the edge of the roof area and peered into the sea of dark beneath; it provided no sense of depth, so he had the dizzying sensation that the drop went on forever. Miller refused to come anywhere near the edge; he complained of vertigo and had almost been physically sick when they had processed onto the roof to see the landscape stretched out all around, bathed in the moonlight shining from a clear sky. Daniels lay glumly against a sloping section, wrapped in his cloak, staring at the stars. Gardener sat with his back to the wall, smoking a roll-up.

The roof was structurally as complex as the new buildings it covered: pitched, tiled sections separated flat areas that could be accessed from the many corridors and rooms that filled the roof spaces; towers, steeples with flag poles and lightning conductors protruded upward, along with huge gothic gargoyles that had the same unnerving effect as the ones overlooking the great hall. The knights had decamped in little clusters all around, reflecting the small teams that had been established during the training period.

"It's still difficult to comprehend," Daniels said introspectively. "We don't know what's out there, in the hills and the fields, in the night."

"We never did," Mallory replied. "I reckon they were always there . . . sleeping, if you like, hidden away . . . but they were there, waiting for their time to come around again."

"No one thought anything like this would happen," Miller muttered dismally.

"We were arrogant." Mallory turned to face them, his head spinning as he pulled away from the illusion of the void. "Because we were top dog on the planet for so long we thought we always would be. But there are things more powerful than us . . . and now they're back to show us we weren't even close to the top of the pile."

"You really do have a depressing worldview, Mallory," Daniels said.

"Realistic," Mallory countered.

There was a quiver of excitement as Blaine and Hipgrave emerged from a door onto one of the flat areas further along the roof. Blaine moved slowly amongst the groups of knights, giving short briefings, taking questions. He had the look of a predatory tiger, and was plainly pleased with how things were going.

When he faced Mallory he couldn't hide a flicker of contempt, but he continued in a measured voice. "The target will soon be approaching. We will be allocating weapons and ammunition shortly. The aim of this operation is simple: to inflict massive damage on the enemy, to bring it down, to kill it. Success will send an overwhelming message back that we are to be feared."

"How do you know the target is approaching?" Mallory asked.

Blaine smiled tightly. "We know—let's leave it at that."

"What's the target?" Gardener said.

"You've seen it before," Blaine replied, "on the night we were first attacked . . . when you were on your field operation—"

"The Fabulous Beast." There was a note of disbelief in Mallory's exclamation that drew a suspicious glance from Blaine.

"The flying creature—"

"How can we hit something like that?" Mallory said. "It's huge . . . it shoots fire . . . Anyway, it's not been seen since we were on the Plain. What makes you think it'll be here tonight?"

"It'll be here." Blaine had grown cold at Mallory's questioning of his big plan and turned his attention to Gardener. "Yes, it is a big bastard, but we've got the capability to down it. And we'll be helped by the power of the Lord protecting us—it won't be able to see us. It will be able to strike, but only at random."

"Where are the Blues?" Mallory asked.

"They'll be here," Blaine said, without looking at him. "Now, no defeatism and we will win the day." His comment was clearly aimed at Mallory. "Captain Hipgrave will be giving direct orders during the attack. Be prepared to respond." He nodded to them curtly and moved on.

Mallory had conflicting emotions; like the others, he felt good at being able to strike any blow, but there was something about the Fabulous Beast that he admired, the sense of wonder and magic it carried on its wings. It seemed clearly wrong to him to do harm to such a remarkable creature.

Gardener bore a sly smile; Daniels rubbed his hands gleefully. Only Miller showed a hint of being unsure. Mallory let his hands drop to his sides, then yanked them away; the hilt of his sword was almost too hot to touch. He thought of the dragons engraved there, of Rhiannon's talk of a Brotherhood of Dragons, and wondered if there was some overt link with the Fabulous Beast.

The tension increased a notch as the weapons were handed out. Most got some form of rifle—an Armalite—but one group was handed a cumbersome and dated bazooka. "That should give the bastard a sting," Gardener said gruffly.

"You really think this is enough?" Mallory said, examining the rifle, which seemed flimsy compared to what they were up against.

"If we're all firing at once," Miller said. "You know . . . someone will hit it."

"It looked as if it had some kind of plating to me," Mallory said. "The scales gleamed as though they were made of metal." But the others were too caught up in the moment to hear his doubts.

The only reply came from Gardener. "Don't underestimate Blaine." And Mallory accepted the truth of that.

They spent the next half hour craning their necks to examine all quarters of the night sky while trying to guess from which direction it would come; Mallory still couldn't understand how Blaine knew it *would* be coming. They were interrupted by Miller, who said, "Gosh! Look at that."

The Blues had emerged onto a large platform about a hundred feet away. They were as perfectly drilled as ever, falling into formation with a fluid ease, adopting postures that made Mallory think of Action Man dolls as they faced the eastern sky. Curiously, he noted that they appeared to be guarding something at the centre of their circle, but it was impossible to make out what it was.

A small team broke off and began to unpack crates on a separate flat section. They worked fast and diligently, gradually assembling the contents. The other knights gaped in awe as it took shape.

"Bloody hell, that's a big bloody gun," Gardener said.

Though still old-fashioned, the two-wheeled gun looked as if it could easily bring down a jet. Mallory's heart sank once more.

Silence fell across the rooftop. With the gun complete, everyone waited. Mallory kept his attention on the main group of the élite cadre. Two knights in the centre of the circle ducked down and a second later a blue incandescence flooded into the air like a searchlight.

"What in heaven's name is that?" Daniels said.

Nobody could guess, but the quality of the light reminded Mallory of the crackling energy that had formed a barrier between this world and the other deep in the catacombs. Instinctively, they all knew what it represented, though: a beacon. They turned to face the east, following the gaze of the Blues.

So heavy was the expectation, it seemed as if they waited an age, though it couldn't have been very long at all. The first burst of light in the distant sky raised a cry of exclamation in several quarters. Some pointed, others yelled for everyone to be prepared. It was coming.

Mallory glanced back at the Blues. "What are they doing?" he said. "Are they calling it somehow? What have they got up there?"

But everyone else's attention was fixed on the approaching firestorm. Although they couldn't yet see the beast, a column of flame would erupt down onto the landscape from time to time, followed by a period of stillness, then more flame, much closer. The advance was eerie; all conversation faded away. No one could tear their eyes from the trail of conflagration stretching into the distance.

Somewhere near Old Sarum, trees were burning.

"Nearly here," Gardener said.

Hands closed tightly around rifles; they felt even more insubstantial. The roar of flame sounded like a blast furnace. A house near the ring road exploded in a shower of tiles and masonry. Echoes of the destruction boomed back and forth amongst the high buildings of the city; falling bricks rattled on rooftops, crashing through some. Smoke swept in along the streets like a river fog; they could all taste it on the wind.

"It looks like hell," Miller whispered.

Mallory thought he could see the metallic glimmer of scales, red, gold, and green, in the firelight. The heavy, rhythmic beating of leather wings filled the air.

Hipgrave appeared with one foot balanced on either side of the roof ridge. A hand shielded his eyes as he watched the Beast's progress. "Raise your weapons," he shouted. Across the roof, rifles went up as one.

Mallory had the strange feeling that he was watching the red light of a plane flying across the sky until he realised it was the beast's eye. It moved directly toward them. Although he knew it couldn't see them, he felt distinctly unnerved by its flight path, as if it sensed exactly where they were.

Another column of flame burst from its mouth, this time illuminating the creature clearly for the first time. Its body undulated with serpentine grace, driven forward by the power of the enormous bat-wings that beat deceptively slowly. The scales covered most of the body, more colourful on the undersurface, darker near the top. A gnarled, bony ridge like the fin of some dinosaur ran along the length of its back. A corresponding bone structure protruded in strange, twisted horns from its head, some small, some larger. A tail lashed the air behind it. The blazing illumination of the flames cast bizarre shadows across its features, giving it a demonic appearance that brought a chill to the assembled knights.

"Take aim," Hipgrave barked.

The column of fire destroyed the Woolworth's building on the High Street.

The fire washed and backwashed as if it was liquid; almost, Mallory thought, as if it was alive. Glass exploded out in glittering shards. The bricks flowed like water under the intense heat. Yet it didn't spread to the adjoining buildings. Instead, it sucked into a tight core that was too bright to stare at; the glow illuminated all of the surrounding streets as if it were daylight.

"Fire!" Hipgrave yelled.

The volley of shots was deafening. Some flew harmlessly out over the rooftops, but several struck the target. Mallory secretly hoped the scales were as hard as they appeared, but he was quickly disappointed. The Beast writhed in pain as the shots rattled into it. With a deft twist, it performed a rapid manoeuvre and soared straight up, too high for their ammunition to reach. But once there, it twisted and rolled in the high winds in some discomfort.

"That was good," Hipgrave shouted. "Get set for when it comes back down."

"What if it stays up there?" Mallory said. "What if it turns back?"

He saw Blaine away to one side, grinning triumphantly. He looked as though he wasn't expecting any retreat from the Beast at all.

Just as Hipgrave said, it did one final roll and swooped back down, directly overhead. They all raised their weapons and fired randomly, more out of panic than anything. It was still too high for most of the bullets to reach it.

"Wait for the order!" Hipgrave bellowed.

The Beast came down with the speed of a jet fighter, and it didn't appear to be letting up. The thought ran through all of them at the same time: it was going to smash into them, destroy them and the hated cathedral in a suicide attack. Several knights threw themselves flat and covered their heads.

"Get set!" Hipgrave ordered. "Fire!"

Another volley of shots burst skyward. This time Mallory heard numerous tiny *clangs* as some were deflected by the scales, but others pierced their target. The beast writhed in the air, still driving down fast.

"Oh, God!" Miller mewled.

Mallory saw those gleaming red eyes bearing down on him and sensed something numinous lying just behind them. While the others dived for cover, he remained standing, strangely calm, locked into their depths.

At the last moment, when it was about to pile straight into the cathedral, it appeared to sense what lay below and twisted into a horizontal flight that rushed mere feet over them. Mallory was buffeted by turbulence and fought to remain standing. The beating of the wings was deafening, the air filled with the foundry smell of the beast.

As the knights climbed to their feet—some of whose who had cried out now sheepish and furtive—Miller muttered, "And now it's raining."

Mallory checked the wetness on the back of his hand. "Not raining. Blood."

His skin was flecked with droplets of a dark liquid that didn't have the consistency of human blood. There was an odd texture to it, like oil, and he was surprised to feel a sense of well-being from its contact. It remained for a second or two, then faded away as mysteriously as it had come.

"At least we've hurt the bastard," Gardener grunted. "Blaine was right—they're not as big and powerful as we thought."

"Flesh wounds," Daniels said. "We've got a long way to go yet. Look at it."

The Beast swooped and rolled on the currents above the city, filled with grace and power; it was a sight that brought awe to all of them, despite themselves.

"I'm not sure about this," Mallory said, marvelling at the Beast's flight.

Gardener flashed him a suspicious glance. "What do you mean?"

"It's not right to kill it. What good would that do?"

"Send a message," Gardener said.

"Is that a good enough reason for destroying a living thing?"

"Steady on, Mallory. You're starting to sound like me." Miller grinned at him, then turned to the others. "He's right, I think. Look at it—it's an amazing creature. It would be like shooting a horse or something."

"Don't start going down that road," Gardener growled. "Bloody defeatists. Daniels, what do you think?"

Daniels was checking his gun over. "I'm just following orders."

"That's why we have leaders," Gardener continued. "To sort out what's right and wrong so we can be free to get down to business."

"I can't begin to tell you how *so wrong* that line of thinking is," Mallory said sharply. He was interrupted by Hipgrave ordering them to prepare for another attack. Gardener mumbled something under his breath that sounded very much like an insult.

The Fabulous Beast performed an immaculate loop over the city and prepared for another attack. Mallory glanced over at the Blues. The big gun still hadn't been used, though the crew aiming it was poised. The Beast had so far proved too fast and agile, but Blaine's tactics were clear: he would wait to give the order until the Beast was slowed by its wounds.

The creature skimmed the rooftops, eyes blazing, smoke streaming from its mouth and nose. The sight was so terrifying, Mallory saw the faces around him go rigid. Yet he didn't feel that what he saw there was driven by hatred of humanity, or hunger, or some nebulous Christian concept of *Evil*. It was something primal, but also oddly innocent.

The guns on every side were levelled at it. They had seemed pathetic before, but now he was not so sure: a thousand tiny blows were as good as one big one.

Go away, Mallory prayed silently. *Leave, before you're hurt.* He surprised himself with the notion.

He raised his gun with the others, but when the order came he didn't pull the trigger. What was the reason for his odd empathy with the creature? The sound of gunfire made his ears ache. The creature snapped out of its flight path. Every hit made his insides knot.

When it looped around to strike again, its movements were noticeably slower. The wings were beating more heavily and there was a perceivable wobble in its lithe undulations.

"This is it," Gardener said.

Why doesn't it use its fire? Mallory thought. Even if the site was protected, it couldn't possibly know that.

The Beast came in low over the rooftops once again. This time, Hipgrave looked to Blaine before telling them to hold their fire. The Blues manning the big gun moved quickly, tracking the Beast's trajectory.

Mallory's heart took a dip. His gun slipped from his fingers, dropping to the roof with a clatter.

The retort of the big gun boomed across the cathedral compound. The Fabulous Beast was frozen in Mallory's mind just beyond the cathedral walls, its red eyes glowing with a fierce, alien intelligence; not even the explosion of the gun going off could force him to tear his gaze from it. Everyone around was caught in states of jubilation and shock.

And then it all erupted in a chaotic jumble of images. The Fabulous Beast was hit square on. There was an explosion; blue light flashed everywhere. Through his ringing ears, Mallory thought he could hear a sound like the wind in the mountains, and then the Beast was thrown back and up. It came down quickly, its wings unmoving, its eyes no longer burning.

It hit the shopping arcade hard, flattening buildings, raising a tremendous cloud of billowing dust. It skidded for a way, bringing down more shops, before coming to rest. The night was filled with the sound of tumbling masonry.

"They did it," Daniels said in blank disbelief. "They killed it."

A loud cheer rose up from the knights. The Fabulous Beast was obscured by the buildings all around, but there was no doubt that Daniels was right. Mallory turned away, desperately troubled and shocked, not knowing why he felt that way.

Across the roof, the blue beacon winked out as the élite knights ended whatever they had set in motion and then quickly made their way back into the cathedral.

chapter eleven

DEEP CALLETH UNTO DEEP

"Perhaps death is life and in the other world
life is thought of as death."
Euripides

During the "great silence" that followed compline, when the brethren retired to their cells, there was only the raucous talk of the knights and guards echoing through the vast, empty spaces. But as the brothers emerged at midnight for the night office, it was obvious word had circulated quickly: spirits were high and chatter was animated. The might of God had once more been evidenced; a blow had been struck against the Devil.

Mallory was uncharacteristically dismal. He felt out of sorts, unable to divine his own feelings, detached from his fellow knights. Only Miller appeared to hold some doubts, but Mallory certainly couldn't talk to him. All he knew was that something felt intuitively *wrong*.

It was an instinct that appeared to be reflected in the weather. The moment the Fabulous Beast had crashed to the ground, dead, the temperature had dropped a degree or two and a powerful wind blew up from the east, battering the cathedral and howling amongst the eaves as if in mourning. Flurries of snow began to fall shortly after. More, the air itself seemed to taste different, bitter; Mallory hoped it was just the ashes from the burning buildings.

The knights were all cheered as they entered the cathedral. Many could barely hide their pride, though the Blues remained as emotionless as ever. They stood at the rear of the nave, shoulders thrown back, staring into the shadows above the quire, while Stefan climbed into the pulpit.

"Tonight we have achieved a great victory," he intoned in a powerful voice that filled the cathedral to its roof. "We have defeated the great Serpent, the Adversary in the form that tempted Adam and Eve in the Garden, the source of original sin. Defeated!" His passion brought a ripple of admiration from the congregation.

Mallory had decided that he disliked Stefan intensely, but he was forced to admire the new bishop's ability to manipulate through his oration. He had a commanding sense of moment, knowing exactly the right words and tone to control the emotions of his audience.

"And this tremendous victory is all down to our brave knights!" he continued. "With minimal arms, they plumbed the depths of their courage to crush the force of Evil."

Mallory was bitterly amused at this interpretation of their actions.

"We have shown today that we can meet the forces of darkness head-on, and that with God's light shining at our backs we can overcome anything the Adversary places in our way. This has been the first step in establishing the new Kingdom of Heaven on earth."

He continued in that vein for five minutes, playing word games, delivering rhetoric, slowly building hope and optimism amongst the browbeaten brothers. But then there was a subtle, unannounced change in his tone; his face grew more grave.

"To carry out the Work of our Lord as He intended, we need to be pure of heart," he said, moving his gaze slowly across the congregation as if he were looking at each one individually. "We need to be a shining example to all who see us: the most devout, the purest of thought, the clearest of conscience, unsullied by the corrupting material world so that the Lord's light shines out of us, so that all who see us will have something to which they can aspire."

There was a long pause while he waited for his words to sink in, but he didn't stop pressing the attention of his cold, dark eyes on the worshippers. "To that end, we will be instigating more intensive religious instruction amongst your duties. There are many different branches of the Church under this roof, which has made worship understandably fragmented. With the help of the Chapter of Canons and some of the elders, we will be attempting to bring homogeneity to services and ritual so that we can be as one." This brought a faint murmur of disapproval, which Stefan didn't appear to hear. "It has also been noted that there have been . . . failings. In some quarters, even piety is a quality in short supply. And some stand in direct opposition to the teachings of Our Lord. Yes, even here. There has been indulgence in drink and blasphemous talk, in the sins of the flesh when the gates were open and in the sin of sodomy since the gates have been closed. Prayers have been abandoned; the Great Work of God has been allowed to wither. That cannot be allowed. We must be strict with ourselves, for if we are not, how can we ask others to obey the Word?

"It was always my belief that we are custodians of our own path to God. Now, in my new role, I see how naïve I was. Some of us need help along the way. Some of us need guidance. We are all children in the eyes of God. And in that spirit, I feel it is my duty to put temptation out of harm's way. From this day, alcohol is forbidden, as are all narcotics, natural and man-made. They corrupt the senses and lead even the most devout into the arms of Satan."

Stefan checked some notes on the lectern before him.

So many rules he has to write them down. Mallory thought.

"Fornication will not be countenanced," he continued. "But the wrath of all good, honest men within these walls will be reserved for those who commit sodomy." Mallory cast a furtive glance at Daniels; he kept his face blank. "For them, there will be no respite."

He left a long silence before continuing. "The temporary closure of the library will now be permanent. Only authorised books will be available, and then only to authorised tutors. I'm sure you will be happy to be relieved of this burden, whereby impure thoughts and ideas are allowed to sully your minds, often before you realise what is happening. I have investigated the contents of the library in depth, and I was horrified to discover many Satanic texts amongst the books. These are not only dangerous to the minds of novices, but are also door-ways that allow Evil into the very heart of our community. Therefore, they will be taken out to the main gate and burned at the earliest opportunity, to act as a message to the Dark Forces gathered beyond our walls. We are pure; our light shall not be dimmed."

The list continued: music, apart from plainsong and devotional hymns, was banned, as were all forms of technology because they "promoted a mind-set in opposition to God." Mallory couldn't tell if the majority of the congregation agreed with Stefan or was angered; all response was muted. But he sensed they had been so worn down by recent events that they couldn't be bothered to feel strongly one way or the other. It was too much detail, minor compared with the struggle of staying alive. Best to let someone else take those kinds of decisions so they could concentrate on the day-to-day hardships.

Stefan finished his long speech with a warning. "To ensure that these new guidelines are treated with the correct respect, any transgressions will be met with the most serious punishment. I feel that is only right. The system of pun-ishment will, of course, be transparent and will be overseen, once again, by the Inquisition of Heretical Depravity. Through discipline we will grow closer to God. That is the way it has always been, though we forgot it for a while, and that is the way it shall be from now on."

Mallory wanted to laugh out loud, but as he looked around for others who had got the joke, he saw only deathly seriousness. And in some, worryingly, he saw faint smiles of appreciation.

There was one hopeful moment. Just as he left, Mallory looked back to see Julian, James, and some of the others gathering at the rear of the nave. Their mood was easy to divine. They were as appalled by Stefan's repressive dictum as he himself was, and they weren't about to let it stand.

Miller caught up with him as he made his way back to the dormitory, head bowed against the wind that brought increasing flurries of snow. It was already starting to settle on the grass and cobbled path, adding a ghostly counterpoint to the brooding darkness of the cathedral buildings.

"What did you make of that?" Miller asked breathlessly.

"What did I make of it? I think he missed a trick by not having a torchlight rally and a marching knight honour guard."

Miller looked at him askance, then, as usual, gave up trying to comprehend his friend. "He seems to have a strong idea of how to move us forward."

"When you say *us*, Miller, I have this worrying feeling that you mean me as well."

"What is it with you, Mallory?" Miller said, with annoyance. "Why do you have to act as if you're not with us?"

"I'm not."

"Then why are you here? What's your motivation?" He sounded at the end of his tether; events must have been getting him down more than Mallory had guessed.

"The only thing that's driving me now is to get out of this place and put as many miles between it and me as possible."

"That's all you care about?"

"Yep. Self-preservation. Don't knock it—it's been driving evolution since . . . well, since forever."

Miller shook his head in disbelief. "Nobody can stand alone, Mallory. You need us."

"And then you woke up."

Daniels came running up, skidding on the snow-slick cobbles. He had a hunted expression.

"You OK?" Mallory asked.

"Looks as though I've turned celibate."

"Could be worse," Mallory said. "He could have made you shag Hipgrave."

Daniels forced a smile, but it barely hid the anxiety eating away at him. "Where do we go from here?" he said, shaking his head.

Mallory was woken roughly from a deep sleep. He'd resisted the promptings of the others to go to the lauds of the dead, despite Stefan's warnings about what would befall those who missed their daily quota of prayer; he had felt more tired than he had in weeks. He'd been having a very lucid dream about Sophie who appeared extremely upset about something, although he couldn't quite remember what it was. All he could recall were her tears and her distressed voice repeating, "You just don't know what you've done!"

For the first few seconds, Mallory was disoriented, but then he gradually realised Miller was next to him in a state of near panic. "What's up?" he mumbled.

"Come on! You're needed!" Miller's face looked white in the gloom. "He's dead!"

Mallory dragged on his clothes and boots in a daze while Miller jumped from foot to foot near the door. Eventually, he pulled himself together enough to ask what was wrong. Miller was rushing ahead of him so quickly that they were outside before he got an answer.

"Julian's dead," Miller said tearfully. "Murdered . . . just like Cornelius."

The announcement came as a real shock to Mallory. Cornelius had always been a distant figure to him, but Julian was someone he could almost understand. "When?"

"Just after the night office. They found him in the Trinity Chapel. Lord . . . there was blood everywhere."

Miller wouldn't, or couldn't, tell him any more. They sprinted into the cathedral to find Daniels and Gardener standing at the entrance to the chapel. Just inside, Mallory could see Stefan and Blaine in deep conversation with Hipgrave. He began to speak, but Daniels waved him silent. The mood was grave.

Mallory waited silently with the others, casting glances into the chapel. He couldn't see the body from his vantage point, but there were blood splatters across the floor and up the walls. Eventually, Stefan led the others out. He immediately fixed his attention on Mallory.

"You weren't at the lauds of the dead," he said.

"He was sick," Miller interjected. "He needed to rest."

Stefan accepted this without comment. "No time must be lost," he said, turning to Blaine. "This cancer must not be allowed to spread."

He stalked away, head bowed, hands behind his back, a picture of grief; *on the surface*, Mallory thought. It was a coincidence too far for Julian to be murdered just as he was clearly preparing to offer some form of opposition to Stefan and the changes he was planning. Perhaps even Cornelius's murder wasn't as they had been led to believe.

Blaine broke off a whispered conversation with Hipgrave and departed hastily. Hipgrave came over, his eyes gleaming in the candlelight. "We're going after the bastard who did this," he said, with the eagerness of a young boy. "There's a trail of blood leading into the new buildings. We're the only ones who can do this. I convinced Blaine to give us the chance."

"Thanks," Mallory said sarcastically. "It could be a trap, you know. A trail of blood . . . doesn't sound very realistic." He recalled the manner in which they had been led across Salisbury Plain to Bratton Camp by the illusory cleric.

"Do we have to go at night?" Miller said weakly. "Into that place?"

Hipgrave was too excited to hear any dissent. He spun on his heels and marched toward the cloisters, one hand already on his sword, the other holding a lamp he had brought with him.

"It's a trap," Mallory said resignedly.

"Then it looks as if we're off to die." Gardener marched off behind the captain.

The blood was already turning dark as they followed the unmistakable signs down into the tunnels beneath the new buildings. The atmosphere was even more oppressive than on Mallory's previous incursions; it felt as though people were walking just a few paces behind them, fading into the gloom whenever they turned to look. Sometimes noises would come and go, footsteps tracking them or voices entreating them to deviate from their route, or so it seemed, but the distorting echoes continually took the truth away from them. They kept close together, Hipgrave at the front, Mallory watching their backs, all aware the threat was growing.

The splashes of blood showed up clearly on the worn stone flags in the lamplight. Hipgrave knelt down to examine them at regular intervals. "This is going to lead us right to him," he remarked. "Good as if he'd fastened a rope to himself."

"What do you think we'll find when we catch up with him?" Miller's voice was small and frightened.

"You saw the state of the bodies," Gardener said gruffly.

"The more important question," Mallory said, "is why did he kill Julian? Cornelius, OK—he was the figurehead. Whatever his motivation, you could make a good case for Cornelius being a target. But Julian—he wasn't a power anymore."

"Just random," Daniels said. "They were both in the wrong place at the wrong time."

"Too much of a coincidence," Mallory replied. "Two of the Church's leading figures killed by chance? I don't believe it."

"You can't expect to understand the Devil's thinking," Hipgrave's voice floated back.

They came to a branch in the tunnel. Two flights of steps wound down in different directions. Hipgrave hovered uneasily, moving from one entrance to the other. "I can't see any blood here," he said eventually. "We should split up into two groups."

Mallory pushed his way forward. "No, that's what it wants."

"'It?'" Hipgrave repeated, puzzled.

Mallory shifted uneasily. "The building. Or whatever's behind it."

Daniels reached out uneasily to touch the stone walls. "You've lost it, Mallory," he said, but he sounded very unsure.

"You're saying something's organising the layout of the place?" Gardener said.

"I don't know what I'm saying." He tried to find the right words. The darkness down the stairs appeared to be sucking at them, as if it was alive. "I've seen some strange things . . . What something looks like might not be what it is."

Gardener was intrigued. "So what you're saying is, this bloody big heap of stone might not be a building at all. That's just the way we see it—"

"That's the only way we can see it," Mallory said. "Our brains aren't developed enough to see its true form, so they just do the best they can."

"So it could be alive," Gardener continued.

"It could be alive. It could be anything. I think down here we shouldn't jump to conclusions just because our eyes and ears are telling us that's the way something appears."

"You see," Daniels said, "when they did that campaign, Just Say No to drugs, they should have wheeled you out instead. Problem solved."

"This isn't getting us anywhere," Hipgrave snapped. "Which way do we go? Right or left?"

A cold blast of wind soared up from the depths, carrying with it what sounded like the growl of a wild animal.

"What was that?" Miller said tremulously.

Nobody answered. After a while, Gardener said, "We take the right-hand path."

"It's as good as any, I suppose," Mallory said.

Hipgrave's earlier confidence had faded with his inability to choose the correct path. His eyes continually darted around and he had taken to rubbing his palms together anxiously. The others turned to Mallory.

"Let's go," he said.

The right-hand stairway spiralled downward steeply. They had to go slowly, for Hipgrave's lamp kept disappearing around a turn, plunging the rest of them into darkness. Water dripped incessantly from the stone above them, and the air was dank and cold.

When they reached the bottom, Mallory drew his sword. The others followed suit as they moved along a short passage to a doorway. Beyond it, the room glowed white in the lamplight.

"What's that?" Miller's voice was filled with dread.

Gardener peered past him. "Old bones."

It was the ossuary. Mallory felt they would have ended up there whichever path they had taken. Hipgrave hovered on the threshold, seemingly afraid of entering.

"There used to be a graveyard around the cathedral," Gardener said. "They flattened it when they landscaped the grounds."

"I don't want to go in there," Miller said.

"Well, you can always go back. On your own." Mallory pushed past Hipgrave and entered. As the lamp rocked it sent shadows of skulls and protruding bones dancing across the walls.

The remains were heaped against opposite walls, leaving a path between them. Hipgrave had grown sullen-faced and quiet, so Mallory took the lamp from him and led the way. A clatter came from the rear: Gardener had kicked away a thigh bone. "I keep bloody catching myself on them," he said.

Mallory progressed slowly; occasionally an icy breeze would bring grunts or moans from the tunnel ahead. Off to his right, he glimpsed something glittering green amongst the bones before losing sight of it again. Behind him, Gardener cursed; another clatter.

"Go slow," Daniels cautioned unnecessarily.

The lamp swung; the green glittered again. "What *is* that?" Mallory said.

"What?" Miller said anxiously. "What? I can't see anything!"

"Calm down," Daniels snapped; nerves were fraying.

Gardener had dropped back further, swearing profusely under his breath. The green was so incongruous amid the yellowing bones that Mallory was intrigued. He drew to a halt and began to search amongst the pile to see what it was.

"Don't waste time with that," Daniels said.

Hipgrave had started to make a strange noise in his throat that sounded like the mewling of a kitten. "For God's sake shut him up," Mallory whispered with irritation.

The green light glowed again as the illumination from the lamp struck it. Mallory leaned forward over the bones to get a better look, careful not to touch the precarious pile for fear of bringing it crashing down.

A pair of green eyes stared back.

Recoiling in shock, Mallory brought his sword up sharply, but the bones were already erupting in front of him as the concealed figure thrust its way out. He smelled loam, saw the black of a clerical outfit, and then the grasping hands clawing toward his face blocked most of his vision. The lamp went flying, crashing onto its side, still alight.

Across the piles on both sides, more figures emerged, grotesque spectres throwing larger shadows that swooped and struck like crows. Bones showered all around. Mallory recognised the ghostly things they had glimpsed in the wine cellar, now given unpleasant substance.

Gardener's muttered curses turned to an exclamation of horror as bony fingers grasped his ankles tightly. Some of the other bones—the ones that still had some skeletal shape—were moving with a life of their own. They dragged themselves out on splintered metatarsals, sending shanks and ribs cascading, jaws sagging, skulls lolling.

Mallory tried to throw the thing off him, but its strength far exceeded its frame as it tried to force stinking rough-paper fingers into his mouth. Somewhere Miller was squealing like a baby. Sparks showered through the dark as Gardener's sword crashed against the flagstones in an attempt to chop up the bony limbs gripping his feet. Whether by luck or skill, only Hipgrave had escaped. Lithely, he vaulted one of the attacking figures, then dropped low and scurried out of the far door. As he passed, Mallory glimpsed a face transformed by the flickering light into something almost bestial, eyes glinting with a primal determination.

Only Mallory's sword had any effect on the revenants. They shied from the blade's sapphire glow until they could find another path of attack, but they didn't relent. Mallory was forced to move back and forth, defending both himself and Daniels. Beyond, Miller was already down with three of the things forcing their fingers into his mouth; it looked as if they were trying to tear off his jaw. Rigid with fear, his eyes were wide and tear-streaked.

Mallory attempted to get to him, but before he could make contact with any of the attackers something crashed into his waist, knocking him to the ground. The breath was smashed from his lungs, purple flashes bursting behind his eyes as the weight of one or more of the things crushed him down.

When his vision cleared, Miller's mouth was ripped open as wide as it would go; Mallory heard the cracking of his jaw. A cowled, skull-like head hung barely an inch from Miller's lips as if it were ready to kiss him. And then it did press forward, not kissing, but forcing itself into his mouth.

Mallory at first tried to convince himself it was some bizarre optical illusion—the head was so big, Miller's mouth so small—but somehow the thing's face was disappearing between Miller's teeth. Mallory felt a sickening sense of failure when his friend's terrified eyes flickered toward him, pleading desperately, as if Mallory were the only person who could ever save him.

While Daniels and Gardener fought their own battles, he could only watch as the revenant rolled onto its back while somehow keeping its head pointing in the same direction. It was eerie and sickening at the same time. And then it gradually melted into Miller's body until it was he, and he it, the features a bizarre hybrid of the two.

At that moment, the other things stopped fighting and quietly retreated to the edges of the ossuary; the dead bones clattered to the floor, their newfound life lost.

Mallory pushed himself to his feet and advanced on Miller with Daniels and Gardener close behind, but the thing and Miller had merged seamlessly.

"It's possessed him." Gardener's voice was an awed whisper filled with religious dread.

"Why have the others backed off?" Daniels looked around nervously.

"*Hear me!*" A voice boomed out across the ossuary, so unfeasibly loud and distorted that it took Mallory a while to realise it was coming from Miller's mouth.

"This sacred land has been corrupted," the voice continued, "and with each passing day it is corrupted more. When we had life, we raised God's standard on this acre. We built this shining beacon of devotion, and now your actions threaten to tear it down! Our sleep has been broken to warn you . . . turn back before all is destroyed!"

The echoes died away until the only sound in the ossuary was the guttering of the torch. In the gloom around the edges, Mallory could just make out the other things waiting motionlessly.

He looked from Daniels to Gardener, then stepped forward. "Are you warning us about the enemy outside the walls?" he asked.

The force of the reply made him take a step back. "The enemy within! God's Kingdom is built on purity, not lies and murder!"

He exchanged another glance with Daniels and Gardener. They urged him on. "What do you want us to do?"

"We will not see all we believed in destroyed. We will not have our eternal rest interrupted. Your actions have dragged us back to this foul place from the Glory of God! We cannot return to the sublime beauty until this perversion has been averted. You must stop this corruption . . . or we shall exact our vengeance on those who do the Devil's work . . . *eye for eye, tooth for tooth, hand for hand, foot for foot.*" The tone brought coldness to all of them. "Take this warning back with you. Let the perpetrators know . . . we are watching. Time is running short."

Mallory asked who the *perpetrators* were, but this time there was no response. Instead, the hybrid Miller-face grew fluid, then ran like oil. Slowly, the thing that had possessed him rose out of his body. It detached itself foot-from-foot, then drifted past Mallory as if he wasn't there; a faint coldness tingled his skin on the side against which it brushed. The other things followed it in a mute, eerie procession through the far door.

When the last had departed, Mallory and the others started as if waking from a daze. They turned quickly to Miller, who was heaving himself into a sitting position, sobbing gently.

"It felt as if I had a rat in my stomach!" he said as Mallory helped him to his feet, keeping one hand on his shoulder for support.

"What's going on here?" Mallory said angrily. "It's like this one spot is being turned inside out . . . Things that shouldn't be alive turning up . . . buildings coming out of nowhere . . ."

"The Devil's directing all his powers against us," Gardener muttered. "He doesn't want us to—"

"Shut up about the Devil!" Mallory snapped. "Those bastards were talking about something inside the cathedral. *The enemy within*."

"The one who killed Cornelius and Julian, of course," Daniels said.

Before they could debate the matter further, they were disturbed by a blood-chilling howl, part animal, part man, echoing from the tunnel ahead.

"Lord," Daniels said. "Hipgrave!"

Mallory snatched up the lamp as they ran into the tunnel with Daniels propelling a disoriented, still gently sobbing Miller. The echoes of screeches and cries were sickening to hear.

The tunnel opened into a vault which the echoes suggested was enormous. The roof was supported at regular intervals by crumbling stone pillars. The floor was hard-packed mud punctuated by large pools of water that had dripped from above. The atmosphere was cold and sodden, but the more eerie thing were the flickering torches intermittently fixed to the pillars.

"Who lit them?" Daniels whispered.

A shiver had run through Mallory when he entered the vault. He glanced back to see a thin blue line crackling along the threshold, the barrier between their world and what lay beyond. He was suddenly caught between conflicting impulses. They were only truly safe on the other side of that line. Yet Hipgrave lay somewhere ahead, perhaps wounded, possibly dying.

"Look!" Miller exclaimed.

Almost lost in the shadows across the vault, there was movement. At first it looked like a man, then a beast on all fours, then an amorphous cloud that gradually developed wings and tentacles and sharp edges before disappearing into the gloom.

"Back," Mallory said.

"No." Miller caught at his shirt. "We can't leave Hipgrave."

"He's a vindictive little shit. He deserves what he gets." Mallory didn't meet Miller's eyes.

"We can't judge him. That's what the Bible says—we're not supposed to judge. We're all sinful in one way or another."

"Speak for yourself."

Miller let go and backed away. "No, not you, Mallory," he said sarcastically. "But the rest of us." He looked to where the shape had disappeared. "Well, I'm going anyway. I have to."

"Don't," Mallory ordered. "You stupid bloody idiot. You won't stand a chance."

Miller set off across the vault while Daniels and Gardener watched Mallory judgementally. Mallory half turned toward the tunnel, then cursed under his breath. "Oh, all right then. But if he's in pieces, you carry them back."

They caught up with Miller, then progressed slowly back to back, watching for an attack from any direction. Miller suddenly called out, "Over there!"

They could just make out Hipgrave slumped at the foot of a pillar, unmoving. He was still alive but in a daze, his eyes roaming the darkness; and he didn't even notice they were there. He clutched his ribs, but Mallory could see no sign of a wound.

"Hurry up, let's get him back to the tunnel," he said.

Hipgrave stirred at the sound of his words and responded in a hoarse, detached voice, "There are things down here . . ." he began. "Not trying to get in . . . to keep us . . . from getting out."

From somewhere, a cold breeze blew. They all looked around but could see nothing apart from the shadows dancing at the behest of the torches. A second later, Gardener pitched forward, clutching at his forehead. Blood splattered across Hipgrave's face.

"Bloody hellfire!" Gardener cursed. He removed his hand to see it was smeared red; a thin line had been traced from temple to temple.

"What was it?" Miller whimpered.

Something moved through the vault, just beneath the arched roof. Mallory saw it only as a fluttering shadow travelling so fast it could easily have been a trick of the torchlight. There must have been another one, for Daniels snapped his head around, puzzled.

"Now can we get out of here?" Mallory said sharply. Just as he turned toward the tunnel, he felt a subtle change in the air currents that signalled the rapid approach of something unseen. He jerked his head to one side. Something tore at his hair and was gone in an instant. As it passed, he heard something, or thought he did, that sounded like a distorted human voice whispering his name.

Daniels crashed across Hipgrave, holding the back of his head. When he rolled over, dazed, Mallory saw a red patch where part of his scalp had been torn away.

Rapid movement broke out in several areas of the vault at once, rushing toward the five of them; the attackers were like giant bats but with otherworldly elements that couldn't be discerned in the half-light.

Mallory swung his sword instinctively, clipping one of the flying creatures. A high-pitched squeal was followed by a rain of liquid and the thud of something hitting the ground.

"Shit!" Daniels exclaimed. "How did you do that?"

"What can I say—I'm fabulous." Mallory spun around to strike out at another dark streak, missing it completely. "But not all the time," he added.

The death of the bat-creature acted as a spur to the others, which screeched from all directions at once until the air was filled with a flurry of shadows.

Daniels managed to help Hipgrave to his feet, though the flying things tore their flesh with claws and fangs until they were slick with blood. Mallory's frenzied hacking spun him around and the wild activity of the bat-creatures obscured his vision. At one point he realised Miller was near him, desperately trying to fend off the attacks with his inadequate swordplay. As they were driven across the vault, Mallory saw that Daniels and Gardener had dragged Hipgrave into the opposite direction toward the tunnel.

Finally, a wall came into view. Mallory and Miller edged along it, claws tearing through their cloaks and shirts. After a desperate moment they found another tunnel and dived inside.

Mallory had expected to fight a rearguard action all the way, but the moment they left the vault, the bat-creatures dropped back. He didn't question it.

"Come on, they've gone." He pulled Miller upright; tear stains cut through the blood on his face.

"I can't cope with all this, Mallory," he said. "I'm not strong like you."

"Nobody likes a whiner, Miller. Pull yourself together." It was said affectionately enough to bring a weak smile to Miller's face.

"Where are the others?"

"They got driven the other way, back the way we came."

"This isn't the right tunnel?" Miller's voice cracked.

Mallory could see that there was no thin line of blue separating the worlds; they were still on dangerous ground. "Let's see where it leads us," he said as emotionlessly as he could manage. He ducked briefly into the vault to pluck a torch from the wall, then led the way ahead.

They continued for fifteen minutes, the tunnel branching at regular intervals until they lost track of the labyrinthine layout.

"Catacombs," Mallory said to himself. "We could be down here forever."

"We could say a prayer," Miller ventured.

"Don't be so bloody stupid." He fiddled with the hilt of his sword, then said reluctantly, "Oh, go on, if you want to."

He marched on ahead while Miller muttered behind him. In a little while, they came to a short flight of steps leading up to a doorway with a carved surround depicting the sun, the moon, and stars.

"See?" Miller said.

"Coincidence, idiot." Mallory cautiously climbed the steps. At the top, the doorway opened onto a large domestic room. A log fire roaring in an enormous stone fireplace provided the only source of light. A wooden chair as big as a throne sat before it, while the walls were covered with shelves of books and heavy tapestries. It was so incongruous after the bleak places they had passed through that it brought them up sharp.

"Who lives here?" Miller asked nervously.

Mallory advanced into the chamber cautiously, transferring the torch to his left hand so that he could draw his sword.

"I don't like this," Miller said. "We should go back."

"I thought you prayed for a way out. You can't throw back the gift just because it doesn't meet your expectations." Mallory knew it was a cheap shot and he resolved not to bait Miller further.

They made their way to the centre of the room, but couldn't see any other way out. "There," Miller said. "We have to go back."

Mallory had to agree, but there was a soothing atmosphere to the room after the cold and shadows of the tunnels. As they turned to leave, the heavy tramp of footsteps approached. Miller blanched and looked to Mallory. They both glanced toward the doorway, but the sound didn't appear to be coming from that direction.

Disoriented, Mallory looked around in time to see one of the tapestries on the opposite wall being thrust back. A man at least eight feet tall was emerging from another tunnel. At first, Mallory couldn't make out his features—it was as though his eyes were running—but the shape of the frame was undoubtedly that of the killer that had pursued himself and Hipgrave in the tunnels.

Brandishing his sword, Mallory backed away until he realised that Miller was rooted to the spot. "Come on," he snapped, but Miller only had eyes for the giant now striding toward them.

As he closed on them, the features became clearer: long hair the colour of coal, a thick beard and black eyes that glowered beneath overhanging brows. He wore a shift made out of something like sackcloth, held tight at the waist by a broad leather belt. A thong bound around his left forearm was fitted with several mysterious hooks, which Mallory guessed had caused the scraping sound he had heard on his previous visit to the tunnels.

"One more step and I'll chop you into hunks," Mallory said. He didn't know how realistic that threat was. Although the giant wasn't armed, he looked strong enough to have torn apart Cornelius and Julian.

Surprisingly, the giant stopped, though he didn't appear in the least bit frightened by Mallory's threat. "Ho, Brother of Dragons." His voice echoed like a slamming door.

"Stay back," Mallory warned, unnerved that the killer had called him by the same name he had been given in the Court of Peaceful Days.

"Who are you?" Mallory was startled by Miller's small voice at his back.

"I am the Caretaker," the giant boomed. "I walk the boundaries of this place of reverence. I watch over the fabric, close some doors, open others. I turn on the lamps of hope in the dark of the night, and extinguish them when dawn's light touches the sky. I keep this place safe from those who would assault it. I keep it safe for all who come here, by whatever route, from whatever place, whether hope or despair rules their hearts. I am their servant."

"I'm warning you," Mallory said. He was considering a guerrilla attack to disable the giant with a couple of strikes, before beating a fast retreat.

"Sheathe your sword, Brother of Dragons. You have nothing to fear from me."

"I don't think he's the killer, Mallory," Miller whispered.

Mallory wavered. "I saw you before. You tried to attack me and my friend."

"I tried to *warn* you, Brother of Dragons. In these times, this place can be dangerous to your kind."

There was a cold, almost alien note to the giant's voice that was distinctly unnerving, yet behind it Mallory sensed honesty. He cautiously sheathed his sword.

"Where did you come from?" Miller asked, calmer than at any time since they had ventured into the tunnels. The peaceful atmosphere of the room had increased several notches since the Caretaker had entered.

The Caretaker appeared not to understand the question. "This is my place," he said with a shrug. He motioned toward the fire. "Sit. Shake the cold from your limbs." He brought over two stools, then lowered himself into the wooden chair.

Still reeling after all the running and fighting, Mallory and Miller tentatively took their seats, but were thankful for the fire. As they warmed their hands, they kept a cautious eye on the giant. The Caretaker's unwavering gaze made Mallory uncomfortable, yet something about the easy mood the giant radiated made Mallory feel he couldn't have fought even if he had wanted to. Mallory's tension seeped away until he felt he could have slept if he closed his eyes.

"I had not expected to see a Brother of Dragons in this place," the Caretaker said eventually.

"Somebody else called me that," Mallory said. "It must be the sword." He pulled it a little way out of the sheath so the giant could see the dragons entwining on the hilt. "It's borrowed."

The Caretaker smiled as if this was the most ridiculous thing he had heard. "The sword would not have come to you if you were not a Brother of Dragons," he said warmly. "I see it in your heart. The sword only answers that."

Miller looked at Mallory with widening eyes. "He's talking as if you're special."

"I'm not special." Mallory looked away from him into the fire. Though the logs blazed, they didn't appear to be consumed.

The Caretaker shrugged as if it were of no import and settled back into the chair, staring blankly at the shadows above the mantelpiece. In the soporific atmosphere, they sat in silence while Mallory and Miller tried to put the experience into some kind of context.

It was Miller who found the courage to question the giant first. "What is this place?" he asked.

The Caretaker appeared to respond to the deference in his voice. "You are a Fragile Creature," he began. "Your world is one of constraints, where things are fixed, immutable. This place is not of your world."

"So we're someplace else? We've been *transported*? Like in *Star Trek*?"

"That's right, Miller. Now ask him if he thought *Voyager* let down the franchise," Mallory said tartly. He was still ruminating over what the Caretaker had said about him being a *Brother of Dragons*: could someone with his past really be some kind of mystical champion without him realising it? When he considered it like that, it was more than laughable, but both Rhiannon and the Caretaker appeared convinced. Just thinking of it made him feel queasy, as if he had no control over his life.

The Caretaker placed his fingertips together and stared into the space amongst them. "This place lies between your world and the Far Lands. It lies amid all possible worlds. It lies within all worlds. It encompasses all worlds."

"Well, that explains everything," Mallory sighed.

"Oh, Mallory," Miller complained. He turned back to the Caretaker. "But it came out of nowhere," he said. "One day it was just here, attached to the cathedral we knew."

"Aye. It would seem that way."

Gradually, the Caretaker's words began to strike a chord with Mallory. The giant appeared to be suggesting that there was a benign aspect to the new buildings, as if the manifestation wasn't connected to the oppressive presence beyond the walls. "*Why* did it appear?" he asked pointedly.

The Caretaker eyed him. "You have decided to rejoin the conversation, Brother of Dragons?" Mallory looked away. "It was, in a way, summoned, or dragged, or manifested. Your home . . . your Church . . . has always been a place of power. The Blue Fire has flowed through it since the beginning, fuelled by the wishes of worshippers, and fuelling them in return. Yet now it is like a wellspring of the lifeblood of Existence. Its light shines across all time and all place, too powerful by far, warping the very fabric, altering the Fixed Lands and the Far Lands, calling the dead back from the Grim Lands. Too powerful for you Fragile Creatures. It will make you sick."

Mallory considered this new information. What could have made the earth energy stronger, and how was it linked to everything else that was happening? At least it explained the ghosts from the ossuary that had been glimpsed around the cathedral. Yet he felt uncomfortable that the spirit-energy was powerful enough to call them back from what the Caretaker called the Grim Lands.

"But what caused the power to get stronger?" Miller echoed Mallory's thoughts. "And why does it look like our cathedral? Only bigger. And scarier."

The Caretaker didn't answer, but a notion came to Mallory as he pondered the question. "That's just the way we see it, right?"

"We all build cathedrals for our aspirations, Brother of Dragons," the Caretaker said enigmatically.

"And you're with it, wherever it's found," Mallory said. "Some kind of universal sacred place."

"I am the Caretaker."

"Then who's in charge?"

"I don't want to hear," Miller said to Mallory. He looked queasy. "This is doing my head in. I can't understand what it all means!"

"What it means," Mallory said slowly, "is that something happened at the cathedral that brought this place to us, and now it's affecting all of us."

"Then it has nothing to do with the Devil?" Miller looked at the Caretaker. "You don't work for the Devil?"

"He doesn't work for the Devil," Mallory said.

"And he doesn't work for the killer?" Miller covered his face with his hands. At this, Mallory looked to the Caretaker; in his eyes there were stars, whole galaxies.

"You must look to your own kind," the giant replied.

Miller raised his head to fix his attention on Mallory. "One of us?" His voice was almost comical with disbelief. "Not a demon? How could someone from the cathedral commit those . . . horrors?"

"You're a man who obviously knows everything," Mallory said to the Caretaker. "Care to tell us who we're looking for?"

"Since the Battle of London, my kind have sought to distance ourselves from you Fragile Creatures. Your affairs must remain your own." The Caretaker stared into the fire in deep thought for a while before adding, "Look to your hearts, Fragile Creatures."

"So we're no closer," Miller said dismally.

"Look to your hearts," the Caretaker repeated. The imperative in his words prevented his comment from being seen as a throwaway line. A wheel began to turn in Mallory's mind, pulling notions out of the dark.

Despite the warmth of the fire and the calm atmosphere, the Caretaker put Mallory on edge; though the giant appeared human, an alien aspect lay just beneath the surface that made him unpredictable.

Mallory decided it was time to go. He rose, choosing his words carefully. "Thank you for your hospitality, but we have to return to our own kind." Miller jumped to his feet eagerly.

The Caretaker nodded slowly, watching Mallory so intently with those glimmering eyes that it felt as though he was seeing right into Mallory's head. "I am not your enemy, Brother of Dragons," he said. "In other times we could stand together in this place and look into the infinite with open hearts." His eyes narrowed as if he were squinting to see further. "But there is something broken inside you and Existence will not open up until you mend yourself."

Mallory shifted uncomfortably. "Is there a way back so we don't have to go through the vault?"

"There is." The Caretaker pulled himself to his full height. "You must be careful if you venture into this place again. For the terrible crime that has been committed, there is a desire that you be punished fully. You will never be allowed to leave your refuge, I fear. Even here, powers circle to keep you contained."

"We've done nothing wrong. Really," Miller pleaded. "There's no reason why we're being made to suffer."

"There is always a reason," the Caretaker replied, "even if you cannot see it."

"What is the crime?" Mallory asked.

"The crime is against Existence."

For the first time the conversation brought some emotion to the Caretaker's face and it looked very much like distaste; Mallory did not pursue it further.

The Caretaker took them to the doorway through which he had entered. "Follow this way. Do not deviate from the path," he said, holding the tapestry back. "It will return you to your home."

They hurried away, but as the Caretaker faded from view, his voice floated after them. "Cure yourself, Brother of Dragons. Existence and all its wonders await you."

They emerged in the cloisters soon after. Snowflakes shimmered against the night sky, the stonework glittering with a coating of frost. When they glanced back, the doorway through which they had emerged was no longer there.

"So we know something happened in the cathedral to make the earth energy stronger, and that surge of power brought this place here," Mallory mused. "And I reckon it manifested so forcefully that it changed everyone who was here . . . made them think it had always been this way."

"But because we weren't around, we weren't affected," Miller said.

"You know what?" Mallory continued thoughtfully. "I think all the new buildings that appeared are frightening and oppressive because they're reflecting the mood in the cathedral."

"Because everyone's hungry and trapped?"

Mallory looked at the innocent hope in Miller's face and caught the words he was about to say. "If everything was right here, maybe we'd see some kind of shining palace. The Jerusalem that everyone wanted to build on England's green and pleasant land."

"That would be wonderful."

"We all get what we wish for, maybe. So even our secret thoughts have repercussions." That thought frightened him immensely.

They found Daniels and Gardener perched on pews in the nave looking weary and worried. "We thought you were done for," Gardener said.

"Where's Hipgrave?" Miller asked.

"He's lost it," Gardener replied. He looked away uncomfortably.

"You saw what state he was in," Daniels said. "After we got him out of that vault he was nearly catatonic. Trying to get him through those tunnels . . ." He shook his head. "Suddenly he came out of it like a wild man. Nearly tore my good eye out. It took both of us to pin him down. In the end, Gardener had to knock him flat." He looked toward the altar. "The things he was saying . . ."

"Where is he now?" Mallory asked.

"We got him to the infirmary. Warwick's given him a sedative, but I don't reckon it'll do much good. He's completely gone. There was nothing in his eyes at all. It must have got to him, everything we've seen . . ."

"He was never too stable anyway," Mallory said. "So Blaine's lost one of his captains. What's he going to do now?"

Daniels shrugged. "We briefed him about what happened, but he wasn't really interested. Something else is going on, I think. I heard the Blues had to sort out some kind of fight in the kitchens. Some idiots trying to get food . . ."

"This place is ready to blow," Mallory said. "God knows what's going to happen when they find out about Julian."

"So what happened to you two?" Gardener asked.

Miller told them excitedly about the Caretaker and what he had said about the new buildings.

"You don't want to be consorting with the Devil," Gardener said disparagingly when Miller had finished.

Miller began to protest. "He wasn't—"

"The Devil always lies." Gardener's eyes were steely and uncompromising. "The Bible doesn't have any room for things like that. So it's the work of the Devil."

"You can't beat logic like that," Mallory said sardonically.

There was a flash like a drawn blade in Gardener's face. "You can stand there being smart, lad, but the way things are going there's only two sides and you'll have to be on one or the other. And I'm starting to have my doubts about you."

"Oh, I'm wounded."

Gardener held his eye for a moment, then began to clean the mud from his boots with a dagger.

Miller looked to Mallory uncertainly. "So we can't trust anything he said?"

"We trust ourselves," Mallory said. "That's all we can do."

Mallory spent the rest of the night and half the next day pondering the Caretaker's enigmatic comments, before his thoughts turned to Rhiannon. In the Court of Peaceful Days, she, too, had made obtuse comments that had appeared meaningless at the time. Were they both trying to help him in an oblique way, so that they did not feel they were breaking some kind of agreement that their kind didn't assist Fragile Creatures? The more he considered it, the more he thought it was probably true. Her words were lodged clearly in his mind: *Look to learning to understand the conflict.* He considered this until, in a flash of inspiration, he had an inkling of what she had been advising.

Mallory feigned illness to avoid going to Peter's Christian philosophy class, knowing it would earn him the wrath of Blaine, but it was the only way he could guarantee that the rest of the knights would be occupied. With all the other brothers dealing with the rigorous day-to-day routine of the cathedral, he would be free to investigate unseen.

He hurried through the snow to the cloisters and climbed the stairs to the library. It had changed considerably since the first time he had been there, now straddling the boundary between the old buildings and the new. On his side, it was just as it always had been, but through the window he could see it progressing into a vast gothic chamber, its ceiling lost to shadows, with bizarre stone carvings that appeared to watch over anyone wandering amongst the racks, lit by sizzling torches and with shelves of books that must have gone up twenty feet or more.

The door was locked, as he had expected, and he knew there was no other point of entry. He hoped he was as good a judge of character as he believed.

He rapped on the glass gently until he saw James approaching. When James saw who was without, he shook his head and tried to wave Mallory away, but Mallory persisted, pleading silently. After a moment, James relented. He slid back several bolts and turned the key before opening the door a crack.

"Are we keeping the gold chalices in here now?" Mallory said.

"The library is off-limits." James was patently ill at ease with his new position.

"Yes, you can't let those books fall into the wrong hands. There might be an awful spontaneous outbreak of knowledge and open-mindedness."

"What do you want, Mallory?" James said wearily. From the moment he had given Mallory the first guided tour of the cathedral, James had never sounded anything less than good-natured.

"A few minutes of your time, that's all."

"I'm not joking. No one is allowed in the library."

"No one? What's the point of having a library, then?" Mallory tried to appear disarming. "You must be bored out of your mind locked up with only the silver-fish for company."

James couldn't help a chuckle. He leaned out to look up and down the corridor, then opened the door quickly to allow Mallory entrance. Once inside, he drew the bolts and quickly turned the key before hurrying Mallory out of sight of the window.

As they entered the new section, the temperature dropped a degree or two and their footsteps took on an eerie echo that susurrated for an unnatural period. The dark closed in around them, bringing with it the suffocating smells of leather, dust, candlewax, damp paper, and great age. Mallory couldn't have raised his voice if he'd wanted to.

James led a mazelike path through the stacks to a table bearing a flask, a Tupperware box containing sandwiches, and a hissing lantern.

"Most people have to commit a crime to get this treatment," Mallory said. James's expression suggested he felt the same way. "If I didn't know better I'd say they preferred you in here instead of out there."

James's eyes narrowed and his guard came up a little. "Who would *they* be?"

Mallory dismissed the question with a laugh. "You know what I'm talking about, James."

James pulled a couple of chairs up to the table and poured Mallory a cup of tea from the flask. Mallory paused when he felt the touch of the plastic lid on his lip. "This stuff will be antique soon. You'll be able to haggle for it down at the market, along with the polystyrene McDonald's boxes and Perspex shed windows."

James lightened. "If I know human nature, we'll be knee-deep in non-recyclable litter again before too long." He sat back in his chair and surveyed Mallory with a strange smile. "Now, Mr. Mallory, what exactly are you up to?"

"Can I speak freely?"

James sighed. "I have obligations to the Church authorities—"

"But you . . . we . . . surely have a greater obligation to a Higher Power. To the religion itself, and its teachings. And if the Church authorities are working in opposition to that—not consciously, of course—"

"Are you leaping to judgement, Mr. Mallory?"

"All I'm saying is that the only thing we have to answer to is that Higher Power."

"God. Why don't you say God?" He could tell Mallory was choosing his words with caution, but James's attempt to divine his purpose couldn't penetrate beneath the surface. "This religion operates within a structure. It cannot exist without that structure. By being part of it, we tacitly accept that structure—"

"And what if that structure's wrong?" Mallory pressed. "What if . . . God . . . never intended that structure to come into place? What if that's all politics?"

"What if, what if." James waved a dismissive hand. "This is what we have."

"This is it, right or wrong?"

James bit the inside of his lip and stared along the racks of books.

"How about if we just talk? No harm there."

James gave a conciliatory smile. "That would be nice."

"So let's start with a discussion of comparative theology." Mallory sipped on the hot, sweet tea—not tea in the true sense, but an infusion of various herbs and spices.

"You're a strange man, Mallory. Why are you interested in these things? Most of your compatriots couldn't care less."

"Religions around the world are all driving toward a comprehension of a Higher Power. God." He smiled. "To an uneducated person, it would seem that the differences between them are only a matter of mechanics. Different vehicles to reach the same destination." James began to disagree, but Mallory waved him quiet. "Several religions have things in common, but there's one thing you can find in Eastern and Western traditions: the power of the spirit. Something that might seem from one perspective to be a kind of energy that perhaps could even be quantified one day, from another point of view looks like magic, affecting things separated by great distance."

James's eyes narrowed. Mallory felt he was on the right lines. "The religion that existed here before Christianity came . . . a kind of nature worship, I suppose—"

"You're being disingenuous, Mallory. You know exactly what it is. I'm asking you to treat me with respect and to speak honestly of what's on your mind."

Mallory nodded. "OK. I'll be straight. That religion, like the Eastern traditions, believed that spirit-energy existed in the wider world . . . in the wider universe . . . and in man. It linked the inner and the outer, above and below. And it believed it ran in channels across the world, along which were established sacred sites where the power was strongest. The stone circles, the cairns, the raised hills. Leys, right? You've heard of leys?" James gave nothing away. "And along these leys ran—"

"The Blue Fire."

"That's right. You know about it."

"Go on."

Mallory finished his tea. "I'm guessing there are books here that could tell me all about this." When James didn't respond, he continued, "The pagan camp just over the walls . . . it's here because Salisbury is on a powerful ley, apparently. The Blue Fire here is very strong. And the Christian church decides to reestablish itself here, in Salisbury. Not in Winchester, or Glastonbury. Here. Coincidence?"

"Glastonbury is on a powerful ley. So they say," James pointed out.

"Now *you're* being disingenuous. But your answer shows we're on the same page. Anyway, the old Glastonbury site is in ruins. What was needed was a complete structure that could focus the energy. Not a stone circle, but a massive stone building with a spire like a lightning conductor. As far as I know, there's nothing in the Bible that mentions this Blue Fire, yet somebody in the Church knows about it."

James shook his head firmly, his lips clenched tight.

"I'm a good judge of character," Mallory continued. "I'm not saying this to flatter you, because I do have respect for you, but I can tell you're a good man, with the best interests at heart. And I would guess injustice probably gets you down. I would think you wouldn't want to perpetuate injustice, or misdirection, or conspiracy, for whatever reason. Not in a religion that makes so much of truth and honesty and shining the light of righteousness on the world."

"Why have you come to see me about this, Mallory? Why do you feel that strongly about it? Most people are just concerned with staying alive."

"Because I think this *is* about staying alive. I don't know why, or how . . . it's just a hunch. But there's something going on at this cathedral that's the root of all our problems, and I think it's linked to this." Mallory tried to be as honest as possible, hoping it would sway James, but it wasn't something that came easily to him. "I don't know how much you know about what's going on, but I think you have suspicions. I think you're at least uneasy. And I certainly know you want things to turn out well—"

"And if you find the information you want, you think you might be able to do something that might help us?"

"I don't know," Mallory replied truthfully.

"What could you do, Mallory?"

"At least I want to try. There aren't many out there saying the same."

James's smile was a forensic dissection of Mallory's character. "That doesn't sound like the Mallory I've heard so much about."

James sat silently for a moment, then rose sharply and began to prowl back and forth in thought; he looked as if he was tearing himself apart. Finally, he returned to his seat and began speaking animatedly as if a dam had broken. "This stays between us. I don't know you well enough to know if you *do* have best interests at heart, but you're right in your assessment of how I feel about the truth being hidden, or glossed over, or bent. But it must stay between us, is that understood?"

Mallory nodded agreement to his terms.

"You talk about conspiracy," he began. "Someone once said that the history of civilisation is the history of conspiracy. What you learn . . . established knowledge . . . is not always the truth. Secrets lie behind everything we pass down, sometimes big secrets. Everyone thinks they know something of history. The truth is, they know nothing. It is a facet of human nature that the most important actions and events are hidden away so that all we see are their repercussions or the lies designed to cover them. You know this—you can see it in the people and organisations around you all the time, and it was no different in the oldest times, in the same way that we are no different from our ancestors, although we like to think of ourselves as wiser, cleverer, more moral. We know nothing." He took a deep breath, controlled himself, then spoke in more measured terms. "I was part of a conspiracy myself, though a benign one. The Christian Church has been filled with them from the start . . . from the very earliest days. It is the nature of the structure. I was a member of a group called the Watchmen. It was our responsibility to guard certain knowledge—pre-Christian knowledge the Church had assimilated—that could be used when the Fall happened and humanity was under threat."

"You know what really happened at the Fall?" Mallory asked.

"Some of it, yes. There are worlds beyond our own, Mallory, where strange and powerful beings live. Throughout our history, they have passed back and forth, influencing events here, becoming the source of all our myths and legends. On a previous visit they became the template for the gods of the Celtic nations. And at the Fall they came back again. Their power is unimaginable to us . . . the world couldn't cope. On that day, all the rules changed."

"And they're still out there."

"The first time they came they almost destroyed the world with their rivalries and games and wars. Humanity wasn't going to allow it to happen again. Sometime in the ancient past, we discovered that they were vulnerable to the Blue Fire . . . that the Blue Fire was a power above *everything*. That information was encoded in the landscape by many ancient peoples, not just the ones who came to be called the Celts in popular understanding. Secrets in stone, in alignments, a language that did not use words and which only came alive to us when we found the right perception through which to see it. And it was that information that the Watchmen guarded and passed down from generation to generation for whenever it would be needed. We knew about the gods, and the Otherworld they came from, and the secret history, and all the prophecies that went along with it, and we told no one. We had to wait until we were needed, when five heroes would come together to defend humanity."

"You met the five?"

"Some of them. Good people, though they didn't recognise it themselves."

"I would say, from a Christian perspective, that this all sounds a little like blasphemy, or at the very least noncanon," Mallory said.

James sighed. "Yes, contradictions abound. But not as many as you might think. You are correct in saying that the Blue Fire is not discussed overtly in the writings and traditions of Christianity, but that is not to say that it was not known of and accepted as a central tenet from the earliest times. It was, and it was kept away from general view by those conspiracies buried in the fundament of Christianity."

"Don't let the common man have too much knowledge . . . the priesthood might lose its mystique," Mallory said tartly.

"That approach was necessary when Christianity was attempting to gain a foothold—"

"And now?"

"Now we are trying to gain a foothold again." He poured himself another cup of tea, his pleasant humour replaced by a seriousness that didn't sit well with him. "One of the most powerful forces within the Church during its first centuries was a secret group of Christian geomancers. They were well aware of the Blue Fire from ancient traditions and linked it with the spirit of Christianity, and they were responsible for the precise position of churches around the world to take the best advantage of sites where this earth energy was at its most potent. Their greatest influence was during the Middle Ages, during the great period of cathedral building."

"Geomancers? In the Church?"

"You see? Everyone thinks they know history, but they don't. And this has been well documented." James went to the stacks and removed a volume. "*Les Mystères de la Cathédrale de Chartres* by Louis Charpentier. Chartres Cathedral stands on a large prehistoric mound over a buried chamber, which Charpentier identifies as a confluence of four streams of this serpentine earth energy, named by him as *woivres*. A very powerful site indeed, and the Christian geomancers built the cathedral there to be a massive collector of that energy, to empower worshippers and to spread it out into the local area, in much the same way that the builders of the stone circles did. And if you find that hard to believe, I should point out that the cathedral site was also the home of the great Druidic university of Gaul, where ancient wise men were initiated into the mysteries of the Blue Fire. The same place, the same potency, within different belief systems. As you said earlier, coincidence?"

Mallory felt a tingling at the base of his spine; a pattern was beginning to emerge.

"These are the secrets I was privy to as a Watchman—the places of power, the spiritual energy in the land that ties people to it, the importance of it in the Great

Scheme," James said. "There are books in this library that hint at it, some . . ." He tapped the French volume, ". . . that speak of it directly. Guided carefully, a good student could piece together much that has been hidden for millennia."

"That's why the first Christian churches were sited on pagan places of worship. Not because of some kind of spiritual hegemony, but because those places were a source of tremendous energy that could be used to invigorate the religion. And that's why they keep you locked up here with the books—because you know so much about it. And that story about the siting of this cathedral by the fall of an arrow—"

"It is an allegory that tells of the Christian geomancers' art. Old Sarum was a strongly powerful spot, but there was some . . . trouble . . . there, and it was felt this location was even more propitious."

"So we're all here because of this spiritual energy in the land. And that's why the travellers have set up their camp here as well." Mallory tried to develop the information James had given him to understand what was happening, but one thought dominated. "The pagans outside the compound are right: they've been demonised, marginalised, and everything they believe in has been stolen. The Church is a sham."

"No," James stressed. "You misunderstand. The philosophy of Christianity is unmatched, a powerful, powerful force. It was the first religion to offer the concept of charity, of selfless devotion to others. That cannot be denied. It has had many dark periods . . . many times when those who profess to be Christians have warped the intrinsic beliefs . . . but that shining light at the heart of it still shines through. It transcends all earthly transgressions."

Mallory shrugged. "Whatever you say, James. But I can't help thinking that a religion that allows itself to be open to corruption is on pretty shaky ground."

"We are a force for good, Mallory, despite ourselves."

Mallory could see that James believed this deeply, but he was sick of religion—all religion—with its ability to cause strife and suffering in its wake. "You're not very good at keeping secrets, James," Mallory said with a smile. "I come in here, ask a couple of questions, and you blurt it all out."

"Because I don't believe in keeping secrets. Nobody asked me to. It was implied, but nobody came out and said it. I believe the Church would work better if it put everything out in the open and trusted its followers. But you can't take the politics out of any organisation. That is human nature." He offered more tea, but Mallory declined; he could almost hear Blaine's fury already. "You're a good man, Mallory," James said out of the blue.

"Right. I'm just looking out for myself, James."

"All of us are two separate people, Mallory. We're the materialistic, rational person on the surface, and we're the ghost inside who moves our hands when we're not thinking. The ghost is the true *us*, our essence, freed from the petty influences of this world. And your ghost is good, Mallory, I know that."

"I wish I could have called him up to scare a few people on Halloween. Might have got some more treats amongst all the tricks."

James laughed heartily and waved him away. "I enjoyed our little chat. It feels good to get things off one's chest, you know?"

Mallory felt strangely reluctant to leave. The conversation had reminded him of his own life, when he'd had the time and the inclination to ruminate over weighty matters of philosophy; but that was before he discovered how pointless it all was. He was halfway to the door when he turned back. "Thanks," he said simply.

"Do your best, Mallory," James replied. "We all need a saviour."

As everyone feared, Julian's death had a terrible effect on the brethren. Whereas before there had been some hope of salvation, the new murder had unleashed a slowly rising tide of fatal resignation. The main target was the cathedral leadership, though few had any workable alternative plans. Dissent was heard on the way to prayers, or over the refectory tables. Furious arguments cropped up regularly, shattering the atmosphere of pious devotion, and on occasion there were even fights. There was a general feeling that death and destruction were only just around the corner.

The mood was not helped by the repeated collapse of the tunnel under the wall, killing two diggers. Accusations of incompetence were levelled; why couldn't the bishop do something about it? Food was running out; there was no time for failure. On the surface, Stefan took the criticism with humility and sto-icism, but behind the scenes, subtle and worrying changes were taking place. Unable to carry out their true role, the knights were ordered to patrol the cathedral, dampening down disputes and reporting back to Blaine the names of any troublemakers. Most took this job reluctantly, but some, most notably members of the Blues, accepted it with unfortunate relish. The Inquisition of Heretical Depravity took an increasingly active role overseeing the "questioning" of the active dissenters. Their offices in the shadowy heart of the new buildings came to be feared, and the inquisitors themselves were only discussed in whispers in case comments were reported back to them.

But the creeping repression was the least of their worries. As December crawled along and a bitter chill set in, the nightly attacks increased in intensity and lasted longer, sometimes until first light. For some reason, the hordes outside had become more successful; walls were repeatedly damaged and much of each day was spent carrying out repairs with rapidly diminishing resources. Against it all was the constant background of fear that the murderer within the cathedral could strike at any time. Nowhere was safe; no one was safe.

chapter twelve

A JEALOUS GOD

"Things continually shift between being united by love and divided by strife."

Empedocles

The snow started again on December the sixth, floating down from a grey sky just before prime. It was a display of such ethereal charm that it prompted even the depressed and hungry brothers to raise their heads from their struggle and enjoy the moment. By lunchtime, a thin coating had transformed the cathedral and its bleak gothic buildings into a fairy-tale palace, glowing soft and white. Across Salisbury, the rooftops gleamed; everywhere sound and light took on a new quality.

And still the snow fell. By midafternoon, brothers were hastily assigned to clear the paths, the crunch of their boots and the scrape of their shovels echoing around the compound. Afterward, they gathered in the shelter of the west front, stamping and steaming, ruddy-cheeked and bright-eyed, cracking jokes and swapping tales.

Mallory watched them as he returned from a patrol around the bishop's palace, quietly marvelling at how something as simple and natural as a snowfall could have such a transformative effect on human nature. Briefly, they had forgotten the Devil at the gates, though the oppressive nature of the threat had unbalanced several minds in recent days, especially after the horned shape had been glimpsed once again hovering over the city. The apocalypse, they all felt, was now sickeningly close.

The snow provided a break, too, from his own thoughts as they continually turned over the many facets of the mystery without finding any connecting factor; but he was close to a solution, he knew that.

A little further on, he spotted Gardener crouching down in the middle of the lawns, occasionally swinging his arm back and forth. Mallory realised he was surreptitiously feeding the birds a few bits of dry bread left over from lunch. In their increasingly dire situation, some would have considered it wasteful, but Mallory found it oddly touching: Gardener, gruff, hard-faced, occasionally unpleasant, locked in a moment of simple sacrifice for lesser creatures.

He watched until the Geordie had finished, then was overcome with a devilish idea. As Gardener trudged away, Mallory rolled a snowball and hurled it with devastating aim, hitting Gardener squarely at the base of his skull. Gardener whirled, eyes blazing, but when he saw Mallory his face went blank. Mallory had a sudden sense of his miscalculation until Gardener dipped down, rolled a snowball, and launched it with one lightning move. It struck Mallory in his chest, showering snow across his face.

For a second, everything hung, and then they both exploded with raucous laughter, leaping into a frenzied bout of snowball throwing. Within moments, they heard a whoop as Miller and Daniels ran up. Gardener and Mallory hit them both before they were halfway across the lawns.

For the next fifteen minutes, they forgot all the pressures of the daily strife in complete childlike abandon. Mallory joked, "Stay on Daniels's blindside!" while Miller darted back and forth among them, whirling snowballs as if he were crazed. By the end, when they were all covered in white from head to toe, even Gardener was laughing. They collapsed into the snow, exhausted but still in high spirits.

Three members of the Blues walked by, watching their ridiculous fun with disdain. One of them sneered that they were bringing the knights into disrepute, following his comment with a whispered disparaging remark that brought mocking laughter from his colleagues. Mallory gave them the finger, while Miller threw a snowball in their direction. The Blues rounded, spoiling for a fight, until the ringleader calmed them and led them on their way.

"Wankers," Mallory said.

"No sense of humour," Daniels added. "Always a bad sign."

Suddenly something struck Mallory, so obvious that he wondered why he hadn't considered it before. "Why are they called Blues?" he asked. The blue flash on their shoulders had set them apart from the very first.

No one knew, but after his conversation with James, Mallory had an idea. Their very existence, all the mysterious missions on which they regularly embarked, had something to do with the Blue Fire: they were an élite squad in more ways than one.

His thoughts were interrupted by the acrid smell of smoke drifting across the compound accompanied by the sound of crackling fire. Filled with curiosity, they made their way around the side of the new buildings to its source near the gates, where a large bonfire was sending up thick black clouds.

"What are they wasting all that fuel for?" Daniels asked.

It was only then that they saw the lines of brothers emerging from the cathedral with armfuls of books, some ancient with crumbling spines, many shiny leather-backed volumes, even modern pamphlets.

"The library," Mallory said. "He really did it, the Nazi."

"Ah, they're only books," Gardener dismissed.

Mallory turned on him. "They're not only books. They're ideas, thoughts, beliefs—"

Gardener interrupted with a shrug. "That's right, but they're not our ideas, thoughts, beliefs."

Mallory knew there was no point in arguing. He turned back to the sad sight until he noticed three figures watching the bonfire across the way, almost obscured by the drifting smoke. When it cleared for a moment, he saw it was James, his face drawn, shoulders hunched, standing between two upright, characterless young men who were clearly inquisitors.

The red flames contrasted starkly with the white of the snow. He watched for another moment, then trudged slowly back to the dormitory alone.

An hour later he was called to a fight in the refectory. Two brothers were brawling over the size of their portions at dinner. It was a stupid argument—there couldn't have been more than half a carrot in it—but in that claustrophobic atmosphere tempers frayed easily. One of the men had received a broken nose. The lower half of his face was stained red, and it was Mallory's job to escort him to the infirmary while giving him a caution. Miller was taking the other one for a dressing-down before one of the inquisitors.

As they left the refectory, the broken-nosed man was sullen and depressed; he'd lost his dinner in the scuffle and there would be nothing more until the thin gruel they laughingly called breakfast. Mallory didn't have the heart to deliver the caution Blaine had outlined for such occasions, so they walked in silence.

When they arrived at the infirmary, they were surprised to find the place in disarray. Warwick's surgical utensils were scattered across the floor, the contents of some herb jars had been emptied, and the operating table was upended. Warwick sat on a chair in one corner, white-faced and uneasy. He was surrounded by two stony-faced Blues and a tall, weasley inquisitor who was brandishing Warwick's clockwork radio.

"It's not mine, I tell you," Warwick protested.

"Your assistant said it was." The inquisitor examined the radio as if it were filth.

"Well, he's wrong."

"You know the punishment for hoarding banned technology."

Warwick looked as if he was going to be sick. "It's not mine!"

"Why was it hidden amongst your things?" The inquisitor plainly wasn't going to let up.

Mallory wanted to say, *It's just a little radio! We all loved them only a few months ago*, but he knew the object had taken on new meaning in the rapidly developing language of the cathedral. It was a nuclear bomb, a Ouija board, a letter filled with anthrax. He wondered if he was the only sane one in the entire place.

It looked as if the inquisitor was only just beginning, so Mallory abandoned the broken-nosed man there and wandered into the network of back rooms. He was taken with the desire to see Hipgrave, who hadn't been heard from in days.

The main ward was full. With the food declining, more and more people were getting sick and taking longer to recover, while others were being laid low by injuries they would normally have fended off. Every bed was also taken in a makeshift ward in an annexe. Beyond, there were several single rooms with occupants in various states of illness.

The final room was locked, but like the others it had a window of reinforced glass through which Mallory could see Hipgrave lying in bed, arms straight out by his sides, staring unblinkingly at the ceiling.

Mallory hesitated, then rapped gently on the window. Hipgrave's gaze didn't even flicker toward him. He appeared, to Mallory's untutored eyes, catatonic. A rigid man, the strain of all they'd experienced had finally broken him.

For the first time, Mallory felt pity for Hipgrave. Although the captain had been thoroughly disagreeable, he didn't deserve what had happened to him. None of them deserved it.

Back in the surgery, Warwick's radio lay smashed on the floor. Mallory found it hard to deal with the pointlessness of it all; no more information coming from across the country, no more messages of hope. All thrown away, for some stupid idea of religious belief that was as irrational as all the supernatural creatures pounding on the walls. He'd been consumed with thoughts of vengeance against Blaine and the Church authorities for all his suffering, but the pointlessness of everything in the cathedral had worn him down. Now all he wanted was to get away with Sophie. Stefan and the others could stew in the hell of their own making.

Warwick was nowhere to be seen. Mallory didn't try to divine what that meant, nor what it insinuated for all the sick brothers in the infirmary. There was no sense anywhere.

Leaving the infirmary, he had half a mind to go back to the dorm and climb into bed, until he heard raised voices coming from the refectory.

He had expected to find another fight, but the atmosphere was much different. Most of the brothers were standing watching a scene being played out near the serving tables. More inquisitors and Blues were struggling to contain a slight figure throwing himself around in a wildcat frenzy. It was Lewis, Daniels's young boyfriend. When he found a gulp of breath, he let out another burst of shouting so filled with passion that Mallory at first had trouble understanding what he was saying.

"This is wrong!" Mallory eventually deciphered. "I'm a good Christian!"

Eventually, the Blues got a grip on his arms and pinned him between them.

His face was flushed and tearstained. Inquisitor-General Broderick turned to the crowd, obviously feeling a need to explain the arrest of someone so young and unimposing.

"This one has committed a sin against the Lord," he began.

"No sin!" Lewis shouted.

"A terrible sin, against the very order of things. He is a sodomite—"

Lewis shouted him down. "I'm someone who *loves*! Is that wrong? No, it's God's message!" he added incredulously. "Then why am I being punished for it?"

"Take him away!" some of the fundamentalists in the corner were shouting, their faces filled with hatred.

Mallory noticed Daniels standing in the front, not far from Lewis. He looked as if he was about to tear himself apart.

Lewis's eyes fell on Daniels. "If you believe in love," he proclaimed, seemingly to everyone, though Mallory knew it was aimed at his boyfriend, "speak out now! Speak out on my behalf! Because if this is allowed to happen, this cathedral . . . this religion . . . will lose something much more important this day! And you'll all know in your hearts you turned your back on a truth . . . on love . . . on me!"

In the candlelight, Mallory could see tears glinting in Daniels's eye. It seemed he was ready to go to Lewis's aid. Mallory prepared to restrain him, knowing that if Daniels spoke out, he would be dragged away with Lewis to an uncertain fate.

Daniels hovered for a second, then turned and pushed his way through the crowd, his head bowed. Lewis cried out as if he had been wounded, but even then he didn't say Daniels's name.

In the confusion of Lewis's arrest, Mallory forced his way through the mute crowd in search of Daniels to try to mitigate the blow. But Daniels was not at the back of the refectory, nor was he outside, or back in the dormitory. Mallory searched for half an hour and in the end was forced to give up. The day that had seemed hopeful only a few hours earlier was ending so bleakly he didn't want to see the morrow.

Wrapped in his cloak with the hood pulled low over his head, Mallory drifted around the buildings for a while, lost to his own dark thoughts, until he was drawn to the cathedral by the distant sound of plainsong drifting through the cold evening air. With the candles gleaming through the frosted windows and the blanketing snow casting the night white, a sense of peace and hope fell across him.

He felt an urge to be on his own, so he made his way to the kitchens, which he knew would be empty at that time. With the ovens burning around the clock, it was also the only continually warm place in the entire cathedral compound; the list of brothers seeking work there had been long ever since winter had come. But how long would the fuel last, he wondered?

The dinner pots and pans had been rinsed and lay gleaming on the work surface; the ovens had been stoked, the few vegetables trimmings put aside for composting. Dinner had been even more meagre than usual and Mallory's stomach was rumbling, but he resisted the urge to raid the larders out of responsibility to the others.

Instead, he found a space beside the furthest oven from the door and shuffled in. The temperature was just right to begin to ease the aching cold from his feet and hands. When he swallowed the warm air, the contrast allowed him to feel the permeating cold all the way down his throat into his lungs; it felt as though he hadn't been warm for months.

In the soporific atmosphere, it wasn't long before his eyelids began to feel heavy. He fought it—it would be embarrassing to be discovered there—but within minutes he had drifted off.

"You've all done a terrible thing." Sophie walked slowly around the moonlit glade.

Mallory knew what she meant. "The Fabulous Beast."

"How could you do such a thing? It was something wonderful, Mallory." The deep sorrow in her voice made his heart ache. "It was more than just a living creature, it was a symbol, it was the manifestation of the Earth Spirit, the power of life given form. And you killed it!"

"I'm sorry." That sounded pathetic against something so huge. He wanted to say that he hadn't joined in; it wasn't his hand that had helped bring the creature down. But he knew that was no mitigation. As she had pointed out to him before, he was complicit because he *hadn't* taken sides; there was no sitting on the fence. He had known that at the time, and he knew it now.

"We can't begin to guess the repercussions of what you did, Mallory," she continued. "The echoes will run through the universe, through time. Goodness knows what the end result will be, what price we'll all have to pay. And there will be a price, Mallory, make no mistake."

"I wish it hadn't happened, Sophie, more than anything, but everyone in the cathedral is under tremendous pressure. They've been facing a siege for weeks now . . . they're running out of food, and fuel. They feel they're in a fight to the death against Evil, not just to save themselves, but to save the whole world. And they're completely powerless—"

"I know," she sighed. "But that doesn't justify—"

"I'm not trying to justify anything, just explain." He walked over and took her hand; she let him, folding her cool fingers into his. "If there's any way we can put this right, make amends . . ."

"I don't know. It's hard to think how. I'll have to petition Higher Powers, see what can be done."

He tugged gently on her hand and she looked into his face, her eyes lost in pools of shadow. "Against all the terrible things happening in the world, we should be nothing, but it doesn't feel like that to me."

She rested her head on his chest. Even in that place he could feel the tension in her brought on by the weight of all her obligations. Behind her confidence and power lay a woman as unsure as everybody else, desperate for a break from the demands heaped on her, someone who had managed to put her own needs to one side to do her best for others. Sensing that, Mallory felt even more drawn to her.

"We're going to make a go of this, aren't we?" she said wearily. "It would be so nice to have someone to help with the burden . . . of this life."

There was a weight of belief in her voice that suddenly scared him. She was implying he had the strength, the ability, the confidence, to stand beside her, to help support her, and he was very good at presenting that view to the world; but inside, he wasn't half the man he pretended to be.

Once again she appeared to be reading his thoughts. "You're a better man than you think you are, Mallory," she said, her voice muffled against his chest.

"Where do we go from here?" he said. But even as the words had left his lips, he was aware that they were moving apart, not through any conscious will of their own, but as if a rope were dragging him back.

Her voice floated to him even as she was swallowed by the trees. "I'll see you soon, Mallory. In the flesh next time."

He awoke with a start, still wrapped in thoughts of trees and a moonlit landscape. Briefly, he wondered where he was, until the warmth of the oven brought him back to earth quickly. Someone else was in the kitchen. Cautiously, he peered around the edge of the oven.

Gibson, the Canon of the Pies, was opening a padlocked larder built into one wall. It had been constructed to be almost hidden unless it was actively being sought: the doors merged with an area of wood panelling, the keyhole lying behind a swivelling, decorative rail. Only the padlock around the two handles, both disguised as ornaments, gave the game away.

Inside the larder were shelves filled with food. Mallory could see cured meats, dried fruits in jars, pickles in larger glass containers, and assorted tins. Gibson was removing what looked like salt-beef from a large Tupperware box and stuffing it into his mouth till his cheeks bulged. From his anxious backward glances, Mallory understood this was Gibson's own private store. He had plainly stockpiled emergency supplies under his role as head of the kitchens to keep him well fed. Meanwhile the rest of the brothers underwent privations to ensure everyone had enough food to survive. Mallory felt a dull flare of anger. He considered confronting Gibson there and then, but he knew the canon would use his authority to deny his crime and Mallory would be the one made to suffer.

While he considered his options, Gibson finished off half of the salt-beef and followed it with two pickled onions. Then he pulled out a stoppered bottle—some fortified wine, probably brandy, Mallory guessed—and took a long draught.

Just as Mallory had reached the conclusion that he could no longer contain himself, he became aware of a sickening but disturbingly familiar smell. His heart began to pound as desperate images of the labyrinth at Bratton Camp crackled through his mind.

Gibson filled his mouth with dried apple and raisins until the contents were falling out even as he pushed more in.

Anxiously, Mallory searched for the origin of the foul odour. Gibson wasn't aware of it. He popped one whole sugary biscuit into his mouth and began to close the cupboard. At that moment, he heard or sensed something and froze. Mallory saw Gibson's fear that his sins had sought him out.

Mallory drew his sword slowly.

"Who's there?" Gibson snapped the padlock shut and turned, pressing his huge bulk against the larder. His cheeks were flushed, his eyes shining.

Who's there? Mallory echoed in his head.

A shadow moved on the far edge of his vision, but was gone the instant he looked toward it.

The air in the kitchen appeared to deaden. The only sounds were the dim crackling of the logs in the oven and Gibson's laboured breathing.

The key ring jangled as Gibson dropped it into a pocket in his robe. He wiped the saliva from his mouth with the back of his hand.

Mallory had grown taut. He scanned back and forth across the kitchen but could see no sign of any other person even though every fibre of his being told him the threat was there. Gibson, too, appeared to have come to this conclusion, for his expression was now tinged with nascent dread. He shivered, steeled himself, then began to march insistently toward the door.

The shadow reappeared, driving toward Gibson so fast that Mallory had no time to react. Half glimpsed, it seemed to be made of glass, falling almost into view, then vanishing completely, like flashes of light illuminating a statue. At first it was undeniably human in shape, but altering as it progressed: tentacles, wings, a fan of knives, a bulking body with too many arms and legs, each blurring into the next.

Gibson only had time to let out the briefest scream. His twisted, horror-filled expression showed that the attacker had presented itself to him fully. Mallory launched himself from his hiding place, a dazzling sapphire light dancing across the kitchen from his sword.

The sheer speed and ferocity of the attacker made him feel rooted. Though barely seen, its effect on Gibson was of unyielding substance. As Mallory vaulted a preparation table, he was aware of a rapid back-and-forth movement and Gibson simply crumpled.

He reached the canon in seconds, but all that remained was butcher's shop detritus, the final spark of life just winking out.

He whirled, but somehow, even at that close range, the monstrous attacker had become lost to him. Yet as he searched, the light from his sword created a shadow where none should be, away by the doors into the storerooms; and it was the shadow of a man.

As it attacked, he brought up his sword, hoping whatever power it held would be enough. The blue glow illuminated something so foul his conscious mind refused to accept it, but at that point he realised—as he had known at Bratton Camp—that he could never defeat it alone. He turned and sprinted out into the snowy night.

Things only fell into place when he was sucking in the freezing air, finally accepting that nothing was going to come out of the open door. Downcast before, his mood was beginning to fan into despair.

The killer wasn't human at all: somehow they had brought the thing from Bratton Camp back with them.

He ran into the cathedral to raise the alarm. Compline was just coming to a close. Before he had time to yell out, Blaine ran over and gripped his arm. "Shut up, you idiot! Do you want to start a panic?" he hissed. He could see from Mallory's face that something terrible had happened.

Roeser, the Blues' captain, manhandled Mallory out into the night while Blaine attempted to convince the brothers that all was well. After Mallory revealed what had happened, Roeser gathered a coterie of Blues and rushed to the kitchens, leaving Mallory with Blaine, two other Blues, and Broderick, who watched Mallory closely with his inquisitor's eyes.

Stefan arrived shortly with the knight sent to summon him, and spoke hurriedly with Blaine before they both approached Mallory. Blaine looked hateful, but Stefan remained as emotionless as ever.

"Do you swear now before God that you did not kill Gibson, and before him, Cornelius, our beloved bishop, and his assistant, Julian?" Stefan asked abruptly.

At first, Mallory was taken aback, but then he saw the hardness in Blaine's face and realised the connections that had been made. "No, I did not," he said forcefully. "I've already told what I saw."

"He's lying," Blaine said. "I've had him under observation for a while. He can't be trusted."

Mallory didn't flinch in the face of the accusations. "I have not killed. I could never do anything like that."

"Not even in the service of God?" Stefan said slyly. He softened as he turned to Blaine. "We must not distrust this young knight," he said. "He has made his vow before God. He has proved himself in the past as a good crusading Christian."

Mallory didn't believe him for a second.

"Besides," Stefan continued, "we will shortly be putting all of our good souls to the test. Then the truth will be there for all to see."

Mallory wondered what Stefan meant by this, but he didn't have time to consider it for Roeser ran up, looking more worried than Mallory had ever seen him.

Blaine recognised it, too. "What is it?" he barked.

"No sign of the perpetrator, sir," he replied. His lips had grown thin and white. "But the storerooms have been ransacked." He looked from Blaine to Stefan and back. "All our supplies have been destroyed."

The assault on the walls began soon after, with a ferocity that took them all aback. Mallory could hear the clattering against the gates even from outside Blaine's office, where a council had been hastily convened. When Roeser made his announcement, Mallory had seen Stefan blanch for the first time. They all knew what it meant: starvation on a mass scale within days. They were already at a low ebb; there wasn't much chance of hanging on longer without any food at all.

The voices echoed dully through the office walls while Mallory thought of Sophie and whether all that potential would ever be achieved. He didn't fear death. For so long, it had almost felt as if he had been shuffling through life in a dream, simply waiting for the end to turn up. Now that it had, he wasn't surprised. But he was sad that he might not be there for Sophie, as she had hoped.

There were still options. He considered dropping over the cathedral walls and attempting to dodge the hellish creatures beyond; he guessed one or two would try that before long. Oddly, he still had hope; that surprised him. He thought hope had long since been excised from his system.

The council had been talking for a good hour. Mallory stretched his legs, then slid down the wall to sit for a while, no longer caring if Blaine emerged to castigate him for not standing tall and erect as a knight should. He knew they'd only brought him along because they didn't want him passing news of the crisis to anyone else.

Through the window he saw fire erupt against the eastern wall. Part of the masonry crumbled, and the regular crew of guards and knights who manned the defences every evening set about desperately trying to shore up what was left.

As he watched, two things struck him: firstly, that the enemy appeared to know of events within the cathedral—the attack had clearly coincided with the murder and the destruction of the supplies; and secondly, not only had the enemy grown stronger, but the defences had also grown weaker. It was this that intrigued him the most. On the surface there should be no rational reason why the cathedral's defences were starting to fail. But what he had learned over the previous weeks about the nature of the Blue Fire hinted at the reason.

The earth energy, whatever designation was chosen for it, was a power of the spirit, strengthened by belief. To the pagans it was the essence of nature. To Christians it was the spirit and power of God. The same force, different ways of approaching it. The same undeniable pathway to the numinous.

If belief gave it a charge, that explained why certain places became sacred—churches, stone circles, hilltops, springs—sites where the Blue Fire was already strong and made more potent by worshipping humans, creating a spiritual atmosphere that was ripe for connection with the divine.

And as the Caretaker had told him, the cathedral had somehow become super-charged; that had kept the enemy at bay for a long time. But now the rejuvenating faith of the brothers was being knocked by successive blows—the murders, the siege, the diminishing supplies. The site was slowly losing its power. If things carried on the same way, if the brothers found out they had no more food, soon the walls would fall completely and the supernatural forces would sweep across them all.

Of course, we might have starved to death long before then, he thought wryly. But the Adversary had been very clever: it *had* all been linked.

He was disturbed from his deep thoughts by the door swinging open and heated conversation spilling out into the corridor. Wearily, he pushed himself back to his feet.

Stefan marched out, hands behind his back, his face dark with determination. "Do what I say. This is the only way. We have the ultimate obligation. If we fail . . . if God's light goes out because we turned away . . . because we weren't strong enough . . . then we will be damned for all eternity." He marched straight past Mallory as if he wasn't there.

Blaine followed him out, unusually angry. There had obviously been some disagreement. He paused by Mallory. "If you do anything to destroy morale, any-thing at all, I will personally break your fucking neck," he said, quietly and coldly. He turned to Roeser. "Organise the teams. Everyone works through the night. We'll punch the tunnel through by tomorrow or someone's head will roll, and it'll probably be yours."

Daniels, Gardener, and Miller were gathered together in the dorm, clearly on edge. Miller jumped up anxiously when Mallory entered. "What's going on?" he blurted.

Mallory wondered how much he could tell them without prompting Blaine to carry out his threat.

"There are all sorts of rumours flying around," Miller said; he couldn't keep still.

Gardener sucked on a roll-up, on the surface the picture of calm, but Mallory could see from his eyes that he was troubled. "They've cranked us up to the highest alert," he said. "Summat's up."

"Are they sending us out to fight those things?" Daniels looked drained, his face puffy as if he had been crying. Mallory could see he had been crushed by what had happened to his boyfriend and what that had made him face within himself.

"Gibson's dead." Mallory dropped wearily onto his bunk and closed his eyes.

"Oh, no!" Miller whined.

"The same as before?" Daniels asked.

"The same." In the dark behind his eyes, with their disembodied voices floating around him, Mallory made another connection; they were coming thick and fast, each prompting another. Everything had been planned from the beginning. They had been lured to Bratton Camp so they could bring that terrible creature back. A hidden assassin to strike from the inside while the hellish forces attacked from without. How very clever. How pathetically stupid they all seemed in comparison; a stupidity born of arrogance. Even after all that had happened, they still thought they were top of the pile, better than anything else in Existence. They weren't, not by a long way.

But it was the words of the Caretaker that struck him the most: *Look to your hearts*. And then he thought of the severed hand he had seen at Bratton Camp, seemingly belonging to one of them, yet apparently not. Now he could guess what it all meant: the thing was inside one of them, somehow, regenerating what was lost; or perhaps even it *was* one of them, putting on skin and bones and face like other people put on a suit of clothes.

That was how they had brought it back. That was how it survived on the sacred ground of the cathedral where no other supernatural creature could walk, the ultimate fifth columnist.

He looked at the faces surrounding him: Daniels, Gardener, Miller, and then thought of Hipgrave locked in his little room in the infirmary. He had spent hours with all of them since the return and they had all seemed perfectly human: flawed, wrapped up in their own little troubles. How well it hid. How could he ever tell which one of them it was?

"What's up with you, lad?" Gardener was watching him carefully. "You're looking at us as if you've never seen us before."

Desperately, he tried to recall where they all had been at the time of the murders. They had been with him on the walls when Cornelius's body had been discovered . . . but when he had been murdered? And Julian, where had any of them been when he died? Hipgrave had certainly been locked away when Gibson was killed. Or had he? Perhaps he was free, loose in the cathedral.

"I'm just tired," he said, closing his eyes again.

Who could he trust? Gardener was hardened by life, but there was humanity burning inside him. Miller was bright and innocent, all his emotions on the surface. Daniels might have been temporarily broken by what he had seen earlier, but his love of life still shone beneath that. Even shattered, sad Hipgrave, unable to live up to his ambitions, was basically a good man. How could it be any of them?

"Are you all right?" Miller asked, concerned.

But what he did know was that if he gave any sign he suspected, he wouldn't stand a chance. "Fine," he said. "You know they're punching the tunnel through tomorrow, hopefully? Putting a lot of steam behind it. Working through the night."

"Why?" Gardener asked suspiciously. "For the last few days they seemed quite happy letting us munch through spuds while they took their time."

"Maybe they finally realised time's running out," Daniels said.

The snow stopped falling sometime during the night, but by then everywhere was blanketed by a covering almost two feet thick in parts. It was generally agreed by those who came from the area that there hadn't been a snowfall like it for a good few years, not even during the previous year's harsh winter.

The digging, however, had continued frantically throughout the night, with large teams working a strict rota system. They had partially demolished a wall surrounding the bishop's palace to provide stone to line the tunnel, and with wood torn from the rafters of another building, it looked as though they had beaten the numerous collapses that had held them up until that point.

"Amazing what you can do when a crisis focuses your mind," Mallory muttered, forgetting Miller was with him.

"What crisis?" Miller asked. "You're talking as if it's even worse than we think."

"It's always worse than you think." Mallory looked out over the crowd of brothers who had gathered to watch the digging. He saw suspicion and trepidation in their faces as they picked up on the powerful mood of anxiety hanging over those in charge. The brethren were increasingly loath to attend to their duties and some were even beginning to skip services. Although the Blues and the inquisitors were stamping out open dissent, they couldn't control the Chinese whispers rustling through the community. Respect for Stefan and his repressive rule appeared to be crumbling quickly. People had been prepared to tolerate him if he got them out of current difficulties and provided security, but things had rapidly gone from bad to worse.

The dissent, though, clearly had a profound effect on Stefan and his supporters. Mallory could see it in the hard lines of their faces: any jubilation they might have felt at their unexpected triumph had faded, but it was plain that now they had tasted power they were not going to let it go at any cost. Mallory saw them all over the place, though they were easy to miss. Seemingly faceless, they passed through rooms without any noticeable trace, like ghosts; the effects only became apparent later. They were particularly adept at using scripture to support their hard-line views. Most didn't have the time, the energy, or the intellectual rigour to argue against them; sometimes it was easier to allow oneself to be swayed. And again, only later were the results apparent.

"You went to see Hipgrave this morning, didn't you?" Miller said curiously.

"Yes." Mallory had known it was only a matter of time before Stefan did something to bolster his position, so he wasn't surprised to see him striding up to the dig with his fawning entourage.

"How is he?"

"Still locked in."

Miller looked blank at this response, then said, "Are you OK, Mallory? You seem a little distant today. Have I done something to offend you?"

"Nothing more than usual."

They hushed as Stefan prepared to give an impromptu oration, only as he began to intone gravely, it was soon apparent that it wasn't impromptu at all: the words had been carefully crafted.

"I have an important announcement to make," he said, after climbing atop a pile of masonry. "We have had many hardships heaped upon us in recent times, and it would seem to me—and, I would think, to most people here—that we have been failing our Lord. We have not been devout enough . . . pure enough. We have not turned our hearts and minds to the teachings of the Lord God, our Father. We have not expunged the sins of our past lives. Rather, we have allowed them to grow fruitful on the vines of our souls, and to the Lord, that could only be an abomination. And so it is time for us to cleanse ourselves."

Mallory tried to guess what tricks Stefan had planned, but the bishop was always cunning.

"Our sacred relic, which has made this cathedral so strong, is filled with God's power," he continued. "And through prayer, deep in the spirit, our Lord has illuminated me on its workings. It can, quite literally, see into the depths of a soul. It can find out your sins. We—the Chapter of Canons and myself—have decided to use that power to enable us all to cleanse ourselves . . . to make us closer to God in every way, so that we can overcome these trials presented to us. One by one, every brother shall be brought before the relic to have their sins divined. In the glorious light of true confession and personal revelation, we shall all find our earthly redemption."

It took a while for the meaning of his words to filter through to the crowd's consciousness, and when it did it was not welcomed with the universal acclaim of the bishop's past orations. But that was clearly what he intended. It must have been in the planning for a while; Stefan had hinted at it on the previous evening. It was an undoubted masterstroke. In the eyes of the hard-liners, everyone had sinned, and all the brothers knew it; somewhere in the deep recesses of the heart, everyone had a little unpleasantness tucked away. It might not be anything bad—a touch of jealousy, a wisp of pride, a hint of sloth, basic human flaws—but the Bible told them it was wrong and the programming of their religion made it impossible to shake that at the most basic level. Mallory had come to understand how the concept of sin was like a constant buzz in the background of everyday life for the devout.

And Stefan had pointedly failed to mention what he, or the inquisitors, or the other Church authorities would do once they knew everyone's dirty little secrets. Would they simply absolve everyone with a little prayer? Would they hold it in abeyance to gain leverage? Or would they pass judgment?

There was nothing so good for diverting people's attention from dissent as the contemplation of their own inner lives. Their security on earth and their chances of eternal reward—or eternal damnation—lay in the balance. How clever Stefan was.

"I wonder if the relic can actually do that, or if this is another of Stefan's little manipulations?" Mallory mused.

Miller appeared to have no views on the matter—he simply continued to watch the activity of the diggers—but Mallory guessed there would be very few others taking the news so calmly.

The digging continued at a frantic pace under the relentless insistence of Blaine and the Blues. No rest was allowed and when anyone flagged they were instantly replaced. Errors were pointed out harshly, so that work proceeded both quickly and with the utmost care. With the judicious use of the timber and masonry, they managed to avoid any further tunnel collapses, but the removal of the shale and gravel covering most of that area was backbreaking work. Even so, it appeared they would be through before the day was done.

However, the cancellation of lunch after the abandonment of breakfast caused a rising tide of concern, and when the evening mealtime approached with no sign of activity in the refectory, panic began to surface. Whatever denials were issued, everyone knew that the only explanation could be that supplies had finally been exhausted.

A large crowd gathered at the bishop's palace as night fell. There was anger, and fear, and raised voices. Stefan came out, and for the first time Mallory saw a hint of anxiety that events were running out of his control, that his hard-fought position was slipping away from him. But he controlled himself, as he always did, and told them there would be fresh supplies that very evening. The tunnel would be completed and food would be brought through from the adjoining camp; and it wouldn't be a thin diet of vegetables. It would be a time of celebration after all their hardship. They had his word on that.

That made the bishop a hostage to fortune at a time when he had so much to lose, but Mallory knew Stefan would never allow himself to fail. He was a consummate politician who would have succeeded whether his chosen sphere had been in business, Parliament, or anywhere else where hard, driven people could rise to the top.

Mallory saw it reflected in Stefan's expression as he turned to go: the bishop knew that, while his words had eased the minds of some of the protestors, there were others present who had set their hearts against him. That expression said so many things to Mallory, but most of all it showed a frightening determination that transcended basic human boundaries. Mallory was worried by what he saw there.

For that reason, he feared the worst when he was summoned to the bishop's palace as twilight fell. The lack of food had left his stomach aching as if he'd eaten sour apples, and the raw cold was eating its way into his bones. The snow had started falling again in the late afternoon, slowly bringing a pristine covering to the churned-up slush where the mob had waited outside the official residence.

Stefan's personal assistant, a man in his late fifties with a troubling smile and an oily nature, showed Mallory into the drawing room where a fire blazed. The warmth was such a relief that Mallory's heart leaped. He was instantly struck by the glitter of Christmas decorations: tinsel and streamers were strung across the wall and ceilings, and several small candles illuminated a well-worn Nativity scene laid out on the antique sideboard. It was so incongruous in the bitter air of hardship that hung over the entire cathedral compound that he wondered if Stefan had gone crazy from the stress.

Stefan sat in a high-backed leather armchair next to the fire, his face placid but his eyes alive with a disturbing passion. "We must never forget our Lord's birth," he said quietly, noticing the direction of Mallory's gaze, "even amid all this pain and suffering. *Especially* because of it."

Amid everything, Mallory hadn't once considered that Christmas was approaching.

Stefan appeared to read his thoughts. "Compared with everything else that has been happening, Christmas might not seem important. But it is, it is. It is the reason why we must overcome, why even in the darkest hours there is always hope. It is a shining symbol that allows us to put into perspective all the passing misery of this dark world."

Mallory watched Stefan cautiously, trying to see if this was the start of some manipulation. If it was, the bishop had hidden it well.

"I don't truly know you, Mr. Mallory, but I know many like you," he continued. "You have an individual nature. You do not suffer fools gladly, and you have a strong disregard for authority. Unlike Mr. Blaine, I do not believe that marks you out as a troublemaker. I am not so unconfident in my abilities that I feel the need to control everybody. Indeed, it is often healthy in any environment to have voices prepared to point out that the king has no clothes. Of course, that kind of commentary can only be allowed to go so far. It must never undermine the cohesiveness of any community."

Mallory listened patiently; he still couldn't tell if he was about to be punished or praised.

"I know what you think about me, Mr. Mallory." Stefan stared into the fire. "You think me a carpetbagger, someone who has seen a source of power and who has moved in to take it. It is an easy accusation to level. I have no history of good works in the Church. I only came to God as a reaction to the Fall, though I would point out the very many others who fled Him at the same time. But you are wrong, you know. It is because I believe so passionately that I am not going to allow my religion to dribble away. I am prepared to have people hate me, if necessary, but I will not deviate from the path, however hard it may be, to save my God, as He attempted to save us all. These times demand hard choices, Mr. Mallory. And while instincts may call on us to be liberal or gentle, if the result of that is the destruction of Christianity, then some of us must be prepared to make the unpleasant choices so that others do not have to. These times demand that we take a stand, Mr. Mallory—on one side or the other. God or the Devil. There are no grey areas, for even the most basic choices lead along those two roads.

"I could tell you about my personal tragedies, my epiphany, the things that shaped me, but they aren't important. If the sacrifice I have to make is that I may not be seen as a good man, but I do good works, then so be it. Only God can be my judge. And I am not alone in that belief. Mr. Blaine feels the same way, as do several others here. In private, I know Mr. Blaine to be a good man, crushed by sadness at the loss of his family, yet who still keeps a warm, hopeful heart, who cares deeply for his men like a father for his own children, but who must at times use the rod. Every injury, every death amongst the knights he feels personally. But he would never allow you to see that side of him, for he has a job to do . . . the gravest job of all. We need villains in life, Mr. Mallory, and if that is what is required of me, whatever the personal cost it is a cross I will bear for the sake of the Glory of God."

Mallory was uneasy at this surprising declaration. He believed he had an unimpeachable radar for lies and manipulation, but Stefan rang clean of cynicism; the bishop truly felt he was striving to do *good works*. It jarred with the unpleasant picture of Stefan that Mallory had created. The thought that both the bishop and Blaine might be decent, if misguided, people made life more complex, and more troubling.

His confusion must have played on his face, for Stefan smiled. "You are probably wondering why I called you here. It is a simple request in the spirit of everything that I have just told you. Later this evening, the tunnel will be completed and we will be able to surface in the camp of the pagans. Because of an unfortunate event that happened a while back—carried out by some members of the Blue team who have been severely punished—I fear there will not be a great deal of goodwill waiting for us. Quite understandable—my heart goes out to them. But we cannot afford to take the time to indulge in extensive negotiations to win them over. We stand to lose everything. There will soon be death here . . . many deaths . . . but it is for the very fabric of our community that I fear. Though we keep God in our hearts, many here will not be able to take much more suffering. So, time is of the essence." He paused, pressed his fingertips together, and stared into the space between them. "It has come to my attention that you have a good relationship with the pagans."

Mallory wondered who'd been talking out of class, though he was increasingly starting to have his suspicions. "They know me."

"What I ask is that you lead the initial delegation through the tunnel, that you plead our case. Perhaps your word carries weight with them. Perhaps you can convince them that our hearts are good, though we believe in different things— that we have commonality in our compassion for fellow human beings. I fear that because of the gulf between our two camps they may meet us with force . . . attempt to repel us as invaders when we come open-handed. Your involvement may prevent any strife."

Mallory locked eyes with Stefan. Was there some underlying motive, some secret plan at work? If so, he couldn't see it.

"I'll do what I can," he said. "Though I don't think you'll find as much opposition as you anticipate."

"Really? You've had contact with them recently?"

"No. Just an instinct."

Stefan nodded thoughtfully. "Then we can count on you. That is good. With God, together, we shall overcome."

A gale was blowing up a blizzard as they prepared to complete the final section of the tunnel, the flurrying snow shimmering like fireflies in the light of the many lanterns. Mallory stamped his feet to keep out the cold; even through his thick boots and socks he could feel it gnawing at his toes.

There was a heady sense of anticipation amongst the diggers. Indeed, even though it was midnight, many brothers had ventured out into the frozen night to see their escape route finally made real. Stefan had ordered the knights to keep them back behind makeshift barriers; he didn't want anything hindering the work, or the delicate task of the first meeting with the pagans.

Stefan and Blaine approached him together as the last preparations were being made. "We don't want any mix-up when we go through," Blaine said gruffly, by way of greeting. "If they're waiting for us with weapons—"

"They're a peace-loving bunch of old hippies," Mallory said.

"Try telling that to the lads who were on the receiving end of some of their stones and sticks a few months back."

"Now, now, Mr. Blaine," Stefan interjected. "We're approaching this in an atmosphere where bygones are bygones and we can all develop a new relationship. Let's start as we mean to carry on."

Blaine grunted noncommittally. "Just make sure they're not going to attack us the moment we pop up," he said directly to Mallory.

"At least so we have a chance to speak," Stefan said. "I cannot stress how much rests on the success of this. It will be the defining moment of this community, of the future of our religion."

"I'll do my part." Despite Stefan's urgings, the only thing on Mallory's mind was that he would soon be seeing Sophie again. He had spent much of the afternoon considering his options. Although he wanted to bolt with her the moment they were through, she had made it plain she wouldn't abandon the people who relied on her, but he could abscond and creep back to her at a later date. Or should he return with the knights and sneak back through the tunnel when there was no one else around? With much of the pressure eased by the tunnel and a new supply of food through the travellers' camp, he supposed the atmosphere would become a little lighter in the cathedral, allowing him to choose a time that suited him . . . if he could bear to spend another night there. The thought of freedom made his heart start to pound.

As Blaine and Stefan departed, Miller came running up. "I hear you're going through with the Blues. That's a great honour, Mallory."

"It's a great honour if you have no kind of life, Miller."

"Thinking of meeting Sophie again?" He winked.

"I'm thinking of using you as a human shield when we break through."

Miller threw his hood back and looked up into the gusting snow. "You are going to come back, aren't you, Mallory?" he said after a while. "You're not going to run off and leave us here?"

Mallory eyed him suspiciously. "What's it to you?"

"It's everything to me," Miller said plaintively. "We need you here, Mallory. *I* need you here."

The innocence in Miller's face almost swayed him. "Of course I'm coming back," he lied.

Roeser stood at Mallory's side with the rest of his élite squad at his back as the diggers worked on the last few feet of the tunnel. Overhead lay no-man's-land, which separated the cathedral and the few straggling tents that had been sited across the river from the sprawling bulk of the travellers' camp. The air was dank, the silence potent with uneasy anticipation. The gravity of what was at stake was at work behind all their faces, turned grim with dancing shadows from the handful of lanterns.

Five minutes later there was a joyful exclamation from one of the diggers followed by a shower of earth rattling into the tunnel. Mallory felt a blast of cold air. Suddenly he could see a square of night sky and one twinkling star.

Before the diggers could clean up the hole, the Blues surged forward, taking Mallory with them. They pushed the diggers to one side, then forced them back toward the cathedral unceremoniously. Obviously *civilians* were not allowed at the front.

Mallory was eased out of the hole first. After so long staring at the grey walls of the cathedral, the sight of distant horizons was both stirring and a little unnerving. He could see the floodplain extending flat and reedy through the swirling snow, while the river gushed noisily just a few feet away. Across the water, which at that point was narrow enough for him to cross with three bounds, the travellers' camp blazed with light from what seemed to be a thousand lanterns. The sound of fiddles, guitars, and drums was carried by the wind. About twenty tents stood nearby, joined to the camp proper by a makeshift pontoon bridge across the water.

A piercing whistle rose up close to hand, startling him. One of the travellers, a young man with a mass of ginger hair and a beard, was hanging out of his tent, signalling to the other side. Within an instant, the whistle was taken up and transmitted across the camp, and seconds after that people were running toward the other side of the river. Mallory could see them picking up sticks and stones, which must have been stockpiled for easy access as a defence when the tunnel was finally opened.

"Stay calm," Mallory said to Roeser, who had joined him. "They're ready for us."

"I am calm," Roeser said.

The travellers massed on the far bank, clearly waiting. There was some hooting and jeering, but no real threat of violence. Within a minute, the crowd parted and Mallory saw Sophie striding toward him, grinning broadly. She waved and he waved back; he couldn't help returning her grin.

"See?" he said. "I told you there'd be no trouble."

"Early days yet," Roeser cautioned.

Sophie was accompanied by Rick, the white dreadlocks of her right-hand man glowing in the dark. They gingerly crossed the rickety bridge over the rushing water, a small band of travellers close behind.

"Who's she?" Roeser asked uncertainly.

"Her name's Sophie Tallent," Mallory said. "She's their leader."

As she reached their side, she only had eyes for Mallory. Her gaze sparkled as it locked on his; her hair blew wildly in the wind.

"Hello, Mallory. It's been a long time," she said as she stood before him. It was what remained unsaid that struck him the most: her affection for him was clear and untainted, backed by both respect and trust, two qualities he hadn't seen directed at him for a long time. There was such a purity to her emotional response that he felt deeply moved.

"Hello, Sophie," he said. "We need to talk."

"Is this cool?" she asked.

"There's not going to be any trouble. They need help."

Sophie's eyes turned cold as they flickered over the other knights. "Sure?"

"Sure."

She turned around to face her people and said in a loud voice filled with authority, "It's going to be OK. Throw down the weapons. Don't bother manning the defences." Mallory guessed more weapons were secreted in the camp.

The travellers obeyed her instantly. Some looked relieved, others eyed the knights suspiciously. Mallory realised how frightening they must look to other eyes, with their mass of black uniforms and medieval weaponry.

His thoughts had already turned to planning his escape when he realised that Roeser was no longer at his side. He cast a half-glance behind him only to see the captain moving through the Blues, whispering. "They can't help their little soldier-games," he said quietly to Sophie. His ironic tone made her laugh.

"Now!"

The sharpness of the order startled him. Suddenly there were Blues surging past him, jostling him to one side.

"It's OK!" he shouted. "They're not planning anything!"

Two of the Blues grabbed Sophie's arms and began to haul her forward. Her shock quickly gave way to annoyance. She struggled, ordering them to leave her alone. Some of the other travellers overcame their surprise to rush to her aid.

The second they moved, the Blues whipped out their swords. The travellers' eyes widened in fear. Mallory could see their faces, white in the lantern light as they struggled to make sense of what was happening.

In Mallory's head the scene suddenly became silent as his own confused thoughts drowned everything out. His gaze skimmed back and forth, taking everything in. Had Roeser seen something he hadn't? Some secret plan the travellers were hatching to get back at them for Melanie's death?

And then his gaze fell on Sophie. She was staring at him and her eyes were saying, *What is happening here?* He watched her expression change from incomprehension to fear to anger. Then there was one instant of steely accusation that made his heart ache.

"Trap!" she yelled. "Go back!"

Suddenly the tableau exploded in sound and movement. One of the Blues punched Sophie in the face. Her head snapped back and she slumped forward, unconscious. Mallory yelled her name, launching himself to help her, still not truly understanding but feeling a terrible acceptance begin to creep over him. Two Blues turned on him and knocked him back forcefully. He crashed into a tent, bringing it down around him.

When he managed to scramble to his feet, he was transfixed by the terrible sight of a knight ripping his sword up into Rick's gut. The dreadlocked teen's eyes bulged, but the sword kept ripping. A gush of blood shot out, staining the virgin snow. In one swift movement, the Blue removed his sword, flung the lifeless body to one side, and moved on to the next. Rick's corpse hit the ground, then slid into the rushing river and was carried away.

Mallory spun around, trying to take in the chaos erupting on every side, made impotent by the horror of what he was seeing. The knights were in full flow. They rushed across the bridge and spread out into the camp, swords swinging. Tents were crushed; lanterns burst, setting fire to canvas, the flames leaping from home to home. Blood sprayed as the swords moved back and forth. People fell. The hellish conflagration moved with frightening speed until it seemed as though the entire camp had been set ablaze within a minute.

Mallory yelled out something, though his rushing emotions had shredded his consciousness and he didn't know what it was. It didn't matter. He heard a noise behind him and looked around in time to see Roeser swinging his fist. It hit him firmly on the jaw and snapped him into darkness.

He awoke on the snow, his body a mass of aches. He was back in the cathedral compound. Nearby, boots were tramping as the Blues carried provisions looted from the travellers' camp in through the tunnel. His dismay was so acute, hot tears stung the corners of his eyes.

"No," he croaked.

"We do this in the name of our God, to save our God's work." He looked up to see Stefan standing over him. The bishop's face was silhouetted against a lantern that hung overhead, so it was impossible to tell his emotions.

"You didn't need to do this," Mallory said through swollen lips. "They were harmless. They would have helped." He swallowed and tasted blood. "Where's Sophie?"

"We have taken her prisoner. The inquisitors will wish to question her before deciding on a form of punishment."

Panic rushed through Mallory, giving him the strength to crawl to his knees. "Punishment?" he gasped.

"The Bible states it clearly. Exodus chapter twenty-two, verse eighteen," Stefan said coldly. *"Thou shalt not suffer a witch to live."*

chapter thirteen
OF WHAT IS PAST, OR PASSING, OR TO COME

"All punishment is like therapy for a soul that has gone wrong."
Albinus

From the singing pain in his limbs and ribs, Mallory could tell he'd been worked over by a few boots after Roeser had knocked him flat. It was a strain to get to his feet, and when he attempted to walk he was shaky. But he didn't have to try, for two Blues caught him under the arms and dragged him through the thick snow toward the new buildings. But his thoughts were for Sophie, not himself. There was no sign of her, and though he asked his captors, they ignored him as if he were a piece of wood they were hauling to the fire.

As his boots bounced down the stone steps to the basement level, he tried to comprehend how it all could have gone wrong so quickly. The Blues dragged him along a gloomy corridor to a row of small cells with covered grilles punctuating doors secured by large padlocks. The third cell was open. They threw him inside. Dirty straw had been spread on the floor, aged manacles fixed to the walls.

"You've been ready for this," he noted. "How long have you been planning to round up the usual suspects?"

The Blues pushed him against the damp wall, yanked his arms back, and closed the manacles about his wrists so that he was suspended in a crucifix position. They departed without comment, and Mallory didn't have the inclination to make smart remarks at their backs.

When he had first arrived at the cathedral, he could have coped with his current situation with the same blasé acceptance with which he faced all the myriad miseries life threw at him. But now that Sophie had entered his sphere he was troubled by hope, and desire, and the nagging feeling that life might be worthwhile after all.

He had little contact with the outside world for the next three days. The passing of time was marked by the appearance of meals: porridge on the first day, but after that it was a return to the thin vegetable gruel they had been eating for too long. He could get some sleep hanging in the manacles, but the pain in his joints and in his wrists where they had been rubbed raw woke him regularly. Occasionally, he would be stirred by a deep rumble through the cold stone: the attacks from the forces without were intensifying. He wondered what plans Blaine would be making to combat them now that the new route out had been opened up.

He felt physically weak, but after the initial shock and despair wore off, his emotional equilibrium had returned and his thoughts grew colder, his anger harder. The guards refused to answer any of his questions—Blaine and Stefan had clearly decided not to have anyone who knew him overseeing his imprisonment—so in the end he took to mocking and abuse. It was childish, but it made him feel better and countered some of the impotence he felt.

They came for him in the afternoon of the third day. The guards dragged him out, blinking, into the snow white world, still glittering in the fading sunlight. His hanging position had begun to disable him even after such a short time, so that he found it difficult to walk. Little nuggets of constant pain glowed throughout his frame.

As soon as he saw the faces of the brothers he passed he realised something was wrong. Instead of the jubilation he had expected at newfound freedom and food, he saw only grey misery etched into the features, weighing on the bowed shoulders, even worse than before. He looked around for clues, but the gaping black mouth of the tunnel was still there in the white, and the walls still stood firmly.

The guards prodded him toward the imposing Queen Anne façade of Mompesson House, not far from the north gate. Outside the grand building, a makeshift stage had been built out of stacked tables. A small crowd gathered before it, not all the brothers by a long way; many drifted away at the fringes, plainly disinterested in what was happening.

Mallory was forced to stand at the back of the stage alongside another heavily guarded figure. It was shrouded in robes and hooded so that it was impossible to see any sign of its form, but when it tilted its head toward Mallory, he realised from the body language that it was Sophie. Her appearance reminded him of the burka-clad women in fundamentalist Muslim countries, their shape obscured so as not to inflame the passions of the men; the woman as devil, agent of temptation.

Miller, Daniels, and Gardener waited to one side of the crowd with a group of other knights. Mallory entertained a brief fantasy that they would respond to the clear injustice and rush forward to his aid, knowing in his heart it would never happen.

They shuffled around in the cold for another five minutes until Stefan and Blaine emerged from Mompesson House. They both attempted to maintain an air of confidence and control, but the fact that Mallory could see that it was an act told him how uneasy they were. What had happened to shake them so? They'd achieved everything they'd planned.

Without glancing at Mallory or Sophie, Stefan climbed onto the stage and addressed the crowd. "Our Church has been under attack," he began. "Not only from the forces of the Devil, which we know all too well, but from more subtle attacks within our community—subtle attacks which can often prove more dangerous. Those who deviate from the path our Lord has shown us can destroy everything we hold dear by a thousand little knocks, continually chipping away at the edifice of our religion. And when that structure falls, it cannot be erected again. So we must strike now, to root out the weeds choking the vine. We must remain pure and remove from our midst those who attempt to corrupt that purity with sly words or thoughts, or with open opposition. The Adversary waits beyond the gate—many have seen his evil form looming up over the city. He feels his time is near. By purifying the light within us all, here, we can keep the darkness at bay forever."

Stefan kept his gaze fixed on the crowd, but made a slight motion with one hand at his side. Mallory was shoved forward onto the stage, with Sophie beside him.

"Here now, a sight to make a good Christian weep," Stefan continued. "One of our own who has turned his back on God to embrace the Devil and all the Devil's works."

Mallory thought to speak out until he felt the guard's dagger pricking his back.

"And at his side, the woman who tempted him from the path of righteousness, hidden from our eyes so she cannot work her spell on us. A witch. Yes, the Devil's own. She makes no secret of her use of Dark Powers to bring corruption and sickness and death to us all—"

Mallory heard Sophie protest, but the hood muffled her voice so that the crowd couldn't hear her. The guard at her back twisted her wrist until she cried out.

"In our current situation, charges of sedition could be levelled at them. Their actions, whether directed against us or not, could weaken us or bring us to our knees," Stefan said. "In wartime, certain liberties must necessarily be put to one side for the sake of the greater good. However, it is still our intention to give these two a fair trial in a Church court. They will be able to present their defence, or plead for God's mercy. Justice will be seen to be done."

Stefan paused as if he expected some kind of applause or encouragement, but he was only met by a weary acceptance.

Mallory suddenly saw through it all. They were planning a show trial, another of Stefan's little manipulations to divert attention from the hardship everyone was feeling; in the end, in whatever establishment, discipline and fear were the only way to maintain power. But how long would Stefan be able to carry on distracting and obfuscating before his attempts became so transparent that they lost their potency? Mallory wondered.

"We must be pure. We must be devout. It is the only way we can bring God back into our lives." Passion filled Stefan's voice. "The slightest weakness brings the Devil to our door. This one . . ." He pointed to Mallory. ". . . is not the only traitor in our midst. There are others. Though I implored you to be true to the path, it has come to my attention that there are still practising sodomites here."

Mallory flinched. Suddenly he could see what was coming next: Stefan wasn't relenting at all.

"I call now on the true and righteous amongst you to speak out. If you know of any sodomite, identify them. It is our only hope. We can show no mercy to them, for the Bible tells us it is a sin against nature."

A witch hunt, Mallory thought. More fear, more divisions, all to throw the brothers off balance so they wouldn't challenge his tenuous position.

The Blues began to move through the crowd. Mallory thought it was all for show—more fear-creation—until a gruff Geordie accent called out, "Here!"

Gardener had his hand on Daniels's shoulder. Daniels bore an expression of such incomprehension it was almost comical. But when he turned and looked deep into Gardener's face, he understood. The blow was so severe that Daniels looked as if his heart was breaking.

Gardener wouldn't meet Daniels's eye, which was filled with a desperate hurt. The Geordie's gaze remained fixed on Stefan, his hand steady on Daniels's shoulder, but Mallory thought he saw something in his expression, a fugitive shadow, that suggested his betrayal had come at a price.

The Blues seized Daniels roughly, his status as a knight now valueless. As he was dragged away, the scenario was made worse by his abject silence: no protestations, just the awful realisation that life was proving to be as painful as he had feared it would be in his darkest moments.

Never in his wildest imaginings would Mallory have thought Gardener capable of such an act of betrayal. His friendship with Daniels, despite their many differences, had seemed deep and warm. To Mallory, it had been one of the few beacons in his long, dark months at the cathedral. But in the end it came down to the one thing Mallory already knew: blind adherence to a religion meant any act, however despicable, could be justified. Gardener's internal battle between common sense and the pressures exerted on him by his hard-line beliefs had finally been resolved.

Mallory wasn't the only one deeply affected by what had happened. He saw Miller turn to Gardener with an expression of dismay that became disgust when Gardener wouldn't meet his eye either. To see that in Miller, who never showed any sign that he experienced negative emotions, was particularly striking. Miller edged away from Gardener into the crowd. Some others moved away, too, until Gardener appeared to be standing alone.

But any point that might have been made was wiped away by a burst of spontaneous applause from the fundamentalists and evangelicals in the crowd. Gardener gave a faint, relieved smile.

"And by this we begin the journey back to God!" Stefan proclaimed before striding from the stage. His departure was a signal for Mallory and Sophie to be led away by the Blues, who appeared to be the only knights trusted to carry out the serious jobs. Those who had cheered Gardener now voiced boos and cat-calls.

Away from the crowd, Mallory called out to Sophie, asking if she was all right. His guard hit him so hard at the back of the neck, he was knocked to his knees.

"I'm OK. Don't worry about me," she shouted, before her own guard struck out. She took the blow and continued walking, forcing her head high beneath the hood.

Mallory's anger grew harder still. Stefan, he was convinced, had gone insane; the Caretaker had said that whatever potency was in the cathedral would unbalance men's minds. He wouldn't be surprised if Stefan was planning some kind of Dark Age punishment for them, possibly even an execution: a burning or a hanging for the witch and her accomplice. He felt scared for Sophie, not himself; but he resolved to give Stefan no satisfaction whatsoever.

That night in the cells was colder than any other since Mallory had arrived in Salisbury, and at one point he was convinced he was freezing to death. When the guard brought breakfast it was more meagre than ever, but it was warm, and when his chains were loosed to allow him to eat, he hugged the bowl to him until he had leached every last bit of heat from it.

Sometime around midmorning, the door was thrown open unexpectedly and Miller skulked in, checking over his shoulder. Mallory's first response was suspicion—was this the thing from Bratton Camp come to slaughter him while he hung?—but after a while, his weakened state meant he didn't have the energy to worry about anything beyond his capacity to control.

"I didn't know I had visiting privileges," he said weakly.

"You don't. They won't allow anyone near you." Mallory was surprised to see tears in Miller's eyes. "The guards were all called away—I don't think they could spare them anymore. And they don't bother locking the door."

Mallory rattled the chains. "It's not as if I'm going to do some kind of Houdini trick with these."

"Are you all right, Mallory?" Miller said gently. He wrung his hands together impotently.

"I've been better."

"For what it's worth, none of the knights think you deserve this."

"Thanks. That thought will keep me warm tonight." Mallory couldn't help the sarcasm and felt bad when he saw how it had stung Miller. "How's Daniels?"

Miller's eyes fell. "No one's seen him since they took him away. I can't believe Gardener would—" He caught himself. "I suppose we all have moments when we lose the path. We shouldn't judge."

"Why not?" Mallory said harshly.

Miller's bottled emotions finally broke the restraining barrier. "I can't believe this is happening," he said tearfully. "We're barely a year and a half away from society falling apart. How could it go so bad so quickly? All the things we took for granted . . . it's as if they happened generations ago."

"It just goes to show we're all beasts at heart, doesn't it? Let us out of the cage and we quickly revert to type."

"That's awful."

"Desperate men lead desperate lives. And self-preservation wins out over anything."

"I don't believe that." There was a long pause while Miller dried his eyes. "I can't believe it. That makes a mockery of everything God stands for."

"There you go."

"You're reading it too simply, Mallory," he said, with the kind of desperation of someone whose life depended on being proven right. "It's got to be more complex than that. Maybe we can't see the cause and effect. The whole reason we're here argues against that outlook."

"Here on this earth, or here in this . . . prison?"

Miller didn't answer. "I don't want to be disloyal to Stefan—" he began calmly.

"Why not? Because he's got a title? The pointy hat doesn't make him better than you, Miller. If there's one thing I would give to this world everyone's trying so half-heartedly to remake, it would be the end of all leaders." He let his chin drop to his chest; his outburst had exhausted him.

"Perhaps you're right." Miller's voice sounded tiny in the echoing cell. "I believe in what Christ stood for. It's just so right . . . loving one another . . . love as this great power . . . sacrifice . . . redemption. I believe there's hope for all of us, I really do."

Mallory softened at his words. "People get in the way, Miller," he said gently. "Keep your God in your own heart."

"But what can I do?" His constant hand-wringing showed his struggle with deep emotions that threatened to unbalance him. "I don't like what Stefan's doing . . . a lot of people don't. But he's the bishop . . ." His voice trailed away, laced with desperation.

"If you believe in something, stand up for it. Don't let Stefan drag this whole thing down his own mad route." He added, "But don't get yourself hurt, Miller. Look after yourself. It won't do any good if you're sitting in the cell next to mine."

Miller stared at him for a long moment, deciphering his words, and then smiled. "I'll be careful, Mallory."

"Before we all start getting too girly in our emotions, tell me what's happened out there. Something's gone wrong, or Stefan wouldn't feel the need to crank up the repression."

"Oh, it was bad, Mallory. First the travellers refused to help—"

"Hardly surprising after Stefan had some of them slaughtered. What was he thinking? Well, I know what he was thinking—that God was on his side and he could do whatever he wanted."

"They all scattered into the city. And then the camp lost its protection. We managed to bring in most of the supplies they'd got stored there—and there wasn't that much—but Blaine was overseeing the setting up of an auxiliary camp so that they could secure another route out, when something attacked. It was like a . . . a griffin . . . or something, they said. Part bird, part something else. It killed five knights and three brothers before the rest of them managed to get back through the tunnel."

Mallory laughed. "Stupid bastards. They lost everything through their own arrogance. The land around here gets its power from belief. If the travellers aren't there to worship—if their belief has been shattered—it ends up like any old patch of turf and mud. Stefan snatched defeat from the jaws of victory."

"Yes, I know, he deserved it all." Miller gnawed on a knuckle anxiously. "But what about the rest of us, Mallory? Everyone reckons the travellers' food must have just about gone. We're back to square one, starving and with no way out. What are we going to do?" Something dark squirmed inside Miller; Mallory could see the shadow it cast but not what it was. "Do you think Stefan can really use the relic like he said?" Miller continued obliquely. "To dig into people's minds? I can't understand how that can work. I mean, relics . . . even if they've got God's power in them . . ."

He was interrupted by the distant sound of a door opening. Miller hurried to the door before turning. "I'll come back to see you when I can, Mallory. And I'll do everything I can to get you out of here. Try to get some people on our side . . ."

Several sets of footsteps were approaching.

"Go on," Mallory said. "Just stay out of trouble."

He slipped out. Not long after, a Blue ushered in Stefan and Inquisitor-General Broderick. Stefan looked tired, his face sagging through lack of sleep, but Broderick had the bearing of a predatory insect.

"Well done, *Bishop*," Mallory said sarcastically. "Your contempt for basic humanity has managed to destroy everything."

Stefan visibly flinched. "Quiet," he snapped. Then, a little more calmly, "This isn't over yet. We have right on our side."

"You talk about doing good works, Stefan, but *you've* turned this into the

Devil's house. Ends never justify means, especially in religion. If you can't stay true to your beliefs, they're not worth very much."

"You never understood us here, Mallory. I doubt you ever had any true feeling for our religion." Stefan massaged the bridge of his nose, distracted. "There was no way I could leave you loose in the community—you were an accident waiting to happen. I couldn't have you breaking the morale of others. I implied as much at our meeting when I requested your services. You've got insurrection in your blood, Mallory. You're a danger to any establishment. An anarchist. I bear you no ill will. In other times I would have simply set you free from this place to go about your unpleasant business elsewhere. As it is, you must stay here, in this cell, until . . ." He shrugged. ". . . the worst has blown over."

Mallory couldn't tell if he was trying to deceive the others, or if he truly believed there was hope for them. He nodded toward Broderick. "So, you're going to let your torturer loose on me now?"

"No, no, there would be no point." He waved the notion away with his hand. "Mr. Broderick is here for the witch. She has information that may be important to us."

Mallory grew cold. "Don't you touch her."

"The Bible says we should have no feelings for her kind. It says in uncompromising terms that they are a danger to everything we hold dear. Spare her no compassion—she chose her path in life." His eyes gleamed. "Unless there is another reason for your protection of her. Is fornication another of your sins?"

"She doesn't know anything."

"She knows how to protect her land, and other things, too, I would guess."

"She won't tell you anything."

Stefan smiled. "Oh, I think she will."

He turned and led the others out. Mallory yelled and screamed until his throat was raw, but all that came back were insipid echoes.

Through the long hours of the day and the burning pain in his limbs, he listened intently, dreading what would happen when he did hear something. But there was nothing. Either the walls were too thick or Sophie had so far resisted the "encouragement" of the inquisitor.

The raw cold eventually turned on its head to become a warm cocoon, lulling him quietly. Though he attempted to fight it, he found himself drifting in and out of a delirious half-sleep where strange ghostly shapes roamed and nothing made any kind of sense. The hallucinatory landscape was suddenly shattered by an electric burst that imprinted Sophie's screaming face on his mind. It was there and gone in an instant, but he couldn't escape the animallike emotions he saw; he was sure they would haunt him for the rest of his days.

But then, not long after, the mists parted and Sophie was there as he remembered her in the pub that first night he saw her. "Don't worry for me," she said with a smile. "All this is passing." There was another flash like interference on a TV set. "I'm not without abilities, or resilience," she continued. Another flash of interference, only this time she didn't return, but her voice floated through the mists to him. "Be strong."

He could no longer tell what were dreams, what were visions, and what was really happening around him, or whether, indeed, all three were one and the same. He saw himself as Adam and Sophie as Eve, two lovers from opposite sides of the tracks in a garden of stone. And the Serpent was there, tempting them with great alchemical knowledge: of who they were and of where they came from and why there was some secret reason for their time upon the earth; the only knowledge worth knowing, and the most jealously guarded.

No random conglomeration of chemicals only pretending to be, it said. *No simple Darwinian drive of survival, of establishment of the species. That's men finding easy answers to complex questions, as men always will.*

"The Devil is the Prince of Lies," Mallory pointed out.

The Serpent laughed, said *One man's Devil*, before becoming two and mutating into the double helix, twin DNA snakes coiling around each other, promising the only knowledge worth knowing for those who would listen.

And then it changed again, becoming a Fabulous Beast, glimmering with the condensed wonder of Existence, forcing its way into his arteries, into his cells, then into the earth itself, leaving behind it a trail that was bright blue with all the hope of every man and woman denied by those who said they had access to the only knowledge worth knowing.

Mallory woke with the strange belief that Sophie was holding his hand. He knew instantly he was not alone, though he could see no one in the cell with him.

"Who's there?" he muttered through cold, parched lips.

He was answered by the wind soughing through the corridor without. Instinctively, he sensed it was night, though there was nothing in his environment to mark the passing of time. The wind died away but the sighing continued, in the cell with him, not far from his left ear. It sounded like a whispered secret that no one wanted to hear.

The cold in his bones became colder still. He didn't want to look, but he knew he must; it was a primal urge: seek out the threat, then flee. Only he couldn't run. Slowly, he turned his head.

The cowled figure stood close enough to touch him. Where its face should be there was only darkness, deep, unyielding, without the hint of substance.

Except he could feel the weight of its presence, of unseen eyes bearing down on him, of a reservoir of emotion threatening to burst its dam.

He snapped his eyes shut, pretending to himself that it was a fleeting hallucination that had slipped out when the door of his dreams had closed. It was not one of the supernatural creatures besieging the gates, nor one of the risen clerics disturbed from their rest by the awful things they felt had been done to their Jerusalem. Since it had first started haunting him, he had pretended that he didn't know what it was. But he did, he did. It was as clear as a burst of fire in the dark.

"Go away," he whispered, his eyes still tightly closed. "Please."

And in that moment of desperation, the notion of his escape route came to him. "Caretaker!" he yelled. Then repeated the word continuously until his throat was torn and blood trickled down inside him.

Time dragged painfully. His strength, already at a low ebb from the lack of food, leaked from him and he lolled forward on the chains, still mouthing the summoning when he had no more energy to call aloud. His consciousness drifted with his vitality, but he was aware that the next time he opened his eyes the hooded figure had gone.

He didn't know if it was minutes or hours later when he heard a sound beyond the wall at his back. At first he thought it was rats, but as it grew louder he realised it was rumbling footsteps accompanied by a metallic jangling.

"Caretaker," he croaked.

The metallic noise rattled mere inches from him, and then there was a resounding click. After a moment of stillness, the wall itself began to shake. Dust showered over Mallory from the mortared joints. Out of the corner of his eye he could see the stones pull apart, then gradually grind open. A brilliant blue light flooded the cell, so that at first Mallory had to screw his eyes tight shut until he was accustomed to it.

"Who calls?" The voice boomed out all around him, making the manacles vibrate against his wrists and setting his teeth on edge.

"It's me. Mallory."

The Caretaker stooped to enter the cell, bowing his head so that he could fit beneath the ceiling. He wore an enigmatic expression that made Mallory think he had been anticipating the summoning. "Good day, Brother of Dragons," he said sonorously.

"Caretaker, I need your help." Mallory felt like a shadow of himself, but the Caretaker's arrival had uncovered a final reserve. "Help me get free. Please?"

Mallory still wasn't sure whether the Caretaker would do his bidding, but the giant bent forward and effortlessly pulled the manacles from the wall before snapping the chains that bound him. Mallory staggered under the weight of gravity and his weakness, and almost fell. The Caretaker caught him with one hefty arm. He exuded a deep spiritual strength.

"We have to get to Sophie." Mallory pulled himself upright. He was overcome with a yearning desire to have his sword at his side; he hadn't realised how attached he had grown to it. "Is there a way through your tunnels?"

"My place leads to all places, Brother of Dragons." The Caretaker motioned for Mallory to step through the opening in the wall. As Mallory checked up and down the dusty tunnel that ran along the other side of the cell wall, the Caretaker rested a heavy hand on his shoulder. "Before you proceed, you should know this: for every choice there are unforeseen repercussions. Every step leads you down a new road, infinitely branching, taking you to places you may never have guessed. At this juncture, the choices are never keener. Go one way and your life will continue untroubled. Go to rescue the Sister of Dragons and your world may turn dark. You may see things best left unseen."

"We get Sophie and damn the consequences," he said, without a second thought.

A faint smile flickered across the giant's lips. "Existence has chosen wisely."

The Caretaker guided him along the tunnels with a lantern that cast the brilliant blue light. Mallory felt himself strangely drawing strength from it, his limbs becoming less sluggish, his thoughts sharper. The direction of the tunnels bore no resemblance to the layout of the cathedral buildings he had in his mind's eye. Though Sophie's cell was close to his, they appeared to be walking away from it for what must have been twenty minutes before the Caretaker brought them to an abrupt halt and slapped the cold stone.

"Here," he boomed. "She is not alone."

Mallory knew he wouldn't have the strength to fend off Broderick or one of the Blues, if that was who was there. "I need my sword," he said.

The Caretaker smiled again. "Llyrwyn calls for you also. Wait here. I shall bring it to you."

He disappeared into the gloom, leaving Mallory to slide slowly down the wall until his forehead was resting on his knees. Things had turned so sour, just as he thought they couldn't get any worse. Yet his dismal mood was nothing next to the ruddy glow of hatred he felt for Stefan, Blaine, and all they represented.

But through it all, one thought was wriggling: the Caretaker had called Sophie a Sister of Dragons. Did that mean their destinies were entwined in some way? He wondered if some instinctive recognition of those mysterious ties explained why he had been drawn to her so instantly. But he liked the idea, the two of them linked by fate and an overarching mission for good; it was like something dreamed up for a fairy tale.

In the unyielding dark of the tunnel, the blue light was visible long before Mallory heard the thud of the Caretaker's footsteps. Surprising himself with his eagerness, Mallory grabbed the sword and strapped it to his belt. The blue light it radiated was even more potent than the Caretaker's lantern.

"How do I get in there?" Mallory turned to the wall, searching for any sign of an opening.

"Take care, Brother of Dragons. Hard choices lie ahead." The Caretaker slammed his enormous hand upon a stone that looked like any other. Blue sparks flew. Mallory felt a change in air pressure, the oddly aromatic air of the tunnel giving way to something danker. Slowly, the wall tore itself apart and opened outward.

Framed in the trembling stones, Mallory saw Broderick and one of the Blues frozen in disbelief. It lasted for barely a second, and by the time Mallory was stepping into the cell with his sword drawn, they were already moving.

Mallory was only dimly aware of Sophie chained to the wall. While Broderick backed against the wall, weaponless, the knight adopted an attacking posture with the ease and restrained strength of the Blues. Even the slightest movement exuded a lethal skill.

Mallory knew him vaguely, as well as anyone knew any of the Blues. His name was Blissett, his accent still thick with the Worcester burr of his youth. He'd once revealed to Mallory that he still loved his childhood sweetheart and once he was given freer range as a knight he'd return to Worcester to seek her out. He'd seemed like a decent fellow beneath the patina of hardness all the Blues carried with them.

He moved forward with grace and power, counterbalancing easily as he swung his sword in an arc. Mallory parried, never taking his focus off Blissett's face, picking up every subtle movement with his peripheral vision. Blissett drove on, hoping to push Mallory onto the back foot. Mallory responded with a ferocious attack that brought a glimmer of shock to Blissett's eyes.

There was no compassion in Mallory, only an arctic cold. When his sword drove through the soft tissue of Blissett's upper arm, he felt nothing. When he pressed it on, feeling the gritty pressure of the bone fracturing and splintering, he felt nothing. When the arm started to come away, he was already pulling the sword back, ready to disable Blissett with a lunge that would slice open his stomach muscles and send his guts tumbling onto the floor. And Mallory felt nothing.

As Blissett went down onto his knees, shocked at the steaming mass vacating his body, Mallory whipped his head from his shoulders with a single clinical stroke.

Broderick had already escaped. Mallory stepped over the sticky pool of gore and twitching remains, the sight already lost to him. His only thought was for Sophie. When he saw her, a sharp pain shot into the core of him; she looked as if she was dead. She hung on the chains, her chin on her chest. Her clothes were torn and there were bruises on her face and forearms; blood trickled from one nostril.

But as he placed his hands on her shoulders she stirred, her eyelids flickering open. She forced a smile.

"Are you OK to move?" he asked gently.

She nodded.

"The bastard Broderick will have everyone down here in minutes. We have to get out quickly." His sword sheared through the chains easily and Sophie fell into his arms. For the briefest moment he pressed his face into her hair and inhaled the scent of her, and then he supported her toward the opening in the wall where the Caretaker waited impassively.

"Who's that?" she asked weakly.

Before Mallory could respond, the Caretaker took Sophie's hand with surprising tenderness. "Let the Blue Fire heal you, Sister of Dragons." A shiver ran through Mallory as he saw the lantern flame flicker toward Sophie as if it were alive. Mallory could almost see her vitality returning; her skin bloomed, her eyes grew wide, the bruises slowly lost their sheen. "You have been a good friend to my people," the Caretaker continued, "and a good leader of your own. You have a strong heart—the Blue Fire works in you, and through you into the world."

There was something almost deferential in the Caretaker's tone. Mallory looked at Sophie curiously, wondering what the giant saw in her.

She smiled and took the Caretaker's hand. "Thank you," she said.

Through the walls came the distant ringing of the cathedral bells. The alarm had been raised.

Sophie turned to Mallory. "Where are we going?"

"I don't know. I haven't thought that far ahead."

"We need to get out of this place—"

"We can't go outside the walls. Those things are still waiting—"

"They never troubled me," Sophie said, "and now you've renounced your place with the cathedral, they'll probably leave you alone, too."

"It's nice that you're prepared to take that gamble," Mallory said acidly. "And I didn't renounce them. They renounced me."

The Caretaker led them along the tunnels to a door that opened into the Chapel of Ste. Margaret of Scotland in the south transept. The room was bitterly cold and suffused with the soft glow of candlelight from the altar. "Thank you," Mallory whispered to the Caretaker.

"Your call came from the heart, Brother of Dragons. How could I refuse? My people have always cared for lovers . . . and fools."

"We'll debate which side we fall on later," Sophie said.

They stepped into the chapel, and when they looked back, the Caretaker and the doorway to his realm were gone. Beyond the low wooden walls of the chapel, the cathedral was quiet.

"I'm betting they've already blocked off the tunnel," Mallory whispered. "I reckon our only option is to get onto the walls and lower ourselves over," he mused. "Don't know how we're going to do that. The whole of the cathedral is between us and the way out."

"I might be able to help there." She turned away from him, lowering her head so that her hair hung across her face. He heard whispered words that made no sense to him, and then her body grew stiff and trembled with the strain. When she turned back, her face was drawn. Though the Blue Fire had reenergised her, her reserves were still low and easily drained.

"What was that all about?" he asked quietly.

"A little inclement weather to mask our tracks."

Cautiously, he approached the door.

"Mallory?"

The voice made him start. He turned to see Miller standing at the front of the chapel; the young knight had obviously been on his knees in prayer, hidden behind the rows of chairs.

As Sophie went to the door to peek out, Miller rushed over and grabbed Mallory's hand desperately. "How did you get out?" he said, his eyes wide with amazement.

Sophie was beckoning; the cathedral was empty.

"Mallory, take me with you." Miller's fingers closed tighter around Mallory's hand; there was a profound desperation to him that was quite shocking.

"You're better off here, Miller. I don't fancy my chances outside the walls—"

"No, no, you don't understand. You *have* to take me with you." His gaze ranged around the chapel with unbearable anxiety. "Stefan's going ahead with the testing . . . using the relic."

"You've got nothing to hide."

Miller's eyes fell; his whole body appeared to shrink. Mallory had forgotten about the beast from Bratton Camp. Was that why he was so afraid—that the relic would expose him as the one who had slaughtered Cornelius and the others?

"What is it?" Mallory asked.

"I killed my girlfriend!" He blurted the words out, then collapsed in sobs.

Mallory stood dumbfounded, trying to comprehend what Miller had said. "You *killed* her?" He recalled Miller telling him how he had fled his home after his girlfriend had dumped him for some local thug.

"I didn't mean to," Miller whined. "She was the only thing I had in the world . . . the only reason I had for living. I begged her to stay, but she wasn't having any of it. When she started to go, I grabbed hold of her . . . she fought me off . . . and . . . and I hit her." His eyes burned with devastation. "I didn't mean to! I loved her! I just couldn't cope . . . I was weak . . . pathetic . . ." He sucked in air to stop a wracking sob. "She went down . . . didn't get up . . ."

"You killed her?" Mallory repeated in disbelief. Miller's story resonated throughout him with a strength that stunned him.

Miller saw it reflected on Mallory's face. "Don't judge me, Mallory," he pleaded. "Not you. I couldn't bear it if you judged me. You're such a good man . . . you were the one who gave me the strength to keep going . . ."

"You're blind, Miller . . . and stupid." Mallory felt queasily empty, felt like laughing at the stupid irony of the situation. Miller had given *him* hope. He'd seemed so decent and honest, so innocent. But he was just like everyone else. There was nothing to which anyone could aspire, nothing at all.

"I came here to do penance, Mallory," Miller continued amid the tears. "To earn my redemption. I didn't think I had any hope until I met you. You gave me hope, Mallory. You saved my life—"

"Yes, and wasn't I a stupid bastard." He looked to Sophie, who was watching them nervously. She motioned frantically for him to hurry up.

"The relic will show what I did!" Miller continued. "The mood in this place now . . . it's all turned sour. They won't forgive me, Mallory. They won't give me a chance. I'm afraid of what they'll do to me." Pathetically, he threw his arms around Mallory's legs, sobbing.

Mallory pushed him off with the roughness of someone who'd been betrayed. "You made your bed, Miller—you've got to lie in it. Same as all of us."

He marched over to Sophie, untouched by Miller's crying. "What was that all about?" she asked.

"Nothing." Mallory tried to ignore the desolation he felt. "Come on, we'd better move."

They slipped out, and Mallory didn't look back once.

The nave was dark and deserted; Mallory had lost all sense of time and had no idea how long it would be until the next service. Keeping his sword firmly in its scabbard so that the blue glow didn't attract attention, he led Sophie toward the door at the west end.

They'd progressed barely twenty feet into the nave when a cry made them jump. A brother on guard had been sitting unseen in the quire and was quick to raise the alarm. They hurried toward the exit, but before they were halfway to it, the door crashed open and three Blues burst in, brandishing swords. Mallory recognised the group they had ridiculed during the snowball fight.

There were too many of them to confront. Anxiously, he looked around. Several guards had entered silently through the south transept and were approaching from behind. Without thinking, he ran for the only door within their reach.

Once he'd slammed it behind him, he cursed profusely.

"What's wrong?" Sophie asked breathlessly.

"This is the way up," he said angrily. "To the spire. There's no way out here."

"Well, we can't go back," she said. "If they recapture us, we won't have another chance."

Dismally, Mallory took the steps two at a time with Sophie following close behind. It was an exercise in futility, but that had never stopped him before. The advantage of height on the stairs would mean that at least he would be able to take a few of the Blues out with him. Strangely, Sophie didn't appear in the least depressed that they were going into a corner.

The door crashed open behind them and the sounds of pursuit followed quickly. Mallory held back so that Sophie could go ahead, leaving him space to protect her back.

"How high are you planning on going?" he said sourly. "Or are you just trying to give me a workout before the last?"

"Shut up, Mallory," she said, without looking back. "Goddess, you don't half moan."

With the air burning in their lungs, they raced up the interior of the square tower. It was two hundred feet to the top of the second stage—Mallory had climbed up there once for a peaceful view over the city. Timber stays and iron ties and braces held the structure steady. They passed the windlass at the base of the spire that had been used to raise stone from the ground when it was being built, and then Sophie led them out of a door to the base of the octagonal spire.

They were met by a sharply gusting wind so cold it felt as though their skin was being flayed. Snow was driven into their flesh like needles.

"Why don't we stay inside?" Mallory yelled above the gale. The wind buffeted him against the cold stone. His head spun when he looked out across the dark landscape; it would be easy to get blown off the tiny walled area and dashed onto the ground far below. "I can make a stand better at the top of the stairs. It's harder to defend this area."

"We're not defending," Sophie shouted back. Her hair lashed across her face, making a mockery of her constant attempts to pull it away from her eyes. She was shivering from the cold. Mallory went to put his arms around her to warm her. His heart felt like a cold rock at the thought that they wouldn't be able to spend any time getting to know each other. What a stupid way for it to end.

But Sophie fended him off, then pointed over his head. "No. Keep climbing."

He followed the direction of her finger. Iron rungs had been hammered into the stone of the spire. They appeared to rise up to the summit one hundred and sixty feet above their heads.

"Are you mad?" The simple act of looking up brought a rush of vertigo. If he attempted to climb, he would be blown off in an instant. Besides, it led nowhere. The Blues could afford to wait until they fell, froze, or climbed down. "Or are you looking for some spectacular way to commit suicide? Personally, I'd—"

She took his hand. The sounds of pursuit could now easily be heard through the door. "Just trust me," she said.

He looked into her eyes, which were wide and honest, and he surprised himself by realising that he did trust her, more than himself. Cursing, he turned and gripped the first icy iron rung and hauled himself up.

Ten feet up and it took all Mallory's strength just to hang on. The wind attacked like a wild animal, throwing him from side to side. He had to hook his arms inside the rungs to prevent himself from being thrown off the spire. He feared for Sophie, who was physically weaker than him, but though he sensed she was close behind, the stinging blizzard prevented him from looking down long enough to see her.

The crash of the door swinging open, though, came loud enough to rise above the gale. The bark of their pursuers was angry and disbelieving, and he could just make out a furious debate about what should be done.

"Keep going," Sophie called up to him.

Mallory felt delirious. The weakness from his incarceration and lack of food combined with his incomprehension to make his head spin. If he kept his eyes fixed on the dwindling stone column in front of him, he was OK. But the snow made the landscape bright and his eyes would repeatedly be drawn to the white roofs and rolling hills, and then down, down, down to the cathedral compound a dizzying fall below.

It was just as his stomach turned at the contemplation of the drop that a particularly strong gust of wind tore over the peaks and troughs of the new buildings and wrenched at his legs. They were ripped away from the security of the rungs, flying out horizontally away from the spire. The shock tore the breath from his throat. He yelled out and tried to grip onto the rungs, but he couldn't feel his numb fingers, couldn't tell if they were holding or slipping.

He heard Sophie scream, then saw his knuckles sliding over the edge of the rung. The wind tugged harder; the snow lashed his face. He felt the fall before it happened, experienced the air being sucked from his lungs, that final shattering impact, his body exploding at every joint . . .

An eddying gust whipped around the spire and caught his legs just as his fingers were about to let go, slamming him back against the hard stone. Winded, he lost his grip completely and slid down the spire, almost knocking Sophie from her handhold. Somehow he caught onto a rung, yanking himself to a sudden stop, wrenching his shoulder.

He clung there for a second, his heart pounding so hard it felt as if it was going to burst from his chest. But the wind didn't relent and the sounds of the knights below didn't fade; he couldn't rest. With small gusts pulling him to one side, then the other, he continued to climb.

Below, he could occasionally catch the sound of Sophie talking, but he couldn't make out what she was saying. Fifteen minutes later, the rungs ran out: the end of his journey, and probably the end of his life. The spire was now just a couple of hand-spans wide and he could feel it moving in the now unbearable wind, adding to the sickening vertiginous pull. He felt unconscionably weary and didn't have the energy to climb down even if he'd wanted to; he could have put his arms around the spire and hugged it until the end came. Just above his head, the cross on the very top appeared to glow.

Exhausted, he rested his head against the stone, sliding back and forth. His whole body was numb, yet strangely starting to grow warm. He couldn't feel any of it; it was just as if he was enveloped in steam.

Something whizzed past his ear, jerking him alert. A shower of dust fell against his face: a chunk of stone had been dislodged.

As he struggled to work out what was happening, something else whipped past him. This time he saw it: a crossbow bolt. The knights were firing at them, trying to dislodge them. *The bastards!* he thought. *They couldn't even wait for me to freeze and fall.*

"Are you OK?" he yelled out, realising at the same time how stupid it sounded. Sophie's response was lost to the wind.

And then there was only the view, the pristine whiteness of the hills, beautiful in their simplicity. He began to fantasise that he could fly, that he could just kick off from the spire, soar out over them, and keep going to a place where there was no hardship and he could spend the rest of his days in idyllic bliss with Sophie.

Movement caught his attention away over the hills. It became lost to the stinging snow for a while before he caught it again. A cloud, he thought, caught in the rolling wind. It continued to move, free of the subtle undulations of the elements. With purpose.

274

Something was moving inside the storm. Drawing closer.

He was mesmerised. It was natural, yet not natural, dark behind the snow. Another crossbow bolt rattled against the stone. How long before one hit him?

"It's coming!" Sophie yelled. Jubilation sounded in her voice, but a hint of fear, too.

A burst of colour in the black-and-white world. He was back in that moment that would haunt him for all eternity. But no, no . . . Now he knew what it was. Yet it made no sense: it was dead. More fire exploded in an arc, so brilliant that it lit the rooftops red and orange and yellow. The shadow so big now, beating slowly up and down. Enormous wings riding the night winds.

"We killed it," he whispered into the howling gale. But all he could feel was wonder surging up inside him like a golden light, a sense of connection with all Existence.

"Stay with me, Mallory!" Sophie ordered. There was an insistence to her voice. Did she know something he didn't?

The Fabulous Beast soared on the turbulent currents, up and down and then to the side, gouts of flame erupting from its mouth at regular intervals like the birthing of stars in the bleak void. Mallory was transfixed. As it neared, he could see that it was not the one they had slain. Something about it appeared younger, sleeker, the emerald, ruby, and sapphire sparkling of its scales more pronounced.

It came directly toward the spire. The beating of its wings was deafening, like the wind in the sails of a mighty ship, and the conflagration of its breath was like the roar of a jet. Mallory could see its eyes gleaming a fiery red, and for an instant he thought he saw something there: an intelligence, certainly, but also a contact, an *understanding*.

He thought, *It's going to get its revenge for the death of the other one. It's going to wipe the whole of the cathedral from the face of the earth. A purifying flame.*

Languidly, it began to circle the spire. Mallory was on a level with it, and at times he thought he could just reach out and touch it, feel the roughness of the bony protuberances on its head and spine, the hard sheen of the scales; he felt as though he could walk across the air to it.

"Mallory!" Sophie yelled.

He jolted alert. From far below he could hear the panicked cries of the knights. They were calling for support, but found time to loose another bolt. It missed Mallory's temple by a fraction.

The Fabulous Beast went down, rose up, went down again, then turned and soared toward the cathedral.

This is it, Mallory thought.

It passed beneath him. The flame gushed out in a torrent, painting the roof far below a hellish red. In its illumination, Mallory saw everything clearly. Two of the knights dived back inside for cover. The other remained rooted in terror.

The fire hit him full force. It drove him off the tiny landing, and as he fell he burned only briefly before the fury of it consumed him and he turned to dust, sprinkling with the snow.

The other knights were out in an instant, one firing at the Fabulous Beast, which had returned to its circling, the other, bizarrely, shooting once more at the two of them.

How they must hate us, Mallory thought.

"Get ready, Mallory!" Sophie shouted.

He had no idea what she meant, didn't have time to consider it. The bolt hit his shoulder as if he had been smashed with a mallet. Pain drove through his arm and side. Everything went with that—his sense, his grip—and then he was falling, turning slowly, seeing Sophie's desperate, loving face, seeing the snow, going down with it.

He hit hard, though he had only fallen for an instant, and then he was being swept sideways. Desperately, his thoughts tried to make sense of what was happening, but before they could, he was mesmerised by the sight of Sophie floating down toward him.

Time appeared to hold still, then speed up. She crashed at his side, then began to slide. Frantically, she raked her hands back and forth, gulping air in terror as she slipped.

Finally, her fingers closed tightly around a bony ridge; her face blazed with jubilation and she began to pull herself up.

The queasy sensation of being whipped along caught them both as they clung on for dear life. From the corners of his eyes Mallory saw the beating wings, and the retreating spire, the angry knights like flies. Far below, Salisbury was laid out like a fairy city, glorious in white, and beyond it the spectral landscape, beautiful and terrible.

The Fabulous Beast rode the currents, taking them to an uncertain fate.

chapter fourteen
CRYING IN THE WILDERNESS

"Do you want to be good?
Then first understand that you are bad."
Epictetus

Mallory woke from a dream of flying to feel heat on his face and the crackling of fire in his ears. At first he thought he was still with the Fabulous Beast, soaring high over the magical landscape. But there was no wind in his hair and no rolling sense of motion deep in his gut. Only hardness and stability lay beneath him.

Nearby, the blazing ruins of an old barn melted the snow in a wide circle, providing warmth in the chill of the grey morning. A farmhouse with a sagging roof and broken windows stood across a courtyard. Mallory lay on boards under cover of the eaves of a disused cow shed. Old sacking had been thrown across his legs. He looked up to the lowering clouds and felt a brief, affecting sadness for what was gone.

The cold the previous night had left him almost delirious, and his memories of what happened after their escape from the cathedral were fragmented. More than anything, he recalled the flight, seeing the world in white flash by beneath, hearing the beat of the Fabulous Beast's wings and the roar of the otherworldly fire. Transcendental, wondrous, an abiding feeling of something greater.

They had descended on the eastern fringes of the city, and that's where his memories had started to dissolve. He couldn't remember the landing or much of dismounting, though he had a clear image of the Fabulous Beast rising up into the sky, limned by the moonlight as it disappeared into the snowy night.

"Finally." Sophie emerged from a nearby copse, clutching what appeared to be twigs and leaves. Her ordeal in the cells had sloughed off her with remarkable ease—the effects of the Blue Fire, he guessed—and she appeared bright and hearty. She wandered over to him, shivering slightly. "I thought you were going to sleep the day away."

"You controlled it," he said in amazement.

This amused her. "Don't be silly. You can't control something as wonderful and elemental as that. I asked for its help. It answered."

"You're full of tricks."

"Yes, I'm just all-round wonderful." She squatted down next to him and examined his shoulder where the crossbow bolt had struck. "You've warmed up. I was worried last night."

"Stefan didn't provide many creature comforts in the cells. Like food."

Her face darkened. "Revenge doesn't achieve anything, but I really want to pay that bastard back for everything he's done . . . to my people, to me. To you." She looked back toward the city. "I hope most of them managed to escape. They'll regroup. The Celtic Nation is stronger than that weak, scared . . ." She shook her head, overcome by emotion as the memories of the attack on the camp returned to her.

"We're out of it now."

She laid the leaves and twigs next to him. "Most of the goodness is frozen in the ground at this time of year," she said. "It's not a season when you should be homeless. But I managed to scrape together a few bits and pieces. If we can find some kind of pot, we can melt some snow and I can boil up a soup—"

"Yum."

"OK, it won't exactly be Jamie Oliver," she snapped, "but it'll give us some energy, at least to keep on the move until we can find some proper food. I think the bolt might have chipped a bone in your shoulder. At least it didn't embed. But you're a tough guy . . . you'll get over it."

"And the twigs?"

"They're for a ritual to keep us safe. As safe as we can expect to be in this place." She looked around at the snow-draped landscape. A few birds flapped desolately amongst the stark trees; it appeared as if all human existence had been swept away.

Mallory took her hand. "One advantage to nobody being around . . . we could always warm up under this . . . uh . . . sack."

Sophie extricated her fingers from his. "I know you place a lot of faith in your charm, Mallory, but really, it's not as winning as you believe." Despite her haughty expression, some of the depression that had hung around her since the attack on her camp lifted slightly. "I don't sleep with just anyone. I need wine . . . and flowers . . . and wrapping in warm towels. And even then my suitor has to meet my exceedingly high expectations. And frankly, Mallory, I shouldn't hold your breath."

Mallory watched her wander toward the farmhouse in search of pots and pans. He felt at peace, he felt free, and both seemed so unusual for being absent from his life for so long. They'd escaped, and he could barely believe it. Above all, though, he was relieved that the Caretaker had been wrong—they'd escaped with their lives and sanity intact, and there hadn't been a price to pay at all.

"Which way are we headed?" Mallory asked as he sipped on the foul-tasting stew that Sophie had laboured over for the past hour. It warmed his limbs and gave him renewed energy, just as she had promised, though the process was slow. "We could head west . . . maybe go to Exeter. Some of the smaller cities might not have been affected as badly as the larger ones."

She spooned in silence for a moment and then said, "You know I can't leave here, Mallory."

His heart sank. He *did* know, although he had tried to resist believing it.

"I'm the tribe's leader. They're counting on me. I need to get them back together . . . lead them away to a safe place where we can regroup. You're welcome to come with us," she added, without looking at him, though the hope in her voice was clear.

"OK . . . of course." He was loath to go anywhere near the cathedral, with its weight of bad memories and the possibility that he might once again be sucked into its awful gravity. He'd hoped it could be just the two of them, insulated from the demands of a hard world, but he knew that had always been a fantasy.

She appeared honestly pleased by his response, and that warmed him. "Besides, what about Miller?" she added. "I thought he was your friend. Don't you want to get him out of that awful place?"

"He's no friend. He's just some stupid kid who was always hanging on my coattails."

Sophie watched him carefully; Mallory felt as though she could see right inside him, all the lies and the terrible things he'd done.

"That's you down to the ground, isn't it, Mallory? Pretending nothing and nobody matters . . . pretending it to yourself. When are you going to learn that everything matters? That people matter most of all."

He put the bowl to one side and stared at the flames that still roared in the remains of the barn, ignited, he guessed, by the Fabulous Beast. Did it really have the intelligence to provide them with warmth? Was it a beast at all?

"I can't work you out at all," Sophie said sharply. "You just switch off when a subject comes up that you don't want to talk about. And how many of those are there? Like the past . . ."

"The past doesn't matter."

"You're an intelligent man, so why do you say such stupid things? The past makes us who we are."

"You say." He was quite aware how petulant he sounded.

Sophie bristled. "So let's talk about the past, Mallory. I know nothing about you—"

"You know everything about me. Everything you see is everything you need to know. This is who I am."

"Do you know how arrogant that sounds?"

"That's one of those character flaws I just have to live with."

"And me by association, I suppose," she said with irritation. "Have you ever had a proper relationship? Do you understand even the most basic rules . . . of sharing, trust . . . openness?"

Mallory hardened; he wasn't going to be pushed into the forgotten wasteland of his past by anyone. "All right. The past shapes us, but that doesn't mean we have to live in it . . . always revisiting it . . . always suffering. Somewhere down the line you have to try to leave it behind."

Sophie watched his face carefully, picking up subtle clues. Her detailed attention made him uncomfortable.

"You want to know about my past?" he said sharply. "Well, it's unpleasant . . . the details will make you sick, all right? They make me sick. But the details don't matter. I carry it around with me every day, like a big fucking pile of bricks on my shoulders, but that isn't enough. Oh, no. There are still things out there that feel I need to be reminded . . . or punished . . . I don't know, I don't care."

"Is that why you don't believe in anything?"

He kicked over his bowl so that the remainder of the stew flowed into the sizzling snow. "No, no, don't you understand? We're not shaped by *incidents*, whatever stories and movies and TV always told us. We're made by a thousand little things, and incidental thoughts, and half-considered ideas. We're built up like bits of chewing gum stuck together into a ball, and only when it's big enough to recognise do we step back and see what a monster we've made. What happened to me doesn't matter. What I am now matters, and what I'm going to be in the future. Good or bad, that's what matters. That's what matters for all of us. Don't look back, look forward."

"I don't know if I agree, Mallory—"

"I don't care." He stood up abruptly and walked away.

He wandered until he came to the farmhouse, hating himself for uncovering the rawness, for letting Sophie see that big, big part of himself that he wasn't proud of at all. He wouldn't be surprised if she wasn't there when he returned. He probably deserved it.

Half of the farmhouse was little more than a shell, but the remaining half was still habitable. He couldn't understand why Sophie hadn't got them ensconced in there, away from the elements, until he saw the detritus piled high against the entrance: a washing machine, a fridge, a sodden sofa, other pieces of furniture. It would take them an hour or more to pull them away to gain access.

He was just considering returning to Sophie to apologise—a first!—when he spotted a movement behind a filthy, streaked window. His hand jumped to the hilt of his sword, though he sensed no immediate threat.

As he approached the pile blocking the entrance, he noticed a path through it, hidden unless you looked closely enough. He considered leaving be whoever was inside, then shrugged, dropped to his knees, and crawled into the hole; it was preferable to opening himself up to Sophie's questioning again. Halfway in, he thought he was mistaken and would have to wriggle out backward, but then he found himself at a door that hung ajar. He slipped through and pulled out his sword.

"Who's there?" he called out.

His voice echoed. The carpet underfoot was sodden and smelled as if it was rotting, but furniture was still placed around a hearth in which a single ember glowed. The door to the back room was closed. He steeled himself, then wrenched it open, his sword glowing dimly in the half-light.

A painfully thin woman in her early thirties moaned desolately, her face buried in her hands. "Don't kill us," she whimpered. "We haven't got anything!"

Behind her, a man who appeared little more than skin and bone lay unmoving on a camp bed beneath a thin, dirty sheet that would have provided little warmth in the bitter cold of recent days. Mallory looked around the room, gradually realising the couple had been existing, just, for some time in that dismal place. The man was clearly ill, barely clinging on, the woman worn down to near nothing by caring for him.

"I'm not going to hurt you," Mallory said.

The woman didn't appear to hear him. She sobbed, rocking backward and forward, her face still hidden. It took Mallory five minutes to calm her, and then a further five before he could get any sense out of her. His first impressions were right: the couple had been living here since the Fall, eking out a living as best they could on their land while fighting off the occasional looter and the more frequent supernatural visitors. They'd survived, despite the destruction of half of their home by one large band of looters, and from then on had taken to subterfuge to continue existing.

Winter was the hardest time for them, particularly after the looters had gone off with their stockpile of food. The husband had managed to trap a few animals to keep them going, but then he had fallen ill—pleurisy, Mallory guessed after examining him—and the woman had not known how to continue the hunt for sustenance.

Mallory eventually convinced her to come with him to Sophie, who provided a degree of comfort that was beyond Mallory. She gave the woman the last of the stew, which was devoured hungrily, while Mallory was sent out to inspect the farmer's traps. Most of them were filled with animals that had decomposed too far, but one contained a freshly caught pheasant. As he removed the dead bird, he couldn't prevent his thoughts from turning to the guilt that was eating away at him; the background buzz became a frenzy when he considered the repercussions of his decision to leave Miller to his fate. At the least, punishment would be severe, but Mallory had the queasy feeling that with Stefan's current frame of mind, he might have condemned Miller to death.

And all because he had responded like a spoilt child in his hurt that Miller had shaken his faith. It wasn't Miller's fault he wasn't the incorruptible person Mallory had imagined him to be, just so that Mallory could believe in goodness and decency and his own salvation. And it wasn't fair that Miller would be punished so terribly for shattering that illusion. In his own way, Mallory had been as bad as Stefan.

It had been one moment of stupidity, and if he allowed it to stand, he'd be as bad as he had always feared; he'd be damned, for sure.

As he made his way back to the farmhouse, he began to piece together exactly what he had to do, but it was only when he saw the thin, broken woman sitting next to Sophie that he accepted completely the path that lay ahead of him. The woman could no more have abandoned her responsibility to her husband than Mallory could have denied Sophie. Selflessness, sacrifice, hope, and salvation all sprang from one source, but he'd never been able to see it before because he'd never felt it before.

It could have been the exhaustion, or the hunger, or the fading memory of the Fabulous Beast, but his internal barriers crumbled and fell and he was suddenly struck by a blinding revelation, so simple in retrospect, almost naïve, but so much predicated upon it. The consequence of what that realisation meant to him and those around him sent his thoughts spinning wildly.

The epiphany dragged back the memory of his grandfather and the dying bird he had relived so acutely in the Court of Peaceful Days, and now he knew exactly why the symbolism had struck him on a subconscious level. Everything was linked—that was the meaning of the Blue Fire—everything was valuable. And it was the duty of humanity to care for it all because by doing so it was caring for itself. All things were linked; and all tied into that little thing he felt for Sophie that from his new perspective was bigger than both of them, larger than the whole universe.

He stood watching Sophie and the woman for ten minutes while his thoughts raged. He felt liberated, his own burden beginning to lift as he realised that salvation was still within his grasp if he was prepared to take a leap into the dark for the sake of others.

The woman, who finally revealed her name was Barbara, ravenously devoured her steaming meat with an edge of desperation that made Mallory turn away. He never thought he'd see starving people in Britain.

Afterward, the woman took in some of the bird for her husband, though Mallory would be surprised if he ate anything; he didn't seem to have long left.

"What's on your mind?" Sophie asked.

"Why do you ask?"

"You seem different."

He picked at the remnants of the meat. "The way I see it, we've got three options. We can run away together—you've already thrown that one out. We can go back to Salisbury and round up your people, and lead them somewhere else to regroup." He paused, his mouth dry. "Or I can go back and try to put things right at the cathedral."

She smiled as if she'd been proven right. "This is about Miller, isn't it?"

"I've saved his life twice. The third's the charm. Truth is, he's lost without me."

"OK," she began thoughtfully, "so what are you going to do? Waltz up and bang on the gates, ask them to stop being so naughty? Because otherwise it doesn't seem like you've got any alternative."

"Yes, I have. I'm going to see the Devil."

She drew herself up, alert, intrigued.

"On a very basic level, my enemy's enemy is my friend, and at the moment Stefan is definitely my enemy," he explained. "But the fact is, I don't believe Stefan's explanation, which is that the Devil is attempting to wipe out the Church in some final apocalyptic battle between good and evil."

She smiled.

"What?"

"I don't believe in the Devil, anyway. Satan is a Christian invention, something the Church used to demonise my religion."

"So if it's not the Devil, it's . . . something else. And if it's not the Devil, the motive Stefan identified goes too—it's not about good and evil. There's another motive."

"What could that be?"

"All this started when the Blues brought back a relic to the cathedral," Mallory began. "I didn't think twice about it until I realised the authorities have been lying from the start to cover up the Church's use of the earth energy, something that might have been seen as ungodly . . . blasphemous. There's a history of geomancers in the Church who've been attempting to utilise this supposedly pagan force since the Christian Church first established itself, and they've always kept it secret," he explained.

"What's this got to do with some relic?" Sophie asked.

"The relic is the bones of Saint Cuthbert, which had been kept for centuries at Durham Cathedral. Only I don't think it's the bones at all. That was just a smokescreen."

Sophie's eyes narrowed. "What have they done?"

"I think they stole something . . . something vitally important to all those supernatural forces lined up outside the cathedral walls."

"What could they possibly have stolen that would have been that important?"

"No idea, but it's got to be something to do with the Blue Fire . . . something that amplifies its power. That's what the Caretaker was talking about when he spoke of something warping reality—pulling in all those new buildings . . . raising the dead . . . affecting people's minds. Something incredibly powerful. And the Adversary, whoever or whatever he is, wants it back. It all comes down to arrogance—the Church thinks it has some right to take this thing and use it. Instead of winning hearts and minds the slow, laborious way, it's using this mojo to boost the spiritual energy so that the Church quickly becomes a powerful force again."

"Who are the good guys and who are the bad guys here, Mallory?"

"Well, they brought it on themselves . . . maybe they thought they were doing the right thing, I don't know. That doesn't matter now. But if we can convince the *Devil* that we can get back whatever it is he wants—"

"And you reckon you can reason with something that has the power to lay siege to the cathedral in the way that it did? I think you should go back to hammering on the gates and begging Stefan to be good," she teased.

"Yeah, it's a risk, but you know me . . . I'm nothing if not confident in my abilities."

"You're a big-headed bastard, Mallory," she laughed. "So how do we find this *Devil*?"

"No," he said, shocked. "I'm going alone."

"No, you're not."

"Yes, I am. It's too dangerous." If he'd believed she would attempt to go with him, he would have slipped off silently during the night.

"You're nothing without me, Mallory. You'd better get used to it."

He could see there was no arguing with her. But it changed everything: failure was no longer an option.

Darkness fell. They'd stoked up the fire in the barn with any item of wood they could find and by then it was blazing merrily. Sophie snuggled under Mallory's arm, both of them buried beneath old sacking under the shelter of the eaves. A cold wind blew from the north, bringing more flurries of snow.

"Do these count as warm towels?" Mallory held up an edge of the dirty sack.

Sophie laughed. "In your dreams, Mallory."

Mallory brought his fingers up to the smooth skin at the back of her neck and gently massaged it; her shoulders loosened at his touch. "In this world, now, you need to hold on to any comfort you can get," he mused aloud.

"I intend to." Sophie felt under the sacking until she found his thigh. "But then maybe it was always that way."

In the roaring of the flames and the drifting of the snow there was an elemental magic. Mallory could feel it affecting him, pulling out emotions that had been concealed by the crystalline protection needed to make his way in the world they had inherited.

"The universe is a wonderful place," Sophie continued dreamily, watching the snow against the night sky. "When you're with someone you love and you're feeling as though they're the only person in the world for you, think of all the random decisions that brought you to that point. Maybe you decided to stay in instead of going down to the pub that night . . . or maybe you'd taken a different job the year before and ended up in a different city . . . or maybe you'd gone to a different university and had a whole different career . . . and you'd never have been at that point . . . never met the only person in the world for you. Yet all those things aligned to get you to that exact spot when everything was right. And it didn't just happen for you, it happened for people all over the city, all over the country, all over the world, for as long as people have been on the planet. And then people try to tell you that there's no intelligence in the universe."

"Some would say it's just chance. That there's plenty of people for you in the world, and you'd have found one sooner or later whatever you did."

"Do you believe that?"

He thought for a long moment. "No."

"Romantic," she gibed gently.

"If you close your eyes and listen to yourself . . . listen to your heart . . . you *know*. You know in a way that you could never explain to someone who only believed in the Selfish Gene and the evolutionary drive. There is only one person for you."

Sophie rested her head on his shoulder and closed her eyes; the warmth of their bodies together was soothing.

"And you'll find them," she said, "if you trust the universe. That's the thing. You give yourself up to the universe and it helps you out."

She turned to look at him, her dilated pupils reflecting the snow so that it looked as if she had stars inside her. "This is our time," she said softly. "The world's gone to hell and the old order's gone with it. This isn't a place for big business . . . for those who're only interested in making money . . . the soul-dead. It's a place for dreamers and romantics . . . the passionate . . . the hopeful."

"Hippie."

"There's no point being anything else. We make the best of what we've got. Life's short. You've got to love what's around you."

He brushed the hair from her forehead. "I used to be like that."

Her eyes shimmered. "You're still like that, Mallory. You just can't see it."

She leaned forward until her lips were brushing his. They were like velvet, so full of life that Mallory could almost feel the pulse of blood. He moved against them; her mouth was soft and warm and moist, yielding slowly, following his rhythm perfectly. Her fingers touched the back of his neck and it was as though electricity jolted through him. Everything about her was supercharged. In comparison, he was sluggish, like someone emerging from a coma.

The air was filled with energy. Mallory was surrounded by frost and fire, opposites coming together in an alchemical union that made them more than they were before.

"We're special," Sophie whispered in his ear, before nuzzling into his neck.

His hand moved across her breast, feeling the rise of the nipple, the subsequent surge of power in his groin. She didn't resist; she met him move for move, desire for desire. Her fingers eased over his body, down to his jeans, fumbling for the buttons. Their clothes loosened, their temperature soared, hardness and softness lay under their hands.

In their passion they were like beasts clawing at each other, completely consumed by the raw feelings of the moment. When Mallory penetrated her, he thought he would come immediately, so powerful was the rush. But he kept himself going, and they kissed, and they bit, and rolled around half naked despite the coldness of the night.

Afterward they lay in each other's arms, feeling their unified heartbeats slowly subside. Mallory dragged the sacking back over them when they became aware of their breath clouding, and for a long while they said nothing, barely believing what had happened and what it meant for both of them.

Sometime later, Sophie suddenly jerked and exclaimed, "Look there."

Footprints tracked their way across the blue-white snow barely ten feet from them.

A chill ran through Mallory. The prints were cloven, but with a hooked toe or claw at the rear, clearly belonging to something that walked on two legs.

"We didn't see it." Sophie's voice was low and rigid. "It was almost on top of us and we didn't see it at all."

"Fools and lovers are protected," he muttered, pulling her close, aware how fragile they were, how defenceless in a dangerous world.

They moved closer to the fire where the heat made their skin bloom, and decided to take turns keeping watch. Mallory constructed a makeshift shelter with some of the sacks and selected items from the pile of rubbish near the farmhouse to keep the snow off them.

"You still haven't told me what we're going to do." she asked him sleepily.

"Tomorrow," he replied, "we're going to petition the gods."

In the pale morning light, Mallory retrieved a couple more animals from the fresh traps and delivered them to the woman and her husband, before they set off north. They walked a fine line, keeping beyond the edge of the city's built-up area yet not straying into the open countryside. Danger lay all around. The snow had abated, but it was still thick underfoot and the going was hard. Occasionally, Sophie or he would disappear into a drift, but they still found the energy to laugh at each other's misfortune, and that helped the time to pass.

His mood changed when he finally saw the bulk of Old Sarum rising up against the snow-filled sky. "You know we're linked," he said obliquely. She eyed him curiously. He told her what the Caretaker and Rhiannon had said about the Brothers and Sisters of Dragons.

Sophie was shocked, then humbled. "Ruth Gallagher, the woman who taught Melanie," she said, "she was a Sister of Dragons, one of the five at the time of the Fall."

"And now you're following in her footsteps."

"But she was a great person!"

"Yeah, I can hardly believe it either. Somebody must have faith in us."

His revelation appeared to be lying heavily on her, so he changed the subject by telling her about his experience on Old Sarum on the night he met Miller.

"There are certain places where the barriers between this world and the other one are thin . . . where you can cross over to places like that Court you visited," she said. "High peaks, lakes, rivers, springs, the seashore. But the strongest sites have already been marked, and they're places where the Blue Fire is powerful."

"The stone circles," Mallory suggested.

"That's right. And the Iron Age hill-forts, and the standing stones, and all the other sites where our ancestors have left their mark on the landscape."

"How do you know all this?"

"Part of my initiation into the Craft."

"That Gallagher woman passed it on?"

She nodded. "It's the truth behind all the things we learned at school. When the Christian Church came, it tried to colonise many of those old places where the Blue Fire . . . a spiritual energy . . . was strongest. At some it succeeded. At others, the powers that had already laid claim to it were too strong. The war's been going on for nearly two thousand years. It's summed up in a carving at Saint James's Church in Avebury. The building itself is Saxon, but it's believed that some of the sarsen stones may have come from the megalithic monument on the site. On the front is a carving of a bishop holding a book and piercing the head of a dragon with his crosier. It's a symbolic depiction of the old Church conquering the Blue Fire and bending its force to its will. Avebury, of course, is one of the most powerful sources of the dragon-energy in the country. And the Christian legend of Saint Michael, the dragon-killer, is the same symbol. That's why so many sites along the main ley running through Britain—from Cornwall to the east coast—are dedicated to Saint Michael."

"You've got a thing against Christianity, haven't you?"

"Not against the Faith, no," she replied. "There are lots of different roads leading to the same mystery—people take the one that suits them. But I've got a thing against the men—and it always is men—who come to control a religion and impose their own prejudices on it. There's an argument that paganism is weaker than Christianity because it's never provided any martyrs. But then there's not been any oppression, torture, and war in its name, either. And remember this, Mallory: at its heart, Britain is a pagan country. Christianity has standing because it's the State religion. But you go out to Cornwall or Wales or Scotland and the old beliefs still prosper. Even in the heartland of England, in the industrial centres, you strip away the lip service to a religion that's been taught from birth and you find an instinctual acceptance of the old ways, though people don't often realise it."

Mallory shielded his eyes against the snow-glare. He had a sudden shaky feeling they were being watched. "So that could be one reason why the cathedral was moved to its new location. It was in conflict with what was already there." He recalled James hinting at something similar.

"The gods at Old Sarum are still strong. In times past they were stronger still," Sophie said.

"And that's who we're going to talk to," Mallory said. He looked at the lonely, windswept hill, remembered the crackling old man's voice, the presence in the dark that was there and then not there, and felt his apprehension rise.

By the time they reached the entrance to Old Sarum on the main road it was mid-afternoon and the sun was already falling. "We'd better hurry," Sophie said. "I want to get this over before nightfall. They're much more powerful then. They might not let us leave."

They followed the winding path toward the parking lot. As they came over a rise, the ancient fort was presented to them. This time, Mallory saw it in a new light: the history of an ancient struggle written in the landscape. There were the prehistoric outer ramparts dating back to Neolithic times more than 5,000 years earlier; the Iron Age defences from 2,500 years ago when Stonehenge was a great religious centre; the Roman roads converging on the site from several directions, marking its significance 1,900 years ago. By that measure, Christianity had been there hardly any time at all. The cathedral had been built off to one side of the old Saxon town on the summit shortly after the Norman Conquest, less than 1,000 years ago.

As they walked past the deserted parking lot, the old defences rising up before them, Mallory became aware of a heightened atmosphere: tension filled the air, becoming more oppressive the further they advanced.

"Can you feel it?" Sophie said redundantly.

The sun was insipid, the clouds occasionally obscuring it; Mallory tried to estimate how long they had before it finally set.

"I don't know how I'm going to get in touch with them," he said. "I'm just kind of hoping they'll come when I call."

"I knew there was a good reason why I came along," Sophie replied. "I can help." She looked around, distracted. "Magic is about symbolism," she said. "It's all around us. Look over there—yew trees. They mark the passage between this life and another, and grow in abundance at these places where it's possible to cross over. The Church used that symbolism by planting yews in graveyards."

"I'm not ready to cross over in that way."

Sophie didn't appear to hear. They paused at the wooden bridge crossing the ditch to the old Norman castle; the gates that Mallory had scrambled over with Miller had now been torn asunder.

They passed amongst the ruins of the gatehouse into the inner bailey. Within the remaining fortifications, the silence had an overwhelming quality, as if the entire place was holding its breath. The snow lay thick and undisturbed across the circular area of the inner stronghold. The raised ramparts prevented any view of the surrounding countryside and cast a long, cold shadow over half of the interior, warning of the impending end of daylight.

Ahead of them lay the corbelled flint of what was left of the great tower. To the right were the remains of the royal palace. Sophie closed her eyes, swaying slightly, before striding purposefully to the centre of the site.

Mallory waited patiently while she drew a circle around them in the snow and then marked the cardinal points. She had already collected items from outside the site—what to Mallory had seemed only leaves and other pieces of dead vegetation—and these she deposited at intervals around the circumference.

When she had finished this, she squatted down with her back to Mallory and began to whisper so he couldn't make out her words.

This continued for ten full minutes. Despite his thick cloak, Mallory began to shiver as a cold wind blew up from nowhere. Sophie stood, a little shakily, and leaned on him for support. "It's done," she said.

"What now?"

"We'll see." She bit her lip.

The wind continued to blow, and after a while Mallory realised it was sweeping back and forth with a life of its own. He had the uncomfortable feeling that something was searching for a way through the circle.

"Over there," Sophie whispered.

She pointed toward what Mallory at first took to be a glistening patch of snow. It shimmered just above the rim of the Iron Age ramparts, but then began to hover about two feet off the ground. As it neared, Mallory could see something within the ball of light, and when it was only a few feet from them he realised it was a tiny humanoid figure, all gold as if the light was radiating from its skin. Horns protruded from its forehead, but its eyes were black and gleaming, like little windows onto space.

It floated around the edge of the circle, then drifted away toward the royal palace ruins.

"I think we have to follow it," Sophie said.

"Can we break the circle?" Mallory looked toward the sun, now bisected by the ramparts.

"I don't think we have a choice."

Cautiously, they stepped outside. Instantly, the wind dropped and all was still again. The tiny figure waited for them, then led them past the palace and over the edge of the defences. They had no choice but to go down the precipitously steep bank where it was impossible to gain a foothold. They skidded, then rolled and fell in the deep snow, winding themselves as they hit the bottom of the ditch.

Covered in snow from head to toe, they clambered out into the wide expanse of the outer bailey, but their guide didn't slow. They hurried behind it to the site of the old cathedral, the ground plan visible in the stumps of walls protruding through the white. Down rotting wooden steps they stumbled, into a regular area that had once been the cloister, and then into a room that lay lower than the surroundings. Once there, the golden figure soared high until it disappeared.

Mallory felt uneasy; there was only one exit from the room. A fizzing in the snow near his feet attracted his attention.

"There's something in the air," Sophie said, shaking the snow from her hair. "Power . . . danger . . . The whole place is charged."

Squinting, Mallory could make out coruscating blue energy just beneath the snow cover. He squatted down and brushed aside the flakes to reveal a faint sapphire arc crackling across six inches. The urge to touch it overwhelmed him. Sophie rested a hand on his shoulder for support.

It felt cool and soothing; strength flowed into his limbs. He closed his hand around the energy flow, then made to stand up, expecting his fingers to pass through it like water. Instead, the Blue Fire came up with him, more of it rising from the ground in a regular structure: two uprights connected by a crossbar that lay just beneath the arc.

When he withdrew his fingers, it continued to rise until it stood just over six feet high, the energy painting the snow blue all around and throwing dancing shadows across their faces.

"What is it?" Mallory said in awe.

Sophie slipped an arm in the crook of one of his, transfixed by the light. "It looks like . . . a door."

Mallory shrugged. "Well, we can see what's on the other side. Maybe we should . . ."

They stepped through together.

It felt as if warm rain was on their skin, even beneath their clothes. When their feet fell on the other side, they jolted; everything had changed.

They could *taste* the air, a thousand complex flavours stirring their senses at once. The quality of light made their heads spin; it felt like the seaside on a steely bright morning. The landscape was the same—the ruins of the cathedral, the snow—except for the figures standing silently all around, or squatting on the broken masonry, watching them.

At first, they appeared to Mallory like blurred shadows, an aberration that he could blink away. He had an impression of tall, slender figures oozing golden light. But then they diminished and became more squat.

A voice sounded like broken glass, the echoes rolling out across the plateau. "This is how you see us now."

And then everything fell into relief. The figures were barely more than three feet tall, though fully formed adults. There were men and women, young and old, dressed in medieval-style clothing in shades of scarlet and green. Their eyes glittered horribly. From most, Mallory felt contempt and threat potent enough to make the hairs on the back of his neck stand erect. Others appeared curious; a few, amused.

One stepped forward onto a pile of stone that had been the wall of the north transept, a few feet above Mallory's head. He was younger than most, long golden hair falling down from a high crown; his features were cruel, his regard cold.

"We will grow in stature again," he said icily.

Mallory's eyes darted around. He felt particularly uneasy about the ones unseen at his back. Sophie, though, was concentrating on the matter at hand. "Greetings," she said. "How may I address you?"

The spokesman bowed his head slightly, though his mood did not thaw. "You may call me by the name known to your kinsmen: Abarta." He nodded as he surveyed them. "I see you are a Brother and a Sister of Dragons. In some quarters that standing commands respect."

But not here, Mallory thought. Under his cloak he moved his hand onto the hilt of his sword, though he knew he could do nothing if they attacked as one.

Abarta smiled like a sneaky child. "This is our cathedral now. The ground is unconsecrated . . . disempowered." He motioned toward the expanse of the outer bailey. "Welcome to Sorviadun. That is how your people knew it once. *The fortress by the gentle river.*"

"Thank you for allowing us into your home," Sophie said with studied deference. "We come to you with a plea for help."

"We heard your call. There are few who know how to bridge the wall between worlds. You have a fine ability . . . for a Fragile Creature." A ripple of cold, contemptuous laughter ran through the assembled group. Mallory watched one of the men sitting cross-legged on the top of a stone column, cleaning his nails with a long curved knife. He smiled dangerously when he saw Mallory looking at him. Abarta eyed Mallory curiously. "The sword, Llyrwyn, has long been lost to your world, and here it is in the hands of a Fragile Creature. I hope it has chosen its new champion well."

The setting was so alien, fraught with so many potential dangers, that Mallory wasn't comfortable speaking; he felt instinctively that the slightest word out of line could bring the strange, threatening creatures on them in a frenzy. Sophie, though, took the lead confidently.

"We ask for your guidance," she began. "There is a force loose in our world that has tormented our people, attempted to destroy those of a spiritual nature . . . taken our children . . ."

Abarta stayed her with a dismissive wave of his hand. "That will come later. First, let us examine this role of yours, Dragon-Sister. You are both still bright. It would seem to me that the responsibilities of your office have only recently been laid on your shoulders. Is this so?"

"I have no idea what my responsibilities are," Sophie replied carefully in case there was some hidden trap in his words. "I only learned of my . . . *office* . . . secondhand and still do not truly understand what a Sister of Dragons is."

Abarta mused on this for a moment. "Then you have much to learn, yet you are deprived of a tutor. Let me aid you: Existence demands five Brothers and

Sisters of Dragons. In times of hardship, as now, when one group passes another must be formed. The king is over the water—all Fragile Creatures await his return—and the other Dragon-warriors now have new responsibilities. So Existence called to you to take up the mantle. Do you understand?"

Sophie nodded, but her mind was clearly on other matters. She made as if to speak, but Abarta silenced her with a finger.

"The old stories are locked into the very fabric of Existence," he continued. "They repeat themselves as the seasons turn. The kings have different names, or different weapons, but they have the same role. They are all the same king because Existence has a need for this role to be filled. If one king fades from view, another must arise to take his place."

The conversation was rambling, yet the beings remained intent and filled with anticipation. Mallory prickled, trying to read the meaning behind the surface. It was only when Sophie began to attempt to lead the talk back to the matter at hand that he realised: Abarta was seeking to distract them. In that place the sun was still high in the sky, but in their world it would be almost gone.

At that realisation, Mallory became anxious and attempted to catch Sophie's eye, but she had already decided to stop any more dissembling. "I thank you for your guidance on this issue," she began, with a little more curtness in her voice than she probably intended, "but I wish to return to the questions I brought with me—"

"Oh, but there are so many things yet to discuss," Abarta said, placing the tips of his fingers together. "Of your roles and responsibilities, of the states of our respective worlds, of wars fought and ones yet to come—"

"Please. Time is of the essence."

"Not here." His eyes flashed sparks of annoyance at being interrupted. "In your world, alignments may take place that have repercussions here in the Far Lands. But in our place, there is no *then* and *might be*, or not in terms that you might understand, and so no echoes or alignments." He paused, ready to launch into another rambling discourse. Tension spread across Mallory's chest. Abarta tapped a finger on his chin in thought, then began, "Now—"

Sophie opened her mouth and a sound came out that made Mallory's ears hurt. It appeared to be composed of syllables he had never heard before, alien sounds he could hardly comprehend coming from a human throat. Sophie only uttered it, yet it created a deafening roar that cracked the sky.

Fury grew on the faces of the crowd. Mallory's fingers clasped even tighter on the hilt of his sword, so sure was he that they were ready to strike.

"You have made enemies of us through your discourtesy." Rage flashed across Abarta's face and edged his cold voice. "The words of power should never be used lightly. We are not beasts of the field to heed your command."

"I came here to make an offering . . . to put us at your favour," Sophie said sharply, "but you tried to trick us—and that's a discourtesy to us." She was shaking. Mallory could sense her fear, though her confidence masked it from the others. "Now you must answer my questions."

"Three," Abarta said, refusing to acknowledge that she had the upper hand. "Only three."

Sophie looked to Mallory. He nodded for her to continue using her own judgement; time was running out.

"Who . . . or what . . . is the one we are searching for?" she said tentatively.

Abarta gave a faint triumphal sneer. "Someone who wishes harm to some of your kind."

Sophie cursed under her breath. "Where can we find him?"

Mallory flinched; he knew Abarta could give another nonanswer: a name they didn't know, or *on your world*, or *in the Far Lands*. But instead, Abarta smiled. "I give you this, knowing it will do you no good. If you want to find the one for whom you are searching, you must travel to a place in the Fixed Lands . . . in your world . . . known to your kind as Knowlton. There you may attempt to storm his keep." A ripple of mocking laughter passed through the crowd.

Sophie took a deep breath. "How can we stop him attacking our kind?"

"By defeating him." Another ripple of laughter. "Or by surrendering to him."

"Come on," Mallory said quietly. "We have to get out of here."

The door of Blue Fire still crackled at their backs. They took a step toward it.

The ringing sound of knives being drawn echoed across the cathedral site. "Know this," Abarta said. "Old Shuck blocks the way for all who travel to Knowlton. And where Old Shuck leads, can the Wild Hunt be far behind? You will fall before them like saplings in a storm, in the Fixed Lands or in the Forest of Night . . . and then we will see how fragile you really are."

Suddenly they moved as one, knives drawn and glinting, black eyes filled with a hungry horror. Mallory grabbed Sophie and threw the two of them through the door. There was the sensation of warm rain again and then they crashed hard on snow. Night was almost upon them; only a thin line of light lay along the horizon.

They didn't wait to catch their breath. Instead they ran across the outer bailey and the parking lot and along the road out of the site, and they didn't stop until Old Sarum was far behind them.

chapter fifteen

TO EVERYTHING
THERE IS A SEASON

"The Infinite has no beginning. It is the beginning of all
other things. It is divine, immortal and indestructible."
Anaximander

"Time's running out," Mallory said, as they marched through the crisp snow at first light. "If the brethren aren't dying already, they will be soon—either from starvation or because those things will have broken through the walls."

"We're doing the best we can." Sophie walked beside him gravely. The moment they had set foot on the road to Knowlton, the last remnants of elation at their escape from the cathedral had been wiped away by the gravity of what lay ahead. They were under no illusion about their chances of surviving an encounter with the Devil, less still that they could convince the Adversary to call off the attack. But they had hope.

"Still time to back out," Mallory said.

"I will if you will."

"I've got nothing to lose. Your people are counting on you."

"Then we'd better make sure we get back in one piece, hadn't we?" She stamped her feet to warm them. "You really think you can pull this off?"

"No, but I'd never be able to live with myself anymore if I didn't try."

His tone was striking, almost desperate; she wondered what it was in his past that was playing out in his decision to save Miller and the others. "And the same goes for me, Mallory. If you've got the ability to do good, then you've got an obligation to use that ability. That's what my beliefs tell me."

Awkwardly, she reached for his hand. He took it, and for a while their mood lightened.

They had spent the dark hours of the previous night huddled in one of the deserted semis on the northern fringes of the city before searching out a militiaman at dawn. He had never heard of Knowlton, but after consulting a map book in his sentry post, they discovered it was a hamlet of only one or two houses south of Salisbury.

"I wouldn't be going down that way if I were you," the militiaman had warned them. "It's wild country. Not much between Salisbury and the south coast."

Now the city limits were visible away to the west and the road stretched out before them. The sun was turning golden as it crested the horizon. The cloud-free sky was a pastel blue; it was going to be a glorious day.

"At least we know where we're going," Mallory said, without highlighting the anxiety he felt at what lay ahead.

They broke for a snack around eleven. They'd found a stash of cans on their overnight stay that had escaped the looters, and had brought a few tins of beans and fruit, a couple of spoons, and a can opener with them. They found a sheltered spot on the edge of a wood and Mallory lit a small fire to take the chill from their bones. A thaw had set in under the unseasonably warm sun, which eased their mood a little.

"I'm still trying to work out the rules of this world," Sophie said, eating her baked beans with little desire.

"Does it matter?"

"When you're not top dog—which humanity isn't now—it matters more than ever. You don't want to offend some of the things that are loose."

Mallory rubbed his hands in front of the fire. "You want a rule? Never get in a transporter with a fly."

She laughed, but the unsettled mood returned to her features too quickly. Her restless eyes ranged across the countryside; there was no sign of human life. "What Abarta said about the Wild Hunt—"

"He was just trying to scare us."

"I've heard of it . . . something from mythology—"

"Lots of different mythologies. It's very adaptable. A Dark Lord leads a few mates and a pack of ghostly hounds across the countryside, scooping up anyone unlucky enough to be out. The Christians said it was Satan hunting lost souls to drag off to hell."

"Ruth Gallagher met them, I think."

"Sounds as if the Über-Witch passed on a lot of useful information." He paused when he realised Sophie was watching him curiously.

"You know a lot of things, Mallory."

"I'm very well read."

"What did you do in your past life?"

"I ate, I drank, and I slept."

She cursed. "You're as infuriating as those things at Old Sarum."

"I try."

"What are we up against, Mallory?"

"Something that makes us look blind and stupid. It planned everything so carefully, manipulated us from the start. The siege . . . the way we were run to bring the beast in ourselves so we could be attacked from the inside, to break the faith of the brothers . . . even the choice of victims, picked to play off the two factions vying for power, so they'd suspect, and doubt, and hate . . . It knew everything that was going on, knew us better than we knew ourselves."

"If this is supposed to be a pep talk, Mallory, you need to reexamine your material." She dumped the remnants of her beans in the fire, then said, "Why are you doing this, Mallory? Not so long ago, you were saying you didn't believe in anything, and now you're putting your life on the line. Have you finally found something worth fighting for? It must be something big to cause this kind of about-face."

Any answer he could have given her would have been too momentous. Instead, he said, "We should get moving."

She watched him for a long moment, even though he wouldn't meet her eye.

As Mallory stamped out the fire, the snap and crackle of the wood gave way to the deep stillness of the snow-muffled world. Yet the quiet only lasted for a second. In the deep background, Mallory picked up another sound that instantly set him on edge: the crunch of snow, but restrained as if someone or something was sneaking up on them.

Quickly, he caught up with Sophie, who had already started along the road. They hurried as fast as they could through the growing slush, pausing for breath ten minutes later, just before the road went over a rise. Mallory shielded his eyes against the gleaming countryside and looked back. A dark shape emerged from the edge of the wood where they had rested, keeping low, moving slowly but insistently. Not a man, certainly, but larger than any animal Mallory could imagine. It followed the line of their tracks, and at the road turned in their direction.

"What is it?" Sophie asked breathlessly some time later as they jogged along.

"I don't know, but it's not letting up. It doesn't matter what it is—we just need to keep ahead of it."

Sophie was looking exhausted, and he was feeling weary himself. In shaded areas the snow wasn't melting at all and in some parts the drifts were so deep they had to wade through them. The conditions didn't appear to be slowing up their pursuer; in fact, over the previous hour it had gained on them.

They continued southwest along the Weymouth road, through wide-open countryside that would once have felt soothing in its agrarian order but was now wild and frightening. Just after the rolling Pentridge Hill loomed up on their left, they took a B-road that felt even more exposed, the hedgerows too close and too thick.

"I've got to try something," Sophie said. Any rejuvenating effect of the Blue Fire had clearly worn off. "Things don't work well when I'm tired. It peters out, or it has no effect at all . . . but I've got to try. I don't know if I can carry on at this rate." Her face was drawn with exhaustion. Demanding privacy to help her concentrate, she climbed over a six-bar gate and disappeared into a field.

Mallory backed up to where he had a clear view along the road. The shape plodded along maybe a mile away, maybe less. He had an idea of what it was now: a dog, some supernatural entity, bigger than any real-world breed and black as space. The knowledge that it was something mundane yet at the same time alien was somehow even more disturbing. It carried with it an atmosphere that operated on some level beyond ordinary senses; Mallory felt threat and a growing sense of despair. Was this the Old Shuck that Abarta had mentioned?

Movement just on the edge of his vision to his right startled him. His hand went to his sword, but he didn't have time to draw it. A terrifying woman stood before him, as though she had appeared from nowhere. She was as thin as a winter tree, her skin almost grey, barely fitting her bones. A long black dress flapped around her, stained with tree-bark green and the white dust of a dry road. Her hair was grey and wild, untouched by a comb for months, years. But it was her face that chilled him, something that lay beyond its physical appearance, which was upsetting enough: it was smeared black with dirt or grease, making the grey eyes even more striking; they contained thunder and lightning, and the end of him.

She stretched out an accusing finger. "It's coming. You won't escape it now. You can't run any more."

He backed off, almost slipping on a patch of melting snow, finally managing to get the sword out.

The woman began to laugh, sheer venom underlining the mockery in that sound, so palpable it stung him. Thoughts burst in his head, memories or dreams; she was releasing them. He was speeding away in a grey car, his face framed in the rearview mirror, locked in an awful shock at what he had discovered in himself, tears streaming down his cheeks, his entire body racked with such shakes that it was almost impossible to drive.

"What do you want?" he yelled, with a fury that far exceeded the moment.

The old woman's laughter rose several notches and became hysterical, bitter. She threw her head back and her hair shook wildly.

"Stop it!" Mallory yelled. Tears sprang to his eyes.

Slowly, the woman backed away, still laughing, still pointing. There was one instant when he thought he would have to attack her with the sword, to shut her up before she said something he didn't want to hear, but then the sunlight glinted off his blade, blinding him, and when his eyes cleared, she was gone.

He'd just about composed himself when Sophie clambered wearily back onto the road. The dog—and he could finally see clearly that's what it was—was now only half a mile away.

"Are you OK?" Sophie said. "I heard you yell out."

"Did you hear anyone else?"

She looked at him curiously and shook her head.

"Did it work?" he snapped.

"I don't know . . . we'll see."

They turned and hurried along the road.

Five miles further on, they realised Sophie's attempt at masking their presence must have succeeded. The dog had fallen back—only a little, but it gave them some respite.

As they went over another hill, they spotted a house almost hidden amongst the trees to their left, smoke rising from the chimney. Parked next to it was a battered van. The tire tracks in the snow showed it was regularly in use.

"Where does he get his fuel from?" Mallory said, bringing them to a halt.

"Some of the more isolated farms have their own tanks. Maybe he found one that had been abandoned. What are you going to do?"

"Steal it."

Sophie shook her head, the exhaustion making her emotions whirl.

"Don't worry, we'll bring it back. We'll get to Knowlton, do the business . . . bam . . . back tomorrow."

"I don't know—"

"Think of all the people in the cathedral we'll be saving."

His comments made some kind of sense, and she didn't have the energy to argue. He led her to the hedgerow and made her drop down below the line of sight. "If I can get in it, I can hot-wire it," he said. They crept along as quickly as they could.

At the gravel driveway, they paused, but there was no sound apart from the drip-drip-drip of melting snow from the tree branches in the wood that encircled the house.

"You wait here," Mallory whispered. "As soon as I come out, I'll throw the door open and you can dive in."

She glanced back up the road. "Just hurry."

He kept low to the passenger side, which was furthest away from the house. It took him five minutes of working on the lock with his Swiss Army knife before it popped. He listened. Nothing. But when the door opened it gave a loud squeal. His breath caught in his throat. With heat spreading down his back, he listened again: still nothing.

Just as he was about to wriggle onto the van floor, the house door slammed open and the sound of running feet approached.

"Shit," he muttered.

Around the front of the van appeared a dishevelled, large-boned man with the wild-eyed appearance of someone who had retreated from the world. He brandished an old shotgun with shaking hands. "Get away!" he screeched. "Get away! Get away!"

He pulled the gun up and fired wildly. Birds rose screaming into the air. Mallory had thrown himself backward an instant earlier when he realised the van's owner wasn't going to waste any time talking. He landed on his back and rolled onto his feet just as another blast raised a shower of wet gravel an inch from his boot.

His instinct was to sprint to Sophie and get out of there as fast as possible, but the gun had already been reloaded and there would be a clear shot at his back if he ran. Another retort made his head ring. Shot passed his head so closely that his hair moved with the turbulence. Mallory launched himself to one side and bounded into the trees, weaving randomly. Wood splintered past his ear.

"You won't kill me!" The man's voice had the crackling paranoia of someone who had been unbalanced by existing in a climate of fear for too long.

Mallory had hoped his attacker would retreat into the house, but irrationality consumed him. He ploughed into the wood on Mallory's trail, obsessed with the idea that he would never find peace until the destroyer of his equilibrium was eradicated.

Mallory cursed at such a stupid distraction. His only choice was to go deeper into the woods to lose his pursuer, then circle around to get back to Sophie. But his legs were leaden, and as the shot whistled around him and branches crashed to the snowy ground, it was clear that the wild man was more likely to bring him down with his random shooting than if he had been taking aim.

He pressed on, running from one side to the other while trying to keep his balance on the uneven ground, with its fallen branches and hollows hidden beneath the covering of snow. He was faster and more agile than his lumbering pursuer, who was struggling with loading his shotgun on the run, but his progress was slowed by the increasing thickness of the wood and the old brambles and detritus that clogged the ground between the trees. In the shade the snow had not even started to melt and his footprints marked his direction clearly.

He slipped behind a trunk to catch his breath, pressing his back against the bark so he wouldn't be seen. Behind him, he could hear the sounds of ragged breathing and pounding feet against a background of constantly dripping water from the higher branches. The sun gleamed brightly through the branch cover, making the snow glow. With his dark clothes, it would be even more difficult for him to hide.

He drove on into the wood.

Five minutes later, he decided it was time to stop running and to attempt to circle back. Annoyingly, his pursuer had managed to keep pace with him, while the random shooting had kept Mallory permanently wrong-footed. The hunter wasn't going to give up until Mallory was dead.

Mallory came up suddenly on a snow-filled hollow about forty feet across that would take him out of his pursuer's line of sight. He skidded down into it and instantly turned to his left, scurrying low across the bottom. Ahead of him was a large area of bushes, tangled brambles, and dead grass where he would leave no tracks behind him. On his hands and knees, he crawled into it, wriggling past the tearing thorns until he was hidden in the very heart; it would be impossible to get through standing upright. All he had to do was wait until the hunter got caught up trying to follow him in, then rush out of the other side and back to Sophie. Holding his breath, he waited.

It wasn't long before he heard the hunter hurrying through the crunching snow. He had reached the lip of the hollow and was obviously surveying the area cautiously.

Come on, you hick bastard, Mallory thought.

The sound of booted feet sliding down into the hollow: the wild man was picking his way along the mess of Mallory's tracks, the gun undoubtedly pointed dead ahead. Tension gripped Mallory's chest.

When the hunter passed into the thicket, kicking at the brambles that attempted to ensnare his boots, Mallory propelled himself forward, low and hard. He burst out of the other side and hurtled up the bank and over the lip. The gunfire was so loud he thought his heart would stop; the blast ripped a chunk out of a tree to his right.

He ran.

It had worked; he didn't look back. But he'd only gone a few metres when he glimpsed movement on the periphery of his vision. The hunter was relentless; how could he have struggled through the thicket so quickly?

Mallory drove himself on and detoured to his left. The sound of crunching snow was loud enough to tell him that the hunter was keeping pace. Breathless, he paused behind another tree. Perhaps he could catch the hunter unawares, disarm him.

He set off again. The figure was slower, but still stalking efficiently, however fast Mallory ran. The hunter had clearly adopted new tactics, weaving amongst the trees, letting the trunks obscure him so that Mallory couldn't really tell where he was until he caught the most fleeting glimpse.

Steeling himself, Mallory hid behind the largest tree he could find and waited. Every fibre of his body was rigid. The constant drip-drip of water was disorienting; he strained to listen past it.

Finally, he had it: the familiar crunch of footsteps, slow, regular, coming nearer. Mallory drew his sword so carefully there was not even the familiar *zing* of the metal escaping the sheath.

Closer, and closer still. Mallory kept calm, though his chest was as taut as a piano wire. Only a few feet away; Mallory told himself to hold on until the hunter was right beside the tree.

Don't kill him, he had to tell himself.

At the last moment, Mallory lurched out, swinging his sword in front of him. Only it wasn't the hunter.

A black shape lay before him, huge and threatening, like death itself. Blood-red eyes seared intensely, a snort of hot breath like escaping steam rising in a cloud in the cool air. The sight was so terrifying that Mallory turned cold at the sight of a demon with the form of a dog, as big as a small pony, its sable coat sucking all light from the surrounding area.

It was the eyes that affected him the most, not dull and stupid like an animal's, but a man's eyes, crackling with an otherworldly intelligence that spoke of horror and threat and dread beyond his imagining.

For the briefest time, the tableau froze: there was just Mallory and the dog in a world of white. Then a deep bass rumble escaped from its throat and a gobbet of saliva oozed from its mouth, which opened slowly to reveal a monster's yellowing fangs.

Mallory was already moving as he saw tensing muscles ripple across its black fur. It erupted from the spot with the speed and mass of a car. Despite his advantage, Mallory only just got out of the way; the dog clipped his sword, sending it spinning across the ground. Its head turned as it passed and a ferocious snap of its enormous jaws only just missed taking off his face. He yelled out as some of its saliva splashed on his wrist, where the skin sizzled and smoked.

The dog was around in an instant, relentless, driving forward. The ground shook beneath its thundering paws. Mallory tried to dodge; it smashed into his leg so hard it felt as if the bones were splintering. He spun, slammed into a tree, and saw stars.

By the time his fumbling consciousness had returned, it was too late: the dog stood a few feet away, teeth bared, ready to tear him apart whichever way he tried to escape. But he couldn't have moved anyway; those red eyes held him fast. Something emanated from them, drilling into his skull above the bridge of his nose, into his brain, where it scurried and wriggled. In his mind, words that were not words echoed; images and impressions burst like fireworks in the night, so sickeningly alien he thought his consciousness was going to shut down at the contact.

Its muscles tensed again; the bass rumble began.

The blast shocked Mallory out of his mesmerised state. Shot smashed into the creature's skull—he saw the skin flow like liquid—but it made no impression; it kept its gaze on Mallory. Through fractured vision, Mallory made out the hunter lurching in the background, waving his gun, ranting incomprehensibly.

Mallory thought, *Here it comes.*

But the attack never came. Slowly the pinpricks of black at the centre of the fiery red eyes moved to the side. Its head began to follow suit, cranking around until it was staring directly at the hunter. What Mallory's pursuer saw in the beast drained the blood from his face. His eyes widened in terror, and briefly the banal madness that had gripped him was replaced by a startling clarity. Mallory saw how unpleasant true dread looks in a man's face: it stripped away everything that made him civilised, everything that made him human.

He had time to fire one final, useless blast before the thing crashed against him, smashing him to the ground. Mallory saw both of the hunter's shins snap in two on impact, but then Old Shuck's rending head was moving in a blur.

Shaking himself from the horror, Mallory jumped to his feet and ran, pausing only to snatch up his sword. He found an energy reserve he didn't know existed, speeding across the uneven terrain as if he were flying.

Sophie was searching the periphery of the wood, desperately upset. She was overcome with relief when he skidded up to her, throwing her arms around his neck. "I heard the sounds," she said queasily.

Mallory threw her off. "No time." He dragged her behind him as if she were feather-light, then scrambled into the van and deftly hot-wired the ignition.

"What about the owner?" Sophie asked, anticipating the truth.

"He's had it." Mallory was filled with lightning. He thrust the gears into reverse and roared backward, the wheels screeching in protest. Through the trees he could see a low, black shape approaching, now bizarrely part red.

Mallory spun the van around in the road and sped away.

There was more than half a tank of fuel, easily enough to get them to their destination. They had to drive cautiously along roads that had barely seen any traffic for a year, where the snow drifted so deeply they had to dig a path through with a shovel they found in the back.

Sophie began to doze intermittently and seemed on the brink of complete exhaustion. It left Mallory alone with his thoughts at a time when he really didn't need to be. Fragmented, buried memories surfaced, mingling with stark images of another world, another life. Once, he glanced at the side mirror and saw the hooded figure that haunted him standing in the middle of a field, lonely and stark amid the ruts of snow and sweep of mud and grass, scavenging crows bucking and diving around it. The sight made him cold and sick, and left him with a feeling that he was rushing toward a reckoning. The past wouldn't be staying behind him for much longer.

A mile from their destination, and with twilight coming in hard, the van suddenly lost all power and drifted to the side of the road.

"What's wrong?" Sophie mumbled as she stirred from sleep.

The next ten minutes were spent checking everything under the hood, but the problem remained a mystery. "Back to walking, I think." Mallory looked up at the darkening sky, then forced a smile. "Maybe we're just jinxed."

The warmth of the day faded quickly. The black dog was a way behind them, but a strange, troubling atmosphere was rolling out across the deserted landscape. The road wound amongst oppressive clusters of trees heavy on both sides. The occasional isolated house appeared, dark-windowed and uninhabited, but still with curtains and hanging baskets, as though the residents had been driven out and no looters had dared to venture in.

This far from the city, the fields were now clogged with thistles and weeds, the grass unclipped by cows or sheep. Soon the only mark of farming would be the wild hedge boundaries. The wind blew across the land, cold and shrill, stirring the rooks' nests in the tallest trees. The birds occasionally broke the silence with their raucous calls.

"We can't be far off," Mallory said, consulting the book of maps he had brought with him from the van.

Sophie fumbled for his hand. "Are you nervous?" she said, manifestly feeling so herself.

"No," he said reassuringly. "But I still wish we were walking in the opposite direction."

"We're a Brother and Sister of Dragons," she said ironically. "We're only allowed to do the right thing."

As they passed a deserted pub standing lonely at a junction, Sophie started and looked out across the fields. "There's someone out there," she said urgently.

"I noticed them about half a mile back," Mallory said. "They've been tracking us, keeping to the hedges and the shadows."

"What are they?"

"I don't know. At first I thought they were animals, deer or something . . . I thought I saw horns . . . I don't know." He adjusted his cloak so he could reach his sword easily if necessary. "But then they looked as if they were walking on two legs sometimes."

"Oh."

"I think they're waiting for dark."

"They like that, don't they?"

"I've been wondering," Mallory said obliquely, "do the gods you worship come to your rescue if you pray? Or aren't they that hands-on?"

"I think whatever created the universe would have an interest in the life that populates it, don't you?"

"I thought for a long time that there wasn't a God," Mallory mused. "You look at all the random suffering and the mean-spiritedness and the venality, and you think if there was a God He needs to be deposed pretty damn quick."

Sophie sensed the gravity at the end of his comment. "But?"

He sighed. "Anything I say would be too twee. No one would take me seriously anymore."

"Go on, I won't tell." They both knew the conversation was a distraction to keep away the void that lay at the end of the day.

"Well," he began uncomfortably, "take love. The evolutionists say it's a mechanical impetus, perfectly designed to create a bond between two breeding partners and then to provide an atmosphere of security so the offspring can thrive and perpetuate the species. But anyone who feels love *knows* that's not true. Inside your head you know exactly what love is but you can't express it in words because it's too rich and complex . . . so otherworldly . . . so nonhuman . . ." He was struggling to find the words. "That's it. It's not *of* us. It doesn't exist within our frame of reference at all. It comes from . . . somewhere else . . ."

"Are you trying to tell me something, Mallory?" She smiled teasingly.

"Tallent, the only people who could possibly love you are the kind who'll come up to you in a park in piss-stained trousers and do a dance for twenty pence."

"There's hope for you yet, then, Mallory."

The road sloped gently down, curving around the edge of another thick copse. A house stood dark and forlorn amongst the trees. Sophie eyed the dying light anxiously; they couldn't pretend the dark wasn't coming any longer.

"Are we nearly there?" she asked.

Mallory closed the map book with a bang. "It should be around here somewhere. Which is good. Because they're getting closer."

A tiny B-road branched off past the deserted house. A little further on, they saw their destination, the symbolism so striking it brought an instant frisson. A ruined church stood at the centre of a large field, while encircling it, enclosing it, forever linked to it, was a Neolithic henge monument consisting of a raised bank and an internal ditch with a ceremonial entrance. The scene was heavy with the resonance of ancient mysteries in conflict yet at the same time inextricably joined.

The wind whistled across the countryside, buffeting them as they ran for the church. On the edge of the world the light was now only a pencil-width. Across the fields on all sides, grey shapes scurried and jumped and ran, neither animals nor beasts but something of both, all converging rapidly on Knowlton.

Mallory and Sophie slipped past the iron gate and sprinted through the gap in the ringbank. Instantly the wind fell, but the grass continued to ripple.

The church was no shelter. The roof and the outer wall on the far side were completely missing. The bell tower standing erect at the heart of the feminine circle offered a feeble defensive position, but it was still open to the sky and the doorway was wide enough to ensure Mallory wouldn't have to make a stand for long.

Mallory spun around on the crunching gravel, sword in hand, then said, "This is it, then." He tried to make it sound positive, but the fatalism wouldn't stay out of his voice. He looked to Sophie as if to say, *Now's the time—do your stuff.*

She leaned in the doorway and looked out across the henge, mesmerised by the shapes sweeping toward them. She guessed there must be hundreds of them.

Mallory's sword was growing bluer with each passing second. She turned to him and said, "Drive it into the ground."

He didn't question her. Once it was embedded in the gravel, Sophie squatted down and muttered. A second later, she threw her head back and gasped. "So powerful here." The words sounded like steam escaping from a pipe.

Mallory knew better than to interrupt. He was disturbed by the sound of a horn, a distinct blast that sounded somehow ancient and eerily threatening. The light was almost gone and everything had taken on a ghostly greyness. Across the sky, clouds swept in that looked strangely like men on horseback. He fixed on them until Sophie exclaimed and pointed through the doorway.

Two red lights approached the perimeter of the henge. They floated unsettlingly in the dark, and it was a second before Mallory realised they were eyes. Old Shuck had found them.

Urgently, he turned back to Sophie—threats were converging on them from every side and their time was almost gone. In the split second his attention had been away from her, she had changed. Her eyes blazed with blue light, her muscles holding her as rigid as wood while sapphire sparks flashed around her limbs. From the sword, lines of the earth energy radiated up into the stone structure of the church and, even as he watched, rushed out into the henge.

Blue lightning flashed all around. Mallory heard a voice that wasn't Sophie's, or his, or anyone he knew, saying, "There are worlds beyond worlds. Which one is real?"

And then the night snapped shut.

Darkness lay heavily over everything. Only the glow of Mallory's sword provided any illumination. They stood in a dense forest, the trees so tightly packed that they couldn't see a beginning or end of it. The thick canopy of branches and leaves made it impossible to tell if it was night or day, but they guessed from the cool, strong aroma of vegetation that it was dark.

"Where are we?" Mallory said.

"I don't know." Sophie sounded dazed; the effects of whatever she had done had taken their toll.

As Mallory shucked off his disorientation, the words of the strange beings at Old Sarum came back to him. "The Forest of the Night," he muttered. The place where they would become the prey of the Wild Hunt.

As if in echo of his thoughts, the dim sound of a hunting horn rang out through the forest. The density of the trees made it impossible to tell if it was distant or close at hand. He slipped a hand under Sophie's arm to help her to her feet.

"Come on," he said insistently. "We have to move."

"Where to?" she said, confused.

And that was it: he had no idea where they were supposed to be going. "Just move," he replied.

The forest was unchanging, never-ending. There was a faint ambient light, enough to guide them, but Mallory couldn't comprehend its source. They ran as fast as they could amongst the trees, occasionally tripping on creepers or ploughing through bushes, jumping gently trickling streams or clambering through boulder-strewn hollows. Most of the time Mallory had to help Sophie along; she was drained of energy, at first a little delirious even, but gradually coming to her senses.

The sounds of pursuit drew closer. He heard the yelp of hounds above the crackle of his footsteps on the dry forest floor, felt the rumble of horses' hooves in the soft leaf mold, and always the intermittent threatening dissonance of the hunting horn.

"We have to find him," Sophie gasped, during one of her occasional moments of confusion. "The . . . the Devil."

"The Devil," Mallory repeated bitterly. He wondered what hell would look like, recalled the last days of Stefan's rule in the cathedral, and thought perhaps that he had seen the start of it.

The first inkling he had that the end was near was the appearance of shapes moving fast amongst the trees on both sides. They bounded low, like ghosts in the gloom. He found it hard to look and run in the obstacle-littered environment, but eventually he realised they were hounds, long, thin, and whippetlike, but with an unnatural colouring of red and white.

Running, he thought with a sick desperation. *He was always running.* A metaphor for his life.

The dogs began to close in with a pincer movement. It was hopeless; it had been hopeless from the moment he had set off from the cathedral, but he had tried his best. He wondered if that was enough.

A storm of hoofbeats filled the air. And still they ran. A laugh escaped his lips. It was crazy. They should just lie down and be trampled or torn apart.

They leaped another stream where white water cascaded over glistening rocks and almost became bogged down in the mud on the other side. A rider jumped it easily. In the thin light, Mallory had an impression of furs and leather, and of a long pole with a sickle attached to the end. The horse, as he glimpsed it, looked like a horse in every way, yet he strangely felt that it was some unrecognisable alien beast. It danced amongst the trees in a way no horse could ever achieve. Mallory sensed more riders at his back, just the slice of a sickle away.

The rider to his left began to close in, raising the weapon to his underarm in a jousting position. *Not long now*, Mallory thought. At his side, Sophie was lost to her running and her thoughts.

The rider drew closer. The sickle glowed silver, cruelly sharp.

Suddenly, Mallory grabbed Sophie's hand and yanked her to a halt. "What are you doing?" she asked, dazed. He pulled her to him and wrapped his arms around her, a feeble protection and a final act of communion with the woman he loved. He smelled her hair and kissed her gently on the forehead.

The closest rider reined in his horse and came back. The others circled in a wide, lazy arc, the hounds baying and whimpering in the gloom beyond. Mallory held up his head, waiting for the killing stroke, but the huntsman lowered his weapon and waved it curtly to prompt them to move forward.

They continued that way in silence for ten minutes, Mallory's arm tight around Sophie's shoulders, until they came to a clearing. In a circle of well-worn grass at the centre was a standing stone slouching to one side. Overhead, Mallory could see the stars for the first time, but no constellations that he recognised. The full moon, though, looked down brightly. There was a cathedral-like stillness and gravity.

The riders brought their horses to a halt around the edge of the clearing and a deep silence descended; even the hounds were quiet.

Not long after, the black dog padded out into the moonlight on the other side of the clearing. When it reached the standing stone, it dropped down to its haunches and stared at Mallory and Sophie in such a human way it made Mallory's flesh prickle.

"We come with the night," it said in a voice like iron on gravel. Mallory started in shock.

Its red eyes looked as big as saucers. Sophie surfaced from her daze, gripping Mallory's arm tightly.

"What you seek lies beyond," the dog continued. "Follow the path. Do not turn from it, whatever you might see." The dog rose up and began to leave, pausing halfway to turn its head back to them. "Nothing is as it seems. Ever," it said. It lost itself beyond the riders.

"I can't see a path," Sophie whispered.

As Mallory scanned the tree line on the other side of the clearing, the moonlight illuminated the standing stone at just the right angle and a trail of energy ran out from the base of it into the forest. It was undoubtedly of the same essence as the Blue Fire, but this had a milky luminescence, like the moon on waves.

Sophie's eyes were wide and distant. "I suppose we should go," she said.

When they passed the standing stone it felt as though they were moving through a gauzy veil. Briefly, they appeared to lose touch with each other, although they had been holding hands, and were again shortly after. And then they were across the clearing and plunging into the dark beneath the branches.

A night wind slipped amongst the trees like a spirit, bringing with it aromas of pine and grass and sleeping flowers. Mallory was filled with something close to peace.

This is the end, he thought dreamily. *We're going to see the Devil.*

As they followed the shimmering white path, they became aware of movement amongst the trees: shapes drifted by, as insubstantial as mist, some human in form, some animals, some a combination of the two.

"What are they?" Sophie asked.

Before he could answer, they were both overwhelmed with a tremendous sense of presence, as if the ground on which they walked and the trees and vegetation were all one being. They gripped each other, rooted to the spot, Existence spinning all around them. Their own thoughts and emotions were intermingled with something from outside, so far beyond them in every aspect they couldn't begin to comprehend it.

Eventually, they found the strength to progress in faltering steps, unable to speak.

They were suddenly aware that they didn't know how long they had been there; it could have been years, or just a second. Their own sense of personality appeared to be dissipating too, or at least growing weaker, merging with what was around them.

At the point where they felt they were about to cease to be, the path wound down a bank and into a dense mass of vegetation. They tried to pause before it, not seeing how they could pass, but some force pulled them in, the leaves and creepers, brambles and ivy parting and then enveloping them so hard that the mass pressed against their faces, chests, and backs.

Mallory could no longer see Sophie. Desperately, he called out her name.

"I'm here!" she said. Her fingers fumbled for his and locked on; not there, but there, always.

They continued that way for a while, drifting in a world of green. But then the vegetation became more hard-packed. Leaves pushed into Mallory's mouth, pressed against his eyes. He lost touch with Sophie's hand, fought for it but couldn't find it anywhere. And when he tried to call her name, the leaves and creepers forced further into his mouth, pressing against the rim of his throat, making him gag. The prick of thorns was sharp against his wrists, growing sharper still until he would have yelled out if he had been able. With a sickening realisation, he knew the brambles were breaking into his veins, forcing their way along them. Yet the veins weren't being torn apart, in the same way that he wasn't choking as the creepers found their way down his throat—though he gagged and gagged—and continued on into his stomach. The vegetation was consuming him from the inside out. Soon there wouldn't be any him at all; just green.

Before he lost consciousness, a voice echoed around him, repeating the words he had heard before. "There are worlds within worlds. None are real."

"The Devil . . . the Devil . . ."

The car sped away. Blood trickled over his knuckles, splashed on the steering wheel. In the rearview mirror, he saw his face . . . saw into himself . . . Horrible . . . horrible . . .

He could feel it looming ahead of him, a shadow so big it threatened to block out the moon and stars and all of Existence. He could feel subtle fingers reaching into his brain, twisting the very essence of him, tweaking memories and half-thoughts. There was a darkness like that experienced only in the thickest forests where human feet never trod. It was coming, across space, across the worlds, through the trees, toward him, daring him to scream, entreating him to break apart in fear.

Mallory fell from here to there and back again, falling still.

It was coming . . .

"You have the smell of my enemies on you." The voice sounded like branches swaying in the wind, yet strangely like his own voice reflected back at him.

Mallory stood in another clearing, much smaller than the last. Before him sat a man composed of leaves and branches instead of flesh and bones, clear eyes staring beneath a brow of fronds. Antler horns protruded from his head. He lounged on a throne made of living willow, oak, rowan, and ivy, appeared to be part of it, and both of them part of the surrounding flora, which was as dense as a wall on every side. Mallory recognised echoes of Green Man carvings he had seen in ancient churches, hints of Robin Hood in the way the vegetation arranged itself like clothes; here was Pan, the living mind of nature. Or the Devil, depending on your point of view.

Through the hazy dream-atmosphere that swathed everything, Mallory felt his thoughts stir with anxiety, laden with the burden of propaganda subtly insinuated from the moment he had set foot in the cathedral; from the moment his education began. He recalled that same profile looming, ghostly, above the city, considered every picture he'd seen of Satan—it was all here in the figure before him.

"I have been with your world since the earliest times," the Green Man said, as if he could read Mallory's thoughts.

The sense of presence was so powerful—much, much bigger than the figure before him, bigger than the world—that Mallory could barely speak. His mind couldn't cope with what it was perceiving, his thoughts like quicksilver, slipping away from him before he could get a hold on them, the gaps in his consciousness filled with visual and aural hallucinations so that he couldn't tell what was experience and what was imagination.

Panic, he thought, grasping at reason. *The dread of the beating heart of nature, of Pan, the mind that lay behind it all.*

He was dwarfed by everything, expecting to be destroyed at any moment, eradicated by a thought or a whispered word.

And then, in some strange way, he was standing on the downs with the warm summer wind at his back and the moon beaming down on the circle of standing stones, the atmosphere heavy with mystical possibilities. Below him, men wearing the antlers of their totem spirit moved on two legs, then on four, howling at the moon and the stones in a dance that was ancient even then. The Neolithic world called out to him, not with the brutality of a mean existence, but with spirituality and a sense of something greater.

"Here." The disembodied voice sent tingles up his spine.

The world fell away and he was in the sacred grove where the sickle cut the mistletoe, and gathered around were naked men prepared for battle, their hair bleached and matted with lime so that it stuck out in nail-like spikes. The wise men who kept the oak-knowledge, the great knowledge, whispered and moaned and felt the universe move through him, and all those assembled sighed with wonder.

"And here."

And he was in the golden fields where the workers made the corn dollies and left them in the silence of the harvest night. And then in the greenwood where the villagers crawled through and under the crushing yoke of the rich and powerful, impeaching the trees for aid to bring back the wealth to the poor. And he heard the answering call of the hunting horn and glimpsed the movement of a green-clad hero in the emerald depths. In the thundering, sulphurous heat of the iron foundry as the Workshop of the World made cities and empires, he heard the apprentice knock on wood. The rural churches where the vegetative face stared out from pew and column, the other churches where the horned faces had been disfigured, made into a grinning devil, a feeble attempt at supplantation that would never, ever work.

"Here, here, here."

Then, like some god, he was above it all, with a vista over all time, all place, hearing the whispered names—Cernunnos, Puck, Jack o' the Green—seeing how they were stitched into the fabric of everything, from the very beginning to the very end.

No Devil, he thought. And no Evil anywhere, just shadows and light, inextricably bound. Tears welled up at the wonder of it all; the meaning that he knew he would never grasp when the glue of his thoughts returned.

"I am part of it, and part of something greater, of Existence," the Green Man continued, his eyes filled with a gleaming, unearthly light. "An aspect. One face. To attack me is to attack everything."

They were back in the grove. Mallory could smell lime, then cherry blossom, then decomposing leaves; everything was so rich it was all distracting. With a struggle, he forced himself to concentrate on why he was there, still amazed he had made it that far, doubting he would ever leave. "Why've you allowed me to come here . . . to you?" he asked cautiously.

"All may come to me, if they do so with an open heart. I care for all living creatures, for life itself."

"You attacked the cathedral." Awe made his voice a whisper; still he feared he would be knocked down like an oak before the tempest, like the sand before the wave.

The words hung in the air for a while before they were obscured by the whisper of leaves. "I defend Existence. When it is attacked, I strike back."

"They took something—"

"They stole from Existence. They attempted to control the very essence of everything for their own aims. And in doing so, they caused disruption . . . and suffering . . . and death . . . the opposite of life."

Mallory's mouth was dry. Power lay everywhere; a scratching feeling at the back of his mind hinted at some tremendous consciousness circling him. His dread began to flourish again. "There are good men who are suffering. If I return what's been stolen, will you leave them alone?"

"If wrongs are righted." The quality of light in the Green Man's eyes became more intense. "You have it in your power, Brother of Dragons."

Mallory flinched; was this mysterious quality in him so powerful that even such a force acknowledged it?

"You are part of me," the Green Man said, answering his thoughts, "and I am part of you."

Mallory began to search those troubling eyes, but snapped his gaze away as they began to suck him in. He felt as if he was staring into a vast ocean of intelligence, one that stretched to infinity; unknowable, dangerous in its alienness, one that could swallow him whole in an instant, so that he would be lost to everything as if he had never existed. Worse than that, it knew him, knew his deepest secrets, his worst fears, appeared to want something of him; or wanted him to want something of himself.

"You have a choice," the Green Man said. Mallory had the strangest feeling he was talking about something other than the matter at hand.

"If you call off your army, let me get back into the cathedral . . . I'll do what I—"

"You have it in your power, Brother of Dragons," the Green Man interrupted. There was a lull; a rustle moved through the vegetation. "This is your time," he continued. "There are two paths before you. Everything hangs in the balance. Your choice, Brother of Dragons. Your choice."

Again, Mallory could tell he wasn't talking about the cathedral and the stolen relic. "I don't know what you mean," he said desperately. But another voice at the back of his head appeared to be telling him that he did, but it was lost, driven back, as always.

The Green Man only smiled.

Mallory had no idea what happened next; it was as if a light was switched off, but things continued to go on in the dark. The next thing he knew he was back in the church in Knowlton with Sophie standing beside him. It was daylight, but it felt as though days had passed. Where there had been a thaw before, the snow lay thick across the whole landscape, frosted in place. For a moment, they stood, still lost to the place they had been, but gradually it faded, like the wind across the fields, until it was almost as if they had never been there.

"What happened to you?" he said, dragging her into his arms with a force born of euphoria, and love.

"What happened to *you*?" she replied, also giddy with her renewed life.

"I saw the Green Man."

"So did I."

They stared at each other for a moment, then burst out laughing.

"They had it all wrong from the start—Cornelius, Stefan, all of them," Mallory said, as they walked across the henge in the bright sunlight. "He was the good guy and they'd badly wronged him—"

"It was more than that, Mallory. In their language, they sinned against God . . . my god . . . Existence . . . nature. They thought they had a right to take anything. That everything was created to be bent to their will, for the ends of their religion. Nothing else mattered but what they believed. And now they're paying the price."

Mallory remembered the Green Man's eyes and shivered. "It felt as though he was . . . more than he was. Does that make sense?"

"In ancient times, pagans believed there was one true God, so far removed they couldn't know anything about him, and all the other gods were aspects of him, symbolising different facets." She looked up at the blue sky. "It feels like the solstice."

"Time's strange in . . . those places." Mallory wasn't really aware of the vocabulary to describe the experience. "How do you know?"

"I just . . . feel it."

They paused at the gate, enjoying the sun on their faces, despite the cold. "We have to go back, then," he said.

"It's down to us to put things right. For . . . Existence." She leaned over and gave him a kiss.

"I can't believe we're alive. I never thought we would be." He took the measure of himself inside. "Everything's changed."

"Then we'd better not throw it away," she said.

*"How lamentable it is that men blame the gods for their troubles,
when their own wickedness brings them suffering over and above
that which Destiny decrees for them."*
Zeus in the *Odyssey*

The gates of the cathedral remained closed, but they bore the innumerable scars of the vicious attacks inflicted during the time Mallory and Sophie had been away. Now they only hung by a thread; one final push could have broken through. Repairs didn't appear to have been carried out for some days.

In the twilight, the place looked mournful and desolate. No guards patrolled the walls, no sounds of activity came from within. Mallory stared at the imposing gates apprehensively, afraid of what he might find. The killer of Cornelius, Julian, and Gibson was still loose, but it was a more personal fear that was eating away at him. The past felt hard at his back; his time of running was nearly done.

Salisbury was unusually quiet. The people had retired to their homes early, as if anticipating something awful. Even the pubs were deserted, their doors open forlornly, casting candlelight across the frozen pavements. But the Green Man had kept his word: his forces were nowhere to be seen.

"You should stay here," Mallory said to Sophie as he craned his neck to survey the top of the wall.

"Can I weep gently until you come back, as well?"

"Sarcasm is a very unattractive quality."

"So is being an asshole. You can waltz off waving your little pigsticker; just don't forget who has the real power around here."

"It's not what you've got, it's what you do with it."

"Yeah, yeah, that's what all men say. Have you ever noticed how women smile tightly when they hear it?" She examined the gates closely; although they were insecure, any attempt to break them down would attract too much attention. "Any idea how we're getting in?"

"Well, you know, there's a thing called foresight." From under his cloak he brought out a length of rope he had picked up from one of the houses they had rested in on the day's trek back from Knowlton. He tied a noose in one end and then took five attempts to throw it onto one of the defensive barbs protruding from the top of the wall. He hauled himself up easily, then dropped quietly onto the walkway. One brother trudged lamely through the snow near the cathedral. Quickly, Mallory hauled Sophie up and they climbed down the ladder into the compound.

As they hurried to the shadows at the base of the wall, Sophie grabbed Mallory's arm and held him tight. "Look!" she said.

On the far side of the cathedral, near the eastern wall, five stark, black scarecrows rose from the snowy wastes. Two were failing to do their job, for three large birds were fluttering around them, cawing discordantly. Mallory dismissed the sight quickly, but his eyes were drawn back by the muttered expression of shock from Sophie. And then he saw truthfully.

"No," he said in disbelief. "They wouldn't."

But Stefan had clearly given in to the madness of his religious zeal. Snow began to fall lazily, casting an eerie, dreamlike quality across the scene. The five crucified figures didn't move.

Sophie tugged at Mallory's arm, but with his new eyes he was transfixed. One of the figures looked familiar in some subtle shape of head or limb, despite the dusting of frost and snow that made all five seem like siblings. He shook Sophie off and began to run, slowly at first, but as the horror rose up in him towing the guilt behind, it became a sprint. He didn't care if anyone saw him, didn't think anything at all apart from what a truly terrible person he was and how he'd never, ever be anything else.

He stopped in front of the figure, his breath steaming all around him, hot tears burning his cheeks. It was Miller. His hair and eyebrows were white, his shoulders and arms glittering with frost. It made a sharp contrast with the dried black blood on his wrists where the spikes had been hammered into the fencing posts.

Sophie arrived at his side breathlessly. When she saw Miller, tears filled her eyes, too. "Oh, Mallory, I'm sorry . . ."

She might have said more, but he didn't hear it. His head was filled with a fantasy of what would have happened if he'd taken Miller with him when the young knight had made his desperate plea for help. Self-loathing consumed him and he had to turn away so Sophie couldn't see it eat at his face.

Bitterly, he drew his sword and cut the ropes around Miller's ankles and then gently prised his wrists over the spikes while Sophie supported the slight frame. Finally, the limp form fell into Mallory's arms.

Gently laying him on the snow, Mallory blinked away his tears, which splashed across Miller's face. "I'm sorry," he whispered, knowing it meant nothing.

"Wait!" Sophie said. "I saw his eyes move!"

They flickered again. Mallory brushed the snow from Miller's eyebrows; his skin was as cold as the surrounding ground. His lips moved a little, as if he were trying to speak, but no sound issued.

"It's just the end of him. Look at his hands," Mallory said quietly. Under the white layer lay the deep purple of severe frostbite. "He's been out here too long . . . the shock of what they did . . . all that time without food . . . he won't last much longer." He glanced back at the thin form until he couldn't bear it any longer, than looked up to the darkening sky.

After flailing around for a moment, he found another emotion that would help him go on. "You stay with him," he said, sheathing his sword. He was ready now, and he wouldn't fail.

"But I need to—"

"No. I don't want him to die on his own."

This made sense to her, but he could see she still felt he was jeopardising their success by leaving her behind. "When he's gone," he said, "when you're sure he's gone, catch up with me."

He picked Miller up and carried him to the steps of the west front; the body was as light as a bundle of sticks. He laid Miller down and covered him with his cloak. "If anyone comes, hide," he said.

"I'll fetch some blankets for him," she said. "Make him comfortable."

Mallory dropped down beside Miller and briefly rested one hand on his chest before hurrying into the twilight.

The cathedral was dark and cold; no candles had been lit, no one was preparing for compline.

In the Trinity Chapel, the cordon still lay around the relic box. Before, Mallory had always felt a faint charge in the air around it, but now there was nothing. It had to be the relic; all the terrible things had happened after the Blues had brought it into the compound that night. He recalled the burned knight, the speed with which they had carried the box through the gates as if they were being pursued. Whatever it was, its power was phenomenal, he mused. The cures it had wrought were astonishing. What wonders could it carry out if it was used wisely by someone in the community? He thought of the dying husband and his pitiful wife. Instead, it had been locked away as some arid object of veneration. If it was a gift of God, would He want it wasted in that way?

Yet that very same power made him anxious. Could it kill as well as cure? Cautiously, he stepped over the cordon and paused in front of the box, flexing his fingers in anticipation. He had little choice. In one rapid movement, he flung open the lid and stepped back.

The box was empty.

"It's long gone, man."

A knight was sitting in the shadows behind him, the cross on his shirt glowing in the dark. Mallory couldn't see the features, but the voice was distinctive.

"Gardener," Mallory said coldly. The Geordie must have been sitting there all along, so still and quiet that Mallory hadn't seen him.

"Never expected to see you back here," he said gruffly.

As if it was a natural movement, Mallory lowered his hand onto the hilt of his sword; was Gardener the one who harboured the thing they brought back from Bratton Camp? "Bad pennies and all that, Gardener."

"Aye. But I always figured you for a bloke with good sense, Mallory. A smart man would be putting miles between himself and this fucking place. I'd be doing it myself . . . if I was smart."

Mallory picked up no sense of danger, but he wasn't going to take any chances. "I thought this was the New Jerusalem for you." He couldn't keep the bitterness out of his voice.

There was a long silence that was almost painful. "I was just praying. I don't even know if He's listening anymore." The bleakness in his voice was almost unbearable. "It all went to hell pretty quickly after you left."

"It started down that road a long time before."

"Aye. Aye, it did, man." His voice grew muffled as he bowed his head; although Mallory couldn't see, he thought Gardener's hands were over his face. "They started testing everybody . . . using that bloody thing in the box. We all thought hard-line was the way to go, but it got out of hand."

"Miller . . ."

"Aye." A sob. "Bloody harmless lad. Did a bad thing, but you know him . . . Poor bastard." He was wracked by a juddering sigh. "There's been no food since you were gone. The old ones started dropping like flies, and the sick. We buried them at the start, till none of us had the strength to dig. And still that cunt was doing his bloody tests!" His voice rose sharply before bursting in another sob. "We put the bodies up in the old infirmary . . . till we found someone had been at 'em."

Mallory was sickened, but not surprised. He tried to imagine the desperate atmosphere that must have permeated the cathedral: a world filled with food just beyond the walls, but everyone trapped in an intense, claustrophobic jail, unable to reach it, the wild energies of the relic unbalancing minds.

"Then we started burning them . . . until we ran out of strength even for that," Gardener continued desolately. "Now we just leave 'em where they fall." There was a pause. "No, that ain't right. James and some of the others . . . they still try to do the right thing. But the rest of us, the miserable ones . . ."

"Lost your faith, Gardener?"

"No." The denial was adamant. "I was only trying to do the right thing . . . we all were. It just got out of hand—"

"That's one way of looking at it."

"You don't have to get on your high horse, Mallory. You're as bad as me. Worse . . . you don't believe in anything."

Mallory could have argued, but there was no point. The facts were clear for anyone with the eyes to see them.

"Stefan . . . Blaine . . . they've gone mad," Gardener said. "We all went mad, and the thing is, I don't know when it started. When that thing got here . . ." He waved a hand toward the box. ". . . or a long time ago. Hundreds of years ago."

"Where's the relic gone?" Mallory asked.

"Stefan took it. The Blues came with him one night and transferred it to another box. Stefan . . . Blaine . . . the Blues . . . I think they've got a secret stash of food. Not much, but enough to keep them going."

"Where did they take it?"

Gardener sat up in the pew, a hiss of air escaping between his teeth. At first, Mallory thought he wasn't going to answer, but then he said, "I need you to help me. You do that and I'll tell you."

"I haven't got time—"

"You do this or you'll never find out!" His voice cracked with hysteria again.

Mallory sighed. "What do you want?"

"I want you to help me to rescue Daniels."

There was an odd note to Gardener's voice, and Mallory could tell it was because he didn't want his betrayal mentioned. The act weighed on him, had probably been the thing that finally broke him.

"Where is he?"

"They took him to the infirmary."

"The infirmary?"

"They were trying to cure him . . ." Gardener's voice trailed away, the silence carrying the weight of too many unspoken words.

They were trying to cure Daniels of his sexuality. It sounded insane, but Mallory knew it was only an extension of views that had common currency within living memory. "Come on," he said with restrained anger.

Their footsteps echoed loudly up the stairwell to the infirmary. They had to rest at regular intervals to allow Gardener to gather his strength for the climb. In the glow of the candle Mallory had lit on entering, Gardener's face looked like a skull, with hollow cheeks and sunken eyes, the skin hanging from his bones; the only thing keeping him going was the hardness that had always set him apart.

The white-tiled room had grown filthy since the last time Mallory had seen it, and the sickeningly fruity smell of decomposition still filled the air, although the bodies had been removed. Gardener appeared oblivious to it.

"He's down here," he said, limping with a strangely innocent eagerness.

They hurried through the deserted wards, the stained sheets left in disarray on the beds. In the corridor beyond, Mallory glanced into the room that had been reserved for Hipgrave and was shocked to see the knight still there. He lay on his bed in the dark, staring wide-eyed at the ceiling and looking remarkably well fed and healthy.

"He's off his rocker," Gardener said without pausing. "Nobody let him out in case he was dangerous."

"Very compassionate," Mallory muttered. He resolved to break down the door on the way back.

Daniels's room was at the far end of the corridor. The lock shattered easily under a few blows from Mallory's shoulder. Daniels lay on his bed, too weak to get up, but he rolled his head and smiled wanly when he saw Mallory.

Mallory quickly poured a cup of water from a jug next to the bed and supported Daniels's head so he could wash some onto his dry, cracked lips; it didn't look as though anyone had been in to care for him for a couple of days at least. In the background, Gardener shifted uncomfortably as if he was getting ready to run.

"Well, isn't this a pretty picture." Daniels tried to laugh, but it became a hacking cough.

Mallory was drawn to a black stain on Daniels's trousers around his groin.

Daniels saw him looking and began to weep uncontrollably. "They cut it off, Mallory! They cut it off!"

In horrified disbelief, Mallory turned to Gardener, seeking a denial. Gardener wouldn't meet his eyes.

Daniels's crying turned to a low giggle; his awful trial had left him balanced on the edge, his emotions untethered. "I think they mustn't have tied off their stitches properly!" he said. "Those boys . . . can't do anything right! But at least the bleeding's stopped now."

Gardener was crying silently, too, wiping his eyes repeatedly in an anxious manner that suggested he, too, was on the edge of a breakdown fuelled by guilt and self-hatred. Mallory felt sickened: so much suffering and hardship, so many broken lives, and a pointlessness to it all that made it almost incomprehensible.

His thoughts were disturbed by the echoes of several pairs of feet rushing up the stairs.

"Don't leave me!" Daniels pleaded.

"You stay with him. Block the door with the bed, if you can," Mallory said to Gardener.

"Stefan's got the relic with him all the time now," Gardener said. "He's locked himself in the bishop's palace."

As he drew his sword and slipped out, Mallory saw Gardener drop to his knees and falteringly take Daniels's hand. Daniels smiled weakly.

Mallory moved tentatively into the corridor. The running feet had slowed now; they were cautious, ready for him. The flickering light of a lantern playing down the corridor told him they'd entered the ward. If they wanted a fight, his best bet was to take them in the corridor where they could only come at him one at a time. He gripped his sword ready, his mind focused, but as he passed Hipgrave's room, the play of faint light told him it was empty. Curiously, he tried the handle; it was still locked.

Before he could understand what had happened, a huge outcry erupted in the ward. He rushed to the end of the corridor to see eight Blues in furious attack caught in the glitter of a lantern lying discarded at the foot of a bed. The uncertain illumination made it difficult to discern what was going on. There was movement, hacking swords, constant running back and forth, faces caught for just an instant, white with concentration and tinged with fear. But their adversary remained firmly in the shadows so that all the motion with no result made the scene faintly comic.

But then there was a wet sound like the contents of a paint tin being thrown against a wall. One of the knights staggered back, trying to hold in his intestines. A second later, an arm skidded across the floor. Someone else backpedalled with a stump where his neck and head should have been. The butchery was so fast and clean it was mesmerising.

The flash of something that resembled an enormous arm stuck with knives snapped Mallory from his trance. He knew what it was, and he now knew who it was. Hipgrave was the host for the thing they had brought back. Of course, it had to be Hipgrave, his madness growing as he was eaten away by guilt, knowing of his crimes but unable to do anything about them. Mallory had no idea how it had passed through the locked door of the room, how it worked at all, but he did know he would be as dead as the Blues would inevitably be if he didn't move.

Mallory slipped along the wall and then clambered over the beds, ignoring the blood that sprayed over him as if it had come from a hose. He couldn't help one look into the heart of the shadows, but whatever lay there resisted any attempt to identify it.

The sounds behind him grew worse, turning his stomach; soon the thing would be finished and free to pursue him. He skidded out into the white-tiled room and came face to face with Blaine lurking in the gloom of one corner. The commander's sword was drawn.

Blaine didn't speak, didn't feel the need to for the benefit of someone so far beneath his contempt. Mallory could read it in his cold, hard eyes: Mallory was just a distraction to be dispatched at the earliest opportunity. Blaine's attention was partly distracted by the noises coming from the ward, which were winding down now.

Mallory stepped in quickly and swung his sword. Blaine was quick to block it, the collision sending jarring vibrations into Mallory's arms. But the fact that Mallory had almost caught him unawares clearly irritated Blaine. Anger flashed across his face and he launched into a calculated but relentless attack that drove Mallory onto his back foot.

Blaine was an excellent swordsman, moving with grace and strength and an eye for his opponent's weaknesses. What added to his threatening pose was an icy composure that made him a brutal machine; his features remained fixed, his arm moving with strokes timed to the millimetre and the microsecond. Mallory had learned his lessons well, but he wasn't even close to Blaine's ability.

It was all he could do to keep Blaine from driving straight through his defence into his heart. In fact, as he batted away the curt moves while backing across the room, he felt that Blaine was simply making him suffer before he decided it was time for the killing blow.

In the ward, the sounds of attack faded away.

This time, it was Mallory's turn to be distracted. Blaine saw an opening and rammed his blade through. It cracked against Mallory's shoulder blade, cutting through the skin, but Blaine whipped it back before it did any more damage; still toying.

Mallory recoiled in a brief burst of pain, but somehow managed to parry the next stroke. Cold sweat sprang up all over him.

Another blow, this time just missing Mallory's cheek but nicking his ear. Instead of defending, Mallory launched into a swift attack. It surprised Blaine, who backed off a little. Mallory kept it up, forcing Blaine to keep parrying.

Mallory knew that the Hipgrave-thing had arrived a second before a shadow fell across him, and across his soul. The monstrous gravity of it drew Blaine's gaze instantly, despite the intensity of the fight. Mallory saw the awful realisation cross his face, the ice flooding into his limbs holding him rigid. It was too late for Mallory to stop the swing of his sword. It crashed into Blaine's rib cage, sliding up to sever the artery in his armpit.

Blaine went down on his knees, clutching the wound as blood gushed out across the floor, but his face was still turned to whatever was at Mallory's back, so consumed by the horror that he wasn't even aware he was dying.

In a cold sweat, Mallory leaped forward, casting one glance at Blaine's trans-fixed, final expression, not daring to look back. He could sense the thing beginning to move a step or two closer behind him. As he raced for the stairs, he heard it fall on Blaine.

More snow was falling and it was already a foot deep across the compound. As Mallory reached the edge of the cathedral, with only a short run and a few small walls to climb between him and the bishop's palace, he couldn't resist looking back. Just at that moment, the aberration emerged from Malmesbury House. At first it was Hipgrave, then something that made Mallory's mind fizz and slide, then Hipgrave again, limping, looking around deliriously as if he couldn't quite tell where he was. The ground was losing its faith-driven power under the desperate, cruel rule of Stefan. Increasingly, the beast could move freely.

Mallory ran.

Candlelight glowed in one downstairs window of the bishop's palace, a faint warmth amid the darkness and silence of the cathedral compound. Stefan must have been watching, for as Mallory approached, stark against the snow, there was the crash of the front door as the bishop emerged at a run clutching an antique wooden box, his robes billowing behind him.

Mallory set off in pursuit. As they rounded the edge of the cathedral, Stefan plunged down some steps into the new buildings. Within their constantly shifting architecture, unbounded by logic, it would be easier for the bishop to evade capture. Mallory picked up his pace, but as he reached the doorway a strange winnowing, like the cry of a wounded bird, echoed eerily across the compound. He looked back to see the Hipgrave-thing sweeping across the snow toward him. Mallory slipped inside and pulled the door shut behind him, knowing it would offer no defence.

He sensed the change in the new buildings immediately. There was an unbearable atmosphere of *potency*, of a sick, crazy power leaking from every part of the fabric. Shadows were distorted; others were thrown by no obvious light source. At a distance, straight lines appeared to bend as if they were being warped by some magnetic force. This was most apparent in the long, columned corridors and the great hall, where the pillars rose to an enormous height and the roof was lost to darkness.

And the further he progressed into the building on Stefan's trail, the worse it got. Logic was cut adrift, replaced by a dreamlike chaos where nothing quite made sense. Mallory would realise that the Hipgrave-thing was behind him only intermittently, when he heard that strange bird-cry or was overwhelmed by a smell like battery acid, but mostly the corridors and rooms at his back were filled only with darkness.

After a while, time lost all meaning. It felt as if he was on a Möbius strip, passing through the same places, experiencing the same emotions. But a single thought had taken root in his mind and that was enough to drive him on: to make amends.

It was in a room lined with statues of people he didn't recognise that he met the Caretaker. Some of the statues resembled ancient Greeks, Egyptians, and Celts, while others appeared vaguely nonhuman with pointed ears and an unusually delicate bone structure, and the Caretaker was at first lost amongst them, his giant form silent and unmoving in the shadows.

He stepped out and held up his hand, startling Mallory. "You will never reach your prize by running, Brother of Dragons," he said in his deep, echoing voice. "You will be adrift in here forever, never quite making up lost ground, till your time is gone or the world winds down around you. Only by going back will you achieve your aim."

"I can't go back," Mallory said desperately. "There's something behind me . . . death . . ." He glanced over his shoulder.

"You know this door, Brother of Dragons." The Caretaker motioned to a portal that hadn't been there before.

And Mallory did know it, though he tried to pretend he didn't. It had a look of the fairy tale about it, with mysterious figures intricately carved around the stone jamb. Mallory was suddenly overwhelmed with inexplicable emotion, terrified yet trembling with an abiding sadness at the same time. "I can't go back," he said desolately.

Mallory took a step away from the door and found himself in front of it. "No," he said. He had no choice but to pass through into . . .

"Did you get it?" Stevens barked at Mallory the moment he stepped through the steamed-up glass door of the café. He was sitting at his usual table in the corner, smoking a cheap cigar, while his hard-eyed cronies sat around, laughing at his jokes.

"Yes." Mallory was shaking. He dropped the haversack on the table.

Stevens chuckled, looking around at his dismal associates. "The only good bitch—" He paused midsentence, his eyes growing wider, the familiar fury rising in his face. Suddenly he grabbed Mallory's wrist. "Is that blood?" he snapped. Mallory snatched his hand back, letting the sleeve of his leather jacket obscure the telltale sign. "Go and wash it off, you fucking idiot."

As he headed toward the toilets at the back, Sylvie caught his eye. She was carrying a plate of egg and chips destined for a Geordie man in his eighties who always sat at the window smoking roll-ups. "You didn't do it?" she hissed with a condemnatory expression that he'd hoped he'd never live to see. She looked tired, her face made hard by too much work for not enough money.

"I didn't have a choice."

"Everybody has a choice, Mallory."

She barged past him in a way that suggested she'd finally written him off.

He had to get out. Filled with despair, he stepped through the door into the toilets.

Mallory skidded down a pile of rubble from a wall that had collapsed from great age, tumbling into a vast vault whose extremities were lost to the gloom. At the bottom, yellow bones protruded from a shattered crypt.

Stefan's footsteps echoed like gunfire, but they were now accompanied by a pathetic whimpering; he knew he'd never get away. Mallory picked up a chipped thigh bone as he ran and hurled it with force into the dark. Stefan's cry came back sharp and sweet.

"I'm going to get you, you bastard!" he yelled, though strangely he couldn't remember who he was trying to get; or, indeed, who he was. He had a name—Mallory—but that was all he knew. It probably didn't matter.

He sprinted across the dusty floor, bones flying right and left. The air smelled of chalk and damp, and was as cold as the grave.

The sound of tumbling rocks behind him snapped his attention back. Hipgrave was at the top of the rubbled slope, all sense gone from his eyes; the beast ruled him completely now. As Mallory watched, horns burst through his skull in a circle around his head at forehead height, became knives, then retracted.

Obliquely, Mallory realised that Hipgrave was closer: he was catching up.

He leaped forward, plunging into the dark.

"You can't trust Stevens," Mueller said with surprising insight. He never looked as though he was paying attention to anything.

They sat on the balcony watching the crew, under the guidance of Denny, setting up the sound system near where the altar would have been. The pale wintry sunshine still brought a dazzle of cascading colour from the stained-glass windows.

"Whose stupid idea was it to turn an old church into a club? It was a crappy idea back in the eighties when the Limelight set up shop," Mallory said.

"Did you hear me?" Mueller turned to him, then slowly relented. "The Devil has all the best tunes."

"I know. It's a metaphor." Mallory plucked the ice cube from his glass, placed it in his mouth, and began to crunch it up. "Stevens thinks he's smart, but he's not. He's a thug, an East End barrow boy made bad. He's no match for my educated, wily ways."

"Educated? You dropped out," Mueller said. "But he's got one thing you haven't. He believes in what he's doing. You watch yourself, Mallory."

"You're such a moaner, Mueller. Moan, moan, moan." The engineer checked the balance by playing an oldie on Mallory's decks. "Beth Orton remixed by the Chemical Brothers," he noted. "Good taste for a monkey." There was a plaintive element to the song that made him introspective. "Do you ever get the feeling that the world isn't the way it should be?" he said, lost to his thoughts.

"What do you mean?"

"Which word don't you understand?"

Mueller sipped his drink quietly. He'd been here so many times over the years, he knew better than to get riled by anything Mallory said.

When Mallory saw that he wasn't going to bite, he made a face and continued, "Look at it—what a sour, miserable existence. If there is a God, is this the best He can do? A place where people like Stevens thrive." He grew introspective again. "Sometimes I think this is all an illusion . . . a mess . . . and there's a better world somewhere behind it. Sometimes, if you catch this world sleeping, you can look at it just right and see straight through it to that good place on the other side."

"Sylvie's addled your mind, Mallory." Mueller tittered.

"Shut up, Mueller. You never did have any sense. I don't know why I ever took you on board."

Doors opened onto rooms that vaguely resembled ones he had passed through before, though each had a slight difference—a carving, a gargoyle, a column. There was stone and shadows, and dust, steeped in antiquity and quiet centuries of deep reverence, where no words were uttered but thoughts were offered up to the heart of Existence. There were chapels and vaults, tombs and halls, galleries and corridors, places of sanctity and places that felt alien and unwelcoming.

Mallory crashed through them all, knowing that if he slowed Hipgrave would be behind him, but never quite managing to lessen the distance between him and Stefan. He had the unnerving feeling that sooner or later he would forget the reason for running, that it would simply be something he did, like eating and breathing.

And each new doorway provided a new room, a new sensation, a new way of looking at life, and each time he lost a little bit more of who he was.

"You do it," Stevens said, "or that little waitress you like gets taken out back by my boys, done over, then popped in the head and dumped in the river. Do you hear me, you little fucker?"

Mallory picked himself up off the floor. His ribs felt as if someone had stuffed a firework in them. "You really think I'd do something like that?"

Stevens smiled slyly. "Well, I don't really know. I suppose we'll see, won't we? I mean, I'm just a thick boy from Bow—what do I know? You're the one with the good education. I expect you'll be putting me straight sometime soon."

"Irony works best in a single sentence. You spoil the effect when you drag it out." Mallory wiped his mouth with the back of his hand; it left a dark smear.

Stevens didn't have to retaliate for the attitude; he knew he had Mallory between a rock and a hard place. He simply watched and smiled, relishing his position of absolute power.

"You've got to be joking," Mallory said, starting to realise with mounting horror that Stevens wasn't.

Stevens shrugged. "Well, bang goes your bitch—in more ways than one."

Mallory began to backpedal. "Now, look—"

"No. Let's not look. Let's deal with the offer on the table. It's simple—even I can understand it. You can do this . . . or this."

"I'll do anything else. You wanted a cut of the takings—"

Stevens made a dismissive hand gesture. "That's all gone now. This is what's happening."

"But . . . but . . . it doesn't make any sense. You don't get anything out of this—"

"Well, that's where you're wrong, my son." His expression told Mallory everything: what he got was the brutish satisfaction of seeing Mallory torn apart by a choice no one could ever make without being destroyed.

"What you want me to do—it's inhuman."

"Yes, it is, isn't it?"

Mallory felt as if he was drowning.

"A couple of other things while you . . . ruminate . . . that's a word, isn't it? You try to run, the waitress gets it. You do anything at all apart from what I've asked you and she gets it. Anything at all. But you do what I ask and everything'll be sweet."

Mallory's mouth was dry. He couldn't see Stevens anymore, just the horrendous images playing across his own internal screen. "How do I know you won't kill Sylvie anyway?" he said, dazed.

"I'm an honourable man, Mallory. I stand by old-fashioned values—I'm not a slippery, fast-talking fucking intellectual like you. When I give my word, that's it. I believe in the things that made this country great. The world now, it's gone to pot. Being honourable, that's all we've got to hold everything together."

The irony would have been funny if Mallory hadn't felt like being sick.

Things changed as he emerged from a tiny door into a room that contained an enormous subterranean reservoir. Echoes of lapping water bounced off the walls, while light from an unidentified source provided shimmerings in the gloom.

Walkways crisscrossed the stone tank, but they were barely wider than a man and it would be impossible to run along them without slipping into the black water of unknown depth.

Stefan was making his way cautiously across the network of paths, unbalanced by the box he was carrying. If Mallory was careful he would be able to make up lost ground.

Watching his feet, he stepped out onto the nearest walkway and moved as quickly as he could. Where the shadows were thickest the water looked like oil. But in some places, where the mysterious light fell across it, he had a perception of depth, and he had the unnerving sensation that things were moving in it. Stefan, too, appeared to have noticed the same thing, for he regularly cast worried glances into the water on either side.

As he passed the first crossway, he realised he was indeed closing on Stefan, who was edging forward very slowly, as much for fear of what might lie in the water as of falling in. Mallory's growing confidence was shattered when he glanced to his left and saw, floating an inch or so below the water, a woman who appeared maddeningly familiar yet had no place in his life as he knew it. He was overcome with a feeling of affection, even love, but the woman's eyes were wide and accusing.

Other bodies drifted silently nearby, and although he thought of them as *bodies*, another part of him was convinced they were alive in some way he couldn't explain. They, too, were at the same time recognisable and not.

The shock of seeing them there like dead fish almost made him lose his footing, and he feared what would happen if he fell in amongst them. He was only distracted from his uneasy thoughts when he realised there was a disturbance in the water around Stefan. Rising on every side were the cowled figures of the dead clerics from the ossuary.

Stefan cowered before them, terrified, as if he knew why they were there for him. "I have nothing to fear from you!" he cried out, his voice reverberating insanely up to the vaulted roof. As one, the clerics each raised an arm and pointed at him. Their silent accusation gave Stefan added impetus and he bowed his head and hurried past them.

Mallory ignored the figures in the water around him and followed quickly, allowing just one glance back. Hipgrave was on the walkway, shifting back to his human form from something that had wings like a bat.

Mallory realised there probably wouldn't be an escape for any of them.

"I'd do anything for Sylvie." Mallory blinked away tears of frustration and pain.

"You think she'd be happy with you, knowing what you'd done?" Mueller was incredulous. "Stevens has won. Whichever way you turn, you're damned."

"She doesn't have to know—"

"She already knows. One of Stevens's monkeys told her this morning. He's just turning the knife—"

"How do you know?" Mallory leaned back against his bookcase for support, as if gravity was suddenly too strong for him to keep standing.

"She called me up . . . wanted to know if it was true."

"What did you say?"

"I said I didn't know!" Mueller paced about the lounge, rubbing his fingers through his hair anxiously. "But she knows Stevens wouldn't make something like that up . . ."

Mallory covered his face; everything was fracturing. "I don't have a choice."

"You had a choice two weeks ago . . . if you hadn't let your pride and your arrogance—"

"Oh, shut up, Mueller."

There was such desolation in his voice that Mueller was briefly stung into silence. "I'm sorry. That doesn't help." He swallowed and ordered his thoughts. "You can't do it, Mallory. Not something like that—"

"I can't let Sylvie die, can I? It would be as if I'd killed her myself."

"If you do it, Stevens will probably kill you and Sylvie anyway . . ." Mueller's voice faded out.

"You always manage to find the silver lining, don't you, Mueller?" He took a deep breath, but it failed to calm him. "No, I believe him. He's a fucking psychotic thug, but he thinks if he sticks by some personal perverse code of ethics it makes everything he does all right."

Mueller chewed on a fingernail; he looked on the verge of tears. "You can't do it, Mallory. No decent human being could do a thing like that and not be destroyed."

Mallory slumped onto the sofa and looked at the records and the books, all the trappings that made up his life. "I love her, Mueller. I love her so much, nothing else matters. I'm a cynical bastard and I tried to pretend it was just infatuation or sex, but it isn't. I couldn't bear for anything to happen to her."

Mueller fell silent, staring blankly at the spines of some CDs. When the pressure in the room finally became too great, he said, "You know this won't be the end of it. Stevens might not hurt her this time, but sooner or later he'll come back at her to get at you . . . to punish you even more, just because he can. He's going to kill her sooner or later, Mallory."

"I know." The desolation he felt was painful.

"What are you going to do, Mallory?"

Doors and rooms, and rooms and doors, stretching off into infinity. After the reservoir there was another series of corridors and indistinguishable halls where no feet appeared to have trod for hundreds of years. But he had indeed closed on Stefan. The only drawback was that Hipgrave had drawn nearer to him; he could now hear each transformation, like a silk sheet being torn by a knife. Things were converging.

Out of the gloom loomed an enormous trilithon that reminded him of the ages-old monuments at Stonehenge. As he passed through its massive portal, he fell into deepest shadow, and when he emerged on the other side he was in the strangest place he had seen so far. It was a vast underground cemetery: crypts and mausoleums, obelisks and gravestones, crosses modern and Celtic, and old markers that were little more than crumbling lumps of rock. Instead of the usual flagstones, there was dusty, water-starved soil beneath his feet. All around, torches blazed on the houses of the dead, creating stark pools of light and shade.

A veil appeared to lift from his mind, and with it came a clarity of who he was and what he was doing.

Stefan was nowhere to be seen. He had obviously taken the opportunity to lose himself amongst the jumbled layout. Just before Mallory threw himself into the network of byways that ran through the necropolis, he checked back on his own pursuer; the Hipgrave-thing writhed on the other side of the trilithon, seemingly unable to pass through it. Mallory's relief edged into a cold focus on the matter at hand. He set off in silent pursuit of the bishop.

The cat-and-mouse game continued for an age. Sometimes he would catch a glimpse of Stefan's robes against the bare white bones of a mausoleum. Mallory would run and hide, dash and squat, all emotion driven from him by the long, wearying chase. The only thing that gave him comfort was the sword singing gently against his leg, its blue light seeping into the very fibre of his being.

After a while, he realised the energy was coming in soothing pulses, but there was a pattern to it, as though it was calling out—or guiding him. Through trial and error, he matched his directional changes to the strong pulses until the flow of energy was constant. And that was when he saw Stefan creeping along the next byway.

Moving as quietly as he could, he used a stone cross to lever himself up onto the roof of a mausoleum and wriggled out to the edge. As Stefan edged beneath him, Mallory threw himself off, knocking the bishop to the ground and sending the box flying. A cloud of white dust billowed into the air.

When it finally cleared, Mallory was standing over Stefan, his blade resting against the bishop's throat.

"Kill me," Stefan said calmly, "and I know I will find peace with my God. Can you say the same?"

"After all you've done . . . after all the misery and suffering you've caused . . . you're going straight to hell, matey."

Stefan only laughed; he was so locked in his worldview that he would never understand, Mallory realised. And for the first time, Mallory felt dismal that there was no hell; Stefan would go unpunished in this world and the next, while Daniels, Gardener, and all the others would carry their hell with them. And what of Miller and those who had died? Somehow it didn't seem fair.

"You never had God with you, Mallory." Stefan was looking up at him with bright, passionate eyes; Mallory was surprised to see almost a hint of pity there. "For you, life is an empty parade of sensation with no meaning . . . no reason even to shuffle through it."

Mallory smiled. "That's where you're wrong, Stefan."

The bishop was puzzled by this clear display of confidence. As if to distract himself, he bowed his head and muttered a short prayer. "There. I have made my peace. Now you may kill me."

"I'm not going to kill you." Mallory sheathed his sword.

This puzzled Stefan further, then began to trouble him.

"I don't hold a grudge. I can't hate you. I should do—for Miller and all the others—but I can't," Mallory said, emotion making his voice crack. "I just think you're wrong, but you're not alone there. You simply took it a few more steps down the line than anyone else, but it's the same pig-ignorance . . . blindness . . . stupid-simple understanding of a complex theology—"

Stefan laughed. "Someone like you could never understand the love of God . . . the light . . . it's beyond you."

Mallory looked around, distracted.

"You're afraid to kill me because you're weak in the face of God's power." Stefan sounded as if he was trying to convince himself, and Mallory realised it was because he thought he had such a clear view of who Mallory was, of how the world worked; but he was wrong on both counts.

Mallory spotted the box and picked it up. "This is what I want." It felt warm to his touch.

"That belongs to God." Stefan's voice trembled.

"Everything belongs to God, Stefan." He opened the lid.

A brilliant blue light flooded out, painting the entire area. Mallory felt swamped with vitality, with warmth, and love, and goodness, and in that instant he realised how its power had unbalanced so many of those who had walked on the charged land of the cathedral. In the familiar blue glow, he understood that this was the thing that had been used to summon the Fabulous Beast to its death; somehow they had known the creature would come once the box had been opened.

Gradually, his eyes cleared and he could see into the depths of the box. Something small and dark lay at the bottom; something alive. It squirmed and tried to scramble over the edge. Mallory almost dropped the box in shock.

"The Devil can do God's work," Stefan intoned gravely. "Indeed, there is a delicious irony in bending Satan to His will." The thing appeared over the lip. "Beware the Serpent, Mallory," Stefan warned.

And then Mallory could see what it was. It was small, almost fetal in shape, and although the glittering sheen of scales had not yet appeared, its wings were perfectly formed.

"It is the first one born to this world for many an age." Mallory looked up at the booming voice. The Caretaker stood next to the mausoleum with Stefan cowering at his feet.

"That was why the Fabulous Beast came," Mallory said. "They killed it, but all it wanted was its young." Suddenly he knew why the glorious creature had been flying back and forth across the countryside, why it hadn't used its cataclysmic flame to destroy the cathedral in its final attack. There was something so desperately sad in it all.

"How can you justify this?" Mallory said in disbelief. "It's a living creature."

"The Devil can take many forms," Stefan replied, and, because he clearly believed a supporting argument was necessary, "God's will overrules all."

"It was a crime," the Caretaker said dispassionately, "against Existence."

"A crime against nature . . . the world . . . everything," Mallory added. "That's why the Green Man threw everything into getting it back." He turned incredulously to Stefan. "Don't you understand—these things represent life?"

"It's the Serpent," Stefan said, unmoved. "This is the thing that corrupted humanity. In the very first times it led to the expulsion from paradise. It is knowledge—"

"Yes," Mallory interrupted, "knowledge . . . meaning . . . the force that holds everything together. You've made this the enemy, but you know in your heart it's the same thing you want, the same power that fuels your prayer . . . the same path to—"

Stefan shook his head vehemently. "The Bible tells us what this thing is."

"You idiot," Mallory snapped, his emotions running away from him. "You put all your faith in a book when you had salvation in your hands!"

Stefan was unmoved. "The only important thing was to save our religion—that was our sole motivation. We understood full well what this . . . thing could do. It's a generator, providing an energy that those of a devout mind could shape to their will . . . to God's will. With this charge, the force of our faith could enable the Church to thrive, to spread out rapidly. We would have saved Christianity from extinction! That was a prize worth any sacrifice."

"Tyrants always think the ends justify the means, Stefan." Mallory watched the tiny creature wriggle around, enjoying its freedom. It was not yet able to fly, but the awe it generated was palpable, and came from some place beyond its form. "There's no logic to any of your arguments," he continued. "A central tenet of Christianity is the power of faith—if you believed that, wouldn't it have done the job on its own? If you believe in the omnipotent power of your God, would He allow His own religion to die?"

"He did not. We were his instruments—"

Mallory sighed; there was no point in arguing—Stefan could justify anything through his belief system. "What do I do with it?" Mallory asked the Caretaker. "We can't just let it free, can we? It won't survive on its own."

The Caretaker smiled with what Mallory thought was a hint of sadness. "It is not a creature as you imagine it, Brother of Dragons. It is more . . . it is an idea, a convergence of hope and belief and symbolism of something greater, given form. But it is still only partly formed, and without the care and guidance of its guardian it will not survive."

"It's dying?" As Mallory watched the tiny Fabulous Beast, he gradually realised the true tragedy of what had happened: the first glimmer of hope in a very dark world had been extinguished.

The Caretaker watched Mallory intently. "If its guardian had not been slain, this new one may well have given up its power to the Fragile Creatures," he added. "The forces aligned against them would not have been able to stand—"

"So if they hadn't killed the Beast, they might have got everything they wanted?" Mallory looked back at Stefan. "Well, there's irony for you."

The acceptance of his monumental error slowly dawned on Stefan's face. Mallory wanted to rub more salt in the wound, but he knew it was a childish impulse and, after all that had happened, quite insignificant. Instead, he bent down and picked up the tiny Fabulous Beast, which was enjoying itself wriggling in the dust. It was velvety soft and warm to the touch; the blue light appeared to be radiating from the very pores of its skin. Mallory experienced another surge of transcendental emotion at the contact before he dropped it into the box and closed the lid. The light snapped out. "Sorry," he whispered, a simple word filled with the depth of his heart's emotion. He turned to the Caretaker. "Isn't there anything we can do to save it?"

Before the giant could respond, Mallory caught sight of movement amongst the mausoleums and stones. He drew his sword and pressed his back against a wall, at first thinking that the Hipgrave-thing had somehow found its way into the mysterious cemetery.

It was Stefan's fearful reaction that made Mallory realise what was happening. The cowled figures of the clerics emerged from every side with slow, purposeful steps, the gravity of their intention creeping oppressively over all. Their approach was silent and eerie; they were like an execution party. Mallory guessed that they had followed with the same slow insistence from the reservoir; and now they had what they had always wanted: the man who symbolised, they felt, the betrayal of the devout traditions to which they had dedicated their lives.

Stefan had left it too late to run. The clerics were on every side, pressing him back against the mausoleum. His eyes ranged with an awful awareness, not because of the fate that awaited him but because he finally appeared to recognise his shortcomings; his own kind had judged him and found him wanting.

Even after everything, Mallory still considered rescuing him. He gripped his sword and took a step forward, but by then Stefan was lost behind a wall of black. There was one final cry, quickly muffled, and then the haunting figures began to drift slowly away, like shadows fading in the morning light. When they had departed, of Stefan there was no sign; Mallory couldn't tell if they had dragged him off in their midst, or if he had been consumed by them. Whatever the answer, Mallory had an instinctive understanding that there had been some kind of justice.

As the tension dissipated, Mallory felt suddenly deflated. "What now?" he asked.

"Now," the Caretaker replied, "there will come an ending."

"Yeah, I can dump this box and get back to Sophie," Mallory said, brightening; still not quite accepting his triumph. "And then it's just me and her—"

"No," the Caretaker said. "That is not how it will be."

Mallory couldn't meet his eyes; although he shouldn't have had any inkling, he somehow knew what lay ahead, and it left him with a desolation that made him tremble.

"There is one more door to pass through, Brother of Dragons." The Caretaker motioned behind Mallory. The mysterious door with the carved surround through which he had first passed now stood behind him. He could feel the weight of it, as if it would suck him through.

"I can't," Mallory said. "I need to get back to Sophie."

He sheathed his sword and broke into a run, zigzagging randomly through the grave markers. When he was finally exhausted, the Caretaker was waiting. "Take me back to Sophie," Mallory pleaded.

The Caretaker led him to the trilithon and then through the corridors and halls beyond, though they never passed through the reservoir or anywhere else that Mallory recalled. Finally, they came to a halt at a blank wall. Mallory waited patiently until he realised that the Caretaker was staring at him.

"What?" he said a little too sharply.

The Caretaker appeared to be choosing his words carefully; though his face was held rigid, some deep emotion shifted behind it. "Existence is fluid, Brother of Dragons," he began. "It is what we make it. Each of us, individually. Nothing is real. Everything is real. Worlds spiral out of mind, disappear into the void, split in two, and then again, into infinity. The only world that truly matters is the one inside because that is the one that affects everything else."

Mallory couldn't quite tell if the Caretaker was apologising for something, or warning him, or trying to offer some kind of guidance. The blank wall opened out to reveal the rolling snow-covered lawns beneath a dawn of majestic pink and purple.

Mallory made to step out, but the Caretaker's heavy hand fell on his shoulder to hold him back for a second. "When you pass through this door, you can never come back to this point again," he said. "When you pass through this door, everything changes."

Mallory nodded, not understanding, and stepped over the threshold.

Mallory sprinted through the foot-deep snow, clutching the box to his chest. In the rosy wash of first light he saw Sophie huddling inside a blanket. More blankets had been heaped over the still form of Miller. Her head was bowed, her hair falling across her face so that he couldn't tell if she was asleep or watching her charge intently. Emotions frozen within him for so long now moved easily: hope that finally everything was going to be all right for them in an idyllic, well-dreamed future; a warm, unfocused joy at the perfect resolution when all had seemed hopeless; and, most of all, love, as sharp as sunlight on snow.

Sophie heard the sound of his boots and turned. The smile was there, as he had hoped. He gave a curt wave—no point in being *too* out of character—and held up the box to signify his success.

Her smile faded; a shadow fell across her face. A shadow fell across him.

It felt like a car slamming into him. His breath rushed out, the box went flying, he hit the ground, saw stars, skidded, and somehow pulled his senses back from the brink.

The Hipgrave-thing raced toward Sophie, a black cloud sweeping across an unblemished sky. Mallory didn't stall, didn't think; he was moving instantly, sword unsheathed, blue glow on snow, driving forward. The tearing-silk sound destroyed the dawn stillness. It was more thing now than Hipgrave: insect arms becoming slashing swords becoming a cloud of snapping mouths becoming something that made his stomach heave; his mind just wouldn't fix on one shape.

He found energy where he thought he had none; the distance between them shortened rapidly. But it was not enough. He saw in frozen instants: Sophie looking up; a true shadow falling over her; her arm rising in feeble protection;

her mouth opening, an exclamation or a scream, he wasn't sure; the Hipgrave-thing smashing down.

And as quickly as it had been there, it was gone, moving out across the compound to new territories, a storm, nothing more, a force of nature that came from beyond nature. And Mallory ran, and dropped to his knees beside her, but it was too late. Clearly, too late. A pool of blood flooded out, staining the snow in a widening arc. Her eyes were wide and fixed. She was already gone.

In that instant, he reached the extremes of human feeling; the acuity of the sensation almost destroyed him. One thought flickered briefly across the tempest: what was the point? Why did humanity exist at all?

"When you pass through this door, everything changes."

Mallory sprinted through the foot-deep snow, clutching the box to his chest. Sophie heard the sound of his boots and turned. He gave a curt wave—no point in being *too* out of character—and held up the box to signify his success. But the smile wasn't there as he had hoped.

"He's gone, Mallory."

He followed her gaze down to Miller's still form. The face was as white as the surrounding snow, the cheeks and eye sockets so hollow that it didn't look like Miller at all. In a rush, Mallory remembered dragging Miller into the car as the monkey-creatures attacked them on the approach to Salisbury; recalled searching for him on Salisbury Plain when it would have been easier to leave him to die. The Chinese believed if you saved somebody's life you were responsible for it from then on; and he had saved Miller twice, but the third time, when Miller had really needed it, had pleaded with him from the pits of his soul, Mallory had given up on his responsibility. Mallory might as well have killed him himself.

What was the point . . .

"When you pass through this door, everything changes."

Mallory sprinted through the foot-deep snow, clutching the box to his chest. Sophie heard the sound of his boots and turned. The smile was there, as he had hoped. He gave a curt wave—no point in being *too* out of character—and held up the box to signify his success.

The Hipgrave-thing raced toward Sophie, but Mallory had already dodged out of its path when the shadow fell across him. He was close enough to swing his sword; even such a powerful blade was not strong enough to kill the shifting creature, but it hurt it badly. There was a screech that made his ears hurt, and it turned on him. He saw movement and darkness and a glimpse of the man he had once known, and then it fell on him. Its first attack sliced deep into his shoulder blade, but after that burst of pain the rest became a wash of nothing. He saw the sky, pink and purple, dark at the extremes, and he saw Sophie, her face so beautiful, so torn with emotion, and then he fell backward into the white, and further backward into the dark, finally warm, finally rested . . .

The Caretaker was standing beside him. "He waits," he said, pointing to a solitary figure standing dark against the thick snow. The emotion carried with the hooded figure that had haunted him for so long was no longer threatening but so potently desolate that it ignited a deep dread in Mallory. He wanted to run anywhere so he didn't have to face that thing and what it represented.

"You know it?" the Caretaker said.

"I know it." Mallory's voice broke.

"There is no more running," the Caretaker said. "Go to it."

His legs felt like stone, but somehow he found himself walking toward it; he knew with a sickening fatalism that there was no escape from something like that.

The figure stood, unmoving, arms at its sides, its features lost in the thick shadows of the hood. Mallory approached it as if walking to the gallows, unaware of the movement of his legs, the sound of the crunching snow, the cold wind against his face.

He stopped in front of it. A shiver that was not from the cold ran through him. He was in a daze, lost to the sucking shadows that covered its face; but his subconscious knew exactly what he had to do. Trembling, he slowly brought his hands up to grip the hood. Then he pushed it back.

It was his face, a true face, an inner face, ashen, with black, black eyes that looked at him as if it was pleading with him to put it out of its misery. But it was not him, just a spirit of place that had taken on a sense of him; an echo; a reminder. He couldn't outrun it, couldn't ever leave it behind.

Hot tears burned paths down Mallory's cheeks. Here it was, then.

Over to his right there was a sound like thunder and the stone door with the carved surround stood there incongruously in the snow with no walls to support it. Lightning danced around its edges; the thunder rolled out from it repeatedly.

One more door to pass through.

It was dark and he had a gun. He hated guns, but really, he had no choice. The barrel bit into his temple. How do you do these things? he thought. No one ever tells you, so you go with the movie version. What's to stop you ending up like one of those freaks they used to feature in the *Sunday Sport*, with half their face missing, not able to talk, but with their brain as active as ever. Wouldn't that be hell? But what did he care about hell? It didn't exist. No hell, no heaven, nowhere better and you couldn't get much worse, no chance to put things right, no going back, and now no going forward.

But Sylvie would get the money and Jemas would get everything he needed to do Stevens. That was the best he could do, and it didn't come anywhere near to wiping out the debt of what he had done. But it was the best he could do, and he had no choice. He pulled the trigger.

The burst of fire was like the breath of a Fabulous Beast in the dark, filled with purifying flame. It imprinted on his mind and there it was, high over the city, high over London, destroying the Tower of London, destroying all the corruption and the filth and everything that was bad about this life.

And you know, he thought, it looks like a better world.

"Take my hand."

The Caretaker gripped Mallory's wrists tightly; all around was darkness. "You have a choice," he intoned gravely.

Mallory didn't have to think. "I want Sophie . . . I want a chance to put things right . . . to be who I could be. I want a better world."

The Caretaker nodded slowly. "Very well."

He breathed a lungful of cold air as if it was the first breath he had ever taken. Every sense was heightened: the snow so bright it was almost blinding, the dazzling colours in the dawn sky, the smell of woodsmoke on the wind; and the crunch of snow behind him, like explosions drawing nearer. He whirled, sword singing as it leaped from the sheath; the blue glow from the blade gave him comfort and helped to focus his mind.

The Hipgrave-thing swept across the lawns from the cathedral like fury, like rage and hate and bitterness. Mallory saw eyes and teeth and wings and claws. He swung the sword with the full force of his strength and felt the vibrations slam into his shoulders as the weapon smashed into the monstrous force. The blade bit deep but didn't slow the thing's progress. It powered into Mallory, sending him flying head over heels. He skidded in the snow, rolled, and came up on his feet, winded and dazed but still ready.

This time he side stepped and struck at the same time. A chunk of something flew through the air and landed in the snow, sizzling.

Teeth-rattling sounds were coming off the Hipgrave-thing, screeches that flew off the register and deep bass rumbles, each one triggering a specific emotion—fear and horror and despair. Mallory fought them down and hacked again.

With each strike, the thing became even more furious, its reactions faster, its strength greater; it was obvious to Mallory that he couldn't beat it, couldn't even hold it back for much longer.

On the next sweep, it was impossible to get out of the way. He felt a rib snap; pain flared up one side. He flew backward, crashed to the ground and lost consciousness.

When he awoke, the Hipgrave-thing was rising above him like a tidal wave of oil. A bone-numbing cold radiated out over him.

Mallory turned his head and yelled to Sophie, who was watching, horrified. "Call him!"

She realised instantly what he meant, though the panic that crossed her face showed that she knew it was already too late. She bowed her head and began to mutter.

Mallory fumbled for the sword and held it ready to ram into the thing when it came down, hoping he could do at least some damage, to save Sophie with his dying stroke.

The crash of the gates falling signified that Sophie didn't have to call out; the powers had been watching. The Hipgrave-thing was wavering, distracted, as if it sensed something Mallory couldn't. Through the broken gates came a tremendous flood of bodies: the pale-skinned, black-eyed army of little people, moving hastily as if fearful of the coming light, and like a stallion amongst them was Old Shuck with its gleaming red eyes.

The Hipgrave-thing pulled away from Mallory, who was now the lesser threat. Its attention was fixed on Old Shuck, which had broken away from the swarming little people and was moving ominously toward Mallory.

Everything was like a dream, hazy, fractured, sometimes moving too fast, sometimes in slow motion. The little people appeared to be scattering something across the cathedral compound. Soon after, there was a rumbling in the ground as of some great beast stirring. Green shoots burst through the snow, sprouted, prospered, and became creeping strands of ivy, saplings, bushes, flowers. The ivy soared up the walls of the cathedral, beginning to smother the lower storeys of the other buildings.

The Hipgrave-thing was hypnotised by the activity. Mallory saw his moment. Despite the pain flooding his side, he pulled himself to his feet and moved behind the creature. With the last of his energy, he heaved the sword over his head and thrust it so hard into the thing's back it burst out through its chest.

It trembled for a moment, the sensations taking their time to reach whatever passed for a mind within it. Then it crashed to the ground like a falling tree. It was clear that even then Mallory had not delivered a killing stroke, for it writhed and thrashed, screeching insanely.

Mallory scrambled backward and found Sophie, her arms going around him easily. He dropped down into her lap, watching what would happen next, too weak to play any part.

Old Shuck advanced until it was close to the Hipgrave-thing. It bent forward, peering with those flaming eyes as though it could see into the creature's head. Mallory had a sense that on some level communication was taking place. Whatever had happened, the Hipgrave-thing slowed its wild movements as though sedated.

The little people swarmed around, lashing ropes with the thickness and strength of wire across the beast. Within minutes, it was completely caught. The strain of the ropes was taken by a hundred small hands, and with great effort, the Hipgrave-thing was hauled gradually toward the gates, Old Shuck keeping pace, never taking its red eyes away. Left behind in the snow was a desiccated husk that had once been Hipgrave; and it was missing one hand.

When the cathedral compound was finally deserted, Mallory and Sophie felt as if they had awoken from a strange dream. She looked into his face, her smile wiping away the strain and worry. "You did it," she said, brushing the hair from his forehead. "Not bad for a man with a penis substitute."

He tried to lever himself up, but the flaring pain in his side sent him crashing back down. "Broken rib," he said weakly.

"Don't worry—we can sort that out. A few herbs, something really foul and disgusting to drink . . . back on your feet in no time."

He rolled his head to see Miller, who lay like death next to them. "How is he?" he asked. The guilt rose in him again; he knew he would never be able to forgive himself for this.

Sophie felt the pulse in Miller's neck. "Nearly gone, I think," she said sadly. "I liked him. He was decent."

They were disturbed by a strange, melodic fluting. It drifted through the thick vegetation that now covered the compound, haunting and oddly unearthly. They eventually located the source: sitting amongst a copse of young trees, almost lost against the pattern of leaves and branches, was the Green Man, trilling gently on a set of panpipes.

Mallory and Sophie listened to his music for five minutes, strangely comforted, but then he stopped and said, "You have redeemed your people."

"They're not my people," Mallory said.

"No. But you have redeemed them." The Green Man rose and walked toward them, shoots wriggling through the snow wherever his feet fell. "This was my place, long before the Church came," he said. "*I* can share it, for its power should be available to all." The implication in his words was clear.

"You've won," Mallory said.

"There is no victory here, only grief, and pain, and destruction." His voice sounded like the wind through the trees, and despite the cold of the morning, Mallory and Sophie felt as though they were basking in the warmth of a summer's day. "Now is the time for new shoots," he continued, "for hope and growth, for all living things to thrive as they are infused with the mysteries of Existence."

"The creature . . . the creature that was Hipgrave . . ." Mallory couldn't find the voice to continue; the pain had put him on the edge of blacking out.

"There are things beyond this place that occasionally pay an interest in your world. It is best not to discuss them." He stared toward the dawn, his eyes reflecting the morning light. "But something has stirred beyond the lip of the universe and it has noticed you . . . something so terrible that even the Golden Ones fear it." He looked to Mallory and Sophie sombrely. "And it is coming this way."

Sophie shivered. "That thing—"

"It is an outrider, a scout, the merest thing compared to what it serves . . . lying here since this place was newly formed. In recent times, it was awakened." A robin alighted on his shoulder; he watched it askance with a touching warmth. "It was mindless, easily manipulated. It could not be allowed to abide, and so—"

"You used it," Sophie said, "controlled it. And now—"

"Now it will be destroyed. But that is not the end of it." He waved his hand as if to wipe away all talk of dark things. "The darkest time of year has passed. Now we look to the light." He stooped down and plucked the box from where Mallory had dropped it. He smiled as the blue light flooded out and the tiny Fabulous Beast wriggled into the palm of his hand. "Is it not wonderful?" he said. "Is this not something that should be raised up to bring warmth into all hearts?"

"It's dying," Mallory managed.

The Green Man squatted down next to them. "It is beyond that. It is life. It is a part of Existence itself." He looked from Mallory to Sophie and in his vegetative face they saw something powerful and moving. "Hope, Brother and Sister of Dragons. Hope and life."

He pressed his face close to the Fabulous Beast, then leaned over and threw the blankets off Miller before carefully laying the creature on the still form's belly. Mallory and Sophie watched in puzzlement. The brilliant blue glow began to pulse, gradually at first but then with increasing speed, growing brighter all the time until they had to shield their eyes. When it reached a peak, the tiny black shape at the heart of the glare appeared to be melting. A few seconds later, Mallory realised that this was not the case: it looked as if it was sinking into Miller's belly. When the last of the dark smudge disappeared, the light winked out and all was as it had been. There was no sign of the Fabulous Beast.

The Green Man had retreated to the nearest copse, and when he spoke his voice was rich and florid; he was smiling warmly. "We shall meet again when there are five of you. And then, once again, the Brothers and Sisters of Dragons shall stand shoulder to shoulder with the Golden Ones in the name of Existence."

And then he was gone, swallowed up by the vegetation as if he had simply allowed his essence to dissipate amongst it.

Mallory and Sophie were transfixed until the sound of rustling disturbed them. Miller was sitting up, puzzling as to why he had been lying in the snow. His cheeks were full, his skin pink with the flush of contentment.

He looked from one to the other, then said, even more puzzled, "Why are you crying?"

BEAUTIFUL DAY

"If you see things as they are here and now, you have seen everything
that has happened from all eternity. All things are interrelated Oneness."
Marcus Aurelius

The Christmas bells rang out across Salisbury, lying sedate and gleaming beneath a thick covering of snow. The sky was a brilliant blue and the sun shone brightly. In the cathedral, the brothers gathered to give praise to their saviour. Many were too weak to stand, but after Mallory had arranged for rations to be brought in from the city, they had at least pulled back from the brink.

Compared with the massed ranks that had greeted Mallory and Miller on their arrival, the congregation was small. Some had died; many had simply wandered away, their faith broken. But the biggest departure had been the followers of Stefan, who had gone off to maintain their strict creed elsewhere, away from the corruption of sinners.

The mysterious buildings that had sprawled out from the cathedral were gone; indeed, no one seemed to remember that they had been there, apart from Mallory and Sophie. But there was much marvelling at the mass of vegetation and mature trees that now grew all around the grand old building.

Miller had little remembrance of his suffering during the last few days. He was flushed with a new sense of vitality that manifested as unbounded joy, bringing a smile to everyone who met him. He confessed his crime to anyone who would listen, and professed his desire for salvation; he was forgiven by all.

But the biggest change was only noticed later, just before noon. A ripple of excitement ran out from one of the old wooden shacks where the brothers lived. Mallory was drawn, wheezing in pain from his heavily bandaged ribs, to find Miller slumped in a chair and several brothers gabbling excitedly over a scrawny man who lay weakly on one of the rough beds.

"What's up?" Mallory asked, wondering what stupidity Miller had offended them with now.

"He cured him!" one of the brothers proclaimed, hands raised to the air.

"Get a grip," Mallory snapped.

"No, really." The brother motioned to the man in the bed. "He was one of the last to come here before the gates were sealed. In the last few days, he developed some kind of plague. He was sealed up in here . . ." He lowered his eyes in shame before the excitement gripped him again. "Miller came in to care for him this morning and—"

"I cured him." Miller sounded tremendously weak, but he was grinning like an idiot. "He was covered with the marks of the plague. But when I touched him, this blue light came out of my hands in a flash. It blinded me, I tell you. But when my eyes cleared, he was . . ." He nodded to the man on the bed, who looked remarkably healthy, if exhausted. "Though I couldn't do it again in a hurry, I reckon. I'm knackered."

"Stop grinning, you'll hurt your jaw, you stupid idiot," Mallory said before marching out. Alone in the beautiful morning, he thought he might cry again.

In the afternoon, he sought out Daniels, who had taken a shack near to the cathedral. Gardener was there, sitting quietly next to the bed in which Daniels slept peacefully. The Geordie looked up, but his face gave nothing away.

"What do you miss about the old days, Mallory?" he asked by way of greeting.

"I miss never being able to hear The Wannadies again. And all the other oldies."

Gardener mused. "I used to like The Animals, meself. Local lads, you know." He glanced at Daniels and seemed happy that his breathing was regular. "It seemed simpler back then. I mean, the bloody world was a mess, right? But it was simpler. When you did something, you pretty much knew what the repercussions would be. And they were never *that* bad . . . know what I'm saying? Never life or death."

"Yeah, these are bastard times, Gardener." Mallory noticed that the Geordie's hands were shaking continually. "How's he doing?"

"Aye, he's a strong lad . . . for a queer, y'know." He bit his lip. "I'll be keeping an eye on him . . . making sure he pulls through."

"He's got a tough life ahead of him. One eye. No . . ." He nodded in the direction of Daniels's groin.

"I'll be keeping an eye on him."

There were a million things Mallory could have said—accusations, castigation, blame—but he could see that Gardener had been through them all himself. He settled on, "You staying here?"

"I think he'll be sticking around. The reasons why he came here haven't changed. He'll be needing some company, I suppose. Some of the blokes around here, they're right miserable bastards. They won't understand him." A juddering sigh made him catch his breath. "How about you?"

"Moving on. Pretty much outstayed my welcome, I think."

344

"You'll be missed, Mallory."

"Yeah, but not by you, you Geordie bastard." He made to go, but had the urge to speak the truth, for once. "There's hope for you yet, Gardener."

The gratitude in Gardener's face was so intense it was almost childlike. "We all want saving, Mallory," he said. "All of us."

At four p.m., Mallory was saddling up the horses he had bought in town with an excessive chunk of the cathedral gold. He'd also acquired some food, a tent, cooking utensils, a blanket, and couldn't think of anything else he needed in the world—apart from Sophie. As he finished up, James wandered into the stables looking ten years older than the last time Mallory had seen him.

"Are you sure you won't stay?" James said, after they'd got the usual perfunctory conversation out of the way. "There's even more of a need for the Knights Templar now." He smiled. "More importantly, there's a need for good men like you."

"You're such a bullshitter, James. God knows how you got wrapped up in all this religion shit."

James laughed heartily.

"See, you're not even offended. They'll be drumming you out of the Christian Army."

"Well?"

Mallory checked the straps of the pack on the horse so that James couldn't see any truth in his eyes. "No. Despite all your flattery—and believe me, I love to have my ego massaged—I've got places to be."

"Oh?"

"Yeah, Sophie—the bane of my life, apparently—she's leaving that Celtic Nation bollocks to the rest of her shiftless, lazy clan. She's decided we ought to be searching for the other three Brothers and Sisters of Dragons so all us losers can get together for a party. Or something. She thinks it's important. And if it keeps me off my knees, praying, I'm all for it."

"You'll make a good Brother of Dragons, Mallory."

"Shut up, you old fool." He stifled a laugh. "You're a sucker for punishment if you're thinking of making a go of it here."

"Someone has to. This religion has a lot going for it, you know: salvation, sacrifice, redemption, universal love."

"Well, that's an opinion. But if you want to get back on Sunday prime time, you'd better choose your leaders more wisely. And here's a tip: don't forget the one rule."

"What's that?"

"Be good."

Mallory mounted the horse and led it and its partner out into the fading light. "You've got to start believing in something sometime, Mallory," James called after him. But it was delivered in such a way that the irony was evident.

Miller came running up before Mallory had got far out of the stables. "You weren't going to go before I had time to say good-bye, were you?"

"Apparently not."

Miller looked up at him with something a little more sublime than hero worship. "I'll miss you, Mallory."

Mallory winced; his failures were still too close for him to move beyond them. "Just be careful they don't lock you up in a box in the cathedral, Miller."

Miller smiled. "It's a good job you're going, Mallory—for you. I know all your secret codes now . . . in everything you say. You can't fool me."

"Miller, you are so wrong, you've got *wrong* tattooed on your forehead."

"Just tell me one thing, Mallory."

"Go on—hit me."

"What did you do before you came here? I need to know . . . so I can understand you."

For an instant, Mallory felt as though night had fallen in his mind. But then it cleared, and he looked around him, at the brothers shuffling toward compline, and the buildings, and the darkening sky where the first stars were appearing. "You know what, Miller. It doesn't matter." And he was right.

They spotted Sophie approaching from the flourishing groves where she had been meditating quietly. She smiled and waved.

"Don't let her lead you astray, Mallory," Miller teased in his innocent fashion. "She's an infidel. And, by God, she's a woman."

"She's my Combat Honey, Miller, and don't you forget it. She could hold her own with any knight."

"You're a lucky man, Mallory."

"Yeah, that's the bit I don't get. Everybody keeps telling me I'm a lucky man, but nobody tells her how lucky she is. What's that all about?"

Sophie gave Miller a big hug and whispered something in his ear; they both looked at Mallory and laughed. He looked away impassively, and that made them laugh all the more.

Then Miller came over and shook Mallory's hand. "You look after yourself," he said, both seriously and honestly.

"I'll do that. And you, too, Miller."

Miller flashed them both a smile before slipping off into the twilight.

"He's got great things ahead of him," Mallory said. "I tell you, in a few years' time they'll be writing stories about him. That'll never happen to you and me."

"Speak for yourself." Sophie mounted the horse and together they trotted out toward the shattered gates. "You sure you still want to do this, Mallory?" she asked.

"If you go, I'll go with you. If you stay, I'll wait."

She glanced at him askance. "Are you being sarcastic?"

"I don't know the meaning of the word."

He spurred his horse, and they moved out into a better world.

If you would like to know more about the world of
The Devil in Green, and how it came to be, seek out the three books in
The Age of Misrule series:
World's End
Darkest Hour
Always Forever

AFTERWORD

This book is one part of a puzzle.

A puzzle that draws on clues scattered across more than two thousand years of human history. In the alignments of stone circles, and mysteries encoded in the great cathedrals and castles. The secrets locked into old fairy tales and ancient mythologies. The learnings of seers, magicians, and philosophers. And, too, the kind of clues you might find scattered through a detective novel, which point into the dark recesses of the human mind.

More than ten years ago now, I found myself on a sun-drenched island three miles off the coast of Wales. I'd reached something of a turning point in my life, or so I felt, and I was thinking about the path ahead, and all that had come before.

Sitting on the beach, looking across the stretch of water to the pastel-painted houses of the resort town of Tenby, it felt the perfect place for reflection. If you visit Caldey Island today, you'll notice, I'm sure, a peculiar atmosphere—one of great peace, evident under the dark canopy of the woods that run down to the shore and the hidden coves, as well as, surprisingly, on the wind-swept cliffs where the waves crash relentlessly. It's only a tiny island. You can walk around it in a morning.

Caldey is owned and managed by a small community of monks resident at the white-walled Cistercian monastery that sits at the heart of the island. There's a handful of other residents who help work the fields, but that's it apart from the tourists who make the short boat trip from Tenby—only twenty minutes away, but the two places might as well be a world apart.

The monastery is relatively modern, with the current order moving to Caldey in 1929. But as I explored, I discovered that other religious people had been drawn here too—a group of monks came in 1906, a Benedictine foundation was established in 1136, and a Celtic monastery had been founded as long ago as the sixth century. The beauty of the island and the relative isolation made it attractive, I supposed.

But then I came across other information that made me think deeper. A strange inscription in the mysterious Ogham alphabet had been left on Caldey. Ogham is a secret writing, possibly invented by the druids, with only four hundred surviving inscriptions, mostly in Ireland.

And then I found the cave, partially excavated by archaeologists. They'd uncovered flints and bones suggesting humans had come to this place more than twelve thousand years ago. And there was evidence, too, of rituals and funerary practices on Caldey throughout the later Stone Age. Neolithic people also found something special in that place.

What was it about Caldey Island that drew people there across thousands of years, from different belief systems? Was that potent atmosphere more than just the sum of trees and rocks and sand and sea? Something buried in the very fabric of the island itself? I wondered.

Stories start with the smallest of thoughts.

Feverishly, I sketched out an epic story that would take in the full sweep of human history, ancient mysteries and occult secrets, and the world's great mythologies too, tumbling across three separate worlds—our own, modern-day world, the mystical Celtic Otherworld, and the world beyond death. The detailed research would take months on the road around Britain, and then across the globe, visiting mysterious places, reading old texts and scholarly papers, and talking to the contemporary custodians of that information.

This sprawling story would eventually be told across nine books—a trilogy of trilogies that could, just about, be consumed in any order, complete in and of themselves. But read together the three trilogies would reveal an even greater story.

The Dark Age is one of those trilogies, and, as I mentioned at the start, part of a puzzle. As you move from *The Devil in Green* to *The Queen of Sinister*, it is not immediately obvious how this story hangs together, but the clues are there. All is revealed in the final book, *The Hounds of Avalon*, but you may enjoy trying to work it out for yourself as you go along.

If you want to know how the world of The Dark Age came about, read the three books of The Age of Misrule (also published by Pyr)—*World's End*, *Darkest Hour*, and *Always Forever*. This series tells of magic returning to our modern world, and five unlikely people who came together as champions, known as Brothers and Sisters of Dragons, to fight a terrible threat. They are Jack Churchill, the troubled leader of the group; Ruth Gallagher, a lawyer who learns to wield old magic; Ryan Veitch, a reformed criminal; Shavi, a mystic; and Laura DuSantiago, which may or may not be her real name, who has a big mouth and a strange destiny. Their shadow falls across The Dark Age, if you look carefully.

Many strange events and odd coincidences dogged my trail while I was researching this story. One of them even cropped up while I checked my facts for this afterword: the Welsh name for Caldey Island, I just discovered, is Ynys Byr, meaning Pyr's Island. Now check the spine of this book.

There are puzzles and mysteries everywhere.

ABOUT THE AUTHOR

A two-time winner of the prestigious British Fantasy Award, Mark Chadbourn has published his epic, imaginative novels in many countries around the world. He grew up in the mining community of the English Midlands and was the first person in his family to go to university. After studying economic history at Leeds, he became a successful journalist, writing for several of the UK's renowned national newspapers as well as contributing to magazines and TV.

When his first short story won *Fear* magazine's Best New Author award, he was snapped up by an agent and subsequently published his first novel, *Underground*, a supernatural thriller set in the coalfields of his youth. Quitting journalism to become a full-time author, he has written stories that have transcended genre boundaries, but is perhaps best known in the fantasy field.

Mark has also forged a parallel career as a screenwriter with many hours of produced work for British television. He is a senior writer for BBC Drama and is also developing new shows for the UK and the US.

An expert on British folklore and mythology, he has held several varied and colorful jobs, including independent record company boss, band manager, production line worker, engineer's "mate," and media consultant.

Having traveled extensively around the world, he has now settled in a rambling house in the middle of a forest not far from where he was born.

For information about the author and his work:

www.markchadbourn.net
www.jackofravens.com
www.myspace.com/markchadbourn

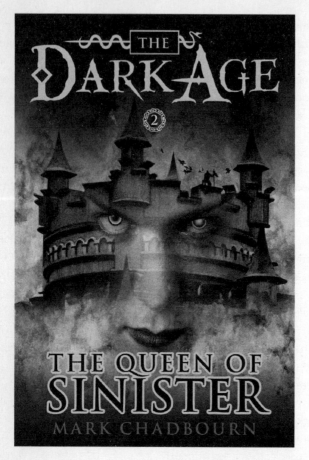